The Girl Who Loved Cayo Bradley

Books by Nina Romano

The Other Side of the Gates
Cooking Lessons
Coffeehouse Meditations
She Wouldn't Sing at My Wedding
Westward: Guided by Starfalls and Moonbeams
Faraway Confections
Time's Mirrored Illusions
Prayer in a summer of Grace
Writing in a Changing World

Wayfarer Trilogy
The Secret Language of Women
Lemon Blossoms
In America

Coming Soon!
Dark Eyes

Darby's Quest series
Star on a Summer Morning
Book 2

For more information
visit: www.SpeakingVolumes.us

Park City, Utah
December 19, 2021

For: ██████ —

Enjoy reading this historical

The Girl Who Loved Cayo Bradley

fiction and romance!

All best wishes —

Nina Romano

SPEAKING VOLUMES, LLC
NAPLES, FLORIDA
2021

The Girl Who Loved Cayo Bradley

Cover design by Hannah Linder

If there are any errors in representation of the culture and the way of life of the Jicarilla Apache Nation, during the late 1800s in New Mexico, I humbly apologize—these descriptions were simply used as part of the fictional story depicting the circumstances of the author's invented character, Cayo Bradley.

ISBN 978-1-64540-539-9

This book is dedicated to:
Jane Brownley
Friend— Reader— Raindancer
and
in lovingly memory of
Buddy
my first cowboy hero

"In the beginning there was nothing
where the world now stands:
no ground; no earth; only darkness,
water and cyclone; no people, fishes or living things."

Jicarilla Apache Nation (INDE)
Creation Narrative
Dinetah Gray Jar

"I remember every single spot of light
that ever gouged a shadow
beside your bones."

Zelda Fitzgerald

"In the end,
the love you take is equal
to the love you make."

Paul McCartney

Cayo Bradley

Oh lady, lady love,
I'm consumed by your image in a locket
escorting me down corridors of time
where facts and fictions kaleidoscope into verse,
letters, long in the longing, written only in my head.

The taste of mesquite on the air, juniper on my tongue,
I'm leaving the one who loves me, back-tracking,
leading my horse in the direction of the one I love.

In reveries and pipedreams, I drift along—
dry sagebrush, tumbleweeds blowing past
with serene zephyrs, though at eventide rainfall scatters
and nothing remains save the sultry, summer night
when the swift pain of loneliness starts again.

I'm sure you know it hurts to leave,
to cross this river wild, wishing I could stay to comfort;
yet as I depart, faraway reveries beckon on the distant shore,
the broad expanse of onrushing waters. At the top of the bluff,
lighter in the embrace of soft, sun-warmed air where bees
rejoice summer, grasshoppers travel farther, I sleep less,
watch the zithering beetles flit-flying to narrow-escape
landings on the escarpment.

By nightfall, a starry backdrop
of sky appears

whilst a curtain of haze halos the moon to shine
in the lee of the hill on the cabin;
as I step up to a pillared porch,
a view of the valley stretches below
and behind me in harmony and in tandem
with every fiber of my being.

A spirit in an afterlife image . . .
     you
         opening the door.

Chapter One

The McPhee Ranch

A keen, sleek whistle, intense for a fleeting instant, yet insistent as moonlight on prairie grass, captured the attention of Darby McPhee—the sound of independence. She thought of a cloud covering the slice of the moon as she listened to the remains of the whistle's sibilance with longing, wanting to run away. How long could she stay in the ranch house slaving away her youth for her four brothers and father? Darby was days shy of her sixteenth birthday when the five o'clock whistle blew. She'd made up her mind. The day after tomorrow she'd be on that iron panther heading east, to her Aunt Bea's, an education and a new life.

There were several obstacles she'd have to overcome not the least of them the fact she might never return. She would take her courage in her two hands, like her Pa told her so many times when she faced a fearful thing and she'd tell Cayo just how she felt about him. And it would be tomorrow. She pictured his face with sharply cut cheekbones and bronze skin—saw his lean body, his rugged work shirt straining over wide shoulders, the collar opened at the neck, and wondered what it would be like to kiss him. She rolled up her sleeves.

Her dreams were filled with Cayo. She remembered the first time she saw him. It only took that one glance to rivet him in her bones, and to know that he'd be as important as blood coursing through her heart. In dreams, he moved but didn't speak. In the morning, she recalled watching him put out a fire, and when she worked she thought about what it meant? What did fire symbolize? Was it destruction? Passion and desire? Or did the dream indicate that Cayo would fulfill her? Maybe in some biblical sense. Was it an insight, cleansing, or transformation? Would her leaving to go east quench the fire? Was seeking an education going to bring anger, or pain? How many times had she been warned off something with the expression, You're "playing with fire."

The next day, Darby awoke, unrefreshed and groggy, dwelling on the significance of that dream. She went about her chores disembodied, until finally she reached for the piggin and poured in the cream she'd skimmed off the milk from the spout into the butter churn. Her thoughts followed the white stream, and then they veered askew. After all, she might never see him again, and a man ought to know if he's loved, even if it's a starry-far-away love that might never be fulfilled. She placed the piggin down on the ground. Her trepidation and fear were pushed on to every forceful slam of the churning paddle. She'd make butter all right and she'd cream away every worry and dang thought about the long train ride east. Leaving Pa and telling Cayo. What if he didn't feel the same? Wouldn't matter, she'd be leaving anyway. But a man should know.

Darby rushed to set the table, pull the biscuits from the oven, turn the bacon, and whisk a dozen eggs with a big splash of milk and farm cheese she'd made earlier that morning. Standing in the doorway, she clanged the iron triangle, calling the men to breakfast. She felt a chill, and rubbed her arms briskly.

Of a sudden, her thoughts drew her back to last winter and a sleigh ride with Hanna, the Pedersons, and Cayo Bradley, who had held the reins on the horses. Then her mind reached further back to last autumn, when the church had taken the parishioners on a hay ride. She was one of the last to mount for the ride. She remembered Cayo's strong arms around her waist and him practically lifting her onto the wagon seat right next to him. He mounted and their hips kissed in the fading light.

"Evening, Darby."

"Good evening, Cayo."

He looked at her, but didn't say more and didn't move; neither did she. Her older brother Garrett had seen Cayo help Darby onto the wagon and, for propriety's sake, got up on the wagon to accompany her along with the driver and another two frisky cowhands that worked on the Pederson spread. Garrett sat behind her, his breath hot on her shoulder, closer than it needed to be, but she understood that was his way of protecting her, like saying, I'm here, don't you worry none, little sister.

Her thoughts trailed back to the present. *When will I tell Pa?* She patted the pocket of her apron which held Aunt Bea's letter stating all the arrangements had been made for her niece but there was an undertone of something else. Had Aunt Bea set her up as a mail-order bride? All her recent letters talked about some Pastor and how kind he was and how devoted to the congregation and how he'd gone out of his way to help her out of the buggy when she'd gone and turned her ankle.

Darby slapped the butter onto a daisy form cut-out made of an oval piece of sorrel wood, closed the three inch high wooden mold with scalloped edges around it and hooked a curved nail over the head of another nail to secure it. She ran to the barn giving a hoot to her eldest brother Garrett and buried the butter shape under the ice to cool it just a little. It always amazed her how hay kept the blocks of ice from melting, but this would be the last time she'd have to concern herself about farm chores like this. Aunt Bea had an actual ice box. City folk lived so much better.

The omelets were made and served. Garrett reached for the strawberry preserves that Darby had stored last summer. "Pass the biscuits," he said to nobody in particular.

"Hey, girl, where's the butter?" Bix asked.

"I've a given name, Bix, just like you," Darby said. "I'll go get it. I put it to cool in the barn."

"Probably just going to cuddle that dumb old sheep dog is all," Darby heard her father say. She muttered, "Na-huh," and sauntered out the kitchen door.

Garrett and Pa. She'd miss them. Pa especially, the only one who recognized the fact that she was the opposite sex—she'd have to admit that was a slight exaggeration, but her other brothers, Bix, Randy and Chad were inconsiderate. Darby thought of them as irresponsible asses, the kind that kicked and threw wild punches—verbal or otherwise—uncaring if they got a thrashing from Pa or not. Pa and Garrett were always at them to fix something they'd messed up, or to get going on a task or chore that should have been finished days before. Lazy bunch of oafs. Serve them right to have to clean up after themselves.

When Darby came back from the barn—the sun still wasn't full up.

Darby pointed to a sign she'd made propped up on the sideboard that read: NO SMOKING in the house! "Can't you read?" she asked the men.

"Sure," Pa said. He pushed away from the table and was about to light a cigarette he'd just rolled.

"Pa, out of respect for your dead wife and my Momma, please don't smoke inside," Darby said. She took hold of another sign she'd made. It was pinned to the gingham curtain on the window nearest the big oak dining table where her family sat.

She read, "Close the window coverings before the sun is full up."

Darby let the curtain fall and closed the Scotch Holland linen shades beneath that Pa had bought for a handsome sum at the General store for Momma. Then Darby picked up a sign that was leaning on a milk bottle used as a vase for wild flowers.

"More stink weeds in this house than milk," her younger brother Bix said.

"Hush up," Darby said. She read from this note. "It says here, Pick up your dish and bring it to the kitchen, or you can wash it yourself or eat off the dirty doggone thing, oink oink, next meal."

She tossed the paper on the table and began clearing away the breakfast remains.

"Skinny as a broomstick, child. You eat?" Pa asked.

"Not a child any more, Pa. Sure, I ate at four o'clock when I got up to start my chores." Now's my chance, she thought. "I got a letter from Aunt Bea. Been meaning to let you read it." She took it out of her pocket. It was dated June 27, 1874.

"I'll have a look see when I come in at sundown," Pa said.

"Not now?"

"No. Got to get a move on. Let's get those britches walking to the door, boys," he said.

A man of few words, thank Heavens. "Pa, I'll set it by the wash bucket for you. Have to rush myself now. Mrs. Miller expects me at the store early today, it being Saturday. There'll be lots of farmer wives and hands coming in for supplies."

Her father caught her around the waist and gave her a squeeze. She felt a twinge of guilt. Looking at her father, she thought of a dozen kindnesses he'd gone out of his way to do for her. She'd miss him, but she couldn't sacrifice her life any longer. *Momma's been gone four long years.* "But I'm not his wife," she murmured.

Darby often felt like a mother hen to her brothers. That was the thing her father would have to reckon with when she left. Darby mulled this over in her mind many times. But now, a day before her departure, it was a tune that was wearing itself out. Her thoughts were not happy ones: Momma's dead, and I'm leaving Pa. She'd talked about Aunt Bea and going east to learn how to teach school so often, but now she felt determined that this time she was really going. She felt badly about so many things, including the fact she'd miss going to church one more time because she'd be readying herself for departure.

Chad had gone out and come back in. He was holding a piece of paper in his hand. "Hear ye, hear ye. I found this note nailed to the outhouse door. Says: Throw in lye after each deposit."

Everyone at the table laughed. Darby went to the kitchen to finish washing the dishes. A note she meant for the boys was propped up against the sink. "Always, prime the pump." *They'll get on just fine without me.*

She'd exhausted dozens of possibilities of what the day would bring her by the time she went off to town in the buggy with her Pa. Then her thoughts brought her to last week, when Fern was out of the store and she'd waited on Cayo. All alone in the mercantile, she was able to engage him in a conversation of what he wanted from life besides being a ranch hand for Captain Pederson.

He spoke of ranching and all the things he'd learned about raising cattle. How he'd someday like to go back to where his people had farmed. The look on his face when he spoke of the land and what it offered was wonderful to behold. It seemed as if Cayo had grown a new spirit right in front of the counter.

On the ride to town, her father interrupted Darby's thoughts. "Awful quiet this morning."

"I didn't sleep all that well."

"Oh? Why's that?" Pa asked as he yanked the reins to maneuver the horse to the left, avoiding a rut in the road.

"Had some disturbing dreams of fire," she said and quickly shifted the conversation. "A lot of potholes now that the rain's stopped."

"Ever wonder where that word came from?" Pa asked in between clucking his tongue at the horse.

"Never did. Where's it from?"

"In olden times, potters couldn't afford to buy clay to work making pots. In towns that had clay, they'd dig holes in the road to steal it and lay it away. In the morning, Teamsters drove over them, many wrecking wagons in the holes. They cursed those damn potters and their potholes."

"How do you know so much, Papa?"

"Your Momma used to read to me at night when the boys were small. Then you came along and she made me promise you'd get an education."

Darby thought about that for some time and the next thing she knew they were in front of the shop.

"I'll be walking home today, Pa. No need to wait around."

He gave her a thumbs up. "Plenty to do at home."

Chapter Two

Coyote Bradley

That dusty summer of 1874 found Coyote Bradley working as a hired hand and sometime cowpoke on the Pederson ranch in Parcel Bluffs, New Mexico, just miles from the McPhee spread. He was long-legged and lean, soft spoken, slow to anger with a deep cleft in his chin. Never had a day off, but some Saturday afternoons he'd hitch up the wagon for Miss Hanna and Mrs. Pederson and take them to town. Hanna was nothing like her friend Darby. The Pederson girl was spoiled and arrogant. He overheard Darby tell Hanna once that her Daddy ought to give his daughter a once-and-for-all-time good licking to straighten her skinny ass out. He had a chuckle about that, picturing Hanna across her father's knee.

Captain Pederson tossed Cayo a full pouch of chewing tobacco for the ride to town and said, "Watch the ruts and gopher holes, Cayo, and have a high time, ladies."

The Pederson women would go to visit in the Hotel Ryder parlor, drink tea and with scissors-sharp tongues cut to pieces every other woman in town. Sometimes they'd go to the dressmaker Fanny Oates, or tend to some other womanly tasks. Before they headed home they would stop into Fern and Harris Miller's General Store where Darby worked as a shop girl.

The Millers were childless. Fern was able to handle the regular trade during weekdays, but on Saturdays things were hectic because the farm folk turned up in town to replenish their stores. Darby was hired to take up the slack and deal with the weekend rush. Fern was a motherly figure for Darby and tried to draw the girl out. Cayo liked Fern but wasn't happy that she was partially responsible for Darby's thinking to leave Parcel Bluffs for city parks in the east with her Aunt Bea instead of wide open spaces and pastures here.

He knew people saw him as part Apache. Others claimed he was left for dead by *bandoleros*, and because of his aloof and stealth disposition, and the fact that he was shy and non-confrontational like the animal, people believed that's how he came to be named Coyote. Somewhere along the way, Coyote's nickname became Cayo. He didn't care what people called him as long as they did, and for sure he knew his name didn't matter because he'd never fit in anywhere. Once you've lived wild and free, it's near impossible to return wholly capable of fitting into refined society. He knew others like himself, children who had been taken and lived with Kiowa or other tribes, and what he saw in them he knew was the same for him. They were the same outcast breed he was, not a trace of Indian blood, but Indian in the way they thought. He'd never completely forgotten his own language, English, so when he finally decided to go back to living the white folks' way, he listened to speech, carefully repeated words, and held himself close, like a gambler in a poker game, keeping his cards to his chest. He shouldered these thoughts about himself and that other life he lived before as a yolk on an ox. It weighed on him, but he could do nothing to shirk it.

Nobody in town knew him by any other name. Whatever his component parts were, it was for certain he was known as a man quick with a Bowie knife, swifter with a whip. That was because nobody had ever seen him shoot a deadly arrow. He wore chaps every day but Saturday when he drove the buckboard. Cayo carried two Colt pistols in his holsters and never rode his horse without a Winchester 1873 rifle strapped to his saddle. He was a man people respected, a man who kept his mouth shut and eyes peeled, even the eyes they said he had in the back of his head.

***

On Main Street, Cayo stopped to talk a spell with Sheriff Bob Jones. Cayo had ridden with a posse for Bob when the train had been held up the year before. Bob didn't care if Cayo was a man with a past or not. All Bob knew for certain was that Cayo could draw fast, shoot sure, ride and rope better than any damn cowhand he'd seen since his own father died, and he could track—keen as any Apache. Cayo had also ridden with Bob Jones to apprehend several renegades from justice. And because Cayo joined last year's posse, Jones was able to apprehend Rick McAlister and his brother Greer. But Cayo wanted no part of the lynching, and, afterward, when he was offered Rick's new, tooled boots, he refused. He'd owned dead men's boots before—not only did they hurt, they carried with them a piece of the ghost.

Being it a Saturday and all, Cayo strolled to the bathhouse for a shave and bath, paying his two bits, with a thumb snap underneath, flipping the coin in the air for the owner Sarah Beach. An hour later, trim and tidy, he meandered over to Miller's General Store flanked by a telegraph-assay office on one side and a bank on the other.

When Cayo opened the door to the general store and stepped inside he was surprised at the cool dank air that hit him. Like a cellar. Rich and loamy. Smells recalled from a youth he could not conjure entirely. The next thing he sensed was the autumn smell of dried apples. When his eyes became accustomed to the dark, he noticed, almost tripped on, a keg of dried fruit. He began to make out clear images. Not in the least was the tall, straight young body of Darby McPhee in a blue gingham dress and white collar standing behind the counter. The shelves and woodwork behind her were beautiful intricate patterns of flowers, deer, and mountain goats. The carvings were graceful patterns straight out of the mountains of Bavaria designed by the capable chipping and scaling of the carpenter Heinz Schroeder. The shelves were lined with Mason jars of peaches preserved in thick syrup, and glasses of homemade raspberry, blueberry, blackberry and strawberry jams, covered with wax. There were tins of black strap molasses, hurricane lanterns with extra-long wicks, boxes of four inch wooden sulfur matches and bottles of tomatoes.

On the counter were burlap sacks of strange dried spices marked with names like parsley, peppercorns, bay leaf, sage, rosemary, thyme and dill. On the floor in front of the counter were larger gunnysacks of white beans and Jacob's Cattle beans, rice, lentils, cane sugar, flour, and cornmeal. He stepped around wooden crates filled with potatoes, onions, butternut and acorn squash and one with pumpkins.

Darby said, "Say, Cayo."

Cayo tipped his hat. "How do?"

"Good," she said, and smiled her father's smile.

Cayo looked about and seeing the owner absent asked after her. "Miss Fern?"

"Over to the tinsmith. You needing something besides your shirt? Need tobacco? Special blend costs a three-cent piece a pouch, but this here one's just as sweet" she sniffed it. "And it's just a penny."

It was like there were no other customers in the place the way she looked at him. Not yet sixteen, but a woman made.

"Make it a penny worth." He walked up to the counter and extended his beaded doeskin pouch with fringes, and a small covering flap of rabbit fur.

Cayo looked at her, drew in the scent of her freshly washed hair and skin. *She deals with all these cackling hens, boisterous drunks. Cooks and cleans for her Pa and four nasty suckers she calls brothers. She cares for me. More than cares for me. I feel it. Know it. But then, I thought that a lot of women cared for me: Red Willow, Barbara, Utahna. But Darby does take extra care of me and she does have an intense look in her eye.* He watched Darby as she folded his ironed shirt and started wrapping it in brown paper.

"Hold on," Darby said, "Let me tend this first so's it don't smell like tobacco."

Cayo put a nickel and an Indian head penny on the counter.

"Too much," she said. "Only one cent for work shirts. Five's for dress ones, if they got ruffles. None of yours have."

Was she saving me money here, too? She could charge what she liked. Fern Miller let Darby take in ironing and she made her own prices. Cayo's face flushed and he was glad of the darkness, and the cooler inside air. He switched a shiny penny, taking up the 1874 shield nickel from the counter. Opening his pouch, he waited. Not just for chewing tobacco. For what? *I'm nine years her senior, yet when I see her I'm a school dunce.* He looked at his hands, the palms began to sweat. He wiped his hands on his pants.

When I'm at the spread I think of things I'm going to tell her—how a calf is warm when he's born, and after—how he's all wet with his momma's juices. The thanks in the mother's eyes when you've helped pull her baby free. What it feels like to rope a steer and how the air smells when you burn his flesh with a branding iron. I'd like to tell her of the high full moon over the prairie and stars you can touch with all the shooting arches of light that make you think there's another universe somewhere out yonder. I'm wanting to give her cornflowers and butter-cups and Hanna's bell-shaped tiny lilies of the valley. Tell her I'd like to have her for my own. To smell the skin of her, to wake up to her tousled hair on my pillow and arm. There's that knot again in my stomach. If I don't eat Johnny cake for a year I wouldn't miss it. But it ain't corn bread, it's this little filly right here. When can I tell her? How do I say it? I never used words with those others. That was different.

Darby's fingertips grazed Cayo's. That bare slight touching was an electrical bolt that shot up his spine, and somehow reminded him of Rolling Thunder, his childhood friend. Darby and Cayo looked at each other. Long and hard. She lowered her eyes and drew her hand away as if she had all day to do that one thing.

Then she turned her back and started putting things on the shelves and said, "I'm home bound at four o'clock today. I take the back path by the old curved road. It's earlier than I usually leave."

Why is she telling me this?

Darby faced him, dusted off the counter of the spilled tobacco with her apron. "I'll be doing some packing and such besides preparing supper for the boys and Pa. Tell Hanna for me I'll ride by later around eight. They'll be finished eating then, won't they?"

Cayo stood there like a storefront Indian. A wooden statue had more life. He felt no blood course through his veins. Time stood still. *She's leaving. Leaving Parcel Bluffs. Leaving me. Without ever having told her how I feel about her but she must know by the way I look at her. I should have said something to her at the church gathering two weeks ago.*

"Can I walk you home, Darby?"

"It's a ways, Mr. Cayo Bradley, but I'd be pleased of the company. And . . ." she pulled her hair behind her ears, and gulped some air, "and" lowering her voice said, "there's something I've been meaning to tell you."

"Something I've been meaning to say to you, too," he said, swallowing sweet words before they hopped out of his mouth.

13

"Oh," she said, her mouth the exact shape of the letter, and tilted her head a bit sideways like she always did when she's thinking on something.

A customer came in with two small children. Cayo held the door for the woman, tipped his hat, and walked out.

Chapter Three

Little Things

On that hazy early summer day, Darby took in the laundry for Fern from the line out back of the store. Her mind filled with thoughts of Hanna. Darby knew that Hanna liked Cayo and wondered if she wanted his attention because Darby already had it, because it was a game, or because it was genuine.

Darby didn't want to dwell on Hanna. Darby didn't want to be concerned with all the little things that annoyed her. What bothered her? Sometimes she couldn't hone in on all of the things, like today, but a feeling of disquiet surrounded her. Other times her mind was overloaded with questions. Most of them unanswerable. Did Hanna hope Cayo didn't feel the same way about Darby? Or did Hanna understand that Cayo cared for Darby and had eyes for only her and nobody else? Or was this wishful thinking on her part?

Was Cayo in love or desire or whatever with Darby? How can a girl tell if a man cares deeply for her? Was he serious or playing her like strings on a guitar? Hadn't Hanna considered Darby her best friend since they were children and their mothers sewed together in a quilting bee? But Hanna changed. She became more self-indulgent and drew inwards since her momma got sick with influenza, never recovered and died. Something broke in Hanna. She had held her father's full attention while her momma lived, but now she was jealous when her father, Captain Pederson, remarried way too soon after her mother's funeral. People talked. People wondered how long he had known or courted Zora, the new Mrs. Pederson. Hadn't Hanna confided in Darby how much she disliked this woman, so different than her mother? It didn't help matters the fact that her Daddy insisted she refer to the woman as "mother."

Darby noticed how at times when she'd be talking to Hanna, she'd get that far away look in her eye, and seemed to be wandering someplace else. Mind traveling. But at the mention of Cayo's name, her ears would prick up and her nostrils wriggle, a prairie dog catching the scent of prey.

There were other things. Little things. They bothered Darby, who realized that she couldn't define them all, but she noticed the signs—signals there for anyone interested enough to read them. And she was interested. How her dear friend would often question Darby about when she'd be leaving, going east on a train to her Aunt Bea's in St. Louis. It was as if Hanna couldn't wait to be rid of Darby—was it in order to pounce on Cayo? Darby hadn't told her father of her plans. Hanna voiced her opinion that it was a mistake and Darby should have done so a long time back in hopes that he wouldn't oppose her leaving.

Last night, Darby hadn't slept well due to the excitement of her parting. On the ride to town to go to work, another thing preoccupied her and it was the keen possibility of Hanna really taking hold of Cayo's lonesome heart. Was Hanna capable? Was Cayo fickle? Did Darby matter to him?

Darby's secret about leaving was one that Hanna promised to keep. Darby had bargained Hanna would keep it quiet, but in this situation, Hanna held the upper hand understanding by the little things Darby let slip out and instantly regretted—indeed she bemoaned sharing anything because Hanna was a chatterbox, and could have it all over town. Did Hanna want to make sure Darby actually left Parcel Bluffs before jumping for joy and reaching out to Cayo? It could take years before Darby's return. How long would her studies take?

***

While Darby folded the laundry, her thoughts ferried her back to Cayo, an ever-present shadow. What did he like about her? Why didn't he go for Hanna, whom Darby always thought was prettier—certainly better dressed and who had a Daddy that gave her everything.

Woodpeckers fussed somewhere with their morning tapping. On a back road, buckboard noises reached her: the clip-clopping of the horses, and an occasional whinny and snort. Darby listened carefully lest she miss something—a sound, a sight, a fragrance—she wanted to bundle them all up and take the surroundings with her, but would she be able to remember the environs in far off St. Louis?

She thought about Hanna's constant chattering and how often Mrs. Pederson said, "Hush now, Hanna, you're bringing on one of my migraines." Why did the girl prattle so much? Was she searching for her true self?

Darby wasn't sure, but could swear Cayo had smirked at the mention of some of Hanna's antics. It seemed he kept the corners of his mouth controlled as they worked to turn upwards. *Thunderation and damnation. What do I see in him anyway he's so ornery and mean-tempered? He could look under my skirt and still never crack loose with a smile. I hate him now and for always forever. Well, until I see him later anyway.*

Inside the store, Fern asked Darby to deliver an order of cloth, needles, threads, buttons and ribbon to Mrs. Ryder, the dressmaker, who was now holding a mid-morning social tea. Before Darby knocked to be admitted, she peered through a window to see Hanna had joined in with the ladies for their usual catty talk of the other women in town. Darby saw how Hanna sulked, got up and looked out the other window. Bored?

17

Darby wondered. Or was her bratty friend calculating Cayo's whereabouts? He always went to Miller's to shore up his stores, but who knew just what time. It was like Darby could read Hanna's thoughts: he'd go to the bath house first, so he'd look his best for his ladylove.

His ladylove. Why that's me!

A chance to become lovers. Darby figured Hanna would somehow interfere afraid to give that opportunity to them—Cayo and Darby becoming lovers. Thrilling though. Frightful, too. A gamble to declare rightful feelings for each other. Did Hanna wish to ruin Darby's bittersweet departure—a probable promise of letters and a future meeting?

Were Darby's thoughts going along the right tracks where Hanna was concerned? Darby read the notions in Hanna's mind: *Probably die and go straight to hell, trying to break up something right as raindrops on windflowers. But why can't he look at me the way he looks at her? Why can't his thoughts be taken up with images of me instead of Darby?*

Darby's hand poised to knock, she peeked through the curtained upper glass portion of the door and listened, transfixed. She heard a bit of conversation.

"I declare," Mrs. Ryder said to Mrs. Pederson, pouring tea into a porcelain cup, "your gal's a might quiet today."

"Thank the Almighty," said Mrs. Pederson. "Hanna was a mockingbird on our way into town. Attention seeking for the driver's behalf." Mrs. Pederson took hold of the honey pot and heaped a generous spoonful into the steaming brew.

Peeved, Hanna was breathing fast. "Mrs. Ryder, Mother, I'd like to take my leave now and get a breath of air; maybe set a spell with Darby over to Miller's. It's always cooler there."

"You do look a bit peaked. You all right?" Suddenly there was a note of concern in Mrs. Pederson's voice.

"Um-hum," said Hanna. "Really. Fine."

"All right, then," Mrs. Pederson said.

Hanna was about to walk out the door. Darby listened to Hanna's mother tell Mrs. Ryder, "A flibbertigibbet, and worst tempered-soul the Savior ever put in Parcel Bluffs. Why the only person who can hold rein on that girl is Cayo."

On the other side of the closed door where Darby listened, Hanna turned and said, "Now that is just not so, Mother."

Darby heard Mrs. Pederson's reply. "But he ain't interested in you, Hanna. He's got eyes only for Darby."

"Your girl sure is a handful you didn't bargain for, Zora," Mrs. Ryder said.

"That is God's own truth."

Darby jumped back clutching the dry goods package she was carrying, ran to the end of the store front and stepped into the street. She dashed all the way back to Miller's.

Out of breath, she entered the store. "Sorry," she said to a perplexed looking Fern.

"I'll deliver the package later." She deposited the package under the shelf by the cash register.

"No explanation?" Fern said, and peered out the window to see Hanna amble toward them with her most genteel walk. "Ah, well, now. I see. Here comes your friend Hanna, and using a Mexican lace parasol as a walking stick. Sooooo fine. Prim and proper." Fern snickered.

Darby joined Fern at the window to see Hanna on the boardwalk, sashaying towards Miller's.

Fern put her arm around Darby's shoulder. "Bet she's calculating what she'll buy as a pretext for walking in here without her mother. Rock candy, you think? Or maybe she's hoping she's timed the visit right and perhaps Cayo hasn't been here yet."

"I declare!" Darby said, surprised that Fern had an inkling about Hanna's feelings for Cayo, and moved out from Fern's hold, fanning her face with her apron. She went to assist a lady with her shopping list.

Darby watched Hanna from the corner of her eye. She had come inside and glanced around. Hanna waved to Darby, who was still waiting on the customer. When Darby finished, she nudged Fern's arm to tally up the customer's bill. "I need to have a moment's privy to tend something personal, if it'd be all right?"

Fern straightened. "Go ahead, Darby." Fern gave her a knowing smile.

"Morning, Miss Fern," Hanna said.

"Good day," Fern said in a formal, stiff voice.

Hanna followed Darby as she stepped into the back storeroom behind a beaded curtain. They perched themselves on a bale of cotton. Both girls fanned themselves; Darby with her apron and Hanna with a lace smock.

"Did you get my message?" Darby asked.

"What message?" Hanna closed her parasol and placed it next to her.

"I told Cayo to tell you I'd be over after your supper tonight to say my farewells."

Hanna's face flushed. "Cayo was here already? Where'd he go?"

"Left to finish the rest of his town business. Mighty interested in a hired hand, aren't you, Miss Hanna? Thought you'd be caring to hear the particulars of my departure east."

"I sure am. It's just I'm surprised is all."

Darby flicked her hands down her apron and smoothed the folds. "Surprised at what?"

"He came in so early," Hanna said and kicked at a wooden box.

"He always comes for his ironing. Came in early today 'cause he's plum out of chewing tobacco."

"That's untrue, Darby McPhee," Hanna said in her know-it-all voice.

"You calling me a liar? What's got into you? The man bought chewing tobacco—"

"He couldn't possibly chaw a whole pouch in two hours." Hanna's hands fidgeted.

"The pouch was empty." Darby stressed the last word, scrunching her eyes for a better look at Hanna.

"I saw Daddy fling a small bulging purse to him this very morning—"

"We're arguing over something real dumb, you know that? I don't give a tinker's damn—"

"No need to curse." Hanna patted down the front of her dress.

"Why you're jealous, and flushing red. Got a hankering for your Daddy's ranch hand, now don't you, little Miss Hanna Pederson?"

"No—"

"That's a sin of covetousness. And a lie. You know how I feel about him. Known it always. Out the sky drops a hawk, no, a vulture. Some friend you are." Darby jumped off the bale. "You could have leastwise had the decency to wait till I was tucked in at Aunt Bea's."

"Did you tell him your feelings yet?"

Darby stood straighter and put her hands on her hips, tapping her fingers. She swayed slightly. "That's for me to know and you to find out. None of your concern. And forget the message. I won't be riding out to see you tonight. Or ever."

"For a shop girl, you sure got a lot of sass." Hanna stood, took hold of her parasol, and turned on her heels.

Darby parted the curtain of beads and accompanied Hanna to the door. "Allow me." Darby opened the door; then slammed it shut behind her.

The bell jangled so loud that Fern came from behind the back counter to see what the fuss was about. "My oh my, that spoiled young lady needs a solid whooping."

Darby smoothed her apron front and looked at Fern. She sighed. "She's not a lady, by any means. She's a slithering snake in the grass—hissing and striking when you least expect."

Fern stepped closer and put her hands on Darby's shoulders. "I've never seen you so upset. What is it? You're crying."

"I'm not. It's just vexation." She wiggled out of Fern's grasp and walked to the storefront.

"She ain't worth your exasperation or weariness," Fern said.

"Trouble is I'm more than hurt. To think I considered her my best friend, even wanted her to be my maid of honor on my wedding day."

"You certainly don't have to worry your pretty head about that—why that's way in the future."

"I'm a woman grown, Fern. With real feelings for a man. Just that you, Pa and the boys can't see it yet."

Just then, Fern's husband Harris bustled through the door with news about some bandit caught red-handed trying to hold up the stagecoach at Raton Pass.

"Was anyone hurt?" Fern asked, concerned.

"No. As luck would have it, two lawmen were on the stage, one riding inside and the other on top next to the whip. The lone outlaw tried to make out he had a gang behind a bunch of pinon trees and scrub pines on a bluff nearby. But they managed to waylay him instead of the other way round. If he'd have gotten hold of the box, he could've retired from his highwayman's life for good."

"What took you so long to get back?" Fern asked, re-stocking the lower shelves, covered with oilcloth.

"I heard the news in Santa Fe Plaza, so I stayed put to see if they'd bring him in, but then saw it was getting late, so I left." He shrugged.

"Did you get a sample of that special feed Captain Pederson asked for?" Fern said, a worried look creasing her brow.

"Plum forgot," he said, exhaling. "I'll send a boy round in the morning."

"Cayo's in town, maybe he can do you the favor since he'll be heading back that way in a while," Darby offered.

"Nah. My responsibility and I'll look to it," Harris said, tying his long black apron in front of him.

Darby breathed a relieved sigh. *Good. Now Cayo's sure to be able to walk me home.*

***

At four o'clock sharp, Darby said goodbye to Harris and Fern Miller. She thanked Harris and hugged Fern, who then put Darby's pay with a little something extra, in her pocket. Darby thanked her and walked out the delivery entrance at back of the store. Cayo slouched against the wall of the general store, his hat pulled low over his eyes. He tipped it back and stood up straight just as Darby closed the door behind her.

She walked outside and shielded her eyes. As soon as they adjusted to the brightness, she dropped her hand. She wanted Cayo to take hold of it, but knew he wouldn't even if he was dying to. How to begin?

"You'll have to walk back, too. Are you sure—" She faltered.

"Don't mind," he said. Overcome by shyness, he looked away.

After about ten minutes she began to speak but faltered trying to make small talk. He took up where she left off, but his efforts were clumsy, more endearing.

Sagebrush rolled across the path. A slight breeze came down from the mountains. Scrub pines, pinons, dandelions, yuccas, thistles and nettles covered the dry patchwork of red earth adjacent to the pathway. Her eyes raked the horizon and traversed the nearby fields sparsely populated with prairie sagebrush, milkweed, and cattails. Wild iris interspersed yarrow and sand verbena. And in the far off foothills, cactus.

Cayo linked his thumbs in the belt loops of his pants and Darby walked with her arms in back of her, right hand grasping her left thumb.

She stopped to pick a piece of prairie grass and kept on walking as she chewed the flat blade till it gave up the last of its juices. Then she tossed it, watching the slight breeze glide it to the ground like a kite to the right. She stopped again in the middle of the path.

"I've been meaning to tell you about my Aunt Bea's letter."

"Don't think I want to hear if it's to do with them bags you'll be packing."

"I need to get away from my brothers and I lack book learning. I'll miss Pa, but he'll get on, and before you know it I'll be back in Parcel Bluffs—"

"Not so sure there's such a thing as coming home. Once a critter leaves the nest, he gets a taste for flying high. Things look mighty different from up there."

"How'd you know? You a bird?"

"I been a bird sometimes in Indian country. I've tasted ground herbs make you fly like a feathered arrow, make you know life from the inside of an eagle."

Darby and Cayo continued walking, shoulders almost touching.

"What's it like?" she asked.

"Like to bust out your skin, wanting to hold on tight to a girl. Never let go, if that girl be you."

Darby opened her mouth to say something, but stopped and merely looked sideward. She was afraid to start walking again, kicking up little squalls of dust for fear she'd never recapture this moment. But she had to look at him, see the moonless night of his blue eyes almost the color of ink, his sandy hair the shade of summer wheat blowing in a breeze.

"I've been dust-deviling all over—a tossed tumbleweed. It's time I settled down. My folks have a ranch—had a place, and I still got the deed to it . . ."

"How'd you get the deed?"

"Long story. I lost my folks."

She slowed her steps. "I'd like to hear it."

"Take forever," he said.

"But you'll think on it now when you leave me, won't you?" Darby stood dead still in her tracks.

"I will."

After a while, she took a piece of the brown wrapping paper she used to parcel and pack things up in Miller's. She opened it to show him a dried, pressed yellow buttercup. She handed it to him. He looked at it for a long time, then folded and put it in his shirt pocket.

Darby saw the hallowed bone and bear claw necklace he wore at the open-collar of his work shirt, but was too shy to ask him about it.

When he put his hands in his pants' pockets, he pulled out three seeds: corn, squash and bean. He handed them to her saying, "My grandmother planted these—they're the three sisters." Then he shrugged his shoulders.

She hesitated a minute, looked at the seeds. "Do you always carry them?"

"Most times. To remind myself of where I been. Never want to forget people I cared for."

Darby handed him back the seeds. "Thanks for telling me. I think of you sometimes ... when I'm pitching hay, or milking, or rag-washing the kettles, or dusting Momma's Bible. I read the names inside sometimes and think on someday seeing my name and kin in it." Darby brushed back the hair off her face. "Even with my eyes open, looking at something else, I see you. I see your face. I see your eyes looking at me."

Cayo spat the rest of his chewing tobacco through his teeth. "I seen you churning butter as I flew over the cottonwoods," he said, pointing to the sky. "Even before I knowed it was you. I saw the black metal beast riding east, too, when it winged past Indian country." Cayo pulled out the folded paper next to his tobacco pouch, looked at it, put it back in his shirt pocket.

"Maybe that was today and not a day in the future. Are you sure it was me? Or are you just saying that?" Darby's eyes followed his movements, remembered the feel of the doeskin, rabbit fur and bead-work of his tobacco pouch that she'd touched just a few hours ago. Who had made it for him?

"Hanna came to Miller's after you left. She told me her Daddy gave you a pouch full of tobacco this morning."

"That'd be true."

"You bought tobacco from me. Hanna—"

"I gave it to Bob Jones. Don't cotton to gifts with tie strings, makes a man indebted. I didn't ask for it." He took off his hat and wiped his sleeve across his forehead.

"Miss Hanna," he said. "Well, now, she's got some real learning to do. She ain't no Darby McPhee."

Darby felt her cheeks get hot. The McPhee ranch was in sight. Cayo took Darby's hand in his and squeezed the fingertips gently, opened her fingers and laced his through hers. He dropped her hand, took a strong hold of it and walked her to the shade of a piñon tree on top of the bluff.

The whole valley lay before them like a painted postcard. Darby leaned against the tree. They stood inches apart. Cayo rested his hand on the trunk just above her shoulder.

"I ain't much with words, Darby, but I got lots of feelings. If you want, I'll talk to your Pa. Tonight if you say, and you can pack your duds, not to travel east, but to come set up house with me."

Darby looked a little frightened and puzzled, until Cayo added, "It'd be a proper wedding with a preacher or a padre. Don't much matter to me. You tell me if and when you're a wanting to get hitched."

He put his other hand up above her shoulder.

Bird in a cage.

She noticed that not all of his hair was sandy-colored some of it was speckled with white in this light. How old was he?

"I'll be moving— heading back to see about my family spread. Probably laying fallow all these years, but with a good hand, she'd be mighty pretty. He nudged his chin in the direction of the Sangre de Cristo Range. "Soon as the summer corn's in. For now I got a cabin tucked up in the woods, needs a woman's hands to give it warmth."

"I was banking on learning to be a teacher." She heard herself hedge. "Where've you been all these years? Why hadn't you settled on your family's ranch?"

He took hold of both her hands.

"No one here knows my past, and for now I aim to keep it that way. My life's the present and future. There's things I can teach you ain't in no books. You can school your own tiny tots. Ours. Time I settled— been a tumbleweed in wind too long."

She listened, her heartbeat pulsing faster with every word he stammered on. Her mind raced. Will he ever share his past with me? No fair asking a man to wait. *And me afraid he wouldn't want me. But he does.* Darby grew so still, she thought he'd hear the pounding in her chest.

Finally she said, "Never been east, nor seen the ocean." *But the deep pools of his eyes will be forever. A safety net.*

She let go of his hands.

"You'll glimpse it all when our baby calls you in fright 'cause he climbed a perch too tall, and you catch him in your arms. Lots of folks never go east or travel to the sea. Besides your Aunt ain't near the ocean."

She took a deep breath and blurted out, "I can't chance leaving you to make high-cheeked babies with the likes of Hanna Pederson."

Cayo smiled a small smile.

Darby returned the smile. "Got some yellow gingham I was fixing to sew into curtains."

"Yellow'd be mighty pretty on them cabin windows. What do you say, Darby?"

She hesitated, thinking that it would mean not seeking an education and then her heartbeats sped up with the thought of losing him. "If that's a proposal, Cayo Bradley, my answer's yes. I best get home afore Pa sees Aunt Bea's letter."

"I'll come round to talk to your Pa at eight."

"Make it 8:30? Got to write to Aunt Bea."

Time sped to no time. Before she could even dream it, Cayo took hold of Darby's sun-warmed arms and clasped them around his neck. She closed her eyes and tilted up her chin. But the second Cayo covered her lips with his, she opened her eyes. A kiss for all times. A kiss to remember.

Chapter Four

The Bradley Spread
Rio Arriba County, New Mexico

Cayo left Darby after that kiss and thought of what she'd said to him. Sure enough on the walk back to town, his mind hurtled back to how he'd lost his parents and his sisters. He hadn't mentioned them to her, just the word, folks. He'd been called by another name then; a name different from the one he went by now, even the name he knew as his own in his head: Cayo, shortened from Coyote—his totem animal, the one he drew energy from—the one the Jicarilla called Trickster. The animal had intelligence, skill, wisdom and guile—all wrapped up into what he'd become.

But back then in 1859, the name of that boy, the one that had ceased to exist on the day he recalled so vividly, was Connor Bradley. The minute Cayo conjured up the ten-year old boy Connor, he saw his life unfold on the Bradley spread as clearly as if he were watching a stage play.

It had been the hour just before dusk. Connor stood by the window, a sentinel on guard, awaiting his father's approach. Only that morning his father had told him no matter how much you prepare for events, most times life surprises you, and things seem to happen of their own accord—actions and deeds have consequences that cannot be undone, never reckoned with, or have a cause and effect unimagined. His father finished the discussion, saying, Surprises ain't always happy.

Connor's father, Robert Cullen Bradley, had readied them for such a day, but it was the long string of days to follow that Connor was ill-equipped to handle. In case the Apaches attacked, Connor's father had laid stores in the nearby cave they could escape to through a tunnel from the house. When food was scarce, the Indians were known to attack farms and ranches. There were many rumors about how ruthless they could be at inflicting torture, but Robert hadn't seen any of that, and believed most of the tales were exaggerated. Still, he was taking no chances.

Their dog, Lady, scampered about, barking a greeting for Robert who came riding in hell-for-leather on a lathered horse. Connor came out and caught the horse's reins.

His father dismounted. "Bring Pinto back of the house, boy," he said. He took off his hat and wiped his brow with his shirtsleeve. "Don't put him up in the barn or the corral. Feed and water him and wipe him down. Bring the saddle and the horse into the mudroom. Get a dry saddle blanket. Tie him to the back door. Where are your mother and the girls?"

"Ma made the girls take a nap in your room after they ate. She's gone over to McGrath's to warn them."

"She ain't back yet?"

"Ma and me got the pails and water buckets filled—ready inside. I soaked down the roof. Then Ma took off. Gone to get little Douglas. I told her to stay put—that I'd go—"

"She promised Meg McGrath if there was Indian trouble she'd get the baby and let him go out with you through the tunnel. A promise is a promise, son. Did your Ma have time to cook?"

"Cooked and stored." When she'd finished, Connor's mother tied pemmican, a sausage-like staple of dehydrated, pounded meat mixed with melted fat and dried berries to his belt. He fitted it into an inner side pocket so it wouldn't interfere with his crawling. The girls stashed theirs inside an apron pocket sewn to the side.

"Water in the tunnel?"

"I filled the Army surplus canteens and set them out at the end of the tunnel."

They walked towards the rear of the house. "Got coverings?"

"Blankets to wear as ponchos."

Connor unhitched the saddle.

"I could eat half a steer," Pa said.

"A dish laid out for you on the table. Biscuits too. Cold by now."

"Candles and sulfur matches ready?"

Connor nodded.

Robert took off his gloves and tossed them with his hat on the ground next to the trough.

He unbuttoned his shirt and washed his hands face and neck, grabbed a piece of gunnysack on a nail by the hitching post and dried off with it.

"Every gun and rifle loaded—a store of ammunition on hand at the windows, and all windows shuttered and bolted—only shoot holes opened—like you said."

He tousled his son's hair. "I'll eat. You finish up with Pinto. I'll ready the girls soon's your Ma's back and we're in the house and all locked up. You start your run with the girls and Douglas soon as I tell you. You make it a game with them, you hear me? Quiet as church mice."

"Ma said when you got back, to get the girls up and help them stack their mattresses at the door and window."

"Soon as I eat."

When Connor came in and asked if something was wrong.

"Sit a minute, son."

His father took a few spoonsful of the beans. He washed it down with a jelly glass of water, staring off into space.

There was a little silence; then his father began to talk and Connor knew it was to fill the spaces and take the edge off his frayed nerves. "Remember when we were digging out the tunnel and the clay was micaceous?"

"Micaceous?"

"I explained that the clay has mica in it—"

"Oh yeah, those shiny bits—like the clay pot Ma uses for the beans."

"The earth is filled with wonders like this and with wondrous people we know nothing about. My father Jesse Bradley worked as a miner in California."

"He the one taught you how to dig the tunnel?"

His father nodded. "One day your grandpa drank water from a bronze cup with a strange green handle with a carved dragon. The stone was jade from China. He handed the cup back to the Chinese coolie who had a black braid that hung down his back to his waist. My father told me he didn't understand all the jabbering the Celestials spoke—that's what they called themselves—the slant-eyed people. The man bowed when my Pa returned the cup to the water bearer. Frustrated not to grasp another man's tongue or ways, he bowed back, and the man smiled. Always try to understand the other's point of view, son. It keeps the peace."

Connor wanted to say something, but just nodded.

"I'd turned sixteen, reached my Pa's height of six feet two inches when me and my brother George lit out of Sacramento the day after. No way in hell I wanted to be a dirt farmer like Pa. George and me got work slinging sledgehammers, mining in another town, like my Pa done when I was your age, only this one was far from California. We never did see that country or my Pa again. The country's wide and I had good eyesight and intended to see much of it before I decided what in hell I wanted to do in life. You can figure the rest."

"You met and married Ma?"

"This is her family's spread, and here I am a dirt farmer, cattle rancher in godforsaken, Rio Arriba County—just like I never wanted. Upper River," he paused, "so named because the Rio Grande runs through it—the only grace God gave this place. What I'm saying is things don't always pan out like you plan. You just got to do what you got to do to scrape together a life. You don't go finding your life, it finds you."

He patted Connor's hand and though Connor wanted to pull away from such a soft gesture, he knew enough to let his father talk and keep touching his hand.

"Something else." Pa got up and went to a highboy and opened the drawer. He took out a ledger, set it down on the table and opened it. He took out an envelope and extracted a piece of paper folded in three and showed it to his son.

"This here's the deed to our spread—house and property. When Ma gets back she's going to sew it in the hem of your trousers. Keep it with you always. Never lose it. No matter what." He refolded the paper, pleated it into a narrower piece, and placed it on the table.

Connor pointed to the paper. "Shouldn't you keep that?"

The father looked at his son, and in an instant, the boy knew that after this night, he might never see his father again. Connor stood, threw his arms about his father's waist and sobbed.

Pa stood back. "Look here, you've got to be strong. I'm depending on you. Remember last year when you couldn't slit the nanny goat's neck? Never again back down on anything you must do. Understand me?"

Connor pulled back, dropped his arms, looked up at his father and nodded.

"Say it."

"I'll never flinch from my duty again."

"That's a promise, I reckon."

"Yes, sir."

Pa sat down and picked up his spoon. His eyes looked glassy, like marbles. In the light they shone a rust-red, like Connor's aggies.

When Pa had given Connor the marbles he'd said, "Sure as shooting, Cain and Abel didn't have them pretty as these. Must of had little mud balls for fighting. All boys love to play at war. The Indians teach them from the cradle to be warriors. A few years ago there was a huge battle near Taos. About two hundred and fifty Jicarilla and Utes fought against the Calvary. Our men lost brutally. The Battle of Cineguilla. Your Uncle George was a Dragoon, and was killed. Indians are fierce fighters, brutally strong. Stronger when being starved."

His Pa had finished eating when they heard pounding hooves. Lady ran to the door barking, wanting to get outside to welcome Agnes, Connor's mother. She rode to the back of the house and dropped the reins of an old bay called Gypsy. She held a bundle in her arms which was partially covered by her flaming red hair. Lady chased her tail and barked with joy.

"Douglas wouldn't leave his Ma," she said, breathing hard. She handed over an infant to Connor and pushed back her long hair, retying it into a horsetail with a piece of calico. "Here, take this papoose cradle, too." She untied it from the back of her saddle and gave it to Connor. "I'll strap baby Audra to your back, Connor. I'll give her chamomile tea now and a small dose of laudanum when I need to. I don't want her crying out in the woods once you get there."

She slipped off the horse just as Robert asked, "Why in God's name, woman, did you take the infant? Connor could've managed with our girls and Douglas, but to give Connor another burden—"

"What would ye have me do, then, leave her to certain—"

"Hold your tongue. Not all Indians are murderous. When they're hungry they raid—they're marauding now for lack of food. You know it and it's common knowledge. This recent trouble and the uprising of small bands was the cause of our own kind—white men. Thieves, the lot of them."

"That's grand, Robert. You defending the Apaches? Tell me why, then, did we go to all of this trouble of digging and excavating a tunnel?"

"Calm yourself, woman. Get in the house."

"Hand me the baby, Connor," Ma said.

"Ma's horse, too, Pa?"

"Indeed." Pa exchanged the horse's reins for the cradle Connor held, and his mother took the baby. Ma pushed passed the men, went inside directly to her room to put Audra in the cradle, where the baby boy she'd lost to fever had lain not but a month before. She awakened the girls.

Connor led Gypsy forward. The horse reared at the door but Connor managed him.

Once inside, he unsaddled and wiped the horse down, then re-saddled him. Gypsy watered but only after he'd cooled down, but he wouldn't eat. Connor lugged some hay into the mudroom, went out and got Pa's horse, brought him inside and bolted the door. Pa and Connor heaved his mattress against the front door and pushed a small vanity behind it.

"All Ma's care gone for naught and shot to hell," Pa said, looking at the mess.

"We've made a fort out of our house—a real messy one," Connor said, wiping his brow.

They checked the back door lock and bolts, shoved the girls' mattresses and upright beds in back, checked all the shutters on the windows and shot the bolts on those Connor had skipped.

"Got to be more careful, son, 'specially now. We're depending on you," Pa said. "Sit down with your sewing box, Agnes."

Ma retrieved her kit, giving her husband a pained look, and Connor knew it was from the verbal lashing he'd given her outside.

Pa handed her the folded deed. "I'm sorry if I spoke with anger, Agnes."

She looked at her husband, and Connor sensed unspoken forgiveness on her face.

"Sew it in his cuff," Pa said. "Take off your trousers, Connor. Give them to Ma. Don't ever wash them unless you take the deed out first."

With a pleading look at his parents, Connor begged them, "Come with us."

His sister Maura started to cry and Beth put an arm around her.

"Hush up," Ma said, raising her eyebrows. "There's an end to it now."

She snipped the thread of the hem partway around, and leaving the pants on her lap, threaded a needle. She worked the folded document, wrapped in a soft piece of doeskin, into the hem and sewed it closed. "No matter what, never lose the deed," she said, handing the boy back his pants. "Remember your father's and my blood and bones are in this house, on this land."

Connor buttoned up his pants and looked at his mother, his understanding so complete she couldn't hide her desperation nor her tears.

"Come give me a hug, Connor, and mind your sisters," Ma said. "Pa and I'll ride out when we can." Ma kissed each of the girls. She took off her chain and locket and placed it around Maura's neck, tucking it inside her blouse. "God bless my children."

"Wait," Ma said, "Connor—" she struggled taking off her wedding ring. "Connor." She took his right hand and put the ring on his middle finger.

"Ma, no—please."

"Stand tall, boy, and remember the important things of life: you're from strong stock, you have an angel beside you, and everything in this world can be righted with love and forgiveness." She took his face in her hands and kissed his forehead and each of his wet cheeks. "Now go."

Pa said, "We'll circle round and when it's clear meet at the cave. Don't light nary a candle, no fire tonight. No matter what. And stay put till after noon. No matter what you hear or think you hear. Are we clear?"

"As water in the well." He cleared his throat and tried for a mature voice. "Pa," Connor said, "I'd like to take Lady."

"No, son, she'd give away your hiding place with warning barks at someone's approach. She'll come with us when all's clear. Remember, no fire tonight. Tomorrow you can get the wood piled up in the back of the cave and light the dead mesquite. It don't hardly smoke none."

"Girls, did you put extra petticoats on like I told you?" Ma asked.

"Yes, Ma," they said, bleating sheep in unison. She helped them into their dark, long woolen capes and fastened the loose-fitting toggles in front.

In the distance, a call like a whippoorwill. Three short owl hoots in response.

It had begun. Pa grabbed Connor and held him close. He released the boy and pushed him away. Pa kissed the girls and gently shoved them to the false floor opening in the back room that led to a narrow, below-ground alley between the house and a hillock. Pa was a careful man, and had done many practice runs with his children in the event that such an escape would be necessary.

37

Conner looked at his mother, memorizing her face, then pushed past her to get baby Audra. He put his arms through the thongs of the papoose and tied it round his waist and chest. His mother wrapped the sleeping baby in a shawl and placed her inside the papoose. Ma spun Connor around and pulled him to her. She held him tightly by his shoulders, showering his face with kisses.

"Don't let no savage take my baby girls, Connor," she whispered in a hoarse voice. She held his face like a vise with her two hands and looked him in the eyes. "Lord forgive me! And you, too, but you know what I'm saying?" She released her grip and reached for the gun on the table. She handed him a loaded Paterson revolver which he took hold of by the varnished walnut grip and shoved in the back of his pants held up by a belt—the baby resting on top of it. He then took a small knife from his mother's hands and sheathed it to an attached leather ring, drawing a leather thong around his calf and cinched it. Then he kissed his mother's hands.

"I feel like a bear, loaded down with all this stuff."

"Connor, promise, no swear to me—" she said, pleading in her words.

"Yes, Ma'am, I swear."

"Here." Pa said and flung a tarp to Connor. "Cover the baby—get moving," he said, and sent the children down the trap door and inside the tunnel. Connor heard his father maneuver a huge, thick slate slab over the tunnel opening. The girls had already begun belly crawling along, using forearms and elbows to move fast ahead of Connor, the way they'd been taught. He blew out the candle and started crawling with little Audra strapped to his back, asleep with the drops Ma had given her. She weighed more than he thought she would and the papoose cradle was uncomfortable.

Thudding noises. Pa covered the trap door with earth and rocks. Then silence. Connor knew Ma and Pa were scattering hay and piling on bales. He knew enough not to listen anymore and kept moving, breathing in and out his nostrils, keeping his mouth shut.

At various intervals along the tunnel, there were lit oil miner's lamps. Connor blew them out one at a time as he passed them. As they crawled on they heard muffled war cries and whoops that made their blood congeal worse than any ghost story old grandpa McGrath told. They stopped. The earth pounded with horses' hooves.

A fissure leaked in some silt, and sand sifted down from above lightly at first. Connor was afraid of a cave-in, but kept on, remembering his father's last words to him, "Get moving," despite hideous cries and shouts, and gunfire cracking above him. The noises slowed his crawl, but he picked up, hoping to gain momentum to recapture his pace.

His father's voice was in his ears again, saying, "Don't rush, Connor, get an even speed for yourself." He must conserve breath for the run at the tunnel exit. The gun in his belt felt like a fat-barreled ax handle in the small of his back, the weight of the papoose on top, and the gun rubbing against his back seemed to triple the weight he carried. He was glad he'd cinched the knife to the outside of his right calf and it'd stayed in place.

At the next turn in the tunnel, Connor doused the second to last lamp. Ahead he saw the girls struggle out of their ponchos.

"Girls," he said, sharpness in his tone. "Put them capes back on." He was sweating, took off the tarp, and folded the underneath blanket like a serape. He put back the tarp and hurled his poncho over his shoulder. Audra strapped to his back, and the impediment of the rough tarp made him wonder if she was still breathing. The girls waited for Connor huddled up and wild-eyed ahead of him. He blew out the last lamp.

"Good girls, you're set. I'll stick my head out first for a look see. Scrunch back."

39

As they scooted back, he struggled with the trap door to slide it across and dirt, grass, shrubs and rocks fell in on his right shoulder. He climbed the wooden rungs of the ladder, and grabbed a branch of a dead juniper jutting out of the earth that his father had planted deep at the tunnel top. He broke off a small branch, put this in his belt and stuck his head outside to survey the land. The tunnel had been completed a month ago and they'd tried a run, but now the breach between the hole and tree line seemed staggering. The exit was supposed to be in a thick woodsy copse of junipers and slash pines for cover. In his father's haste to finish the tunnel, it was short by at least a furlong. Connor wished he'd practiced the run from the tunnel to the cave at the bottom of the foothills.

Dusk had settled, succumbing into night. He swallowed hard, hands clammy with the realization they'd have to run under cover of a shower of stars, which he knew would make them more visible and the distance seem longer. "Dang," he said hoarsely into the opening. He cleared his throat—backed down into the tunnel. He stepped off the ladder and wiped his hands on his thighs.

"Dang," he repeated.

"What's wrong?" Beth said.

"Nothing. Follow me. He clambered up first and pointed. "Just run for that stand of cottonwoods and keep low—when you reach it, lie down. Maura was on the last rung of the ladder. "Now you, pretty Maura. Don't' cry. Just run to Beth."

When she was out, he watched the girls run ahead. Then he scampered behind to see if they'd gotten to the safe point. They were belly down. Connor peered into the darkness till there was no movement on the ground. He looked back toward the house and saw the barn on fire. He had a sinking feeling in the pit of his stomach, and shook his head as if that would stop the forlorn ache, as if that would make his tears cease. Then he remembered his father's words, when he was riding Pinto before the horse was fully broken. "A man crying loses his sense of what to do next. Get hold of yourself, Connor, and stay that horse." With that he remembered Pa had said to cover the opening and hide their tracks. He slid the door in place, tossing stones and dirt, broken branches over it. As he did, he pictured Lady, like him, ever obedient. The baby squirmed and fussed. He loped off toward the girls, took off the tarp and papoose and gave the baby over to Beth.

He wanted to tell them to run for the cave, but thought it better to lead them.

"I'm going to hide our tracks. When I get back we'll move and start our climb. Be careful and go slow. Don't bend branches. We'll go in the same line like we just done. Beth first with the papoose, then Maura and me last, covering tracks. Keep flat down now."

"The barn's on fire, Connor," Beth said.

"Hard to tell from this distance—maybe something else," he said, stunned he could lie so fast, and loped off toward the tunnel at an even pace.

On the trail back, he brushed over tracks with the branch of leaves he'd tucked in his belt. Hunched over with the juniper branch, he swept some more. They were covered, but he prayed for rain. Glancing at the starlit sky, there was no chance of that. If it had been rainy season ditches and arroyos would be flooded and he wouldn't be worrying about disguising tracks because the tunnel would've been washed out, and he would have been back at the house fighting Apache. How long could his parents hold out? Would they get to ride the readied horses to safety? Would his faithful dog Lady escape to find him?

Once in the cave, the children spent the night, cold and fretful. In the morning they ate some meager provisions. Beth fed the baby with tied pig gut that served as a teat. The baby suckled the milky liquid laced with laudanum his mother made to keep the child quiet and sleepy so as not to cry.

Beth changed the diaper cloths and put the dirty ones in a small pouch. "I'll have to wash and dry these soon. We're running out." Beth rocked the baby.

"Not for a spell. Can't leave here till I scout about and look for Pa's all clear signal," Connor lied, knowing that if his father had survived the fight, he'd have come for them by now. The boy made his way to the cave entrance and peered out, but dense foliage blocked his view. He removed and cleared a small corner, turned toward Beth, rocking and crooning to the baby. "Stay hushed while I look around. Quit yammering, Beth. Baby Audra's already asleep."

Beth stopped rocking the baby and wedged her in between the rock and the rolled up tarp.

"Be back in two shakes of a lamb's tail," Connor said in a low voice, and crawled out. He climbed to the top of the ridge. His family's homestead smoldered. His eyes stung from the windy acrid air and tears blinded him. He forged another way back to the cave, wiped his face and nose with his shirt sleeve.

Connor, afraid to be afraid, felt he had no time for it. He was decision-maker for himself and for the sisters his parents had trusted into his care. He brushed hair out of his eyes, as tendrils of panic threatened to overtake him, as if the terror inside him became a live, crawly thing.

Burning. He smelled charred wood wafted on the wind as he rearranged the cave covering. The girls spoke in whispers. Connor heard horses. He signaled his sisters to hush up. He looked at the gun. He looked at the girls. He knew this might be his first, last and only chance to use it. But how could he? What if the riders weren't an Indian scouting party, but just some miners, or mountain men passing through? Couldn't they be just as dangerous? Hadn't his father also warned him against them? He'd have to decide. Their approach was imminent. He hid the gun in back of a rock with a small overhanging lip, pushing it toward the rear, undid the knife, slipped it into his boot and rolled down his pant leg. Baby Audra whimpered, and Beth held the baby so close that Connor thought that Beth might smother her.

A strong odor of sweat and bear grease closed in on them. Then, a huge Indian with black braids wrenched aside the camouflage and stood in the cave opening. The girls screamed in terror. Sunlight lit the ochre and red slash marks across his cheeks, glancing off his knife blade, the hilt of it in one hand, the barrel of a rifle in the other.

"*Dábeenésdzi'é*," he called out. He repeated it loudly, "*Dábeen-ésdzi'é.*" He brandished his rifle.

Connor somehow understood this to mean: they're afraid. He stood in front of his sisters, summoning courage instigated by the Indian's sneer. With a thud, another Indian dropped through a hole from above. How had he done that? Had they known about this cave? Two more rushed into the cavern and flanked the first one. More screams from the girls, and now the baby was crying. Connor trembled with the memory of what his mother had asked him—to kill his own sisters—before they got scalped or raped. How could he?

The massive Indian pointed to the cowering girls, and the boy understood the expression meant: they're afraid. Connor stood straighter, summoning courage, wishing he could kill his sisters, pronouncing the word *dábeenésdzi'é* mentally, committing it to memory, though no sound ushered from his lips.

"Mbai', Mbai'" said the Goliath. He pushed Connor aside and yanked Beth to her feet by her hair, the same texture but shades darker than her mother's.

His mother's words came to his ears as if she were speaking them. Fear is only the absence of knowledge of how to combat something or someone—it's the quaking in the presence of power, a warning in the company of danger. Think, Connor, she'd said, facing the charge of a bear, what do you do?

So the boy understood that he must not cower, that he must appear bigger than he was to this giant before him. Connor spread his arms like an eagle in flight and started barking out orders to the girls. "Put the baby down, Beth." His startled sister wrenched herself away and did as her brother commanded. Standing in place, moving arms like a bird with an injured wing, he yelled in a loud voice, "Maura, curtsey to the savage, for the sake of Christ Jesus our savior and redeemer," sounding like his father in a fit of rage. "Stop blubbering. This Chief ain't going to eat us alive," he said. *No and worse he ain't going to kill us either.* He wanted to die himself for not carrying out his mother's plea, knowing he'd subject these girls to a life of servitude among heathens. Chattel, his mother had said, and whores. *How could she have given me this dastardly mission?* Why had he hesitated? So cowardly a deed. Could he do it now? Redeem himself? Reach behind the rock and blow his sisters' brains out and smash baby Audra upon the rock?

He shuddered as the Indians advanced closer.

"Stand up proper. Look him in the eye," Connor screamed to the whimpering girls. Both girls sobbed, but their cries had ceased. Only silent tears gushed down their cheeks. What if by the grace of God, his parents weren't dead, and got a posse to hunt for them? No time for distractions. *Be present.*

The Indian that the others were calling Mbai' whirled around toward them and pounded his chest, mimicking Connor's barking orders at the girls. Mbai' had the face of a wolf, and Connor wondered if that was his name.

Connor had heard stories often enough and knew the fate of these girls, mere children. They would be separated from each other. They'd be made squaws, become slaves to other women in whichever camp they'd be taken. His mother's girls would be forced to break camps, trudge behind horses, carry heavy loads like pack mules, become nomads on the move, who'd dress the meat of the hunt, cook, carry wood, haul water, beg for scraps of food like mangy dogs. He pictured his white-skinned, freckled-faced sisters forced to fornicate and do unseemly deeds with savages—men twice and three times their age. Old men would spread foul-smelling bodies upon them, ripping open their private parts.

It was then he saw the red-headed scalp still tied with a calico ribbon on one of the huge warrior's belts. Connor knew, then, that this was the leader of the raid, and not the one they called Mbai'. All in all he counted eight men, but he saw ten horses outside. Maybe two Indians had been killed, he thought, but no—those were his parents' horses.

Rocked to his core by the sight of his mother's hair, Connor dove behind the rock, rolled onto his shoulder, reached and grabbed the gun, cocked and fired it into the back of Beth's skull, as she faced the Indian. She fell clutching at air. Then Maura half turned in his direction, and he shot her through the temple—pretty Maura half-facing the Indian, half-facing her brother. He hurled the gun at the giant, which caught him in the chest as Connor whirled around, picked up the baby, and was about to dash her head upon the rock when the huge Indian tore her away. Connor pounded his chest as the Indian had done and screamed the most blood-curdling yell he could muster—pain cleaved and hacked his gut, seized his heart, clenched and squeezed off his life supply. Breathless. Connor found himself spun around and held in the air by another huge Indian. Connor contorted, kicked and flailed. The stunned Indian watched Connor's macabre dance. He stilled and the Indian let go.

Connor screamed the only name he'd understood. "Mbai', Mbai', here I am, come kill me!" He swooped down, stuck his hands in his sisters' blood, and drew a line across both his cheeks, down his nose, then swiped it, crisscrossing hands in opposite directions across his forehead. Then signed himself with the cross, yelling, "Kill me! Kill me now! Kill me, kill me," he screamed over and over until he was felled by a rifle butt to the back of the head landing in a heap at the feet of Mbai'.

Chapter Five

A Picnic

All last evening after Darby had pocketed Aunt Bea's letter, and told her father that it didn't contain anything urgent or important, she thought about Cayo. His broad shoulders, his slim waist, long legs—the way he sauntered with a slight sway and sometimes clicked his heels. What kind of a man was he really? She knew so little about him, much of it hearsay. But if she could judge by her feelings for him, she credited him with a heart capable of love.

She cooked dinner and cleaned the kitchen, hardly saying a word to anyone. All the while, her brain buzzed with reflections of everything she knew about him, had heard about him, wondered about him. She kept looking out the window, opening the door at the slightest noise, but he didn't come and the night grew dark. Was he a man who kept his word? After she wrote to her aunt, Darby finally surrendered to bed and a sleepless night.

The questions that made her toss all night were: Why didn't he come? What if he wanted to take possession of her before marriage? Would she be able to relinquish her prim and pure virginal body to him, and enslave herself forever to the whims of this coyote man? She wondered if she were a femme de glace—a woman of ice, frigid, cold and incapable of letting a man love her physically. This was a type of woman she never knew existed until she'd read about it in a novel. Her aunties didn't know her Momma had "borrowed" the book from Darby's dead uncle's private library and was now tucked under Darby's pillow. But no, she wasn't like that. She couldn't be.

***

Since she decided not to leave for St. Louis, the next morning she hurried to finish her chores and go to church services with Pa. Her brothers always managed to find something they needed to do that absolutely couldn't wait, and Pa never pushed them. Not that he was a religious man, but he tried to be out of respect for his departed wife and also to please his daughter.

Darby was glad she attended service for it gave her an opportunity to thank the Lord for all that was happening in her life. But when the pastor started preaching, she tuned his droning out and gazed through the open window at a monarch butterfly doing acrobatic somersaults in air. This gave her the chance to think and dream about how things might soon be as Mrs. Cayo Bradley.

She changed her Sunday best into comfortable riding clothes: a calico shirt and a wide soft suede skirt. When Cayo finally did come to call on her early that afternoon, she said without prelude, "Thought you were supposed to come to speak with Pa last night?" She pulled her long hair in back of her head and fixed it into a horse's tail with a piece of cord.

"It's not I don't have courage to ask." He stood at the bottom of the steps, hat in hand.

"Why didn't you show up?" She picked up her apron and fanned herself with it.

"Is he here now?"

"Gone into town to a meeting of ranchers. Mr. Pederson, too."

"That's why I'm here now. Couldn't get away last night."

Darby inspected his face for signs of truth in what he said. Finally she said, "Come set here on the porch a spell. I'll prepare a picnic basket and we can go for a ride."

"Sounds like a swell idea."

"Care for some lemonade while you're waiting?" she called from the window.

"That'd be mighty fine." He sat on a rocker and put his hat on his knee while in the kitchen, Darby put together what she thought of as a haphazard lunch on the fly.

They mounted their horses and rode to a secluded part of the river where she'd never been before. Riding beneath the tree crowns, the canted light sifted down though the branches and leaves lending the spot an ancient air, as though entering an old cathedral whose roof and eaves had been desecrated and destroyed by time. An air of solemnity surrounded her, the nature of a consecration.

Cayo spread a blanket and they ate the chicken and leftover breakfast biscuits and drank water from a canteen. When they'd finished the slight repast, it was hot and he said he wanted to swim.

It was early July and in the heat of the afternoon sun, Darby sat with Cayo in what he told her was his favorite place. She unlaced her shoes and took off her stockings. She wiggled her feet in the green grass.

Cayo said, "Watch out a little snake doesn't start crawling in and out your toes."

She immediately recoiled and pulled her feet up and tucked them under her skirt. She yanked a fistful of dry grass and rubbed it on her dusty shoes. The effect wasn't perfect, but they seemed cleaner.

A slight breeze ruffled his hair, but he was hot and sweaty. He sat and pulled off his boots and socks, one of which was darned. He took off his hat and tossed it in the high grass, then stripped off his shirt.

"Turn around if you don't want to see a naked jay bird."

He started to pull off his waist overalls—the denim pair made by Levi Strauss with the new copper rivets she'd sold him at Fern Miller's. She knew they cost $1.46 and nobody in the whole town looked as good as he did in them. Everyone else had to shorten the hems, but not Cayo.

"Turn around, Darby."

She felt brash, determined, yet skittish. "And miss the best spectacle I'll ever get to see? You go right ahead. I've seen men stark naked and pointing upwards before—I've got four brothers, you do recall, don't you?"

"I'm going to take me a swim to cool off. You wouldn't want to jump in with me, now, would you, sweet pea?"

Nobody had ever called her that before. It sounded so good to her. Sitting barefoot in the grass by the stream under a stand of cottonwoods, she forgot his warning about snakes and watched him finish pulling off his pants. Sure enough, he stood naked, stiff and pointing. He sauntered over and came to stand over her. He offered his hand. "Ain't you going to cool off with me?"

"Turn around. I'm slower than you."

"Not for every silver dollar carried on the Wells Fargo."

She stripped down to her bloomers and camisole and ran into the water ahead of him. She was treading water in two senses—the actual water she was in and the shallow pool of her head. This could only lead to trouble. How daring—she was risking her reputation. Forget her reputation. It was her virginity she was gambling. The secluded woods by the Rio Grande would never betray her. She knew there wasn't an actual road out here, and unless you knew the spot like Cayo did, you wouldn't be making a foray into these foothills. Her brain said, Caution, but her body, young, firm and hot from the external heat of the afternoon sun, and the internal furnace Cayo had stoked, ignored prudence. She heard

Hanna's voice in her ear, You give it away only one time. Darby resisted: *No use saving myself for worms. Then a conflicted inner voice, like hers, whispered: You shouldn't have agreed to marry so fast. You know nothing about him and you're going to break the solemn promise you made to Momma.*

She shuddered, and then swam to him. "Can you touch?"

"Sure." He reached out his hands to cinch her around the waist.

Pulling away, she said, "I mean the bottom."

"Yup."

"You know I've never been with a man before, Cayo."

"Yeah," he said, "a man knows, Darby, but I'm only asking you to swim."

"Well, then, why not?" She said with a conviction she didn't feel and swam a few strokes before he reached for her hand. He yanked her close, gripped her around the waist and nuzzled his head in the crook of her shoulder and kissed her neck with his hot lips and scratchy stubble. Grasped in the arms of a totally nude man—the man she loved—she felt him hard against her and she thought she'd swoon, but she was not that kind of girl.

He boosted her upon his hips and walked toward shore. Her legs tight around him, riding him, wrapped around him like a vine swirled around a tree trunk. She nipped his ear the way he did to her in the water, and passed her hand over his chin, and said, "You need a shave. I'm going to have chapped and burned skin if you don't stop."

He laid her down on the grass, her feet in the sandbank on top of pebbles, water washing over her calves.

He began to kiss her and she knew she was going to get what she thought she wanted. The kissing became intense, the pressure of their open mouths. Their lips came apart, and they breathed softly. She felt giddy with trying to still her breath. Her hands crept up his arms, and she pulled him into her. Her chest crushed under the weight of his. With a sudden frightened movement, she pushed him away and rolled out from under him. She ran to grab her clothes and headed for some scrub pine. "I can't," she yelled. "I just can't. It's not right. Not that I'm afraid of you. I swear it, but my Pa. My Pa would die if he found out, and I'd be disgraced and could never face him again."

"I gave my word, I'll marry you. A promise is a promise. This concern's between me and you—it ain't no matter for your Pa. This is you and me," he hesitated, "forever."

Bashfully, her cheeks crimson, she came back to him. She stood for a moment, undecidedly, then dropped her clothes. He stood up and pulled her into his arms, kissing her nose, her cheeks, her chin and neck, testing the delicate swirl of her ear, back down her neck to slide his lips along her collarbone. Moving slowly, he began to untie ribbons with his teeth, gently tugging at interlaced pink satin strings. When he'd exposed her lacey undershirt, cut low and exposing the gentle rise of her breasts, he moved his mouth across her chest. He looked up into her face and stroked her lips with his thumb, and in an instant she learned to respond. He'd inched closer, removed his hand and put it at the small of her back, drawing her close. He kissed her and she kissed him back, her mouth open, her tongue hungry for him in an unbridled passion she didn't know she possessed.

They fell to the ground on their knees and then they were side by side. His hands were all over her and found the slit in her pantaloons. A shocked shriek issued from her and then she willed herself to calm down.

It was nothing like she was prepared for or had expected as he fondled her and stripped her naked to make love to her right there in the shallows. Something hot oozed out of her, and she understood it to be her virgin tide carrying him along. When he was spent, he lay back and said, "I'm sorry for the rush, next time, I'll be more gentle. Now I need to wash you." He stood, pulled her to her feet, picked her up in his arms and carried her into the water, where he set her on her feet and began to gently cleanse and massage her legs all the way to her pulsing crotch. When he was done, he lifted her once more and carried her ashore to the blanket to put her down. She instinctively brought her knees to her chest. He reached for his shirt and dried her back and arms and then forced her legs down and dried her breasts. He tossed the shirt aside. "I've been with women, Darby, but never a girl like you, never someone untouched but by me. It don't make me proud I've taken you, but I couldn't help myself. You're like the breath in my body. And I sure as hell can't tell myself to quit breathing, now can I?"

He didn't stop kissing her, touching her until he took her again and then he lay down beside her and dozed, until the descending sun mellowed the grass, trees and river and some cloud cover lent lengthening shadows to the surroundings.

What seemed like an hour later, she marched her fingers like tiny toy soldiers up and down his forearm. "It wasn't like Hanna said it would be."

"We didn't do anything against nature. All's I did was kiss you, let you see me in the raw, and do what I've had a hankering to since the first day I saw you over to Miller's."

"It's just that I don't know much about this, and it seems that Hanna does—"

"She's getting a reputation. A bit on the wild side. She likes men and she likes them taking notice of her sashaying all over town. How old is she anyway?"

"A year and some months older than me. Seventeen."

"Let's don't talk about her, especially now, and pay attention here, girl." Cayo took her in his arms and touched her face with curled fingers and great tenderness, outlining her cheek and jaw as if he were a painter taking notes on what angle best to face her toward the sun.

Darby felt something strange stir inside her that made her want his touch in all the wrong, or maybe right places. She started to speak, but Cayo silenced her with a kiss, his heat matching hers in the hot afternoon. All afternoon.

They slept under the cottonwoods and though she knew he wanted to make love to her again, and she wanted to give in to his mounting desire, she was sore and hurting and so they held back and remained chaste.

"Your skin smells sweet as peaches." He sniffed her in the crook of her neck as if he were an animal trying to catch the scent of his prey in the wind. When he couldn't take being near her any longer he dove into the shallows and swam till he was exhausted. Then as the sun started its descent they ate honey and biscuits, and drank sun-warmed tea. Then he did the damnedest thing, he dripped and spread the rest of the honey all over her arm, as she squealed enough to rouse the dead, while he licked it off.

Cayo looked at the sun. "You'd best be getting that arm washed before the bees and locusts follow you home."

"Is it late?" She stood and pulled him to his feet.

"We've got to set off soon," he said.

She almost said, *a shame*, but didn't want him to misconstrue, or to dishonor or to degrade what had occurred, and merely said, "I could stay here forever."

"Yup. A little bit of paradise on earth," he said, his voice raspy with yearning.

They dressed. He hugged her once more, but with such ferocity, he stopped her breath. When she'd taken in some air, they moved toward the horses, and she reached for his hand. He took it momentarily, and then dropped it, and she knew in that rapid refusal to continue touching, how difficult it was for him to show outward affection. What had this man suffered to make him so reticent when they had just been so close, so intimate? They saddled the horses, mounted and rode off in the direction of the ranches.

Chapter Six

Jicarilla Apache Life
Tipi, Wickiup, Totem

The soft glow of evening was settling by the time Cayo reached town after accompanying Darby partway home, he was thirsty and headed for the Nameless Saloon. He tethered his horse at the hitching post in front of the saloon, and stroked the horse gently and whispered in Wind's ear. Cayo was too spent to ride back to the ranch. In one bound, he jumped two stairs and stepped under the colonnade, pushed open the swinging batwing doors and ambled up to the bar for a drink to quench his parched lips and burning soul. He ordered a glass of water and a shot of whiskey.

If there was one person in the entire world he didn't care to see, it was Captain Pederson, who happened to be sitting at a baize-covered table, drawing a hand of cards close to his chest, a drink and some silver in front of him.

No escape.

"Join us for a hand, Cayo?" the Captain said.

"No thankee, sir. I'll be getting on soon's I wet my whistle." He lifted his shot glass in mock salute.

"Suit yourself. I see you're having 'firewater' as some people call it," Captain Pederson said, practically yelling it.

Cayo glared at the table of men, tried to compose his face into something less than contempt and ignored the slur. He asked the barkeep for another quick one and tipped his glass toward his boss, chugging it down in one gulp. Cayo slammed the glass down. "Same feeling some men get when they take a scalp, I'll bet."

He tipped his hat, picked up his gloves and strode through the paneled doors. On the ride back to the Pederson's ranch, Cayo's mood was elevated and he relived the entire time he'd spent with Darby at the river. When he had finished recalling every minute detail, something he saw in the distance forced his mind in another direction. It was the sight of what looked like a cave in the foothills.

Involuntarily, his mind shifted and he envisioned the scene he never wanted to recall, but couldn't stop. It was the intense revolting feeling he had after he'd slain his sisters and what happened next. In the aftershock, the boy he used to be, Connor, had been bludgeoned, tied, dragged, beaten again, and finally tossed over a horse and carried miles over rough terrain until sunset, when the small party stopped by the Rio Grande, watered their horses and drank their fill. He was thrown off the horse like a sack of shucked corn near a swift-moving stream of water. A thin, wiry man dunked Connor's face repeatedly into the water till he came up sputtering.

There were five Indians. What happened to the other three men and his parents' horses? He imagined the others had taken them to trade. Where had he heard about Indians trading horses? Maybe from his Pa?

He watched these men as they each ate a handful of dried berries, some nuts and strips of what looked like jerky. The lean man who'd dunked Connor's face in the water cut loose his bound ankles, wound the cut leather thongs and stuck them in his pants' waist. Then he heaved the boy onto his horse to straddle it in front, and when the horse started to trot, Connor grabbed some of the mane with his hands between tied wrists. Others had mounted their horses, driving them forward, riding up ravines and into steep gullies and canyons, riding forest and foothills till the little dipper was close enough to touch—they rode till the silver sickle moon had all but disappeared.

Connor thought about the knife he'd stashed in his boot and determined he could do one of three things. The next time the small band stopped, when his guard wasn't looking, he could reach for the knife and cut himself free, steal a horse and make a run for it. How far would he get? He reckoned not very. Or, he could kill one of his captors and the result would be his own death for sure. Or he could just wait. He opted for patience and prudence, as his mother would have told him, and to delay all action; stay and watch for his chance.

Connor existed in an isolated time frame, a perpetual state of horror, detesting himself, from the minute he'd committed the brutal acts. He sought penance with every punishment meted out by his captors as he re-experienced the horror of killing his sisters over and over in his mind. With each denial and with the dispensing of pity for himself, he begged God's forgiveness. Finally, as he began to suffer a more acute, physical agony, he forgot somewhat. He smelled smoke from cookpots and saw lights from fires in the not too far-off distance.

The small party rode into a village of wickiups—tent-like dwellings made of branches, brush and hide, and other cone-like lodgings—tipis fashioned of animal skins.

Dogs barked at them, as they rode into the encampment. One black and tan wolf-like dog nipped at Connor's heels, growling, pulling back his mouth and exposing gums over his sharp teeth. Connor kicked at the dog. His riding partner smote Connor with a glancing blow on the back of the head. He was yanked off the horse with his hands still bound and hurtled to the ground like excess baggage off a stagecoach towards a group of snarling women. The Indian he'd ridden with pulled the thongs from his waist and retied Connor's ankles.

The dog seemed friendly compared to these waiting women. He was flung into their midst as into a gauntlet—a double line of them, yelling and screaming. Their whoops and ululating increased his fear. He was shoved off balance and hurled into a tunnel of jeering females. He was scratched, gouged, jabbed, punched and kicked. Caroming blows made him fall. He crawled, got to his knees and then to his feet once again, hiding his head and face with his arms to deflect the flogging. No shelter. He hopped forward and was struck with sticks. He was taunted and urged to run, hindered by his tied feet, jumping and falling, as the women heckled, hissed and spat upon him.

Then he was lugged and launched, dumped on a pallet of fur that covered the hard, packed earth. His eyes filled with blood and salt tears, then went a hazy gray. He sank into turquoise, then cobalt blue, then midnight, not a twinkling star left to guide him home. He slept where he had been heaved, inert as a sack of oats, remembering nothing of that sleep. Not the position of his body, nor a dream, nor if his hand had moved to search for the knife or for a blanket to cover him. Nor if the scruffy dog he'd seen, with menacing teeth had approached and sniffed him while he slept. Did the dog recognize him as foe, and did he count coup while he licked blood and sweat off Connor's scratched face?

He half-woke in a dreamscape to chanting voices, to the smell of meat roasting. His stomach gurgled with hunger. A while later when Connor was fully awake, he felt fear, and ran his hands through his scalp to see if it was still attached to his head. He knew he was in a sleeping hut. His cheeks grew hot from the close quarters and with the shameful memory that his sisters would never eat again. The odd turbulence of his stomach churned this way and that, hungered and nauseated from the smell of cooked meat. The chanting had ceased. He saw food had been laid out for him on a leaf. He wanted to eat, but it all looked unappetizing and smelled strong. Maybe it had been put out for the dog. He looked around. The dog was gone.

Connor thirsted. He remembered a sermon about Christ tasting gall. His mouth felt like the cotton wool his mother had used to stuff handmade dolls for his sister. That seemed like years ago. His eyes searched the tipi and came to rest on a gourd. He drank water from it in huge gulps and then threw it all up until dry heaves left him exhausted and once again he fell back upon the pallet. He felt uncomfortable, and realized he'd been leaning into the pemmican his mother had given him. He reached into his pants and took it out. It smelled of sweet herbs. He took a bite, tasted pungent juniper berries. Then he gnawed the end. After only a few more bites, thoughts of his mother and the girls made him weep uncontrollably. When the sobs stopped, he drank some more. This time slower, and because of the food, the water stayed put. He reached for his knife. It was only then that he saw that his hands and feet were not bound. He put back what was left of the pemmican.

Connor crawled to the entrance flap and peeked out. A shirred moon swayed in the pre-dawn sky, and he realized his eyes were not fully focusing. He blinked several times and then washed out his eyes with the remaining water in the gourd.

Only a few people milled about, mostly women. He knew he was too weak to attempt fleeing. With escape on his mind, he hid the knife under the pallet. He heard a noise and feigned sleep.

A woman with long gray braids entered the flap of the tipi and began to croon a song. He sneaked a look at her, but she caught him, and with an understanding smirk that he was faking sleep, laughed abruptly. She flipped her braids in back of her and said, *"Hánsinéé?"* with a welcoming expanse of her arm; then went about her chores. Was she asking him how he was? He didn't recognize her from the tunnel of women who'd beat him senseless.

She stoked the fire, sniffed the air, and then she sniffed him and wiggled her nostrils. The crone drew a face, like something stank, tapping her nose with her index finger. With unexpected swiftness, she tugged off his boots. Connor could only think about his hunting knife—thankful he'd hidden it. He scooted back on his haunches as she tried to pull his pants off. She cuffed him one, which startled him, but then she touched his face almost tenderly, and proceeded with her struggle for his putrid pants. Only now he understood, with shame, he'd wet them.

When he was less dazed, he pulled the fur cover over his semi-nude body. The woman cackled and held her nose, then made a pretense of beating his smelly clothes with a rock and washing them. She extended her hand in an impatient gesture for the rest of his clothes. She addressed him in a gruff tone, and by it he knew either he would have to give her the clothes voluntarily, or she'd take them anyway. He stripped with hindered movements under the covers, and tossed the rest of his clothes to her. She nodded and walked toward the opening in the tipi. Suddenly he remembered the deed sewn in the hem of his pant leg. He made a dash for her and wrenched the pants from her. He bit savagely at the stitches his mother had made so carefully to conceal the deed. The old woman punched his chest, demanding the pants back. He turned his back to her and she pummeled his shoulders, until he finally pulled the paper out and quickly stuffed it in his armpit so she wouldn't see it, and handed her the pants with a slight formal bow.

She raised the flap. Before leaving she turned to Connor, and pointing to herself, said, "Bichóó." But the fall season would pass into winter before Connor, who'd by then been named Coyote Dinizhi, which meant dark or dun-colored Coyote, understood her name Bichóó meant Autumn or Fall.

His shoulders ached with the assault the woman had made upon them. He fell onto his pallet face down, but before he fell asleep, he saw his mother's ring on his middle finger. He yanked it off, and then cut off a long fringe he'd found on one of the old one's dresses. He looped it through the ring and tied it around his neck. Then he slept.

The old woman tended to him for two weeks. He soon understood that no one was going to kill him unless he did something stupid, like lunge at someone with his knife. At the beginning of the third week, he'd done all of his chores and was bone weary from the old woman's orders, task after task. When he refused to do something, she threatened to beat him with a stick worse than any dog. After a while, he realized she never acted upon these threats, and he'd had it with her and her stick and her commands, so he just walked into their dwelling and sat down.

When she returned from the river, the old woman rummaged around in one of her many packs and came out with a foul smelling salve which she rubbed into Coyote's shoulders. He nodded his thanks, surprised at her kindness. When she went to put the salve back in its place she gave a startled cry.

Coyote looked in her direction and then down on the ground about three feet from where she stood.

"Dásidáo," Coyote said and motioned her with his hand up to stay put, just like she'd said to him when he complained too much about his chores that very afternoon.

He began to hum a soft lullaby, bending forward and inching his upper body very slowly. He reached under his sleeping pallet and drew out the knife. Still humming, he threw it at the huge rattler who'd invaded the old one's tent, and severed its head. The snake continued to writhe, but Coyote wasn't concerned about that. He motioned for her to step back farther because the head could still lash out and strike with its venomous fangs for about an hour more.

"Now you'll have a pretty snake skin and we've got dinner," he said in triumph, holding up the body."

She had moved back slowly, frozen with aftershock. Pointing first to the snake and then to the knife, a swift look of amazement came over her. She shook her head in disbelief, the expression on her face understanding that he could have chosen to use it on her.

Later that night he learned that they didn't eat snake, and after he'd eaten and was ready to sleep, Mbai' came to the old woman's tent and asked to see the knife. Coyote stood, handed over the knife by the handle, the way he'd been taught. Mbai' held it by the hilt to check its balance, passed his thumb over the blade, then threw it into a rack of hanging antlers. He pulled it out, and handed it back to Coyote. He said something, like "Nice knife."

Coyote, confused, thought he'd take it away, but when Mbai' didn't, Coyote thought perhaps he should offer it to Mbai'. An awkward moment passed and he left. It was when the flap of the tent closed that Coyote realized what had just transpired. He was beginning to be trusted.

***

In the months to come, Connor grew into his new Apache name, Coyote, but sometimes he was only referred to as *Dinizhi,* and he became linked with the spirit animal for whom he was named. His hair grew long, and the clothes he outgrew were changed to buckskins around the time he turned thirteen. He learned to ride bare back, to hunt with a lance, bow and arrow. He used snares for small mammals, learned to whistle like the bleat of a fawn to lure it to its death, and set up head nooses threaded beside traces. He alone fished and ate the fish, but none of the others ate it, and soon he gave up trying to convince them to taste it. He also learned that along with fish, the People abstained from eating bear, mountain lions, coyote, turkey or owls. When he hunted antelope, he wore a head mask.

Although sometimes he was forced to be in the company of his captors, he avoided these warriors, remembering his mother's hair hanging from a belt he never saw again. He recollected his mother's stories about these barbarous men in between Bible lessons. He felt a horrible sense of guilt towards his mother and sisters, yet was somehow gaining the respect of the men, which was essential to his own well-being. How could this be? His ways and thoughts were changing. How had he seen that the Apaches were not beasts, merely men, doing what they needed to survive and keep their camp safe from white intruders. Why had they kept him alive? Perhaps because he fought like them, begging to be killed after he'd taken the lives of two beautiful little girls. This would haunt him forever. Maybe had he been taught and instructed differently, he would have spared them their lives, now knowing if they would have been adopted as daughters.

However, it was through the contact he had with these men that he came to understand he owed a great debt to Mbai'. Coyote had killed two children that Mbai' would have taken as captive slaves, but treated as family, like he himself now was.

Coyote often wondered about Audra. Where was she? And then one day he found her, toddling around. He gave her a quick hug, but she looked startled and began to cry, so he backed off. But his need to see her was great, so he returned every day until he became familiar and she began to play with him and soon accepted him as a friend.

Apparently she had been adopted by a childless couple who named her Little Fawn, because as a child when first starting to walk, she resembled a little fawn trying to walk. One day after he'd discovered her, he stood behind a tree to watch the new mother comb the child's hair with great tenderness, even though she fidgeted and wriggled and tried to run away. The mother spoke in dulcet tones in a soothing manner. The child quieted, and embraced her. Seeing that was like an arrow in his heart. Maybe that would've been his sisters' fate too, but now he'd never know. *What did you think the new parents would do to the child?*

Whenever he saw Little Fawn's adoptive parents, he spoke politely to them, but never explained his relationship to her, or his desire to see she was well taken care of. Coyote hadn't seen Little Fawn for quite some time and was shocked to see how much she'd grown when he stumbled across her at play.

At times, though, Coyote was uneasy with the knowledge that his treatment among the People hadn't been especially harsh. He'd broken the Fifth Commandment: Thou shalt not kill. He'd committed murder for no good reason, and this thought and the image of their dead bodies gave him nightmares. How many mornings had he woken up screaming and in a sweat? He'd lost count. But what was it his mother had said when she handed him the gun? And how many times had he heard his father say things like: "Raping savages will tear their tender bodies apart in pleasure and make whores of them." How little they'd known. How ignorant his parents and many other whites had been of Indian ways. Savages? What was he, then, who'd misjudged them and taken innocent lives? He vowed to learn; to be open to things he at first did not understand. To become aware. To study and recall all he saw and heard. To become a proud warrior like them. Fierce. Courageous. Loyal.

It was by keen observation and practice that Coyote absorbed the Jicarilla language and soon his vocabulary grew and he was able to communicate without hesitation, yet he was reticent to do so. He practiced the words alone walking by the river—sometimes jumping and turning or ducking and squatting in quick movements as though someone were spying on him and might think he was losing his mind.

When he became fully conversant, he sought out Little Fawn. Her first language was his second, but they communicated well, until he began to teach her English. At first she resisted, but then, with much patience on Coyote's part, and because he invented so many games of it, she began to mimic him and learn words, phrases and finally sentences. She was clever and quick to learn.

Coyote had many chores and duties to perform, but so did the other young braves whom Coyote worked alongside. He was taunted and teased, tolerating blows without retaliation. He fended pelted rocks, as a dog with mange. He was an outsider, who never hoped for tolerance or sought acceptance. Many times he thought about leaving the camp, but where would he go?

He received all manner of slashes and beatings stoically, believing he deserved worse for the heinous acts of murder he'd committed. His demeanor somehow won him respect, and soon the jostling, the jabbing, the pushing, the taunting stopped. He never shirked work, but rather welcomed any occupation that kept him alert and thinking of the task at hand because it made him forget for a little while the abomination he'd committed.

***

Eventually, these same young braves were also those with whom Coyote began to enjoy games and recreation. And in the time-honored way that children speak an international language of play, the boy also began to learn in earnest his new adopted language, but first he learned to sign.

After learning how to sign, Coyote began understanding more and more words. At first these word sounds ran all together as one jumble, but gradually he was able to pick out a word he knew the meaning of, and then another, and he began to fathom what was being said and fashion a vocabulary. What his father had told him was true. "It was frustrating not to grasp another man's tongue and ways."

He began to ask questions, at first only to the women, and then to the old holy man, Red Hawk, who was considered a great seer. As his fluency began to take hold, and his tongue formed words no longer strange to him, he found he was losing his shyness to approach others of the village, especially boys, and to converse with them. Many months later he became fluent.

One night, Coyote was caught in the midst of an intense summer thunderstorm. His sense of direction was confused, until he saw the familiar dwelling of Red Hawk. He approached the tipi, but instead of the customary scratching on the hides to gain entrance, he merely entered, thinking that the blind man would be unaware. Coyote thought, *Even if the old man can distinguish light, it is so dark out from the storm that he won't know.* Coyote crouched like his namesake, opening the flap just enough to wiggle his body beneath it. The howling wind covered over any noise, and his movement disallowed any entrance of light.

Red Hawk's back was turned away from the entrance and he was smoking a pipe. The scent from the pipe and the logs burning were pleasant to Coyote. The warmth of the fire invited him to go near and dry his wet clothes, but he hung back for fear of detection. When he had settled himself, leaning upon a backrest against the tipi wall to the right of the old man, he closed his eyes and could have dozed were it not for the thundering voice of Red Hawk, calling out, "Welcome, grandson. Come near the fire and dry your clothes."

Coyote didn't answer, thinking that the old man was expecting his own grandson. He made to leave, but again Red Hawk, cried out, "Coyote Dinizhi, it is to you that I speak. Come close."

How could he possibly know it's me? he thought. Maybe he's faking his blindness, but he'd not turned a hair from where he sat.

Coyote hesitated.

"I have been waiting for you," Red Hawk said. "You are a long time coming to me."

"A storm rages, Grandfather, a mountain lion in a briar."

"Why did you not scratch to let me know I had a visitor?"

"I didn't want to disturb you if you slept."

"And upon coming, seeing me awake, you made no noise to let me know you'd entered my dwelling." He made a lifting motion with one hand. "Take off your shirt. Here is a blanket."

Coyote did as he was bade and then approached the fire. "You knew it was me."

"Your scent gave you away and your bad manners. You entered without permission. What if I was entertaining a young maiden?" he said and laughed.

Flustered, Coyote didn't answer for a minute and then when he realized something was wanting, he said, "I apologize."

"But why?"

"For impolite behavior. It will never happen again."

"Never and always are two words which should be contemplated before uttering. Sit. I will tell you a story. You do not believe in my blindness. You must lose your mistrust. It is your own blindness that makes you guard your heart."

The old man's face was benign, like a placid river, the furrows of his brow tiny ripples from an unexpected change in weather when the wind picks up and a sudden squall comes out of the hills, moving the water of streams. And though he felt the story would be serious, Coyote smiled, thinking of the old man's remark about a maiden.

Red Hawk began his story, and Coyote listened carefully, not to miss a word hidden by the wind's savagery.

Red Hawk put aside his pipe. "When I was a boy, I was sick with the White Man's disease."

By this Coyote knew he meant smallpox.

"The sores were watery beneath my skin. These I plucked and put the water into my eyes. I recovered, but I never saw my mother again."

"She died from the sickness?"

"No, I was blind."

They sat in comfortable silence for some time but when the wind and rain abated, Coyote asked permission to leave because he didn't want Grandmother to worry.

Red Hawk smiled and lit his pipe. "She is the mother of Mbai' and our culture is maternal. You need not fret for she is sturdy and works still. She tends her pottery. Have you not seen the way she scours the earth for the clay with the shiny bits in it to make into cooking jars?"

"I helped her gather the clay some time ago," Coyote said, and remembering the shiny pieces of mica infused in the clay, became saddened at the memory of his mother's bean pot. "But now she has released me from what she calls woman's chores."

Red Hawk continued. "What do you know of our Jicarilla tribe?"

"The tribe has two bands. We are the *Olleros*. Potters. I have helped build the fire for the clay pots. The heat is sometimes fierce, but worse yesterday before the rain."

Red Hawk puffed on his pipe. "The other band is known as the *Llaneros* or plainsmen. The Spanish gave us our names in the dim and distant time when they came over the great waters with horses. Now, in place of war between our bands we hold races, and the runners decide which is the strongest group. Have you not seen these races? Would you like to partake of these next time?"

So many questions. So much information. Coyote found it hard to grasp it all, but finally blurted out, "Yes, I have seen the races. Of course I want to be part of them, but—"

"But?"

"I have never been invited. Maybe because I am as fast a runner as White Feather, who is fast as the wind." He hesitated. "Perhaps even faster."

"You will think on these things, and soon you will know what your heart tells you and how to be part of the ritual."

Cayo thought for a moment and then said in the language he'd come to learn, "*Inheed.*" Coyote said with a contrite heart filled with thanks.

"Stay. Make yourself invisible to the young warriors as they practice and learn their methods."

Coyote stood and waited. Red Hawk came to him and put his hands on his shoulders. "You will be invisible, *ligai.*"

Coyote was glad that Red Hawk had not used the word ghost after "white."

"But how is invisibility obtained?"

"There are many ways. Our tribe, the *Olleros*, paints themselves with white clay when they cross the plains for battle. To our men, turning into the white clay means self-protection—a scheme to bring our warriors home in one piece. This using of clay is like the desert moth changing its spots. With the practice of prayers to summon mystical and sacred protectors for safe-conduct, our fighters return to us unharmed. It means survival."

"But not all, and not always," Coyote said.

"True. But look to Chief Huerito Mundo—"

"The one with the longest braids and earrings?"

Red Hawk nodded. "Our tribe is often on the move, and this leads us into different territories now. In the remote past, all the land was ours. We are invisible because we intermarry with the Pueblo and Spanish— even Utes and Whites. You, too, will be invisible when you leave us."

"But I'm not going to leave," Coyote said with great agitation in his voice.

"Be calm, Coyote. The Great Spirit ordains. We merely follow heavenly directives. There is no shame in it, but I tell you there will come a time for you to go out into the world you came from. It will happen."

Coyote felt as if he'd stopped breathing so he could think. A surge of emotion enveloped his mind: I was Connor. I was a prisoner. I am Coyote. "I am Apache now."

"Lessons to be learned are many. Listening and time helps. We, the People, are like a woven fabric. If you look at it, you see the whole piece, not individual threads, not the indistinguishable parts that make it whole."

Coyote donned his shirt to leave, listening to the old man whispering a blessing over him.

The women packed up the tipis for the march to the winter camp. Leaves swirled in windy eddies and the air was tinged with frost. Snow flurries whirled about, the winds lifting them. Coyote watched the dancing leaves, wondering if they'd ever touch the ground. It would be a severe winter he knew because he had spoken with Red Hawk, who, because he was a holy man who was blind, had been given many gifts by *Usen*, the giver of Life, and one of these was the ability to see the future.

Coyote was curious about a blind man who ironically was often called, Seeing One. On a night when the wind began to howl, a restless Coyote passed near Red Hawk's tipi. He wanted to enter, but stood frozen and was about to scratch on the tipi when a clear voice called for him to enter and told him to come and sit by the fire. *Could he have heard me in the wind?*

Red Hawk sat against a woven twig backrest, puffing on a pipe, blowing smoke in an indolent manner. "Have you eaten?"

"I am sleepless."

"Then speak what troubles you."

"Once when I was sick, my mother carried me to the river and plunged me in the cold water to revive me and I shook. I felt like a bird and wanted to fly," Coyote said.

"Did you?" Red Hawk pulled on his pipe.

"How does the tree teach the wind to fly its branches like a bird? How does the tree learn to cast shade in summer and to hold the nests of birds?"

"Listen keenly to the wind, but even better, listen when the air is still. Sit now and we will speak of a great chief and I will tell you his words about the wind."

Coyote sat down breathing in the exhaled smoke.

"His name in Chiricahua is Goyaałé, One Who Yawns, but he is known now by the Mexican name of Geronimo. He was born a Bedonkohe Apache but now leads the Chiricahua Apache. You know what Apache means?"

"Fighting men."

Red Hawk nodded. "This man moved like the wind. You too can be like the wind."

His words were bracing, a splash of cold water to wash sleep from Coyote's tired face glowing from the fire. "How?"

"With a great deal of practice you can do this and more. You can become invisible."

Coyote smiled. "I will learn this magic," he said, and laid his head down on his hands, falling asleep, his hair grazing the fringes of the old man's buckskins.

Red Hawk cleaned his pipe, setting it aside. When he thought the boy was deep in sleep, he patted him on the shoulder. "And so you shall do this, for I will teach you."

A sleepy Coyote said, "I will learn."

***

Winter passed. Green shoots appeared on the trees and the young men acted as lookouts for herds of buffalo. They traveled great distances farther away from the village. The spring prairie was dry and summer rains were not close, but snowmelt had engorged the rivers. The scouts were in need of water. They got down from their horses and surveyed the area.

"Watch for coyote," White Feather, son of Mbai' said.

"Why me?" Coyote said.

"Not you." He smirked. "The animal. He'll lead us to drink." White Feather turned his horse to a high blackberry bush.

"I've heard that bees are great indicators of where water can be found."

Another boy, Picks-Up-Pebbles, joined the two boys and said, "I know that toads always know where water is."

"How do you know?" Coyote said.

"I kept one once as a pet," Picks-Up-Pebbles said in a confident voice.

"I say the desert wolf always knows for sure," White Feather said.

"Desert wolf?" Coyote asked.

"Coyote has many names. Get used to them," White Feather said, leaning towards a blackberry bush and picking a few berries. He popped them in his mouth, but quickly spit them out. "Not ripe yet. Need summer sun."

They found a wide and windy creek and drank their fill, then watered the horses but only at the water's edge. They did not trust the fast-moving current of the swollen water coursing over stones, forming white waves and eddies. Then they rode back to the village in no rush and a bit slumped with disappointment as they had not sighted bison.

Two seasons had passed and still the boys had not sighted buffalo. A group of boys, including Rolling Thunder, were out hunting and returned to camp with a deer. When they arrived, they gave the news to some of the elders. It was decided to have a ceremonial dance as a prayer and also because they had some invited guests among them.

That night as fires roared, the boys watched every dance, knowing the movements were each a form of prayer. Ceremonial dances continued and were held in the camp especially when guests were present. Some Utes were urged to join in and dance in celebration of the corn yield. There was a harvest moon above. Its reflection seemed as bright as the lighted fires below, which gave the jealous sphere pause to stop its glow momentarily, hiding behind some clouds. When it reappeared, a loud cry of joy exploded from the dancers and drummers.

Coyote was enthralled with the festivities that three medicine men had organized. Men dancers wore intricate costumes in an attempt to imitate Gans, the Mountain Spirits. The headdresses were ornate wooden carvings. The men painted their bodies and wore kilt-like skirts and black masks. Some carried wooden swords.

Coyote watched much of the dancing, but didn't eat, saving his appetite for later after he'd been in some contests. He didn't want a full belly to slow his movements. The night air was redolent with fire and food.

The movements of the dancers brought to mind days when he remembered the rhythm of cutting hay with a scythe, and sickle-cutting the wheat, and threshing it in early winter with his father. For this, the Bradley family had used a flail. He had not thought of his father for a long time, and a wave of shameful remorse washed over him again. He cried out a little, hoping his father's spirit would understand his prayer. He was mesmerized by the chanting, the drumbeats, and the incredible agility of the men dancing.

One of the Utes, a giant of a man, brought his son over to pay respects to Red Hawk. The man's name was Nantan and he was the spokesman for his tribe. His son was called Ndóicho, and when Coyote Dinizhi met him, he knew they would be friends. Ndóicho was short and stocky and hadn't yet begun to grow like the cornstalks Coyote's other friends were turning into. Ndóicho was younger and stronger than Coyote, but when the young Ute challenged Coyote to a wrestling match, he outsmarted the guest, by quickly unbalancing him. They rolled in the dirt and Coyote was pronounced the winner. Other boys wrestled and when they did, the new friends bet who would win. They agreed on the contests, and at the end of all the games, they gripped each other's forearm and laughed. There were fast races, running contests of all kinds, jumping matches, a gambling game called Kah, and a game called Foot. The boys participated in all of them except the gambling. Their energy appeared unbounded.

They ate cactus fruit and seeds from mesquite to hold them though the games. As the night progressed Coyote and Ndóicho went from cookpot to cookpot savoring the delicious food. At one lodge, there was no cookpot, but the flap was thrown back and inside an array of pemmican was being offered: dried meat and nuts and berries packed into the intestines of wild boar were the food that men carried when they were on war parties or hunting without women to cook for them. This same food had been the last his mother offered him the night he fled in the tunnel and left his parents to their fate. He declined the offering of the food. Memory had stolen his appetite.

A few days later, when the ceremony was winding down, the Ute band of visitors said they were satisfied, and with this proper bidding of farewell left the following morning. Coyote was sad to see Ndóicho go, but hoped their paths would cross again, and as the camp began to break up, it was with a full heart that Coyote said his goodbyes.

Finally ready to collapse into sleep, he went back to his own lodge. The old grandmother wasn't there. He sprawled on his pallet, but the excitement of the day and the faraway echoing sounds of chanting made it impossible to rest, and by and by he remembered a song his mother used to croon to him when he was anxious about something. The words came to him slowly and when his head was filled with them they slipped from his tongue:

Come now my child of womb and heartbeat,
Come to me fair and flaxen boy
Hither now, and take my hand
Tenderly nestle, safe within my arms.

Tears flowed as the song came from him, and not recalling all the words, he repeated what he remembered over and over as images of his mother flooded his consciousness.

He sensed rather than saw the old one, but his song did not cease, and by and by he fell asleep. He tossed and turned fitfully all night long. Towards morning he was cold and covered himself with a buffalo blanket, and fell into a deep sleep. He dreamt he was a coyote on a ridge looking at his father, who picked up a rifle and took aim to shoot because he didn't recognize his son. Then he lowered his weapon and smiled. Was his father pleased to see he'd been accepted into the tribe?

Was his father at peace? Did he know that his son had murdered his sisters, thinking he was saving them from a far worse fate? When Coyote awakened, he shivered. He thought about the dream in which his father had stroked Coyote's braids, pleased to see him thriving.

He watched the old woman, but didn't get up from his pallet. He saw her prepare a brew of what seemed to be rose hips, leaves and twigs. She added water from the pouch that was hung on an antler, and carried the mixture to heat inside another pouch. When the brew was hot, she poured it into a buffalo horn, filled it to the brim and carried it to him. She smiled.

"Drink this, perhaps it will dispel your ghosts." She handed him the cup.

"I dreamt of my father, Robert Bradley."

"We do not speak the names of the dead—it offends them." She returned to the paunch and poured out a second cup of the steaming liquid.

"He was so alive." He sipped the herb concoction and felt the warmth spread through him.

"His spirit is with you." She sat next to him. "That is good."

"It was my mother's song I'd been singing. I should have dreamt of her."

"A dream, like life, is not how we want it, but how it is meant to be."

He sipped the brew. "Wise Grandmother," he said in a tone soft as a falling feather, and then added something incomprehensible to her because it was in his own tongue, "I love you."

She understood the power of the dream had opened a floodgate of emotions that now washed over the boy. She moved closer to him and whispered, "Here it is different, but now our world is yours. Why not ask Red Hawk to take you to the sweat lodge?"

"This is the second time someone has told me that, Grandmother."

"And you still have not done it? Do you need a boulder to fall down on your head?"

Chapter Seven

Never Two, Without Three

The following Saturday when Darby's father dropped her off at the Mercantile, Harris Miller greeted her at the door as he was walking out. He waved to McPhee as Darby's father maneuvered the buggy forward.

"Why, Darby, we thought you'd left." Harris said.

"I was going to but had a change of heart, and well—please don't say anything to Pa, will you? Pa didn't know I was considering going to Aunt Bea's."

"Hadn't planned on it," Harris said with a look of dismay on his face.

"I'd like to speak to Fern first. That is if she'd still like to have me for the day."

"Believe me, she can use all the help she can get. There's a Mormon family in there causing quite a ruckus. Ten kids, mind you. I'm off to the feed store."

"I'll go straight in," she said, putting on her apron before opening the door.

Darby entered and cornered three of the whooping and hollering little ones. "Am I ever glad to see you," Fern said. "But why am I seeing you here? I thought you left for—"

"I'll tell you later. What do these people need?"

Fern leaned close, "A cage to keep their young ones in."

Darby smiled and retied the strings of her apron. "Can I help you folks get some of your gear together? What else will you be needing?" she asked a young man with a long beard.

He tipped his hat. "I have other errands to do, so I'll leave you my list and take the children. But my wife's feeling poorly. Can she set a spell?"

The man didn't wait for an answer, but put two fingers in his mouth and gave a shrill whistle. The whistle reminded her of the train and what she was giving up by staying. Nine children lined up. Darby went to hand him the infant in her arms, but he shook his head, and marched the children like the Pied Piper straight out the door and into the dusty street. There was a young girl with them in an obvious state of expectancy but instead of rushing to the anguished woman's side, she followed the man out the door.

Darby gave a quizzical look to Fern and handed the infant to her, pulled over a wooden crate for the woman to sit on, realizing that no possible way could the woman manage to mount it. Her protruding belly looked as if she was going to have another baby right then and there. "Oh my," Darby said, indicating the huge belly. "Would you like some water?"

"Thank you kindly. I'm at my time. Have either of you ever delivered a baby?"

Darby's eyes opened wide as she shook her head.

"I'm childless," Fern said, and went to hang a "Closed" sign in the window facing outward.

The woman gasped. "Set the baby on the floor and block her with some gunny sacks. I'm going to squat right here and grab hold of this heavy barrel. God's going to give you a chance to help me this day, and it's a lesson that may aid you in your own trial someday."

"What about your elder daughter? Why did she desert you and go with her father?"

"Ain't no kin of mine, though he insists I call her sister in front of folk who aren't kin or keen on our ways," she said, and drank the water Darby gave her.

"You mean she's another wife?" Fern asked.

"Yes'um. I do," she said.

Darby's eyes grew large as saucers as the woman began stripping off her pantaloons and squatting near the barrel, her arms circling it.

"If she's living with you, she should at least have stayed to help you. Seems like the decent thing to do. Are you going to assist her when her time comes?" Darby asked.

"Not if I can help it," the woman said, grumbling. She smirked. "Bless the poor young soul—it'll be her first and perhaps her last as she knows not a thing of birthing. Bet she doesn't much know how she got in that condition either."

Fern laughed and Darby tried to hide a smile.

"Not a kindly thought, I reckon," the woman said before a sharp pain made her cry out. "Mighty unchristian of me, but I say tit for tat." She sucked in a huge gulp of air. "Does nothing but simper and sway after that old goat instead of helping me with the chores and little ones." She moaned a long soft tone at first that grew with intensity and made Darby wince. *This is far worse than I imagined.*

Darby comforted the woman as best she could. She helped her into a squatting position, as the woman's grunts and groans increased. She dried the woman's sweaty forehead and upper lip, asked if she wanted another glass of water.

"What I want is to get this here baby out of me, thankee very kind-ly."

When the birthing was over, Fern and Darby picked up the blood-soaked rags and brought them out back to burn them with the trash.

Shortly after, Darby sat with the newborn nestled in her arms considering what it would be like when she had Cayo's child.

After Fern made the woman comfortable with her back propped up and pillowed, Darby handed her the baby. She looked at the woman and then again at the baby. "Why he's beautiful. Every single toe and finger, his fuzzy little head and button nose. He'll grow into a handsome young man."

"Thank you kindly," the mother said. "That's like a little blessing."

Close to a half hour later, when the bearded man came back with his second wife in tow, he rapped on the window and said in a husky voice, "I'm here for my parcels and my wife."

Darby opened the door. "And let's not forget, baby eleven." Darby snapped up the baby from the mother and handed the newborn over to the young woman with mousy hair, who had sidled up next to the man. "Hope you'll help out and get some instruction for yours to come."

"May the Lord, the God of your fathers, *increase* you a thousand-*fold* more than you are . . . because by some miracle of God, your number has been increased," the man said. He smiled and asked, "A man child?"

"Yes, sir, and Amen," Fern said, and helped the recently delivered woman to her feet and out the door. The woman glanced over her shoulder with a grateful look in her eyes and nodded her head by way of thanks.

Fern slipped a small vile into the woman's pocket and whispered something to her.

Darby knew it was laudanum and she patted the woman's shoulder, "Take care now, and ask your sister for help from time to time. From what I saw here today, she's going to need yours."

The woman smiled, nodded her head and lumbered toward to the exit, juggling the next to youngest infant in her arms.

Customers jammed the store all day long after that, asking questions about what had happened, why the store suddenly closed in the middle of the day? Finally Darby got tired of answering questions about the unusual happening of a birth in the shop, and the Mormon family passing by. She swept passed customers and pointed to Fern, who gave brief accountings of the unusual circumstances. When the last customer left, Darby drew down the shade on the upper window portion of the door and brushed up the dried mud, leaves and twigs into a dustbin. "I can't believe how nosy and curious the people of this town are, can you?"

Fern locked the door and said, "A weird occurrence such as this's bound to bring out the curious and the talkers. It's exciting news in a dreary town. Now, put the broom in the corner and sit here and tell me why you missed that train east and why you're here."

Darby hopped up on a barrel and adjusted her skirt. "I came in today to tell you, simply put, I'm going to marry Cayo Bradley."

"Marry? What of your promise to your mother? Your education? Teaching? Are you giving up all of that to settle down with a cowhand?" Fern sighed and shook her head with exasperated emphasis, and sat heavily on the stool behind the counter.

Darby flushed apple red. "I guess so."

"You guess?" Fern all but shrieked. "You'd better be danged certain it's what you want. It certainly's not what you need, my fine girl."

"But I love him."

"And what exactly do you know about love or him? Where's he come from anyway? Rumors are he's part Indian."

"I don't think so, but he might've lived with Indians growing up—"

"You know nothing about him, do you? It's puppy love. Fascination. But love for a lifetime? Oh my, you've got lots to learn. Love or whatever you think it is, fades, child. You can't feed babies on it. And babies will come. Look at the Mormon woman we had in here."

"Cayo's a good cowboy and experienced. He's got a ranch up north. Why with a couple of maverick cattle, he could start a herd. Capture and brand them as his own."

"Got it figured, huh? Maybe," Fern said, pulling her cheek in and biting it, like she did when she was thinking hard.

***

The next week, Darby came down the veranda stairs dressed in her Sunday best carrying a parcel that she tied on the back of her horse. She went back into the house and took hold of a small gunny sack that she'd prepared early that morning with pieces of leftover fried chicken and hard boiled eggs.

At the water trough, she stopped to watch her Pa finish pouring in one more bucket of water for the horses. "Sorry, I can't go today. You say hello to the preacher for me."

"Will do, Pa, and don't expect me till after suppertime. Everything's prepared. All you or one of the boys have to do is heat the stew. Covered biscuits are on the table and don't need heating. Just dunk them in and sop up the gravy. Table's set. Draw fresh water."

"Why ain't you coming home after service?"

"Been invited to spend the day with Hanna and we're going to have a picnic. Before you know, summer'll be over and then we won't get much time to be company for each other." She mounted her horse. "And. Pa, if it gets real late, don't worry about me, I'll stay the night and ride home first thing in the morning."

On her way to church, Darby considered skipping service altogether, but if she wasn't there, people might talk and word might reach her father's ear that she was absent. She couldn't stand the idea of hurting him, or putting him in an embarrassing position with the nearby ranchers. But hadn't she just lied to him? A first. But how could she tell him the truth? She felt a savage hunger she'd never known after she had lain with Cayo by the river.

So she went to church and noted that Hanna wasn't there. That was odd, but wouldn't be the first time she skipped out. Mrs. Pederson was missing as well. Was that cause for alarm? Hanna and Mrs. Pederson were Darby's excuse for not returning after church. She wasn't a liar and certainly didn't want to be called out for being one, but her story to Pa was a falsehood. She hoped she wouldn't regret it.

The summer day was hot and dry and bees droned outside the window—a pleasant distraction from the discourse coming from the pulpit. The fragrant flowers that the lady's guild had placed in the window boxes were perfumed, reminding her not of the church service but of the other afternoon on the meadow with Cayo's arms around her. Whenever she thought of Cayo or came within close proximity of him, she felt a riot of butterflies loose inside of her. Is that what love is? Like Fern said, she knew so little about him. Was it enough? She knew he was wild in so many senses. Gruff. Had he really grown up with Indians? He was feral and strong and would protect her in any circumstance—this she knew instinctively. But, what if her brain become stultified? What if she had no time for reading and studying, tending house for him? Would she be trading one prisoned environment for another?

She met Cayo by the river and they ate a small meal. Then they bathed each other in the water while the sun still streamed down like golden wands. He took a handful of silt and sand and scrubbed her back,

85

rinsed her off and whirled her around. The slight waves washing over her breasts and in between her legs left her goose-skin prickling for more of his touch. He engulfed her in his arms and covered her mouth with his lips—his kiss tasted of the river, corn tortillas, and tobacco; his moustache held the acrid smell of campfire smoke. She yearned for him.

Near the shore, he knelt in the water, sliding his hands upward from her clamped ankles. He stroked each calf, each thigh. He stood. His palms traced her hips, ribs, breasts. Her underarms felt his thumbs imprint themselves in the hollows as he lifted and spun her, his hands slipping to her waist. Cayo settled her upon him, a child in his upright lap, till his grasp reached behind to support her. She gripped him with her legs, and as her fingers cat-crawled up his back, with one thrust he was inside her. She whimpered like a puppy, licking her salty lips, then his, like open wounds, biting her own. She hurled her mouth onto his as if fused by a branding iron. Her leg muscles throbbed, her shoulders shuddered, her back curved into him and their pulsing movements were syncopated to the lashing of thin-armed juvenile branches in the cottonwoods, undulating in the wind. The wind riffled her hair as her head thrashed sideward, whipping his face and neck with long wet ends.

Although he wanted to possess her again, to make them one being, she shook her head and, conscious of her disquiet, he did not.

Sliding away from him, Darby, stilled and warmed, felt blood course through her while the river cleansed and baptized her—a vocation, a calling to an ancient religious belief in nature. She stood profoundly in awe and without guile like this man who faced her.

"Have you ever cleansed a woman like this before, Cayo?"

"I can honestly say I have not, but I saw a close friend of mine make love to her lover like this once. They looked so joyous, but at the time, I was hurt and angry and thought it was disgusting. Yet here I am enjoying every morsel of you. You are the sweetest tasting thing, I ever did come across."

"And all that from a man of few words!" She giggled.

He carried her out of the water, setting her down on a patch of wild cocksfoot—the grass course and cold. She trembled. He picked up a blanket from where it hung on a chokecherry and draped it around her shoulders. He rubbed her back with it. She wanted to say something, waiting for him to speak first, but neither of them did. She thought she'd feel ashamed, and her muscles would writhe and wither of their own accord, she'd fall in a heap, but instead her body flexed, waiting, attending in eagerness while he strode away to get his poncho. He dried himself with it, slung it over his shoulder, but didn't walk back to toward her. He looked at her. She knew by his slight smile that her eagerness showed on her face, her nostrils assailed by the smell of horse and leather, of cooked meat, and singed wool. His blanket. His woman. She waited, but then a reckless, impatient impulse made her discard the blanket.

And still he didn't move, while her heartbeats marked off the months of a calendar year, watching his strong, lean body finally turn and face her and start to advance. Each ripple of his muscles, every sinew, each visible blood vessel set her teetering on a cliff edge of despair, ready to catapult off if he stopped coming for her. The air around her was palpable, and her breath audible in frenetic gulps—a miner trapped in a cave—till her feet ploughed the earth, running for him, her legs bounding upward, vaulting outward and thrusting herself up into his arms. Her legs ensnared him in a circle because she hadn't trusted her senses enough to believe his approach would ever reach to take possession of her. She knocked the poncho off his shoulder as she threw her arms around his neck.

He begged her to stay with him, and though she knew she shouldn't, she couldn't resist the temptation to remain curled in his arms next to the fire for an entire night.

Sunrise found Darby and Cayo heading towards their separate ranches. She ran flat out at top speed and knew she was lathering up the horse, but it was later than she'd imagined, and now distress claimed her. A silent alarm went off in Darby's brain as she dismounted and walked into the barn. She unhitched the saddle. She ran a hand over the sweated flank, and put the saddle on a sawhorse. Then, a noise startled her. Darby turned, and her brother Garrett took hold of both her arms and yanked her close to him. "Pa don't know you been out all night and he sure as hell don't know you ain't been with Hanna."

She tried to put an impassive look on her face, but he was squeezing her arms. "You're hurting me like the devil."

"If that don't beat all. Ain't nothing to what it'd be like getting a licking from Pa with a cat o' nine tails, and your cowboy strung up with two Winchester holes through him."

"Pa wouldn't. You're trying to scare me."

"Maybe not the cat, but you deserve a good horse whipping. Don't put it past him. You've never seen Pa's wrath."

"I beg you. Please, Garrett. Don't tell him."

He let go of her arms. "I know what you were doing. What were you thinking?"

"We're going to get hitched. Soon. We're promised. He's going to ask Pa, he's just not gotten to it yet, is all."

"And here I thought Hanna was going to be the little whore." Garrett spat in the ground and opened the barn door, a look of disgust on his face. "Get cleaned up. I made breakfast."

Darby's hand flew to her throat. "I love him," she sputtered.

"You don't know the meaning of that word. And with a Redskin!" He pushed her back out of his way. She wasn't expecting it, tripped on a rake and plunged into a pile of hay. The shock of seeing her brother's fury rocked her. She stood shaking, now acutely aware she'd over-stepped the bounds of propriety. "He's not Indian," she said, swiping at her clothes to get the hay off.

Garrett turned. "Maybe not in your eyes, but he is around town."

"But you're friends with him."

"That's another matter. I'm a man. He'll treat you like a squaw."

"Such a brutal word." She reached to touch him, but he slapped her hand.

He stepped back and then stood with his hands on his hips. "Rejection hurts, does it? Get used to it. Even if he does marry you, in small towns there ain't acceptance of that kind of marriage. How could you? You been raised to know your place. Why would you toss away your reputation to tie in with the likes of him—a man with a past you don't even know."

"Do you, Garrett? Then tell me. What's he done?"

"Don't matter. Nobody knows for sure. By the way the man shoots, handles a knife, a bow and arrow, and a whip—he ain't no kind of saint."

Darby was shaken as Garrett stormed off towards to house, slamming the barn door, leaving her in shadow. She leaned against one of the stalls. Once she caught her ragged breath, she yanked the blanket off the horse and put it on one of the Mexican tooled tack boxes.

She sat on the box. It wasn't the idea of falling into sin—but was it a sin when you loved someone? She'd been reckless. Darby's understanding was now implicit and complete. She really knew nothing of Cayo's past, although she'd observed him always seeming wary, as if he were being hunted. She must ask him. Only how does one find the mettle to question someone's past life? She felt nauseated and knew there'd be a price to pay—but what? Surely it wasn't just losing Garrett's respect. She could gain it back; if not his regard, then the closeness she'd had with him. Her eldest brother—so like Momma.

She went out to the trough and washed her face, dried it with her skirt, and hoped to put on a good face that would convince her Pa of the lies she was about to tell. And then there was Garrett. What if he told Pa the truth?

Chapter Eight

Bow and Arrow

Cayo rode out from the Pederson ranch before first light with a group of men selected to do the branding. They were slightly ahead of time for roping, branding and wattling, but Captain Pederson was always more than punctual. Dawn's shadow made things somewhat murky but two of the cowpokes rode around and circled at a slow pace, whistling or singing softly some melancholy cowboy song to keep the herd quiet and sleepy. When it was Cayo's turn to do the two-hour night ride-around with someone else, he whistled, hummed, or spoke quietly but never sang because he didn't know the words to many songs.

An old smithy on the Pederson ranch had just died and a new one by the name of Ben Star had moved onto the ranch some days after. He had been working in Cerrillos when Captain Pederson hired him when the old smithy took sick.

Ben Star lived in a cabin that was part forge and part livery stable. The men on the ranch said he was a barn-built man, whose manner spoke of gentle breeding or at least an etiquette that no man around these parts had except for Captain Pederson. Ben Star had been a slave at one time, but was now a free man. He'd been a mere child when conscripted to serve as a Buffalo Soldier during the Civil War. He loved to pass the time of day, but loathed speaking of anything that had to do with his life before or during the war.

When Cayo heard about him, he rode out early one day to find him to see if it was the same Ben Star he'd worked for years before. In

Cayo's mind, there couldn't be two men of the same name, of the exact description, and both of them blacksmiths.

The first thing Ben did when he spotted Cayo coming toward him was nod his head in recognition.

Cayo dismounted his horse and stuck out his hand. He had a firm grip. "The name's Cayo Bradley. If you remember me from another time, I'd take it kindly you forget it. Be seeing you often. I'm working on the Pederson place."

Two riders approached and stopped in listening distance, probably wanting to get their horses shod. Ben reached for Cayo's hand to shake a second time. "The name's Ben. Ben Star," he said loud enough to wake the dead. "Come on in," he hesitated, "Cayo, you say your name is?"

Cayo nodded.

Ben faced the two riders and said, "Bring the horses under the lean-to out back. I'll be right with you. Give me a minute."

Ben turned to Cayo. "I was just going to rustle up some breakfast. How do you like your eggs? Let me guess. I'm not a betting man, but I'd bet a silver dollar you like 'em scrambled."

Cayo smiled, patted Ben on the back and said "I'd love a cup of coffee. Yup, your very strong coffee, not that shit-chicory served around these parts."

Ben smiled and opened the door.

After that day, Cayo noticed that when Miss Hanna went sashaying her stuff about the men, Ben Star looked away. Was he ashamed for the way she taunted some of the men or for his feelings toward a white girl? Cayo had a few more thoughts with regards to Ben Star. He knew him for a kind man; one whom Cayo believed would keep his past relationship with him and the name Coyote forgotten.

Ben was the best man Cayo'd seen with an anvil and hammer. He also had a reputation for staying the hell out of trouble. Then why did he stammer and seem so uncomfortable around when that hot little flame of a girl came sputtering by? Could it be that little Miss Hanna had a hankering for dark meat? Cayo had seen her care for her horse—maybe that's why she sought out the smithy, but the fact was she wouldn't let the stable boy touch her horse most of the time. Cayo rethought his suspicions. Anyone who loved horses the way Hanna did couldn't be all that bad.

"Mr. Star," Hanna said, "would you be so kind as to loan me your long-handled tongs—you know the ones you said you forged during the war?"

"Yes'm," he said and handed them to her, as if they were a bouquet of wild flowers. "Although, I don't ever remember mentioning anything about the war. Yes'm. I'm pretty sure of that."

"Yes'm." She mimicked him and gave him a sly smile. She took the tongs, walked a few steps away, then turned and made an exaggerated curtsey without so much as a "thank you."

The next day, Cayo was out branding with some of the other cowhands, talking, which had momentarily distracted him from the commerce, when he spotted a frantic-eyed calf and began working the rope into a lasso and circling it overhead. Then he thrust it forward to loop over and catch the animal by the legs. He cinched the rope and started dragging it over to the fire, the mama following behind curious to know what was happening to her calf. The branding iron was toasting in the coals. Not too hot so it wouldn't burn through the skin. Cayo tied the legs, while Captain Pederson's head ranch hand, Roddy Dickerson, took the double-P redolent brand and leaned it against the calf's hide. The smell of burning hair and some flesh when the iron went too deep, gave an acrid bite to the morning air. He set about marking the ear for quick identification.

"Whyn't he use a bell wattle?" Captain Pederson's young nephew Oscar asked to nobody in particular.

"Cut's a little different, usually at the jaw or at the neck." Roddy pointed to the spot on the animal's neck.

"My uncle told me."

"He did, did he? The spot's there—nope, a little ways down lower," Cayo said with frosted patience. "The skin fold."

"Wattles are all the same—just different location like I said," Oscar said.

"You didn't say, so here try it, and put a button on your lip." Cayo flipped the boy the knife, and it landed between the boy's feet.

Looking down, the boy said, "Hey, that's dangerous."

"Yup."

"You could've hurt me." He yelped.

"Yup."

"Is that all you know how to say?"

"Learn to catch a knife by the handle and next time, I'll toss it to you," Cayo said.

"I can catch," Oscar said, ready to cut a wattle in the calf's ear, trying to take a stance like Roddy's, then flipping the knife up in the air and catching it badly by the blade. He righted the knife and took hold of the calf Roddy held for him.

"Don't slip with that knife, boy, or you'll be cutting a wattle for your uncle's neighbor, at the Hendrickson's Swallow Fork Ranch," Roddy said.

"I got a name. It's Oscar, and nah, Swallow Fork's a cut out kinda V-like."

"No kinda nothing, it's a V, so don't slip," Roddy said, winking at Cayo.

"You're making me nervous, and besides that cut under-slopes— point of ear and back to his head," Cayo said.

Oscar started to say, "I was trying for an easy way—"

Cayo waited. When he had the boy's full attention, Cayo dipped his head with his hat covering his eyes. Then he brought his eyes up a little at a time. He squinted, twitched them slightly. A look loomed on the boy's face registering menace and fear.

"What's your point, boy? You don't know squat," Cayo said, taking a stance that everyone called "getting his Injun up." He muttered, "A real buckaroo, that one," and mounted his horse. "Wishing ya luck, Roddy, with our boy Oscar here. So expert. Don't turn your back on him. He's got killer in his mean eyes."

"What's he mean, Roddy?" squawked Oscar.

Roddy spat in the dust. "You're gonna need luck if you're to make it here or anywhere," and took the knife away from the boy. "And you might try showing a little respect. A friend in the wilderness is a friend for life."

Cayo rode off a ways, having had enough of the little greenhorn kid, never turning and waving back to Roddy.

Cayo's dally rope was wound around the saddle horn—he held it loosely, bottom of the rope upwards—others held the rope fast and hard. He was used to roping ponies, and roped cattle pretty much the same way he'd been taught. He'd been curious about the name dally rope and asked Miguel, one of the hired hands, who seemed to know just about everything; especially where names came from.

"Señor Cayo, 'dally rope' is Spanish for *dale vuelta*, meaning he gives a turn, you take your lasso and go around the horn of your saddle to stop the horse."

"Yeah, like in English to dally, or delay."

"Us *vaqueros* do cattle wrangling and bullfighting—goes way back to the *conquistadores.* You go to the stampedes and cowboy contests and they say 'the cowboy dallies.'"

"There's an entire cowpuncher language that comes from Mexican ranch hands in Spanish," Miguel said.

"I rode with an outfit in Colorado, learned a few things myself. Just never figured out that one," Cayo said. *"Por lo meno, puedo hablar un poco."*

"Your accent is good. Keep speaking. You'll learn more. I'll help you."

There was still snow on the mountains surrounding them, but the weather could never cool the branding iron heated hot enough to make a good brand.

"Make sure it's not too hot so it'll burn the skin," Cayo said to Miguel. Then Cayo turned his horse towards the cliffs.

Cayo had been scouting some strays as he rode the higher inclines so when he got back to the camp, he was surprised that everyone including Roddy thought he'd gone out to hunt.

"Just out looking for strays," Cayo said.

"Figured you couldn't handle this chow. By the time it gets here, it's two weeks old," Roddy said and snickered.

"Quit your beefing," Cayo said.

"Very funny." Roddy said and shook his head. "You can't stomach it either."

Roddy approached the chuck box, which acted as a portable kitchen when the camp was on the move. He peered in. Dishes, utensils, and some food. "Why don't they just get us a chuck wagon? A trail drive or a roundup needs one—just like the old days. Something complete. This is tosh. Aye, nothing but detritus—worse than a crapper."

"If that's English you're speaking, better tone it down, so's we get your meaning," Cayo said, looked at Roddy and signed to him that he'd go out again. This time for fresh meat. Cayo tossed his rifle to the boy. "Here, youngin', mind that."

"I can't shoot," the boy bellowed.

"Better learn a might quick. Cock and aim it in the direction of a bear if one comes up on ya. Anchor the butt into your shoulder or you're gonna bounce three feet backwards with the kick she'll give you," Cayo said.

"Just like a woman when you think she's yours." Roddy slapped his knee and laughed at his own joke.

"Besides, if you're going hunting, you'll need it," the boy pleaded.

Cayo turned slightly so the boy got a gander of the quiver and set of five arrows he'd just strung to his back. Then he deftly unsheathed his knife and flung it overhand whizzing past the boy's ear, straight into the heart of a nearby juniper.

"Don't guess you'll be needing it, then." The boy touched his non-existent sideburns.

"Don't ever guess." Cayo pointed to the tree.

The boy walked over to the tree and pulled out the knife. "No, sir." The boy handed it back to Cayo, and when he thought he was out of earshot, said in a low voice, "Roddy, is he a Redskin?"

"If'n me laddie-boy, you intend keeping your own precious skin, then watch yer mouth with Mr. Cayo Bradley. That's my advice. And if'n I was you, I'd abide it."

"Can he rope and tie from up there in the saddle?"

"He can. He's a real buckaroo who rides in and ropes a calf by the hind feet."

"Never seen it done. Do you think we can ask him?" Oscar asked. "Not unless you want to play the part of the calf."

Cayo returned with two hare slung in front of his saddle. After the rabbits were skinned and spitted, everyone took a break and, after filling their plates, sat around the campfire chewing the last of their bread crusts and beans. Roddy poured whiskey into his tin coffee cup, sloshed it around, and drank it in one gulp. "Ah, now, that was a might good. Hey, Cayo, you should get you a mail-order bride, you ole' buck. Probably never seen a woman's female parts."

Cayo thought on that, chewed some old tobacco that tasted like shit, and spat a gob of it in the direction of the fire. What he really wanted to do was spit it in Roddy's face, but he reckoned that'd get him wrapped up in a brawl, and today, branding cows he just wanted to do the physical part of it. Didn't want to think. He'd done branding for so long the work was automatic, so that left him plenty of time to think on Darby's female parts, indeed.

The next morning, one of the cowhands wearing chaps, yelled, "I got the earmarking—wattle's what I know best. Nobody but Captain Pederson's gonna have my special brand—it'll be the only one in this here state."

Another cowhand who'd been a familiar face around the animals, Doc Jenson, took care of the inoculations. "Good mark," Doc said, glancing quickly at the cow, "and everyone sees it's gonna know whose she is. Used to be in this here country, a man only branded. Nowadays, there's more rustling and running cows. Makes them gone-by days seem like a fairytale."

"Branding's permanent identification—" Cayo said, thinking he should put a brand on Darby. He'd dwelt on Darby long enough. His insides hurt from wanting her.

"Yeah, but not enough as a theft deterrent," Miguel said.

"I'll start the castrating over by the other corral," Cayo said to Miguel. "Tell Roddy, I'll begin just as soon as he gives me the go ahead."

Miguel had been a vaquero in his Mexican homeland and in New Mexico, and knew everything there was to know about neutering male animals, so as to make them easier to handle. The neutered stock gained weight quicker, driving up the beef price. He knew and understood animal husbandry and treated animals much the way the Apache did. With respect. Miguel told Cayo that some of the traditions had crossed the ocean from Old Spain. "That's why the livestock's kept free-range— so they can feed and water themselves," Miguel said.

Cayo had tended cattle, horses, some sheep and goats. The sheep men hated the cattlemen and vice versa. Sheep ate everything including the roots and left nothing for nobody was the argument. Miguel said many a time: Now a cattleman will tell you that cattle are polite beings, and leave the roots so's the plant will thrive again.

While Cayo thought all this branding calves to indicate ownership, and neutering to drive the price up were beneficial things to the rancher, the poor animal suffered the brunt of all man's greed. Cayo was more Apache than he realized. He watched as one spirited little calf dashed away, sprang, and turned.

"He runs as lickety-split as a dog." Roddy pulled in his reins, and slid off his horse.

"Hey, did ya see that dodge?" Miguel asked.

"No easy task if you don't have the practice, *amigo,*" Cayo said.

"A cowpoke never lets his eyes off his quarry—even in branding season," Roddy said.

That struck a chord with Cayo. He took a deep breath, knowing he had to focus on the job at hand and pushed Darby's sunlit smile to the back of his head. No dallying here. You can get yourself killed.

Cayo's horse, warmed up, was bound to respond to the chase. His horse had two qualities to get the job done well: a fine spirit and an eagerness to run. Cayo was swift on his horse and his horse, Wind, was well-trained and quick—almost as if he anticipated each swerve Cayo wanted to make, each flick of his wrist, or tug of his hand.

With his right arm, Cayo swung the noosed rope, and in a matter of seconds he threw the lasso out so that it landed directly over the shy, running calf's head.

His horse did an instant maneuver on his own: he thrust forward, and the immediate advance plunge, gave a limp feel to the rope. When Cayo felt his rope go slack, he began to wrap it quickly round the saddle horn.

"Whoa, there, beauty, slow a bit," he told his horse, heading on and pulling the calf behind.

"Now relax, youngin'," he said in a soft voice to the calf, "you'll soon be in good hands, and out of that branding station before you can wonder where your *mamacita* went."

Cayo watched as a branding iron redolent from the fire, was taken out and seared, sizzling to the calf. Now, Cayo thought, forever someone's property. "Let him loose, Roddy. Half the kick in this is watching that little heifer run again."

"Always worried about the calves, eh?"

"No need stressing the little guys." Cayo looped in his rope and rode out to catch himself another sweet-faced calf. He pushed his hat back on his head, wiped his forehead with his sleeve. "After this calf, I'm done and will head back to the ranch."

"What about supper?" Roddy asked.

"Nah. Not hungry and don't care if I eat a hot or cold supper." He tipped his hat, a formal goodbye salute.

He'd tortured himself enough all day with thoughts of Darby. Now he needed to go back in time to figure out why he was the man he'd become. What he needed now when day was done was time—a spell to think at sunset when color changes. His youth chanted to him. Would he ever fit in completely in the white man's world with Darby. Cayo separated from the men and took a long sweeping road back to the ranch, conversing with himself about the Jicarilla Apache of northeastern New Mexico.

His tribe. They had called themselves Inde, or The People. Jicarilla meant little basket—for which the tribe had many uses. By the time Coyote had grown to young adulthood, the tribe began to call themselves Abaachii from the Pueblo word Apachu, meaning enemy. In the years of his captivity he learned that these people were not savages, and that they lived by a religious code that was universal and total. They were respectful of their elders and all things in nature. Animals were assigned unconditional spiritual powers.

The Jicarilla hunted buffalo in the plains, along with other animals, but only out of necessity. The never hunted for sport. The buffalo was revered because the animal gave the people clothes, shelter for their tipi coverings, warmth for their sleeping pallets, and food. When Coyote was old enough to follow the hunt, he did so with a feeling of great pride. The day he made his first arrow, he thought about how his father had relished the thrill of the hunt. While stalking a small herd of deer one day, Coyote wondered if his father had had the same exhilarating feeling. He was taught that antelope, elk, and moose were slaughtered only when food was required, and he hunted with a younger group on these forays. They utilized all the parts of the animal—skins for covering, bedding, tipis, clothing, and moccasins, sinew for thread, and meat to eat. Coyote's heart gladdened when he realized that his people wasted nothing from the carcasses of felled animals. He began to learn about totems, the force and nature of all animals, the power that they bestowed in the form of talismans. He hunted coyote to learn their habits and habitats and he listened to the stories of the elders as they told tales and passed on folklore and the legends of his namesake.

Coyote's tribe moved in the high plains country that rose to westerly mesas. They traveled plateaus and the basins formed in between the southern Rocky Mountain ranges, the heights of which soared thousands and thousands of feet into the sky and without much rainfall. He heard Red Hawk say that mountains echoed in a man's heart and spirit, that the tiered and checkered steeps gave way to greening slopes before they turned to rock and shale and splintered cliffs. In the snow powder cups, the shape of an upside down skull, there was protection in winter, but high up above the tree line there was little shelter from the elements. Coyote asked Red Hawk if he'd ever climbed to the top. His answer was no, but that a man who climbs to the top of the mountain might see the Great Father in the sky and would be able to see and know much of the lands below. But no matter what, the climb would never teach him the inner thoughts of men, nor all there was to see on earth.

It was among the short grasses and scrub pines, the skirting hills and knolls of the mountains that Coyote learned the story of how his tribe came to be—these beginnings of his adopted family warmed and comforted him. The elders sat round a fire and recounted how they ascended to earth from the underworld on ladders of sunbeams. He liked that story, and likened it to his own emergence from the tunnel to the cave where he'd been found and taken, leaving behind a trail of tears over his sisters' blood. The ancestors were said to follow trails till they found the heart of the earth. He imagined his sisters and parents there, where one day he, too, would follow.

They planted in the mountains. The women set down seeds to yield corn, squash and beans, known as the three sisters, because they shared the same needs for water, soil and sunshine. The corn sprouted tiny emerald green seedlings that soon shot up into tall, hardy stalks. Besides roasting corn for food, the Apache learned to fashion a type of beer from fermented corn.

One night White Feather and Coyote came upon some braves who were drinking and merry-making. The boys circled the camp to see what else of interest was going on. They passed a young married couple's lodge, and put their ears to the skins to listen for sounds of lovemaking, but all they heard was crying, and backed away.

"Why do you think she was crying?" Coyote asked.

"Maybe he hit her or hurt her. Women cry all the time. When they're sad, but when they're happy too." White Feather made a face and pretended to wipe away tears from his cheek.

"Maybe she wants a baby and he can't give her one. They've been together many moons now. The seasons have changed—" Coyote shrugged his shoulders.

"You think too much. Let us go back to see the drinking party." White Feather said.

The men had fallen asleep, and the young boys sampled the drink.

"It burns the throat, but I feel invisible," Coyote said in a whisper. He took another swig and passed the paunch to White Feather.

"It heats the gut like a gunpowder burn." White Feather said.

"Give me some more." Coyote took a long gulp.

White Feather wrenched the *tulapai* away. "Drink is not the way to learn to be invisible. Do you not see what drink does, my friend? Look at these men. If we're attacked now, it's you and I who'll have to defend our village."

"Since when are you chief?"

"Let's take this to Red Hawk so these foolish ones don't drink more."

"Good idea, but first we'll have some." Coyote said.

"What kind of warrior are you?"

"Like them. Tired," Coyote said, pointing to the sleeping men.

They walked to the lodge of Red Hawk and the flap was drawn back. "You think maybe he's expecting a guest?" Coyote asked touching the pulled back skin.

A voice from within said, "I've been waiting for both of you."

The boys entered and unceremoniously dropped the *tulapai* paunch by the old man's feet.

He sniffed the air and the boys sat down. "You also have tasted the *tulapai,* why did you bring it to me?"

"The braves had too much and fell asleep. We thought it was best to bring it here, so they wouldn't be foolish and have more. Do you drink, *Shi'choo*, Grandfather?"

The old man reached for the makings of a pipe. "When I was young, but now I need clarity of mind."

"This does make cobwebs over thinking," Coyote said, "and movement."

"Is there something else you wish to say to me?" the old man asked.

White Feather looked at Coyote, as if to say, how does he always know? Then White Feather opened wide his eyes. "Coyote feels invisible with the drink."

"This is not the way to achieve it," Red Hawk said.

"We want to know about the initiation rite," Coyote blurted out.

***

Coyote learned a lesson in patience from White Feather who taught him to make arrows. They went past a stand of mesquite trees. First Coyote and White Feather cut down mountain birch saplings, looking for the straightest branches, but White Feather was not pleased with these. They moved along to find chokecherries, and cut several branches. When they had a hulking bunch, they stripped the bark off the straighter chokecherries first, then worked with the pieces that were less straight, bending them by using heat.

They bundled all of these to let them dry naturally. After a few weeks, Coyote undid the bundle and peeled off any remaining bark. Retying these, he dried them until they were ready for cutting.

The process was ongoing and as these dried, others were prepared. A month later, before he cut the dried ones, he straightened those with flaws, using bear grease and heat. The grease protected the shaft so it would not scorch, and the heat made it flexible enough to straighten.

He assembled all the shafts. Then he measured each from the middle of his chest along the length of his extended arm to a bent wrist—that would be the length. He always left more in case of error, and so measured from mid-chest, the length of his extended arm to the end of his middle finger before the cut. Finally, he lined up all the cut shafts.

Mbai' walked by and observed their work. "These shafts are not perfect." He picked one up to examine it. "But, they are hunting arrows. The flaws will correct in flight. Good enough."

Coyote knew by now, that compliments for work well done were hard to come by, if not impossible, but he felt pride push his chest out a little farther as he took his next breath.

It was not long before he was old enough and trusted as one of the People to follow the chase and hunt with the others. First he learned to hunt rabbit and small game, next he hunted deer, which required practice. In the beginning, he mimicked the others, approaching in silence in back of other braves. Soon he acquired the necessary skills—stealth—by crawling long distances in weeds or high brush always against the wind; patience because he'd have to wait sometimes for an hour for the right moment to strike, and fortitude to remain strong in the face of a scattering herd after the first few deer were taken down. At last he became invisible.

Many years after he was abducted, Coyote found himself in a ponderosa pine forest. He put his nose in a cleft of a huge pine tree and the aroma of vanilla and butterscotch ferried him back to his mother's kitchen. He fought hard to banish memory as he swept together bunches of pine needles to soften his berth, tossing his blanket on top. He would sleep here but now prayed softly, his voice commingling with the riffling pines from a gentle wind.

"Hear, oh, Spirit, my need, I ask for rest and a dreamless night before the hunt tomorrow." So troubled had he been by other dreams his adopted grandmother said she wanted to make him a dream catcher. She had said, bring me feathers, but when he did, she looked at them and noted with pity in her voice, "These are dove feathers. You suffer much to be loved, my child. I was hoping for eagle feathers."

When she finished making him the dream catcher, he regarded it as a work of art duplicated from nature, for it looked like a spider's web, and from it hung long, knotted tassels and the feathers he had gathered for her from three eagles, that his brother White Feather gave him.

But he had not brought it with him on the hunt.

He slept badly, waking often in the middle of a frantic dream. Towards dawn he washed himself and drank from a cool stream. The camp was on the move. He and three young bucks were in charge of bringing up the rear in back of the women who were to skin and butcher the buffalo. They ate a kind of hardtack with piñon nuts and dried berries along the trail, riding through the piñon mesas over hillocks and up mountainous terrain till finally he came upon brush flats.

They forded a river that wasn't much more than an arroyo, or a gulch that had filled in from the melting snows of winter. Though the water was swift moving and seemed to pool and gather strength around some boulders, it wasn't very deep. He gauged there was a current, but not a danger if someone were to fall into it. The flattish stones were easy to use as a bridge, and he watched the winsome Red Willow as she hopped and skipped the rocks. In the early morning he rode beside her in the deeper water where the bottom was sand gravel. The larger black rocks to his left were slick, for he saw the maiden try to grip with her toes, but slipped, and using her arms for balance, her hands carrying her moccasins flailed the air. Despite all of her desperate movements to regain her center of gravity, she was thigh high in the cold stream, and a small cry of surprise eked from her mouth. If her mother had been near, she would have chastised her for the tiny yelp. He watched her grapple for a hold on the moss-covered rock, heaving herself upon it.

He couldn't help from smiling at her predicament until his attention was caught by a flock of water birds swooping low in wedge formation. This helped him focus, realizing his job was not to spy upon the pretty girl, but to look for signs of black bear. He saw none. His gaze shifted. He sniffed the air, reined in his horse when he saw mountain lion tracks. It paid to keep sharp eyes, not gawk over a young girl. He looked all about, noting it was but one prey animal, and the imprints weren't fresh; therefore, he did not warn his companions. What if he'd missed these? Stealth was the characteristic of his brother White Feather whose totem was the cougar. White Feather, son of Mbai', had become his ally and best teacher, but Mbai' still declined having any commerce with Coyote.

As the boys rode bareback, at the rear of the hunting party, White Feather complained of a sore thigh that rubbed and chafed. He had been jabbed by a shard of boulder that had broken loose as the boys had kept watch on a bear's lair, hoping to steal some honey.

"Quiet," Coyote said. "Do you want the women to hear the son of Mbai' acting like a girl?" There was sharpness in his voice.

"You're still afraid of my father, aren't you, little brother?"

Coyote snorted. "Of course not."

"If you want to earn respect and pay back my father for not killing you, you must do something spectacular in bravery and put him in your debt."

"Ah. Good. Seeds of wisdom from you who almost snapped your leg like a twig. Now just what brave act would that be?"

"I have no idea, but you could go to the sweat lodge and ask for guidance—" Then White Feather repeated the old saying, *Ni nahii maa at' e, ya nahiika' ee at'e*: The earth is our mother, the sky is our father. We are all part of this, Coyote Dinizhi." He made an expansive swish of his arm.

"I will think on it," Coyote said.

"Remember," White Feather said, "we believe the Coyote is a Trickster, and a hungry one is a danger to his enemies."

"Now what's that supposed to mean?" he muttered in English. "Am I still an enemy?" Coyote took off at a fast pace and tossed back over his shoulder the Apache words, "And you call me brother?"

He saw the hurt in White Feather's face, but kept putting his horse forward. He rode a little way on, when he suddenly jerked up his reins and stopped his horse. He turned and yelled, "The earth trembles," and slipped down from his mount, putting his ear to the ground. They are near," he cried. "*A.yan.de*! The mighty buffalo."

There was no time for the others to return for lance or spear, but luckily that morning, for some unknown reason, Coyote had tethered his to a sheath at the side of his horse. A buffalo hunt started at its own crazy momentum whether or not you were prepared for it. Bison thundered over the bluff into a shallow ravine. The size of the herd was staggering. Nine hunters raced after them intent on cutting off stragglers. The trailing slower beasts lagging behind were snared by six youths bringing up the rear. Those with spears raised surged forward. Sheets of aerial dust floated above blocking the sky, sand cones whipped upwards with cyclonic gust. Within minutes a curtain of red, gray and black descended upon them. Soon the rear back-up party led by White Feather and Coyote were coughing and spitting, their burning eyes tearing and cleansing in a matter of seconds. Coyote squeezed his eyes shut, but knew enough not to rub them. He blinked several times. The squalls of dust were ahead now. His heart pounded to the rhythm of maddened hooves in stampede. The grassy pastures of the wide-mouthed ravine were flattened. The smell of death and blood, the war cries of the hunters hung in the air, incensing the goaded animals. Terrified animals running in a mass, they broke ranks, darting hell-bent at breakneck speed.

With whoops and hollers the more seasoned hunters waylaid and killed the weaker animals that trailed behind, the young calves following their mothers, trying to steer them away from the herd—these were followed by some old bulls. The braves launched their spears, then switched to bow and arrow. After their quivers had been emptied, they rode back, slid from their mounts and retrieved their spears and some arrows to stage a second attack. Dust settled to the rear, but the chaotic crashing herd had veered. The deafening war cries assaulted Coyote's ears. He lost sight of White Feather for a moment, but then saw him galloping in the direction of his father. Coyote was confused as this wasn't part of the strategy they were taught.

"What are you doing?" Coyote yelled, his voice muffled though his bandana, then carried away in the melee.

He yanked down the bandana, cantering in the direction of White Feather, "You're breaking ranks! This isn't our plan," he shouted. "You're—" His throat closed with a mouthful of dust. He spat, but no sound ushered forth, and he was about to replace the bandana. Instead, he put the reins in his mouth and covered the horse's eyes with the cloth, tied it as best he could. Taking hold of the reins again, his horse's gait surged from canter to gallop, racing in time with his heart. As he leaned into the wind, he felt a part of the horse, the horse's breath was his breath; the speed and movement of its withers, neck, shoulders, flanks and back fused to him so they were one fluid anatomy sluicing air, pounding earth. Then he skirted the rear of the coursing tide of on-rushing buffalo. Coyote turned into a small breech, but a ridge forced him around retracing his direction backwards. He slowed his pace and got a bead on White Feather, now understanding why he'd disobeyed and broken rank. He must have seen one of the outriders, Little Wren, a boy of considerable bravery, in trouble. Coyote watched as White Feather tried to reach Little Wren, but he was outdistanced and saw a bull ram the underbelly of Little Wren's horse. The gored horse was hurtling down screeching, as the rider, going down with the horse, jumped off.

Coyote realized Mbai' must have seen Little Wren's wounded horse collapse. Mbai' reared on his mount, turned and headed to where the boy's horse had gone down. But White Feather had already circled back, riding like the wind for Little Wren, standing on top of his horse. White Feather slowed his steed, reached down and with his forearm, linked, locked, and scooped up Little Wren, who bent his knees, and hurled himself upward. White Feather's action was like a hawk catching a fledging in flight, fallen from its perch—a keen and practiced skill he'd honed with Coyote.

Little Wren slapped his savior's back with much joy and enthusiasm, and seeing they were out of danger, Coyote was about to rotate and resume his rear position, when he spotted a surprised Mbai'. Was he surprised because of the heroic behavior of White Feather, or because now he'd been cut off from the other hunters?

In a thunderous explosion, the buffalo changed course, charging, stamping and stirring the parched earth into a frenzy of dust squalls. Mbai' flung his spear with heft and accuracy meeting its target. Then with practiced motion he disengaged his bow from around his head where it had hung to his left side. He clenched it with his rein hand, now drawing an arrow from his quiver with his free hand. He notched the arrow, aimed, drew back, and fired all in one fluid movement, but the arrow only caused erratic behavior in a seasoned bull as it glanced off the animal's hump. Horror gripped Coyote's entrails and his stomach lurched. Next, he rode at top speed toward Mbai', hemmed in, watching the aggravated bull skid to a full stop. The animal veered, lowered his head and pawed the earth with his hoof in concentration. The beast's hooded eyes came upon the warrior who, wary of the beast, had slowed his horse, and notched another arrow. Without warning, Mbai' beveled, his steed tilted and went out of control—dancing in place, bucking, and snorting, sensing the bull was out for blood.

On the far side of the hunt, three riders caught sight of White Feather's exhibition of bravura, coming up to White Feather's hind side with Little Wren still mounted in back of him. All stopped mid–action brandishing their spears and as if guided by one thought, their eyes watched Coyote's race toward Mbai', their tethered gaze fixed on Mbai' with horror and on the spot of his impending doom.

Without a thought for his own safety, Coyote dashed into the fray. Yelling a death cry, wailing the fiercest battle shout he could muster, he charged the bull's path. At the last moment, he yanked his horse's head so as not to receive a frontal blow and crashed his horse into the pummeling beast's side. At the same time, slamming his lance into the raging bull's neck, Coyote vaulted, thrusting upward, heels hurtling overhead through the air, a rotating cannon shot. The horse's legs shattered on impact, its head and torso careening in air behind Coyote in a gruesome dance just before he hit the earth tucking his shoulder, rolling sideward and out from the crush of his beloved steed.

The air had not yet cleared of dust, but Mbai', in control and no longer in danger, urged his horse into a quick trot toward the bull, approaching the animal's injured side. The brave aimed, drew back the bowstring, his thumb resting in the hollow of his cheek. The arrow's feathers grazed his high cheekbone, and in an instant he released his arrow. It punctured the buffalo's hide, finding its mark, the top of the heart where it would die fast.

The mighty animal kept running, head down with the force of inertia until it collapsed some distance ahead. Mbai' did not look at his kill. He shouldered his bow as he rode to Coyote standing in the wake of the bull's dust. Neither spoke. Mbai' hunched forward and extended his arm in a mirror image of what his son had done earlier. Before mounting, Coyote clasped Mbai's forearm covered with red dust.

Coyote said, "I am no longer in your debt."

Hauling the lightweight up, Mbai' said, "My life is yours."

When the rescue was over, Coyote's heart and mind gave thanks to Usen, the giver of Life, instead of to the Christian God of his childhood. Perhaps they were one and the same, for that's the way Coyote had begun to think. The hunting party rode toward the felled beast and Mbai' jumped down from his horse. He cut open the slain animal and offered the liver to Coyote, who took it and bit a chunk off, warm blood spilling off his hands, covering his mouth. Nothing had ever tasted so good as this fresh organ seasoned with glory.

***

That night around the campfire Little Wren and Coyote grieved for the loss of their horses. What was worse was that the boys knew their beasts would be part of the food for the celebration. Nothing was ever wasted. But the boys were not permitted to stay apart from the hunters. There was much rejoicing. Meat skewering on open fires was plentiful. Squirrels were seared and served with nuts, seeds and berries. The women had skinned, cut, butchered and prepared bison and all of the other meat and some fowl for the feast. In a day or two they'd begin the process of smoking and drying the remaining bison meat.

White Feather took Coyote aside and put a hand on his shoulder. "No need for the sweat lodge now, my little brother. My heroic feat pales with yours—the debt is paid."

"To your father, perhaps, but I'll never wash my hands clean of my sisters' blood. I may yet need go to the sweat lodge."

"Don't dwell on that sorrow. There will be more in future days. To-night, we'll smoke a pipe and be happy." White Feather winked.

Coyote's eyes filled. He turned away so that as the tears fell, he would not compound his self-loathing with a shameful, womanly act. "And what of you, my brother? Are you not angry that I eclipsed your daring with my clumsy attempt of —"

"The moon is unaware of what it does but steps in front of the sun anyway."

"I had no time to think," Coyote said.

"If you'd thought too much, my father would be dead. Acts measure a man. Had you weighed the danger, Mbai' would now be feasting with the Spirit Father, not sitting by the fire." White Feather made a wide sweep of his arm. "Look there. Hear how he recounts the bravery of his son's friend."

"He beckons you. Go," Coyote said.

"Not me, Coyote. You." White Feather laughed, gave his friend a gentle shove and said, "Get used to it. He owes you his life, and he's going to be with us for a long time. I'll be along in a moment. Ask for what your heart craves most—go on, hurry."

But Coyote didn't hurry. He ambled in an unhurried gait, aware his station had been elevated despite the fact that he had lost one of White Feather's horses. While he walked slowly, a thought sped through his mind. A horse. Without a horse, he was less than a maiden. But could he ask for one? In some regards, he felt he was still a slave of the people, but the thought of what White Feather had said gave him a sense of belonging. From these words, Coyote Dinizhi drew confidence.

Entering the tent, fire-glow lit the faces of the warriors. The bear grease and their own sweat shined as if they'd all just shaken off river water. There were several elders he recognized: Snow Owl, Spotted Wolf, and Rested Wind, but what he noticed was the usual grave manner on the men's faces was different. The looks seemed welcoming.

"Come in out of the night air," Snow Owl said.

With the closing of the tent flap went the last vestiges of a cool breeze.

Coyote snaked his way round Spotted Wolf and Rested Wind, past Snow Owl until he stood face to face with Mbai'.

"Gayóodi," Mbai' said, but Coyote didn't answer because he was so used to his nickname: dark—*why isn't he calling me Dinizhi?*

A flash of insight passed through his head, and he shivered slightly. He was being called by his formal name, Coyote. Now he finally understood. He'd been baptized by blood with the death of his horse, the crimsoning of his body with the buffalo's blood, and the saving of this chief. Coyote, his true name, the first name he'd been called in the Apache tongue.

White Feather had followed behind him. Coyote looked at his brother and summoned courage.

When he got control of his emotions, he said, "There is something I would ask of Mbai'." He squared his shoulders.

The warrior almost bristled, but his look changed. He was curious. Talking ceased. Silence reigned.

Coyote thought to himself, Mbai' thinks I'm going to ask for my freedom, but for me freedom is—"I need a horse."

Mbai' laughed. And everyone else laughed, too, but not at a brazen boy. They laughed with a growing warrior, a member of their tribe.

"Abáachi, Apache," Gayóodi yelled. "Gayóodi is Apache."

Chapter Nine

Darby's Departure

The wrangle with Garrett didn't deter Darby from seeing Cayo again. Although she turned the argument this way and that and tried to see it from every perspective, she was obsessed by only one thought—Cayo. The brutal words Garrett had used pricked her conscience many times throughout her working days and made her murmur to herself, *Oh God, I'm ruined if he doesn't marry me.*

She walked to the pinon tree just outside the McPhee ranch post with the name *Tess* on the cross stanchion. Tess, her mother's name. It brought back all the things her mother wanted for Darby, but most of all her mother's desire to see her daughter study, learn and become educated so that she'd always be able to care for herself. Darby sighed, thinking of her mother, and picked up a feather from the lower crotch of a tree branch. This was the sign she had devised with Cayo which meant he was free and could meet with her by the river. She walked back, saddled a horse, and rode out to meet him.

He sat on his haunches looking out over the river and turned to face her, a sullen look on his face.

"What's wrong?" she said.

"Don't have all day, Darby. We got to design a better way of seeing each other."

"Hey, I know one. Let's get married. If you'd ever ask Pa, we could be together always."

"Let's not argue. We don't have much time to be together. If I didn't tell you, I'm saying it now. I'm laying aside some pay so we can have a bit of a stake. It won't take long, but somehow I never did get the hang of money. Got something to show you, so don't dismount. Follow me." He was up in his saddle and she followed him north along the river when he veered east and found an old overgrown path. He led her to higher ground into the mountains. Darby followed him until they came up behind thick, rough decaying hacienda walls, nature reclaiming its own. She looked around. Beauty surrounded her. She observed a flitting movement around the cottonwoods: a monarch butterfly, and as soon as she spotted a grouse nearby, a crane alighted from another direction and sailed high above. There was a buzzing in the air that could be hypnotizing if she'd let the sound lull her.

They dismounted, tied the horses to a scrub pine. He didn't wait to take hold of her in his arms, but backed her up against the wall. The sun in her speckled eyes blinded her and she shielded them with her hand. Everything blurred slightly, turning a dark purple haze. He took her hand down slowly, bent over her, leaned one hand on the wall and placed his face in front of hers shadowing everything but her hair. He said, "Your hair's like gold streaming in a creek bed; it lights up this wall." He took a handful of her hair and undid the thick braid, gently tugging her towards him until he covered her mouth with his and pressed his body into hers. Her skirt was up around her waist, her knickers down and his hands fumbled with his belt.

When they'd finished their hasty love-making, she slumped against the wall and looked around. This had been a room with a fireplace that was like no other place she'd ever seen. It wasn't an adobe dwelling like she was used to seeing. This had been a stately mansion, probably one that had been owned by a rich Mexican—either a wealthy rancher or a bandit.

She saw a broken chair and pointed to it. Cayo hiked up his trousers and left her abruptly but now beckoned her. She moved from the stone wall and walked to where he sat, picked up her skirt and petticoat. Darby had no bloomers on as she'd carelessly tossed them by the wall. He summoned her forth and she straddled him on the chair with his pants down around his ankles. He untied her bodice. Her undulating breasts moved untethered across his chest. She felt his mouth slide down her earlobe, down her neck and along her heaving chest. Darby moved in rhythm to his thrusting forward, at first so gentle it could have been the wind propelling him, and then with a certain surge, the pulsing was upward, deep and intense as though she was speared, skewered, spiked. She hardly breathed until his movement ceased, and her crying out startled her as if waking from a deep, dreamless sleep.

"Oh," she said after a long silence, "that was like the beginning of daybreak."

"More like lightning felling a tree," he murmured.

Sure enough, it had started out as a strange day, balmy, like a snow-melt breeze in spring. Like a warm dry wind developing in the lee of the mountain range, which felt like a Chinook wind descending from the eastern slopes of the Rockies raising the temperature to melt the snow to slush and make run-offs muddy.

This swaying felt like spring, breezy in the greening corn, stalks not understanding which way they were supposed to bend. But it was summer, not spring, and the strangeness of the wind lead to a magical feeling surreal as if she were an observer and this wasn't happening to her, to them.

A little later on, Cayo left her for a spell and came back with a bou-quet of wild flowers he took from behind his back and thrust at her.

"Oh, my, bluebonnets." She looked at him, a smile bright as sunshine. "Some call them buffalo clover, but they've got another name that suits them well, do you know what it is?"

"Didn't know these were bluebonnets. Just some wild blue flowers."

"From now on I'll always think of them as that other perfect name for them—wolf flower. And these," she ruffed up some brush in the bouquet. "Coyote brush."

"Well, think of that now, a plant named for the man I am." He bent and kissed the tip of her nose.

Sounds at sunset surrounded them. At the last light of afternoon, she stretched out on the grass, closed her eyes, still grasping the bunch of flowers he'd given her. She envisioned him seated on the tiled floor in the middle of what once was the hacienda's kitchen. He was dressed all in black. Black shirt, black faded pants. He unbuckled his silver spurs, pulled off his black boots and socks, one with a hole through the toe.

While still day-dreaming, she pictured his male figure in the position of an Indian, legs crossed in front of him, knees popped up. She watched him unbutton his shirt, remove it and lay it in front of him. He pulled his undershirt over his head, his back muscles taut and rippling. His back was scarred. Then he put his hands on top of his knees. Was he praying? His back was lined as if scratched by sharp fingernails, or perhaps thin remains of faded whiplashes. Or were these lines keen indentations from chains or ropes that had crisscrossed a much younger back? Or recently made from the lattice chair back—yes, perhaps by the chair on which he'd been sitting before he moved to the room's center and the floor? Some marks perhaps, not all. Why had she not noticed them at the river a week earlier?

She noticed his ears were small and close to his head. Curly hair, sandy with gray flecks at the nape of his neck—a neck that was scrunched and red—dune-colored when the dusk sun is ready to make its descent. She thought of parched earth at the base of some of the low lying hills. His face—sunburned dark and delicious-looking—the color of baked yam in contrast to his back, white, protected and untouched by sun's rays.

The spell of their time at the hacienda was broken when he said to her, "Once I attempted suicide. Hard to believe, isn't it?"

She didn't answer. She sat up and leaned against a tree.

"There are ghosts that haunt me and in the night, in my dreams they invade my space and disturb my peace of mind. Lately, I've been lost in the past, my brain bustling with things I can't control and hardly remember. But there's one thing you need to know about me."

Darby looked at him, an unsettled feeling coming over her, knowing she was about to hear something terrible. And then she knew. "You killed someone didn't you?"

"How could you know?"

"The look in your eyes when you said—"

"I'd kill him again if I had the chance. He raped and murdered—"

Darby jumped up. "Don't tell me," she said, agitated. "I beg you not to tell me her name. I never want to know it."

"Her name? We don't speak of the dead by name."

He got up and took from his saddlebag the dream catcher he always carried with him. It was made of a twisted twig and woven, interlaced leather thongs, and doves' feathers hung from the circle to wing away any disturbing dreams. "My Indian *bichóó,* my Grandmother, crafted it." In the sand, he wrote *Dak'éé.* "That was her name—I think that's how you'd write it by sound."

"How do you say it?"

"I can't say it. I just told you. We don't speak the names of the dead. It means the season when the leaves change color and blow off the trees."

"Autumn."

"Your mother's mother was an Indian? I thought your mother was a white woman who died?"

Cayo didn't answer and Darby didn't want to break his spell or train of thought and question him further.

Then he said, "She was my adopted Indian grandmother."

When he stopped talking, she asked him what it was like to be raised by Indians. Cayo retreated from her. Not in the physical sense, but perhaps in an emotional one, almost out of fear the way a turtle pulls its head into its protective shell. Darby held her tongue but thought about what Garrett had told her. *He was wrong. Cayo isn't Indian.*

Darby sensed he couldn't speak more about it. A queasy feeling swept over her and she knew the moon would be sickly. "I've got to go home to serve the boys dinner."

"What did you leave prepared?

"Bean soup with a ham hock."

"Sounds tasty."

She smiled. "Would you like to come for dinner some time?"

"Not yet."

On the ride back, with the departing light of evening, she knew there'd soon be a smattering of stars, but the sky was sullen, only boasting a shadow of a moon, a moon bereft with clouds—how she felt every time she left Cayo.

As the days of the week wore on, Garrett became less angry when she told him that Cayo was raised by Indians, but he wasn't Apache. Garrett ignored Darby. She had a knot in the pit of her stomach each morning and night when she knew she'd face seeing him. After days of feeling sick and unsure, one morning she resolved to confront him. She determined it would be that night after dinner.

The boys and Pa had gone to bed and she had wiped and put away the last dish. She eased into the great room where Garrett sat at Pa's oak desk by the fire. In front of him were a stack of bills run through with a needle stick bill holder. Papers, bills and envelopes scattered on the desk. Garrett shook his head and smirked with annoyance.

Not a good time, Darby thought. *But better now or lose my nerve altogether.*

"Garrett," she said, and he snapped his head up.

"Thought you went to bed already," he said in a voice less gruff than in the past week.

"I don't mean to distract you from working on the invoices and such, but I need to talk to you," she said, barely audible.

"Sit down and speak up. Since when're you so meek and mild. I need a break anyway."

"Would you like some more coffee?"

"Any more and I'll pee brown till morning." He pushed back in the chair and stretched.

Darby pulled an embroidered footstool close to the desk and sat at his feet.

"What I did might seem wrong in your eyes, but I wish you'd have some compassion. You were in love once. Clara. That pretty girl with blond braids and cornflower blue eyes."

"Don't," he said, his tone curt.

"I'm just wanting you to see that—"

"I would've married her," he said, his timbre more mellow. "Clara was in her buggy after a day's outing, when marauders shot up the town and—"

"I'm so sorry, Garrett. Woeful. A brutal destiny to be at the wrong place at the wrong time." Darby folded her hands in her lap.

"Destiny," he spat out the word. Then he softened. "You think you love Cayo enough to settle with him and raise a family?"

"I do believe—yes."

"Who am I to judge you, or anybody? I owe you an apology. I'm jealous. It'll never come to me again—what I had with Clara."

"I've tried so often to show how contrite I am. Not for loving him, but for offending you, losing your affection. Why it's almost as bad as losing Momma—"

She stood and approached the desk. He moved his chair back and outstretched his arms. She sat on the desk the way she used to when she was young and whispered, "Forgive me, Garrett, for hurting you and making you recall your girl. I need to convince you that what I feel for Cayo is as real and unchanging as what you felt."

"You'd give up your dream of schooling for him? Your promise to Momma?" Garrett picked up a paper weight and set it down a bit too forcefully. "You care for him that much?"

***

Two weeks drifted into three and the drowsy days of summer warmth and buzzing bees seemed to fade towards a welcoming respite of cool weather. Darby and Cayo talked about getting married, but there never seemed to be the right moment for him to ask her father's permission. The longer he put it off, the more she thought that maybe it was better to have some time for them to be promised and get used to each other. She knew it wouldn't be a long betrothal because his desire heightened with each passing day. Now she had to fend him off or make sure they weren't alone so much.

After work one Saturday when Cayo rode Darby home from town on his horse, she squeezed his back and said she wanted to know and understand him better. "I keep trying to engage you in conversations about memories of your past. But—" What were those words she'd written down to remember from the new book Aunt Mary had sent her?

"Hold up a minute, Cayo."

He pulled back on the reins and stopped the horse, half-turning around to see her.

"Why're you so taciturn?" she asked, quite peeved.

"I'm what?"

"Reticent."

"Are you making fun at me?"

"Heavens, no!" she snapped. "I'm just trying out some new vocabulary I read in a book."

"What's it mean? Do you want to get down and walk a bit?"

"All right," she said, and he dismounted and helped her down.

He was still holding her when she said, "It means, Cayo Bradley, you're cagy and reserved and won't talk to me. Why is that?"

"Why can't you just see me for who I am, a man standing holding you, who wants you for his own?"

"I do, but I'm craving to know what's inside here." She tapped him on his chest. "In your heart. The things you've lived through."

"You don't want to know that, Darby. You might turn to hate me." He dropped his arms and they took a few steps together.

She stopped walking. "What are you afraid of? Can't you trust me?"

"Not a matter of trust. I done some hateful things and don't want that part of me to be a part of us. I just want to be horizontally refreshed by you."

"Can't be every time we're together. Think on it, a second. It only takes one time to make a baby, Cayo. It's not my intention to walk down the church aisle to say 'I do' with a bulging middle for the parishioners to gape at."

"I'll ride out tomorrow night and speak to your Pa."

She sighed. "About time."

Cayo left her about a mile from her ranch and headed his horse toward the Pederson place.

The next day as Darby returned from Fern's store and rode toward the barn, her father called her to come up to the porch. She strode up to the house. Darby could see her father seated on a rocking chair, his rifle leaning against the wall.

Before she reached the porch steps, Garrett rode up and hopped off his horse. He threw the reins over the hitching post. "I gave Pa something for you," he said.

Then she noticed a telegraph message on the rough planking near her father's boot.

"From Aunt Bea?" she asked.

"Garrett brought it home from the post and telegraph office this morning." Pa leaned down and picked it up. He waved it in front of Darby. "You're going. You're not going to waste your life out here slaving for your brothers and me. You're going to study and be a teacher and maybe get married to someone who can support you."

"You're right, Pa. I'm going to marry Cayo Bradley. He's coming here tonight to ask for my hand all proper like."

Her father stood up and looked down at her. "I didn't finish. You don't have to marry that eastern fella your Aunt Bea's so keen on, but you're going to get that education you're Momma always wanted you to have."

Darby went quiet and didn't answer her father for a moment. Her reflections about education thrust her through school memories, until she reached that last day of school two years ago. As if seeing a representation cast upon a wall, she saw her teacher, Miss Candace Mather, an unmarried spinster who wore her graying hair in a tight bun at the back of her head. She slapped Darby's knuckles with a wooden ruler when she lost her place in reading. The slap stung, but not nearly as much as the feeling of mortification in front of the class because she'd been inattentive, looking out the window and smelling the fresh cut grass, pungent and ushering in spring. Darby loved the idea of school and learning. She adored books. She craved reading. What was it that had drawn her away beside the sweet soft scent of high grass? It was a cowboy she didn't recognize riding past the schoolhouse. He seemed as big as the seventeen hands high stallion he rode. The rider was dressed in dark clothes, the shiny coat of the horse as black as Satan. She couldn't see his face shadowed by his big-brimmed hat. But instinct told her that he was no ordinary looking cowpoke from Parcel Bluffs. Little did she know at that first glimpse of the rider that she'd fall in love with him.

***

Darby looked at her father, tamping down other school memories and the insistent knowledge that she adored Cayo, even if he'd committed some outrageous deeds. It didn't matter. What did was that she ached for him constantly.

After a while she said, "But, Pa," focusing on the moment at hand and in the softest voice she could muster, "I want to stay here. Teach school here. I want to marry here, to raise my own kids—"

Her father slapped Darby with such force, her head teetered on her shoulders. The shock of it ended the discussion for the moment.

Darby's hand flew to her cheek. She rubbed the spot which stung. "You've never hit me before," she said, vexation in her words.

Her father's face crumbled and he looked remorseful, but merely inclined his head.

"If you think a slap can deter me, you're wrong, Pa." She whirled about on her heels, went into the house and shut the door with more force than she intended. She walked to her room off the kitchen to sulk and sort out her true feelings.

Preparing dinner was a matter of angry tosses of pots and pans. She was more than distracted cutting carrots and potatoes and she sliced her finger. The cut furrowed deep. She rinsed it off and wrapped a strip of napkin tight around it, tying it off with her teeth. But the cut didn't stop her from finishing the chopping and slicing, dicing vegetables, and carving small batonnet carrot sticks for stew. As she worked she was assailed by uncertainty. She was sorry to be such a fence-sitter, but realized this was the decision of a lifetime. Scooping up the carrots, potatoes, onions, turnips, she dumped them unceremoniously into the stew pot with some hunks of sizzling bacon that normally she would've cut into smaller pieces. She was so intent on completing her tasks quickly that she didn't notice her wound was still bleeding on the wooden cutting block. She washed off the board and her hand in a bucket of water by the dry sink and re-bandaged her finger with a hanky from her pocket.

***

After finishing her work, Darby took a long walk. She came back calmer and sat on the porch petting the dog and thinking. She was thinking so much that she decided to pick up a book to distract her. She

127

read only fifteen pages, her eyes rereading over and over the last few sentences and her eyelids weighing down. She closed the book, walked to her room, took off her shoes and stockings and threw herself on the bed. She hugged her pillow, thinking of Cayo, and wishing for blessed sleep to overcome her in hopes of some illuminating thoughts. Why hadn't Cayo come to speak with her father?

The following night at dinner, silence reigned at the table. Finally, Darby said in a contrite voice, "You're right, Pa. I'd be throwing away my chance of education to better myself, and for good. An opportunity like this doesn't come twice, does it?" Without waiting for an answer, she continued, "If I don't go east and get book learning it would be a betrayal to Momma. Worse even. It's been my heart's desire since the day she taught me to read. I've been hankering to learn enough to be able to teach children. School children. My own children." But what Darby neglected to say was that part of her would die leaving Cayo. And just as she was thinking that, he rode up to the house. She peered out the window as Cayo tied up his horse. Each step of his boots on the stairs was a crushing blow of defeat. How could she go? How could she renounce and desert him?

Cayo rapped lightly on the doorjamb.

"Come on in. Darby and Pa've been waiting on you," Garrett said, "since yesterday."

Cayo said, "Evening, folks." As if on cue, Garrett, and the other brothers pushed their chairs away from the table, stood, and walked out the front door, one by one in single file like schoolchildren at recess.

Cayo took off his hat, "Evening, sir. Evening, Darby," he mumbled.

She knew her wet eyes glistened in the lamplight, and was afraid to move for fear the tears would roll down her cheeks. She stood stone still, a deer frozen in the light of a campfire.

"Sit down, Cayo," Pa said, with too much geniality in his voice. "Cup of coffee?"

"Darby, you get Cayo here a cup and then go see if the boys need something more. Looks like they rushed off way too hurried like. Cayo and I—well, we'll set here a spell—and pass the time of day. Haven't had a moment alone with him in quite some time."

As Darby turned and started to go, she glanced at Cayo, sorrow on her face, unbidden tears now washing her face.

Cayo looked perplexed, aware of the tension in the room—energy he'd never picked up on in these rooms, but knew to mean danger. The cowboy in him made him hit the inside of his boots with his hat, one at a time, shucking loose the dust. Then he glanced up, long and steady at Darby, and before she took another step, caught her by the arm and shook his head, whispering, "What's going on here?"

She jerked away from him. "I can't—not now—"

He re-grasped her arm and underneath his breath spit out, "This can't be. You promised me, promised—" his words petulant and fearful as child's.

"Let her be, son. She didn't have my word to give hers to you," McPhee said.

"No, sir, the hell I will. She's full grown and doesn't need her daddy's permission—"

Darby caved then, her feelings making her dizzy and confused. She pitched forward falling to her knees. "There's no way I can please both you and my Pa." Her overriding passion for Cayo had her shaking. She was refusing him. "It won't be forever. You can wait. I'll be back in a year—eighteen months at most."

"Don't go. Don't leave me now. Marry me and be mine like we talked about." He gestured with his hat towards her father. "You don't owe him nothing—"

Darby was on her feet. It seemed as though all the light in the house was snuffed out and in the dark Darby's eyes went sable, so clouded over, she could barely see the shapes in front of her. "Cayo, please, please understand. I took an oath—this is bigger than you and me, for now. I've got to go, but I'll be back—"

"When?"

"Listen. Wait for me. Cayo?"

Cayo shook his head. "This can't be."

"The promise I made momma to get schooled became a promise to myself. I'm going—"

The next thing Darby heard was the door slamming—as if a rock had been thrown at her chest that made the floor come up to reach her whole body. She lay prostrate and looked up. "Papa, you shouldn't had ought to interfere. Nobody stopped you from taking Momma to your bed—a bride of only thirteen."

"T'weren't me, Darby. You asked him to wait."

***

Darby couldn't sleep the whole night long, tortured by her weakness, tossing over and over and over in her mind, her inactivity to move and go with Cayo. She was incapable of courage. She had been dressed, on the verge of running away with him. Why did she falter? Because in her heart she knew she didn't want to remain for the rest of her life ignorant and untutored.

All night she pondered what she could have done to change the circumstances. She thought Cayo would ride back to the ranch, toss pebbles at her window and help her climb out so he could seat her on his horse to whisk her away. But he never came. Why would he? She was a gutless creature to be pitied. Cayo left her to decide her fate for herself, a decision too impossible to consider. Darby was still dressed in her homespun garb as morning approached. She washed her face. She couldn't cook for her brothers or father. Had Pa controlled her life making her move away from Cayo's love and kindness? Of course not. She had herself to blame for her choice, but she couldn't believe why Cayo didn't say, 'I'll wait for you.' Forever is a dream word. An illusion. It really doesn't exist.

Two days later at the station, the train master tipped his hat to her. Darby, embarrassed, considered kissing her father, but merely hugged him. She made a promise to herself she'd never be another man's chattel again. Cayo had given up on her. With mixed emotions of tenderness yet remorse, she watched Bix and Chad place her trunk on board. Garrett and Randy went aboard to settle her hand luggage. She thanked them, but with a bitter heart. The rancor she felt was at herself. When they finally stood all together again, Darby said goodbye in turn to each of her brothers, giving them each a swift hug, and lastly her father. She would think back on this day and realize he thought he was doing his best for her, according to her mother's wishes. And if truth be told, weren't they also Darby's?

She turned towards her father. "Remember, Pa, I'll always be devoted to you and my brothers and will return if it's in my stars. I'll write to you." He nodded.

She glanced around once more hoping for a glimpse of Cayo, but he had not come. Of course he had not come. Why would he salute her and say farewell—she was, after all, the woman who betrayed him.

"You do what the good Lord's intended for you, little miss," her father said, and bent down to kiss her cheek, taking her by surprise. His cheek was wet with tears she'd never dreamed he possessed. When she stepped away from her father, Darby saw a violet haze surround him and brushed at it as though it were a fly. When it didn't dissipate, she knew in that instant she would never see him this way again; full of vigor, standing tall. Maybe not even alive. Her arms prickled with goose flesh and still she refused him any kind of sign of affection and forgiveness.

Bix said, "Luggage is all on board, Darby." He fidgeted turning his hat in his hands.

"Sorry you boys had to miss time away from work for such a foolish thing as my departure," she said, an apology in her voice.

"Ain't foolish at all, Darby," piped up Randy, "hell a half day off is worth it to me!"

"I ain't been at this here depot since almost a year ago," Chad said.

"Yeah, when we herded all them cattle to ship east," Garrett said.

"Then you'll owe me thanks for getting you off work. I'll take it in the form of a letter—be sure to write me."

"As if—" Chad started to say, when the conductor yelled, "All aboard what's going aboard."

"Bye for now," she said and put her stockinged-and-booted foot on the first step to mount the train. She settled herself by the window. The train whistle blasted, punctuating her desire to be independent, yet at the last moment, regret overwhelmed her. She leaped up and waved furiously, and then stopped and struggled to open the window. She leaned out and waved again, slowly this time, as the forlorn sound of the fading train whistle heralded her departure. Did gaining independence always mean the sacrifice of letting go what was familiar and cherished? Would she ever find a balance for both?

When she no longer had sight of them standing like a small band of forgotten strays in the train station, she took off her bonnet and tossed it on the seat. Swept up by the finality of her decision to leave, she jumped to her feet and rushed toward the door to the outside platform, struggled to open it and stepped outside. Hot wind blew her skirt furiously around, no concealment of her petticoats, as she fought to hold them down. Darby stood staring off for several minutes until she finally caught sight of a lone rider. It was him, she knew it. Her heart beat fast—it must be him. She was feeling what he felt. What had she done? How could she have left him? Why couldn't she have sacrificed schooling for love of him? What kind of a woman was she? The rider shadowed the train for a long time, but never approached close enough for her to see him. It could have been a phantom, a ghost, or a figment of her imagination.

The horseman reared upon his stallion in a salute, then turned the animal around. As tears stung her cheeks, he faced his horse in the direction of the Pederson ranch. She knew he'd follow no more.

She stood gripping the rail for a long time. Finally, she returned to her seat. She was riding east away from everything and everyone she loved. Darby felt weary and knew she had to distract herself, but before picking up the newspaper the conductor had left on the seat next to hers, she saw a note on top of a parcel tied with hemp cord. It was Garrett's terrible cursive writing, but what stunned her even more was what the note contained. She read it once quickly and then again.

Darby—

Cayo gave me this for you at dawn. He said it was a parting gift. Oh and he told me something puzzling. Said you're never never coming back to how it is—how could he know that? But he repeated twice that this here ending in Parcel Bluffs was your real beginning. Do you know what he means? I don't be-lieve it. His eyes were glazed over like he'd been drinking but I swear he was cold sober. Hope it's not some Indian curse. He knows when things are going to happen sometimes before they

*happen. Did you know that? Open it when you get to Aunt
Bea's.*

   Send word when you get there.

   ~Garrett

She folded the note that sounded ominous. What if Cayo were right? What if the winds of fate conspired against her and she'd never return? Never see Cayo or her brothers again? Or her father? What if she would never be able to fall into Cayo's arms? To kiss his soft and eager lips. Never to teach in a school in her beloved New Mexico. She untied the parcel and removed the coarse paper to uncover a fringed medicine bag, but she couldn't bring herself to open it. She passed her hands over it, soft as a moccasin.

If she dared open it, she knew her hands would sear like being branded. She examined it as if she'd never seen a piece of Indian handiwork before. She patted the soft doeskin, combed her fingers through the fringes, and ran them across the colored beads. She stroked it over and over, knowing the contents were of importance to the man she loved.

***

With the movement of the train along the tracks, she dozed on and off, and then fell into a light sleep. She woke with a start, and picked up the newspaper beside her to read about President Grant's redecoration of the East Room. The decor was hailed as "pure Greek" but some had already hinted at ridiculing the renovation as "steamboat Gothic," whatever that meant. She skimmed some other articles and news, when something caught her eye. Barbed wire had been invented. The writer explained how this innovation would change cattle and sheep farming— fenced in land with no more free range. The wire was being manufactured in Illinois, a neighbor state to Missouri, the one she was travelling to. How long before it became common practice to employ this caging in also in Arizona, Colorado, New Mexico, Utah and the whole wide west? How long before it reached Parcel Bluffs? What would that mean to her father, the Pedersons, and other cattle farmers; not just her family but to Cayo and other cowhands used to unconstrained boundaries? The words loose, unrestricted, unconfined came to her all at once, and she wondered if, like cattle, a man like him could ever really settle down and stay in one place.

She imagined cattle fenced in by wire. Rural, desolate places unable to be crossed for water or for feed grass, hemmed in all around by man-made fences, no more God's open country. Free. Her fears made her picture a battleground: gunfighters, herds of cattle, bandits, rustlers and prairie grass, all covered with blood. The vision that came to her was of the plains where dead men and animals lay in disordered chaos, bones bleached by sun.

But what of her own future? How would she manage her school work and fare with Aunt Bea? Darby felt confident she could handle her studies, but she was much less sure about how she'd be able to control herself under her aunt's domineering supervision. Bea was nothing like her younger sister, Darby's mother.

Chapter Ten

Cayo's Dream

Cayo rode back from seeing the train depart with Darby on it, cursing himself for not having asked for her hand sooner. Chiding himself for procrastinating brought thoughts of Red Willow, the guilt of his sister's deaths, and the murder he'd committed to the forefront of his mind. Everything from his past seemed to have made him inert to act, and this failure, he was sure, caused Darby to leave him. He hadn't been able to make the proposal of marriage to her father. Although he said he was saving money, the truth was that deep down he was afraid he wouldn't be able to protect her forever. Small town. People gossip. One slur about Darby being with an Apache would have meant disaster. Cayo worked hard the rest of the day until he was exhausted and fell into a deep sleep.

Before daybreak, looking right and left, as if he were being lassoed on both sides of his body, he jumped from his bunk, realizing he'd meandered somewhere in a dream. He awoke, sat back and settled down. It was pitch dark still, the only light from the window coming from the illusive stars and a moon, lean enough to ride bareback.

He sat at the edge of the bed and tried to recall the trancelike sequences. He wanted to remember. He didn't want to lose a thing from that time. The dream had seemed so real. It had been after the hunt when he was still a lanky boy.

Bichóó went with the women who followed the buffalo. She was part of the group that skinned the animals. The hunt had been successful, but what Coyote overheard was his grandmother telling one of the women how pleased she was. *Bichóó* told the woman that she was glad of the news of Coyote's heroism and stories of bravery. Her fearless adopted grandson had pleased her; not because her status had improved, but because she had come to care for him and wanted him to shine like a glimmering star in her own son's eyes.

After the trek back to the encampment when the hunt was over, Coyote saw *Bichóó* filled with contentment. She appeared younger and more energetic than before. Surely, she had eaten her fill of meat, had worked hard at butchering, expended much vigor in traveling, but these physical activities were not tiring. She told her grandson, they were satisfying, heightened in intensity because of her pride in Coyote.

Sitting in front of her dwelling, after the hunt, her son came to eat with her. Coyote had finished his tasks and slouched on his pallet reliving all that had happened when he overheard his grandmother speaking to her son.

She said to Mbai', "I have new feeling for the boy."

"What is it?" her son asked.

"Maybe not new, but added to others, like juniper berries added to wild herbs for rabbit stew to give it better flavor."

"Ah," he said with understanding.

"But also it is like seeing you young with a dove's chest puffing out."

Mbai' laughed. "You are a singer of songs and a poet, my mother. This boy has given you renewed life. This pleases me."

"I will resume work on the deerskins I dried from the kill that Coyote made before the buffalo hunt. Will it please you when I tell you the new garments I make are for him, instead of for my son?"

Stealthily, Coyote peered through a slit in the door covering. If Mbai' was surprised by *Bichóó* 's remarks, his face didn't betray it. "I have a wife and daughter for that."

"Besides," she added, "the girl who has been making his clothes has no talent for it," she said.

She had set aside the skins when it was time to follow the buffalo hunt and softened them into pelts for Coyote as a reward. She was proud of what he'd done in the hunt. She also wanted to show him that he had been accepted into her heart and by his fellow tribesman. One night she spoke to him in an offhand manner as she handed him roasted tongue. "As a member of my family I am making you hunting coverings—you have outgrown yours in all senses." She sat next to him and tugged at his pants. "Too short, ill-fitting, and altogether too small." He knew she had been with the women who had skinned the animals and probably listened to their gossip. He imagined Bichóó watching mothers of young maidens speak of Coyote with new respect. Before long he would be choosing a wife to relieve Bichóó 's burdens.

Coyote brought her a gray fox. After she scraped and dried the fur, she fashioned the parfleche into a small tube-like bag adding deerskin fringe and ties with eagle feathers; this time brought to her by her grandson. When he saw her, he knew that she had waited for the right moment to give it to him, anticipating the light in his eyes when he saw it. And he rewarded her.

Not too many days later *Bichóó* sat by the cook fire with Coyote. She stood up and also made him stand up. She ran her hands along his torso and his back. "Your body is finding its way to manhood," she said. Then she took hold of a braided rope, like a thin lariat, and with it she began to make rough measurements of his chest and shoulders.

He stuck out one arm and she measured, and then he bent his elbow, and watched the expression of contentedness spread across the old lady's face.

"How did you know to do that?" she asked.

"My first mother made me do it, and I watched my sisters do the same when she made them new clothes." The mention of his sisters brought with it a vision of their bloody heads and a current of nausea shook his gut. He stiffened, but not because of the sick feeling possessing him, but because Bichóó had started tugging at his loincloth.

"What are you doing, old one?" he asked, instinctively covering his privates. "I thought your time of interest in these parts was long burnt out?"

She giggled and gauged the inside of his leg from crotch to ankle. "I'm making you breeches and a new shirt. You are like grass after rain—your height has increased so that if I wait till summer your leggings will expose your manhood."

He felt glad to be alive. For the second time in only a few days. He felt proud to belong.

"Sit," *Bichóó* said, and she sat down by the fire next to him, taking hold of a long piece of sinew. With it, she threaded a porcupine quill that served as a needle. Before she started to sew, she passed the tip of the quill in the fire, took hold of his hand and prodded a thorn out of his thumb. "Why did you heat the tip?"

"To purify things unseen without a glass."

He wondered how she knew about glass. The light in the fire drew his mind to another world, another time. He followed his mind's meanderings, like a tracking animal that'd caught a scent.

He'd been a toddler, playing with the roughhewn planks that his father had laid down near the house to build a lean-to for the horses. He took a fall and went sprawling, outstretching his hand in front of him and got a splinter in the palm. He ran inside to show his mother. She sat him down, took a sewing needle from her basket and struck a match. "Watch the flame, Connor." She put the tip of the needle into the hottest part of the flame, and when she withdrew it, it was charred black. "Now it's clean," his mother'd said.

"But when my face is black as soot, I have to wash with a soap and rag."

She laughed and agreed with him, trying to explain the heat had burned away anything harmful that couldn't be seen by the naked eye.

"What's a naked eye? One without a bandage?" he had asked.

"So many questions from such a little boy. A naked eye means one without a special glass that makes you see the tiniest speck of dust."

His mother had removed the splinter and then pointed to his chest. "Look here," she said and when he bent his head down to look, she pulled his face gently upward and kissed his forehead. He felt that kiss now. He pictured his mother sewing with her spectacles slipping down her pert nose, and then his brain spun to an image of his father looking through a long-range looking glass when they hunted from a cliff or high ridge. Then, a memory of air swirling though a pile of burning leaves made him picture his mother turning pages of a brown-leather bound book, her finger pointing to a picture of a microscope that enlarged things—with a high-powered lens, she'd said. She pushed her glasses back to the bridge of her nose.

Bichóó slapped his leg. "Where were you, Coyote?"

"Hmm. Too far back to tell, little grandmother" he said in a weary voice as if waking from a dream.

Bichóó reached under the pile of skins and brought out the fox quiver. Sure as the sun rises at dawn, a smile played at the corners of his mouth and a brightness from within shone in his eyes. He passed his hand over it. Ah, an inner voice cautioned, *Careful not to want it too much—this is not meant for you.*

"This is for my son—"

And there it was. "Oh, I see," he said.

"You see nothing, because you hear nothing. Let me finish."

Coyote nodded.

"This I made for my son's gift to me, for my grandson," she said, passing a hand over the quiver.

"Grandmother!"

"No need to shout. I'm sitting right next to you." She handed him the quiver, but before he put the string over his head and across his chest, he hugged the old woman. She was moved to tears. He understood that her wet eyes were thanks, for his strength, bravery but mostly for his love.

"You are taking my breath," she said, gently pushing him away.

"Oh, sorry, Grandmother."

"My old bones are brittle. Try it on."

She shook her head up and down in approval. He stood and did a full turn, adjusting the foxtail so that it hung down on his hip. "I will make warrior arrows for the quiver."

"Just like White Feather, your brother."

"He is that. Will he be jealous you made this for me?"

"He has one his mother made him. You have no mother, only me."

The realization of her words stung him as he walked out of the tent visualizing his mother's red-haired scalp. Then he did a most unmanly thing. He cried.

Chapter Eleven

The Medicine Bag

Darby was greeted at the train station by her two aunts Bea and Mary, her mother's sisters and their man-servant Clyde, who also drove their buggy. Clyde's son, a young, strapping boy named Tark, was hired for the day to help with Darby's trunk, hand luggage, parcels and a leather saddlebag into which she had placed the medicine purse.

Darby handed over Pa's letter to her Aunt Bea who folded it into a large wallet, and said, "Oh dear, the trip must have been exhausting."

After the luggage had been stowed in a separate buggy and Tark left to bring it to her aunt's home, the ladies settled themselves into their own buggy ride that Clyde maneuvered expertly out of the stream of traffic and into a country lane.

"This is perhaps the longer route home, but it's far more relaxing and pretty," Aunt Mary said and squeezed Darby's hand.

Both of her aunts wanted to know all about the trains and transfers and Darby, despite her exhaustion, explained what the conductor's responsibility was, what the lead service attendant did, and who was responsible for the dining car staff. She mentioned the lounge car attendant in charge of operations in the café/lounge car, and by the time she got to the sleeping car attendant, and the brakemen in the caboose, Darby felt like a railroad engineer. She concluded her explanation wearily by saying all of the staff was most accommodating and pleasant to her. Furthermore, to give them a more complete picture, she explained how she'd taken a branch line from Lamy eighteen miles away from Santa Fe to board the Atchison, Topeka and the Santa Fe Railroad.

"But enough about me and trains. It all seems like ages ago since I left home. I slept badly and was homesick for—" she hesitated but finished saying, "and nightmares kept me up every night of the voyage."

"I'm sure you can't wait to have a bath and climb into a real bed with clean linen sheets," Mary said.

Darby nodded, understanding with that one statement, she had an ally and friend in Aunt Mary.

When they arrived at the house, Mary said, "I'll draw you a bath. Come follow me upstairs."

Two weeks into her stay with Aunt Bea and her sister Mary, Darby was settling in. She wrote in her diary that the night before last she and her aunts and their friends went out for dinner to a fancy club restaurant, but she couldn't remember the name. There had been an orchestra and cake to celebrate Aunt' Bea's birthday. Darby concluded her diary entry with the phrase: "If Aunt Bea hadn't shown me which fork to use beforehand, I'd have embarrassed myself no end."

Darby looked at the 1874 calendar pinned on the wall. September 2nd was circled. If she'd married him last month, she'd have been an August bride. What did it mean to be a bride in any month? Darby scanned the room. Such disarray. Scattered about was every bit of attire she possessed: boots, shoes, petticoats, bloomers, a camisole, a chemise, skirts, dresses, blouses, aprons, and a pearl gray knitted shawl. Her portmanteau lay open on the bed. Two hinged compartments had fit all this!

But today she'd have to choose what she'd wear to the festivities this evening. Her aunts' minister, Pastor Erik, was expected for dinner. She'd met him several times already and although he wasn't a bad sort, he appeared rather stiff. He was more athletic-looking than she fancied him to be. At least he wasn't the pasty-faced fellow she imagined, but definitely not the rugged cowboy she was attracted to.

How she wished she could write to Cayo. Instead, she composed a letter to her father and brothers saying how well her aunts treated her and how her studies were progressing. She put the letter in an envelope and set it aside. There were only a few of her household possessions left to organize. She took the linen towels, her good baking tin, a pair of long tongs and a gardening trowel to the hall closet. Her parents' daguerreotype wedding picture in a pewter frame, her looking glass, brush and comb, Bible, she placed on her dresser and stowed away her scissors and sewing basket in the lower section of the night table. All organized except for the clothes and Cayo's medicine bag that Garrett had put on the train for her. She was grateful for that and the fact that her brother had forgiven her—what he considered a grave transgression.

She gazed about her. Hers wasn't an extensive wardrobe. Some of the homespun she'd left behind in favor of calico and store-bought cloth goods from Fern, and a petticoat with a lace hemmed border. Two dresses were gifts, presents from Hanna's dressmaker and Mrs. Pederson. Why had they given these to her and not to Hanna? Out of the corner of her eye, she saw the bag Cayo had meant for her resting precariously on the edge of the vanity. She picked it up, fingered it and passed her hand over the smooth-textured suede. All the while her mind spelled out the word: *alforja*, as she ran her fingers over it. Why had the Spanish word come to her? Had Cayo ever used that expression? The bed was strewn chock-full and overburdened, so she sat on the floor in her petticoat, crossing her legs Indian fashion, and held the sack in her hand. The pouch had been sewn of soft doeskin and beaded intricately by someone he once knew, Darby felt certain. Pricelessly worn with oils and scents of others' hands. The flap was fringed, and she unexpectedly thought of the coming-of-age dress that the Jicarilla girls wore with long fringes—one of the longest on each side had a tiny piece of wood knotted in it—so they could scratch an itch without ruining their paint or dress.

Some of the tassels on the medicine bag were tied with porcupine quills, sharp enough to have served as sewing needles. She wondered if it had been a squaw's. His squaw. Had she made it for him? Had he lived with an Indian woman? Was she still alive? He had called out a name once when he was dozing by the river and had startled himself awake. Utahna. An Indian name. A woman's name, of this Darby was certain.

There were so many things she'd wanted to ask Cayo but never got the chance. She fingered the note that Garrett had written. She read it again. Why had Cayo wanted Darby to open the bag only after she'd reached her Aunt Bea's in St. Louis? How many times had she looked at the contents of the bag since her arrival? Shame colored her face she knew because her cheeks grew hot—the mere thought of him on his horse, or walking toward her made her longing for him stronger than ever.

Although her conscience tugged her not to, she threw back the flap again, unknotted the leather thongs. She reached for her pristine, freshly starched white apron and laid it on top of the hand braided rug, like an altar cloth. She spilled the contents out onto it by overturning the bag, a narrowly folded piece of doeskin with something crinkly inside and a piece of paper fell upon the other items. She brushed these aside and counted the sister seeds: corn, squash and bean. Her hand swept over an arrowhead of chiseled slate, a lead bullet and a thumbnail size lead ball, and a turquoise stone. She picked up a tiny awl, fitted the heft of the hammered handle into her fist. She put it aside, flicking a piece of obsidian with her pointing finger. Beneath the stone, another rock, like crackling ice, except pink as kittens' paws. An eagle's feather, a bear claw, a hallowed-out piece of bone like the tubular ones in the necklace he'd made for her, a piece of furry buffalo hide soft with washing and combing, a bow and arrow burned into the smooth side, a tiny acorn, a rolled tobacco leaf tied with a piece of hemp. Darby shifted her hands, reached for a folded piece of brown paper, a buttercup pressed in between. She heaved a sigh, realizing he'd given her back the flower she'd given him the day she said she'd marry him. Placing it down, she took hold of a wedding ring, inscribed: Agnes and Robert 7/7/1842, slipping it on and off her finger. His mother's. She picked up the doeskin and unfolded it. There was a folded and crinkled paper inside. It was the deed to his father's ranch. He would never go back to that ranch—the one they were to settle on. Did this mean he had broken with her irrevocably? Did he expect her to someday claim it? She wondered if the paper held any legal value. It must have been written long ago.

Mysterious, mystical, spiritual, supernatural. Heartrending.

She couldn't fathom any of it, but the buttercup made her weep. She'd picked the yellow flower and pressed it in under her mother's Bible—a book that meant nothing to him, yet everything to her. She pictured the look on his face when she'd given it to him on the walk home from Miller's, which now seemed like years ago, yet it had been only a few months. Seeing the flower led her to dwell on the happenings of that day. Then her thoughts brought her to a different day when they'd picnicked under a stand of cottonwoods near the Rio Grande. They swam—him bare—naked, the way these offerings from the pouch touched her now with stark simplicity, truth, and regret.

Her thoughts returned to the day Cayo had walked her home. She'd written words on a paper. Love words on a scrap piece from the dry goods section of the mercantile—and in between, she'd placed the pressed buttercup.

Then that afternoon after she'd presented it to him, she asked if he read the words she'd written.

"Can't cipher no letters, Darby. My Ma was just teaching me when the Apache took me captive." Her hand instinctively moved to cover her heart. He took the paper from his pocket and handed it to her. She read it to him. "I will give all of me to you and love you always."

He leaned his head back against a tree trunk, clenched his fists, and closed his eyes, like she did now with remembrance. She'd uncurled the fingers of his scarred left hand, and placed the flower in it. He opened his eyes, whispering, "*Dá'aadahé'yéé.*"

And somehow she knew that was the Apache word for a long time. Forever.

She sat on the floor for a long time with Cayo's gifts spread before her, curiosity about the contents still unanswered.

***

For the first few weeks at Aunt Bea's she had that same recurring dream over and over again, and would wake up drenched in perspiration from fear and shock. The same fantasy that had awakened her in the middle of the night before she left Parcel Bluffs.

Like a puzzle, piece by piece, she rearranged the dream until she saw herself standing at the back of a dark cabin. Shouts and whoops like war cries, the thudding and thundering of horses' hooves galloping around the cabin. Suddenly the door was broken down, a window smashed in and an overhead skylight crashed. From every entrance an Indian covered with war paint and feathers appeared, brandishing tomahawks or knives. She was surrounded. Outnumbered, a smoking rifle in her hand, two Indians were writhing at her feet, and there was no time to re-load. She crouched in the corner, only it was not her. It was another woman with an Indian looming over her, leering.

As she started to dress, she uttered a prayer of thanksgiving that she'd not been visited by that brutal enactment in her sleep for a while. In days past, she'd been afraid to look out of a window for fear of seeing painted horses with half-clad Indian braves, covered in war paint, riding at a furious pace. Whopping and hollering around a burning cabin. Was the cabin Cayo's? Was the woman his mother? Were these the Indians who had captured him and the baby girl. What was her name? Who was she to Cayo? The vision-dream remained a mystery.

Chapter Twelve

Red Willow

Coyote's life with his tribe had seemed eons ago, when in reality it was only a few short years. Throughout the passing years, his fondness for the old ones, White Feather, and Little Fawn had grown stronger. Coyote often saw Little Fawn by the river bank, carting wood in a woven burden basket made of sumac, strong and flexible or carting roots and berries in a willow basket. He'd catch glimpses of her stretching animal skins for tanning. Coyote would seek her out and talk to her. Often he would see her attempting to use a sling, or to practice with a lance as the older girls did. Girls were taught to use bow and arrow just like boys. This fascinated Coyote, but also made him aware of just how important this skill was in case of a Comanche raid, or if she needed to protect herself and kill an animal.

Little Fawn came frequently to help his grandmother and when the old woman was not near, he taught Little Fawn her English name, Audra, and her native tongue, but this came about slowly and only after the child, like he, had learned the language of the People. He spoke to her in English when no one was around because he didn't want to inflict pain or punishment on the girl. He could tell she relished these times together when he'd tell her stories of ranch life and what he knew of her parents, and especially of the day he carried her on his back to smuggle her out of the tunnel his father constructed when the Indians had begun to attack homesteads. What he never spoke of was that he murdered his sisters. Did she know? If she had discovered this horror, she never said so. She finally gained fluency, and they spoke often, but always alone.

One day, long after she was fluent in her native tongue, he told her he was proud of her and now she'd never forget her heritage. That was the day she confronted him with the tales she had heard about him when he was first captured.

"Where have you heard these stories?" he asked.

She cast her eyes down. "In the women's tipi at the time for their monthly courses."

"I am not proud, and carry this grief forever inside me, but they do not lie."

"And now they speak of your eyes for the girl Red Willow." Little Fawn blushed.

He was stunned into silence and walked off, leaving her mixing clay with tiny bits of shiny mica in it for his grandmother to form and then fire-bake into a bean pot.

The next time he saw Little Fawn, he tried to explain all the things that went through his mind when he had committed the foul act and taken his sisters' lives. They strolled along the river on a late afternoon, a breeze rustling the yellowing leaves of the quaking aspens as he spoke in tones that took on a spiritualism all their own. "They are in Heaven with the Great Spirit," he said, but could not look in her eyes.

"But why did you need to kill them? They were so little."

He explained in fits and starts and halting language, speaking as if it had happened to someone else, so that his emotions would not overcome him.

How wrong of him it was to judge those who had captured him. How ignorant he was of their ways. He'd been taught vile things that they might do to his sisters. To save them from pain and anguish, he had broken the Fifth Commandment of his mother's faith, and yet she was the one who had begged him to do it, begging of the Lord to forgive her.

He had done penance, but it never seemed enough. Now, speaking of this terrible incident, he was wracked with shame once more, and knew he would carry it inside for all the days he walked the earth.

For a year, Coyote watched Little Fawn's family prepare for her puberty feast, how she worked alongside her mother fashioning the yellow ceremonial cape made from black-tailed deerskin. It was painted ochre and decorated with lane stitch beadwork sewn with sinew on the front and also the back. Coyote saw thousands of Venetian beads in bowls that he knew were gotten at the trading post in Dulce. He wasn't interested in this aspect, even though he had been the one to barter the trade for the beads because he spoke English. He marveled at the sheer beauty of the emerging cape. The ceremonial cape that Little Fawn's mother worked on had triple-scalloped oblique edges bordered with three stripes in blue and white. Two small deerskin bags contained horsemint and pronghorn antelope jaw were attached. He wanted to ask what these represented, but surmised they stood for force or power. Little Fawn would wear this cape at the end of the preparation for her coming of age ceremony, known as the *keesda*.

It was believed a girl's puberty rite was of importance for vitality and fertility, so that she could bear healthy children. When a girl came of age to bring forth a child, she was the essence of the moon which brought forth fruit. The moon was cyclical, as was the woman's monthly changes. It would soon be time for this Jicarilla maiden to take part in the ceremony that would last four days to complete. Bathing and dressing in distinct clothing was the beginning. Afterward the girls were not permitted to touch their bodies. If they had to scratch themselves, small wooden pegs tied to long thongs were provided on the dress. Any perspiration had to be wiped away with a scarf. Water must not touch them or it was believed it would bring a vast flood and interrupt the observances which included creation songs, usually by men, and ritual dances. Endurance was essential. The young girl and other maidens would go to the big tipi to pray, fast, wash, and be painted. It was a test of great strength because it also entailed races. Bee pollen, which had been collected from cattails way before the initiation ceremonies began, had been stored in deer pouches and was painted on the girls' faces and on their scalps to insure fertility. Indian tea or mescal was also collected and made well in advance of the ceremony in season. The girls participated in four exhausting runs that represented the stages of life.

Little Fawn was a comely girl, lean and fair, like her mother Meg McGrath had been, with deep auburn hair parted in the middle and woven into thick braids that swayed like the branches of trees in breezes when she ran from him to meet up with the girls of the village. Coyote overheard some of the girls who were envious of her height and hair, but clever Little Fawn cajoled them and told them they were far more beautiful than she because of their black hair and gleaming dark eyes.

Coyote and Little Fawn became faithful friends, but in a secreted fashion, so the people would not separate them for speaking a foreign tongue. He noticed the subtle changes that were occurring in her, the tiny waist, the outline of her developing breasts, the way her hips moved when she strolled away from him, and sometimes he was confused by this and his feelings for her.

Little Fawn knew Coyote admired Red Willow. He cared for her more than he admitted, but Little Fawn tried to warn him off in a sororal fashion. "She's not the one for you. Anyone will tell you. Some say she is of a divided spirit, and cannot help herself." He was confused by this. Was her warning of the jealous nature because she cared for Coyote more than a friend?

Coyote didn't understand his emotions for Red Willow. But this current ceremony for Little Fawn reminded him of a past one when he'd seen Red Willow. She had emerged in a cache of young women from the

Big Tipi when it was her ceremonial *keesda* the year before. Her eyes were radiant and they seemed to take in everything at once, but he hoped that her glances were only for him. He only knew he desired her in a way that was different from the other girls. He felt a jiggling of his heart, the fast movement of his blood through his face and belly when he saw her. He stole glances at her as she did her chores around the campfires. And once, she dropped a feather as she walked toward her mother. He quickly snatched it up and spirited it away under his chamois shirt, next to his heart.

One day, not long after Little Fawn's ceremony had concluded, he spoke to her about Red Willow, who was on the other side of the stream. Again, Little Fawn told him to look for another maiden. Red Willow had been picking berries, and was about to leave the spot, when Coyote called to her and waved. She waved back. In his haste to catch up with her, he ran across a log to cross the stream, but he slipped and fell. In between the splashing he heard her laughing.

He thought she was the most beautiful girl he'd ever seen. In certain lights, her long hair shimmered almost blue it was so black, and her dark eyes held a special radiance when she laughed. He followed her whenever he could but always at a distance. He studied her as she tanned hides to make winter robes and blankets with her mother. Coyote painted mental images of her as she chiseled horns to make cups or ladles.

One cool day Red Willow was down by the river filling paunches—cleaned out buffalo intestines and stomach—with water. He hid behind a tree and whistled. She had been so concentrated on her task that the noise jostled her and she spilled the water back to its source. She looked all around, but still didn't see him. He waited till she had refilled both paunches, and he whistled again, but this time, though she jerked her head up, she didn't tip out the water. She marched by with her hands full. This was his chance. He grabbed her to him, though she flailed the paunches at him, she did it too gently, and he kissed her till she broke free and ran toward the village.

Somehow instinct told him that Red Willow would not choose him so he approached her brother and father and asked to marry her. He had acquired several horses and although unusual, he made an offer in exchange for the bride.

They were married after Red Willow's father paid her bride price. She brought to the marriage a buffalo blanket robe, a ladle, some baskets, a clay bean pot, two buffalo paunches, a large and fringed, leather quiver with six white-feathered arrows.

On her wedding day, Red Willow wore a new deerskin dress with long fringes and blue and white feathers. She had painted a design around the neck of the dress and sewn on colored beads and tiny cowrie shells that had been a gift from her great-grandmother, the only one of the People to own them. She had made ceremonial moccasins for both Coyote and herself, but she showed no joy in doing so.

The sun shone brightly on the morning of the day they married. Then clouds began to form during the ceremony and darkness covered the couple. As the ceremony concluded, Mbai' placed the chain and locket that had been Coyote's mother's and last worn by his sister, over Coyote's head. He stared at it for some minutes. Lifting the chain from his chest, his eyes glassed over. He was shocked, but would not, could not, cry. The heavens opened up, and he welcomed the drenching downpour upon the campsite, hiding his tears. With the ceremony over, he entered his own tipi with his wife, wondering if the overshadowing omen of the gift would be a blight on his soul his whole life.

Later he tried to tell Red Willow of his feelings for her, but he was not a lover, and had not enough experience for her.

They gazed into the fire, and he handed her a box that he had carved.

"I can only give you this box of daylight and my love, and this—it was my mother's."

Her eyes grew wide as she saw him take off the gift. He kissed the locket that held his parents' wedding picture, opened it and showed it to Red Willow. Coyote read the confusion in his wife's eyes, the fear on her face.

"These," he said softly, "are my parents' on their ceremonial day—when they started out, just like us today," and placed the locket over her head, adjusting it around her neck.

***

Coyote and Red Willow lived quietly for almost half a year. The couple moved their lodge closer to his grandmother's so his wife could help the old one who had begun to fail. Coyote thought he'd never become a father at this rate. He would dash about looking for tasks to do to exhaust his energy for it seemed that lovemaking was a chore and very disagreeable for his bride. And yet, somehow he felt she was more practiced than he in this art.

Coyote was angry for forcing himself again on Red Willow. Why was she always so uninterested in him? He wondered if perhaps she were carrying a child. Wouldn't she have told him? This didn't seem the way things should be. Who could counsel him?

It was early when he came back to the tipi, bringing her wildflowers that he'd gathered reminding him of his father coming in with bunches of flowers for his mother. He watched his wife as she moved about and became affectionate with her, but she was standoffish. He spoke to her in low tones of his feelings for her but she pulled away from his amorous advances.

"What is wrong? Why are you behaving like we are not a couple?" Coyote asked with tenderness.

Red Willow looked at him with sadness in her eyes, but did not respond.

After several more attempts, he stormed out of his *kogha midaa me'ña'i*, without a word or glance back at the tipi, or at her. He was angry with her, but also with himself for not eating. He wanted to distance himself from her and breathe clean air from some high perch.

He rode off on one of the mares he had given for Red Willow. Riding away from the village, Coyote thought about breaking tradition and custom by what he'd done, but he had wanted her at all costs and was too eager. Despite the measly dowry paid to him, which was of no consequence to him, he now realized his mistake, and berated himself for not consulting Red Hawk prior to his brash offer. After a while, he slowed and dismounted. He hobbled the horse and walked a little farther to a place he didn't frequent much, because it was near a secluded area where women gathered to wash clothes, bathe, stake skins to dry, share sweet and bitter tales, joys and fears—matters they did not speak of with their mates.

Coyote gathered long thin branches of the chokecherries to make arrows, stripping them of bark and layering them in bundles. When the first cool of morning dissipated, the haze melted into the clouds, the dew sucked dry from the grass by the merciless sun. Having rested poorly, he fell asleep under a cottonwood. The mid-morning air became thick with gnats, butterflies, swarming bees, cicadas and the wingbeats of swallows the only other noise. He woke with a start, sat and watched lizards engorge on a host of flies and insects, the underneath flap of their jowls expanding in a red flash downward beneath their chins. Absorbed by the way they camouflaged themselves by adapting a green or a brown skin. A sound of rock against rock drew his attention.

From a crevice in the gorge, Coyote saw his wife Red Willow. He watched as she washed clothes on a rock, then spread them on the high grass to dry. Her trained movements were like cat shadows on a tipi prancing and preening as though someone were watching—but she couldn't know he was there—and as a cat would pounce gingerly to toy with a ball of sinew, she took off her bone and bead necklace and twirled it in her hand. He noticed that she hadn't worn his mother's necklace. Then she removed her belt, her movements seductive. She pulled the belt through her closed hand, a taunting as if someone were watching. Coyote squatted in the shade of the towering gorge felt his manhood rise, his flesh hot, and he wanted her more than ever.

He gazed at the way she snaked out of her clothes and heaped them in a pile as if the chores at hand had lost interest for her. She was alone. There were no other women about, no washer-companions. She dipped a toe into the water, then laughed and retracted it, arching her foot and muscled calf, playacting like a dancer about to leap. Red Willow looked around, then waded in for a swim, shivering when the chilled water reached to lick her breasts. She stood waist high, then smiled as a shrill call like the trill of a whippoorwill sounded across the water. From behind a boulder in the lush thick brambles came the medicine woman called Starfall in breeches, her braids reaching to the small of her back.

Starfall stripped off her clothes quickly, nothing playful in her brusque movements. She was flat-chested, with a bony torso, and lean hips. She seemed ageless, yet her angular body was built like a boy's before maturity. Moving swiftly to the shoreline, she strode into the water till she was waist high and dove into the crystal pool splashing Red Willow who shrieked with glee.

Red Willow had always been shy and reticent around Starfall, Coyote thought, but now they danced in tandem, twirling like leaves in a gust of wind. What did they remind him of? He watched them till the image of frolicking bear cubs came to him. Coyote felt confused by the swimmers' movements. Then the playfulness changed from rough and tumbling to what he thought was the domain of husbands and wives.

The worst part for Coyote was watching the familiarity with which the two women kissed and touched, the sunlight glinting off their black slick hair. They turned and spun, embraced until a three-note hoot came from some distance. Overhead from a higher ledge, women began to descend. Red Willow scampered out of the water to grab her coverings and ran to hide in the lee of a hillock. She was out of his sight range, but Coyote knew she was fumbling with her doeskins and dressing in haste.

With slow sauntering movements, Starfall came out of the water toward the other women who stopped their giggling behind their hands as she approached. Coyote's stomach knotted with cramps for he knew for sure the women knew of his wife's relationship with Starfall, and he felt rage and humiliation.

Coyote mounted his horse in a fury, leaving behind his stacked arrow branches, riding hard and fast over the plain toward the foothills. His anger was mollified but only for a few seconds when thoughts of Red Willow's tenderness for him surfaced in his brain. He tried to squelch them, allowing the betrayal to magnify: it was not a rival male who'd won his wife's heart. This shock triggered an explosion, the way gunpowder does when thrown in fire. If it had been a warrior he could have sought revenge, but how can one rebuke the medicine woman? Coyote's sinking heart could only remember how he'd admired Starfall's agility, her horsemanship, her ability to heal and to counsel. She was renowned for her marksmanship, unequalled among his people. No man could best her in any competition, least of all this one.

A million thoughts lapped up like the little waves that had washed over Red Willow's breasts. Why had she been so happy? Hadn't she disgraced herself with him yet again only last night? Why had she seemed pleased, before Starfall's arrival, when she should have been contrite and feeling the same miserable desperation he did? In that instant, he knew that his wife's feelings for him had been false, no, invented by him. He had been duped, blinded, his heart beating out her name every hour of the day. He remembered how he had explored her body with love and longing, and how she must have been sickened by it. His mind harkened back to the morning's swim, Starfall's slow, possessive examination of Red Willow, and how her face radiated in anticipation of the woman's touch.

His wife had fooled him. He leaned into the horse's neck, feeling the blood course though the animal's body, and wished he could change places. Coyote's mind and body were fraught with lies and deception, but he could not hate, and whispered, "I've lost Red Willow to Starfall, but perhaps my wife was never really mine." He leaned his head forward. "Your nature is to be a horse, mine is to be a man, but there are other natures we don't understand." Coyote rode hard, thinking of the ways he would take his vengeance out on Red Willow. He would slice off her nose, as was the custom for sure. He'd disfigure her and she'd never again commit adultery, would never again be the willing object of a lustful affair. His thoughts trailed away with the knowledge that this was different. He was not losing Red Willow to a warrior. He had already lost her. What then, was the custom for this? Was this the warning Little Fawn had tried to give him? That Red Willow was a divided spirit like the two-spirited Starfall?

Coyote rushed to Red Hawk's tipi for counsel. He barely entered and the words flew out of his mouth about his wife and Starfall.

"Sit. We will smoke a while and let our mind's ease."

"But what can I do?" Coyote asked.

Red Hawk did not answer but puffed on his pipe. When the tension in the air had abated, Red Hawk said, "It has been so many winters since such a thing has occurred that perhaps no one remembers the ancient chants, the talks, and the powwows, surrounding this kind of behavior."

After a while, Red Hawk stood. "Let me consult with the elders and chief. Do you want to be present?"

"I fear not. My nerves are fraught and I may do or say something regretful. But I will speak to Grandmother, perhaps she will know what to do."

It was, in fact, Coyote's old grandmother who had the solution. The men of the counsel could not remember stories or tales connected with such happenings, and their memories were foggy with the long years passed since their youth.

Grandmother came to see Red Hawk with Coyote and told him that when she had been a girl visiting a Ute camp, a similar situation occurred. Their solution was to break up the marriage, and allow a union between the two-spirit women.

Another council was held, but this time Red Hawk insisted that Coyote must be present. During the assembly, a grave decision was made. It was decreed that Coyote's marriage to Red Willow was dissolved and she would go to live in the medicine woman's tipi as her wife. Red Willow was finally recognized as belonging to the two-spirit people, like Starfall. Red Willow's mother, Swooping Bird's face was impassive when Coyote faced Red Willow as if to strike her, but he merely lifted up the chain from her neck. Coyote looked in her eyes, and dropped the locket against her chest. "A gift is a gift," he said, "one of remembrance and for all times."

He turned and faced Swooping Bird and they exchanged a sorrowful look. Only Coyote felt Red Willow's mother's inner grief as deep as his own, although not even he could imagine the depth of that sorrow. Not until the day after the dissolution of the marriage did Coyote grasp Swooping Bird's regret, when she stepped from a high precipice into the void of the canyon below.

It was believed that two-spirit people possessed special powers. That the love-making of Red Willow and Starfall would follow the proper mandate of the tribe, which was that they would come together only with their legs intertwined, and never any other way.

Two-spirit people owned special abilities, and bound together they were stronger, but even Red Willow and Starfall had to conform to the tribe's rituals and sanctioned methods of love-making, and their union could only be in the prescribed fashion. However, they did not follow these proscriptions, perhaps thinking themselves above the law of their fathers.

A boy and his four friends were out beyond their supposed field of range, hunting small birds, rabbits, squirrels and grouse. The eldest boy appointed himself the leader of the hunting band. Another taller boy argued they were going beyond where they were permitted, but the eldest called him a coward, and so, he too, followed along. They meandered the hills and outcroppings when all at once the eldest raised his hand, a signal to stop. He then crept to the top of a boulder and looked down upon Starfall and Red Willow performing what he knew to be an indecent act. He crept back not making a sound, knowing he would need a witness to what he saw. He beckoned to the tall one who hadn't wanted to venture far afield and the two crept up the same boulder. The eldest, cautioned him with a signal to be silent and watch. The witness's eyes became large as hunting stones and almost gasped when the eldest clamped a hand over his mouth. They retreated back to the band of boys and left that place to go back to the village to report this unseemly behavior.

A council was held, and the conclusion was that the chiefs separated the two-spirit women to live apart for two months. But, the elders and the People came to understand and believe that a great misfortune would befall them because of Red Willow and Starfall's misdeeds.

Chapter Thirteen

One Day at Aunt Bea's

It was Saturday and the hired teacher, Miss Violet Niederman, a spinster who tutored some of Aunt Bea's neighbor children and also Darby, went home early with a headache. Darby was grateful. She just wanted to be alone.

The air was brisk. Swirling, falling gold and brown leaves were like miniature cyclones whirling about her skirt hem when Darby walked outside. In a few days it would be Halloween. Darby walked in the neighborhood and saw jack-o-lanterns lit in many windows and pumpkins on the front stoops of the houses. Some of the leaves clung to the trees, others churned about in little colorful eddies around her feet. She inhaled the acrid smoke of piles of burning leaves and the smell made her nostalgic and homesick. Darby wanted to bolt and go back west to see Cayo, but didn't have the heart to ask her aunt for the money for the trip, or to ask her father, who had worked hard to pay back Aunt Bea for the train ticket to St. Louis in the first place.

By the time she got back from her walk, the temperature had dropped. She had forgotten mittens and muff, and drew her hands out of her warm coat pockets to open the door which was surprisingly locked. She knocked on the door and Bea opened it, greeting her with, "Why were you out so late?"

"Just wanted to clear my head. So stuffy in here," Darby answered.

"I'll be upstairs if you need me," Bea said.

Darby warmed her hands by the fire. Aunt Mary handed her a cup of hot cider. The perfume of the mulled apples reached her nose with a welcoming and familiar smell. Mary had put in a cinnamon stick, and perhaps a splash of vanilla. When Darby sipped, she also tasted a drop of wild field honey and something more pungent and bracing that burned her throat: Cognac. Darby smiled and tipped her cup towards Mary in a toast. "Thank heavens Bea doesn't mark the bottles."

"If you go out tomorrow, dear, put this cashmere shawl on top of your coat. Bring gloves or your fur muff or both," Mary said.

Darby took hold of the shawl and thanked her aunt. When Mary and she finished the cider, Darby put on the shawl over the sweater she was wearing and went out into the back garden. Pulling the shawl tightly around her sweater, she was struck by how much the muted colors reminded her of Cayo's poncho. She wondered if she wrote Garrett a letter for Cayo would her brother give it to him. She didn't think he'd tell Pa, but he might just toss it in the fire. She couldn't chance alienating Garrett.

Darby entered the sitting room off the parlor and sat at her Aunt Bea's desk. From the tiny ladies' traveling desk that rested on top of the larger desk, she drew out a sheet of cream-colored stationery that held a faint watermark. As she reached for the feathered quill and ink, her hand shook with the desire to write Cayo, yet she still dreaded Garrett's reaction. She replaced the writing implements, and demurring felt loneliness rise in the pit of her stomach.

The next day, in the garden, where Darby picked the last of the primroses the week before, she now snipped mums and marigolds to place in her basket. She wandered over to a patch of still-blooming pansies glistening with evening dew. So beautiful, like velvet, she thought, purple and yellow. Darby snipped one off and sniffed—too bad they lacked perfume. Walking past the gazebo towards the back entrance of the house, she deposited the flowers on the kitchen counter. She reached on tiptoes to take down a milk glass pitcher. Behind it was a cut glass vase that her Aunt Bea said had come from Europe. She'd just begun reading and studying European history. Fingering the vase, she wondered which country it came from. She carried it to the sink and filled it with water after priming the pump. While she arranged the flowers, Aunt Bea, spidery fat cheeks flushed, walked into the kitchen from the dining room and greeted her.

"Why don't you take your books and sit out in the covered porch. I'll have Cook light the fireplace and prepare dinner." Aunt Bea adjusted the tiny spectacles slipping down her nose.

"Aunt Bea, you don't have to fuss over me. I'd be happy to cook. It's a waste of money to have someone prepare meals when I can do it. Why, I managed a houseful of men—cooked, baked, cleaned, fed the animals and planted my own vegetable garden."

"Your Uncle Cyrus left me very comfortable and Aunt Mary is used to our comforts—plus we want to spoil you a little. That's our prerogative, young miss."

"I don't want to become fat and sassy." The words reminded her of Hanna.

"Like me? Oh, I can guarantee you won't. Just you wait till after the ringing in of the New Year. You won't have time if you plan to take two years of study in one. Land sake's alive—never heard of such a thing."

Darby exhaled, shrugged her shoulders and placed the vase on the table. She watched her aunt place a doily under the vase.

"Such niceties," Darby said, "they come so natural to you, yet I have to think about them. I guess you're born with a bent for certain things."

"They're learned. Acquired. Nothing's a given in this life, child."

Darby ambled over to the open kitchen window that faced the garden. Soon, with the surreptitious parting of dusk, she'd be alone with her own thoughts and able to contemplate. She heard the cry of a whippoorwill in the nearby woods behind the house. They'd begin hunting insects now, darting here and there. She prepared herself for sudden movements and before long, her senses were alive with sound and a prickly feeling stole onto her arms. The chase had begun. She shut the window.

"Darby?" her aunt Mary called.

"Coming," Darby said.

"There's a letter for you on the silver salver in the entrance way."

"Oh, I didn't see it when I came in." Darby rushed out to get the letter. Hanna.

"And there's a postal card from Cayo. Is that the cowpoke you're so sweet on? I don't see any letters from him, but at least he wrote you a card."

"Cayo? He can't write. Or read." Darby said.

"Oh?" Aunt Bea sat down at the table.

"His mother was teaching him, when the Indians took him. I will teach him. Someday."

"Not such an easy task. Especially if he's a proud man."

"One I fear won't wait for me." Darby fingered the postal card. It wasn't a government issue, meaning one that only cost one-cent. Instead, it was one of the more expensive two-cent picture cards coming into fashion. Her address was on the front side. She turned the card over to read on the message side, in a child's poorly executed script the words: *When? Cayo*. She wondered who had helped him write it? Address it? Why this choice of one word? It had cost him almost as much as it cost him to have a shirt ironed.

Darby decided to write to Fern Miller and enclose a separate note in the envelope for Cayo. She knew she could trust Fern and wrote first to her and then to Cayo. Darby sealed it with wax from her Aunt Bea's desk. She kissed the letter and slipped it into the envelope along with Fern's letter. Now all she had to do was wait for a response.

After Darby assured herself that her note to Cayo was safe in Fern's letter, she tore open the letter. "This is from Hanna. Cayo works on her father's ranch. She's got eyes for him." Darby skimmed the letter. "There's something in here she's not saying that makes me—"

"Now that we're on the subject of young men, when are you going to let me invite our young pastor over to dinner again?" Aunt Bea asked.

"Whenever you think it's appropriate. But please don't think I'm going to fall for him, Aunt Bea. He's, why he's—"

"He's what, dear? Too refined for the likes of you?" Aunt Bea said, sugar dripping from the question.

Darby bit the inside of her cheek to keep herself from answering with like sarcasm. She glanced over to the table where the last of the season's peas waited to be shucked and late green beans to be snapped. She was tempted to take the vegetables with her to the gazebo, but it was too chilly now and the light was fading. It wasn't worth the fuss. Instead, she attended to the waiting vegetables. When she finished, she went to get her books from the parlor, passing the ornate pier glass between two support windows, flouncing her skirt towards her aunt as she passed it, much like a dog kicking up dirt to cover something in back of it. She grabbed her books off the inlaid table, and plopped down with them on the settee.

"Try to sit like a lady, dear-heart. Are you listless?"

She shot her aunt a sly, ornery look, but couldn't rein in her tongue. "I wonder, though, can your pastor break a horse, brand a calf, skin a buffalo, or shoot deer with a bow and arrow?" Darby looked at her aunt with a mixture of anger and pride she hadn't expected from herself, pleased by her response.

"Heaven's above, I do believe you're a lovesick pup."

"Aunt Bea, this isn't puppy love—you see I've—" she interrupted herself, knowing she was about to say too much concerning her feelings for Cayo. To avoid a discussion, she said, "Yes, I suppose it was an infatuation. I'm over it." *Now you've done it. Lied, but worse, betrayed him, you Judas.*

After dinner when she finished her homework, she closed the books and stacked them. "Time to retire, aunties." She blew them a kiss from the staircase.

Darby went to her room and looked out the window toward the urban forest she feared would soon be developed. She'd walked there many desolate days in pathless woodlands, loving the solitude and time to think.

The following day was Sunday. Darby and her two aunts attended church services and stopped in at the confectioner's shop to buy chocolates for Aunt Bea's guests in the afternoon. The parlor turned into a gambling hall as Bea would entertain her whist group at five.

Two card tables would be set up, and Aunt Mary would serve a light supper afterward. This Sunday felt different as the weather was an Indian summer day—warm enough to invite an outdoor activity, so before the guests arrived, Aunt Bea took a nap while Darby and Aunt Mary laid a table in the gazebo. She set up another one in the garden under a pergola, covered with Norton grapes, some still ruby-red, while others had already turned blue-black.

"Aunt Mary," Darby said after all the preparations were made, "Do I know everyone who is coming to this shindig?"

"Wherever do you get these expressions?" Aunt Mary patted Darby's shoulder. "Aunt Bea wants you to see Pastor Erik in a less formal setting than that restaurant outing and after church socials—"

"A set up. I just knew it." Darby huffed and shook her head.

"What's wrong?" Mary drew her handkerchief from her bodice and wiped her upper lip.

"She's going to try and run my life like she runs yours. I'll not have it. Tell her I've got a headache."

"Wait a minute, dear heart. She's gone to a great deal of trouble to do this. She's been patient with you and waited until you've adapted to the move and circumstances."

"No, indeedy, I won't have it. I left my heart back home. This is an interim stay to get me some learning, then I'm going back to reclaim my love."

"Better learn to speak properly then, my sweet. If you can say 'interim' you should follow through with proper diction."

"Dang straight, I will—just not today while I'm livid."

"About?"

"I lied to Aunt Bea and told her Cayo was just an infatuation—why, Aunt Mary, he's the love of my life, and I denied him. Worse than Peter denying Jesus in the garden."

"Don't be so hard on yourself. You don't have to strive for sainthood in these surroundings."

When the guests arrived they played cards. Later, they challenged each other to a game of croquet on the back lawn, and when they finished, Darby served tea sandwiches of fresh baked bread, watercress and homemade cream cheese with large pitchers of iced tea or lemonade.

Aunt Mary brought out the two baked cherry pies she and Darby had made that morning and set out one on a wire rack on the windowsill and the other in the pie-safe to cool.

After Pastor Erik had two pieces, he wiped his mouth daintily. Darby had all she could do to contain her laughter picturing Cayo doing the same thing, but instead using his sleeve for a napkin.

Pastor Erik stood up and reached his hand out to Darby. "Would you care to take a stroll?"

Darby looked at him as though he'd just sprouted a third eye, and said, "Aunt Mary, do you recall I wasn't feeling well and had a headache coming on this afternoon?"

"Yes, dear."

"Well, it's arrived with a legion of other aches behind my eyes. I must have been reading too much, or maybe it's all the baking and setting up we did."

Darby faced the minister. "Will you excuse me, Pastor?"

She turned from him and toward her aunt. "Aunt Mary, I've got to take one of those headache cachets you made for me, so please keep the pastor company for me."

"What's this?" Aunt Bea said, taking hold of a cake dish.

"The girl is unwell, Bea."

Bea cleared her throat. "Really?"

"I'll just be a minute and go up to take a cachet. If you insist, of course, I'll rejoin the company, but Pa always puts a cold compress on my forehead whenever I'd get one of these from bending too much while milking."

He was smiling. Yes, the Reverend Anderson knew what she was up to, and didn't seem to be offended. Well, one point on his score sheet, but no win.

"I'll be right back down, auntie," Darby said with a hand on the bannister and her foot on the first step.

She glanced at the pastor again, and tilted her head in a gesture of thanks for not giving her little act away to Aunt Bea.

***

170

On the subsequent day, the minute Aunt Bea left the house, Darby went rooting around in her deceased uncle's library and came upon several novels by Charles Dickens. She picked up *Oliver Twist*. She'd heard this author's writing was towards gloomier topics and themes, probably not suitable or appropriate reading for her, according to Aunt Bea. Luckily for her, Aunt Bea had covered all of the books before her dear departed uncle left this world. Her hand trailed over books dressed in linen, cotton and silk cloth dust jackets, some were embroidered and embossed with titles and authors, some with other adornments, of ecru stitching on cobalt blue. But to her, the most beautiful ones were the books in embossed leather and two of them were housed in silver filigree. She picked up one and followed the swirls and curlicues as if a road map about to take her far away.

Darby replaced the book and then switched out the dust covers for something more benign. She looked through the swapped-out book, jotted down a few quick notes on a piece of stationery and stuck it in the middle of the binding in case her aunt asked her something about it—she certainly didn't want to be caught in the subterfuge. But, oh how delicious this little bit of chicanery seemed: to put one over on her dear auntie! Reading was so much more fascinating and enlightening than listening to Miss Violet's rhetoric. She wondered what would have happened if she'd stayed in Parcel Bluffs and self-taught herself by reading poetry, history and geography. She knew she'd have failed miserably at mathematics—that somehow was daunting and she needed explanations from others before being able to solve problems.

So, with her prized appropriated novel, she scooted upstairs and made herself comfy cozy in the window-seat and started reading by the natural light filtering through the sheer curtains. She bit into an apple, and somehow the sweetness and the pungent smell released in air made her think of Eve in the Garden of Paradise—sin and knowledge eternally together. When she finished eating and summoning up Bible lessons, she placed the core on the windowsill, washed her hands in the basin, dried them on a fringed-linen towel, and resumed her position, book in hand. A small sigh escaped her lips, that and the choir of birds in the trees, the only sounds.

Chapter Fourteen

Comanche Raid

For days working on the ranch became a daily drudge Cayo found difficult to bear. He wouldn't even have the diversion of taking Mrs. Pederson and Hanna into town on Saturdays because they were going off to visit Mrs. Pederson's sister in Taos. They were leaving by stagecoach. Cayo and Roddy, the Scots foreman, were driving them into town early in the day and then the two of them would have the rest of the day at leisure.

Roddy was a burly man. He stooped a bit and leaned close to Cayo and said, "Shall we have some funnin' with little Miss Sass?"

"What?" Cayo asked, surprised.

"Let me remind her of the good manners to be used while traveling on the coach," Roddy said quietly, smoothing his mustache and clutching his red beard.

Cayo nodded and laughed just as Mrs. Pederson said something sharply to the girl and Hanna sat up straighter and went silent. Cayo hadn't caught the words, so he interjected. "Roddy here's got something serious to say to you ladies. There's customs and behavior most men probably know, but since not many women travel by stagecoach, they ain't privy to. Roddy knows more than I do. He'll tell you."

"Go on, Roddy," Mrs. Pederson said with an encouraging smile.

"Let's see. Well, according to a jehu I know—"

"A what?" Hanna asked.

"You know, the stagecoach driver, the whip," Roddy said.

"Oh, yes," Mrs. Pederson said.

"This here feller I knew worked for the Wells Fargo Stagecoach. He told me they posted notices—lists of proper behavior in all the swing-stations—"

"What's a swing-station?" Hanna piped up.

"Well, missy, a swing-station is a small stage post where the drivers change horses and where they put up poster signs with the rules." Roddy spit over the side of the wagon. "See that what I just done? No spitting, chewing tobacco or smoking cigars permitted—usually. Not allowed to lean a head on another passenger to fall asleep either, but that does seem to happen occasionally," Roddy said, turning back slightly and wiggling his thick eyebrows.

Hanna's eyes grew large as saucers.

Roddy took his hat off and smoothed back his oily hair. "Oh, and a man won't grease his hair so's not to get it full of road dust, and let's see what else—"

"We're women. These silly guidelines don't apply," Hanna said.

A few minutes slipped by. The only noise was the steady clip–clop of the horses, rhythmic but almost too quiet, so Cayo said in a loud voice, "Oh, here's a safety rule to be mindful of—stay in the coach and do not attempt to jump out if the horses get out of hand and runaway."

Mrs. Pederson smiled and fanned herself. "I've ridden a stagecoach before—it's courteous to share a buffalo robe if it gets cold."

"Yup," Roddy said, "and no hogging it all to yerself." He turned to wink at Mrs. Pederson.

Cayo, knowing she always carried a flask said, "No drinking liquor, either."

He saw the color rise on Mrs. Pedersen's neck to her face, and Cayo was sorry he'd said it. His intention was only to give further concern to Hanna, and even there, he thought that Roddy was overdoing it a tad.

Roddy cleared his throat. "But if'n you do, then share that, too."

Mrs. Pederson flushed. "Only proper and gentlemanly thing to do," she said, her emphasis on the word gentlemanly.

Hanna said in an indignant tone, "That certainly does not apply to us."

"Right," Roddy said, drawing out every letter of the word.

Cayo flicked the reins on the horses and said, "Gee up."

"These are outlandish regulations," Hanna said, peeved.

"If'n you don't behave, Miss Hanna, the whip can tell you to walk and you'd best move on out of that coach and start walking," Roddy said. He pulled out his gun from its holster, shined it with his shirt sleeve, blew into the muzzle, and replaced it.

A look of shock registered on the girl's face and Cayo noticed Mrs. Pederson trying to hide a smile behind her fan.

Just to be ornery and put the fear of God in Hanna, Roddy added, "Most important is to remember—no talk of Indian attacks or robberies, murders or the like's permitted neither." He looked directly at Hanna and thought she'd faint dead away.

"You'll do just fine, Miss Hanna," Cayo said, looked at Mrs. Pederson and winked again. "M'am, you still have that small pocket derringer I loaned you?"

"No, Cayo, you must be mistaken, but I've got this," she said, and extracted a bone-handled Colt House Model five-shot pistol from her tote bag.

"Mighty fine piece, you've got there, M'am. I've got a grand suspicion you're handy using it." Roddy tipped his hat.

She nodded, smirked, and tucked the gun away.

After Cayo and Roddy deposited the women at the depot, they went off for a shave and bath and decided to spend the night off in town. Cayo cleaned up and put on freshly laundered clothes, told Roddy he'd wait for him at the saloon. They met up a few minutes later and drank away some of the tediousness of the past weeks.

Cayo, Roddy, and a few other ranch hands were playing a game of poker when two Indian scouts with blue army jackets came in, but the barkeep refused to serve them.

Cayo regarded them with curiosity as they headed for the door. He looked, not with hatred because they were Navajo, but because they put him in mind of the Comanche who had traded for rifles from the French and had raided and killed what he would forever consider his people.

The two Indians left peaceably, but Coyote felt indignant for them, picked up a bottle from the table and stepped outside. Roddy, put a hand on Cayo's arm.

"No worries, Roddy."

Cayo called to the two scouts and beckoned them holding up the bottle. The men were mounting army-branded horses. They stopped, dismounted and walked toward him. He handed them the bottle. He wanted to make reparation for the insults they bore silently inside at the bar. He didn't wait for or want their thanks, but strode away and went back inside, threw some coins on the table for the whiskey and said, "I'm done for the night. See you back at the ranch. Roddy, you coming?"

"When did you turn Indian lover, Cayo?" Pederson's nephew asked and smirked.

"When you were still sucking your momma's teats."

"Yeah, I'm done, too," Roddy said.

The ride back to the ranch was dark. Roddy slunk back and fell asleep almost instantly. Cayo felt lonely, save for a gibbous moon that somehow put him in mind of Darby and her almost flaxen hair in certain light. The kid's remark had gotten to him and watching those Indians get refused service spun his mind away from Darby in a completely different direction altogether.

Once again in his mind he'd become Coyote riding his horse, heading in the direction of the village after a hunt with his brother, White Feather. Coyote had been with most of the braves for some days. When they returned to the village with food, they found a pueblo destroyed, and many lost in a battle with warring Comanche. Women and children and old ones had been brutally ambushed and slaughtered. The Comanche had raided the village just before dawn.

What was left was an eerie sight. His ears ached with the keening of the living over the bodies of recently dead. He looked first at Grandmother's, then at Red Hawk's dwellings. Both of their bodies were lying in close proximity. At this sight, he thought his heart would break and burst out of his body. He asked a young boy about Starfall.

"She's wounded."

"And what of Red Willow?"

The boy was running and the gust carried away his answer.

Coyote's horse snorted with the scent of blood. When Coyote got him under control and quieted him, he felt his own blood pulsing wildly and his heart pounding inside his ribcage, and then his eyes lit on Little Fawn. She was safe. He jumped off his horse and grabbed her in his arms, smothering her into him, begging news of what had happened.

Little Fawn pulled away from his grasp and without prelude began the woeful tale. "I was away—out gathering acorns and wood with Broken Claypot. We saw and heard what was happening. We hid ourselves in the hills for a long time, until the mourning and wailing began, and we knew it was safe to return. We had only our knives and would have been no match for those savages."

"I have seen the bodies of Grandmother and Red Hawk," he said. Did you see the killing? How was their death?"

"I am sorry for the loss of both of them, Coyote. From my hiding place I witnessed Red Hawk who was Red Hawk until the end—ferocious as he slashed at the enemy as if he had eyes to see them, a warrior even in death." She cried.

He tapped her shoulder gently to make her stop crying and continue telling him what occurred during the massacre.

"Blind," she said. "But blind as he was, he died fighting, a lance in one hand, a knife in the other. He was shot in the back. I stuffed my fist into my mouth not to cry out."

"And Grandmother?"

"I didn't see her but Broken Claypot saw the last of the savagery. Your Grandmother came out of her dwelling and used your axe. She drove it into her attacker, and as the blade entered his chest, gave a cry of war and of bravery, but it was her last song. She too, was shot through with a long gun."

"A rifle."

"A rifle."

"I heard Starfall was injured. Nothing of Red Willow. What are the People saying about them?"

She moved her hand as if it were a wand covering the village. "They say Red Willow and Starfall are responsible. They broke the covenant. The trouble that has come to pass—this brutal attack—our People blame them. The women say that two months apart from each other was not enough punishment to placate our gods. Our chief and elders should have been more—"

"How will they make them answer for their transgression?" Coyote hunched down on his haunches, as though standing to receive this news would be too much for him to take.

"There is no further need for they too have suffered pitiless acts at the hands of our attackers. Starfall was gravely wounded, and those wounds caused her death."

"Red Willow?" he asked, urgency in his voice.

"I am sorrowful, my friend, to be the one to bring sad tidings. Worse than dead. Red Willow was carried off by the leader on a high black stallion. Starfall was valiant. She fought like a man, but was slain trying to save—"

"Were you an observer?" He stood.

Little Fawn shook her head. "Only Broken Claypot. Seek her out. Ask her."

"I will tend to the old ones in the prescribed manner of the People. There is nothing more for me here. I will leave. Come with me."

Little Fawn shook her head with vehemence, and as Coyote reached for her, she stepped away. Her whole body shook.

"I will not force you."

She calmed herself and looked down. "You are a man and will find your way, but me?"

He lifted her chin. "What do you see when you look at my face?"

"A man of two worlds. You will survive," she hesitated, "even thrive—you will remember their ways and how to live that life. You will grow accustomed once again to the white man's world. But my heart—" She touched her chest. "I belong here with the People. I remember nothing of that other world of which you still speak."

He put his hands on her shoulders and squeezed gently. Then moved his hands to cup her face. She lifted her eyes slowly and there, in the sadness, he was surprised but saw clearly the words she did not know how to say, but he understood. Little Fawn had always loved him and probably thought someday he would have chosen her once he was over lamenting Red Willow. Coyote's guilt left a cleft in his heart, he knew would be difficult, if not impossible to assuage or heal.

After Coyote had attended to the burials of his loved old ones, he left his brother's lodge and went into the dwelling he shared with Grandmother and threw some of his belongings into a large traveling pouch she had made him. Before he put in the dream catcher she'd made him, he fondled it with great care. He picked up his old quiver for arrows. He hadn't used it much of late because he was given a new one by Red Willow at their marriage. He caressed the sheath, and went out in search of Mbai'. They ate together and then went for a walk.

"It is time, now. I am leaving and I want your blessing." Coyote halted his steps.

"I see you hold the quiver that my mother made you."

"I want you to have it," Coyote said, and thrust it into Mbai's hand. "I have thousands of days filled with memories of her and of Red Hawk."

Mbai' unsheathed his bone-handed knife, and without words handed it to Coyote, who nodded taking it, afraid to look up, because his emotions flooded his eyes. The men embraced.

"I am not sure you will be happy in that other world, but understand, you must try."

"Yes."

"Little Fawn goes with you?"

Coyote shook his head. "There is nothing for her in that other life. She knows only the People's ways."

"You will return for her some day?"

"I cannot say."

"She will not wait for you."

"I think not." Coyote now stood a head taller than Mbai'. He put his hands on the shoulders of the man Coyote once believed was a giant. "I would like to see her wed my brother White Feather."

Mbai' agreed. "It will be a good match. He will care for his brother's little friend."

Coyote mounted his horse. "I go to bid farewell to my friends and family," he said, knowing that this, too, would be another source of grief for him and for many others. "Separation is much like a death," he said. His grandmother had said this many times. And with those final words, he turned Wind and kicked the horse's flanks into the heart of the destroyed village.

Chapter Fifteen

Aunt Bea's Ill Health

Darby couldn't concentrate enough to study. She was concerned with Aunt Bea's health. All of a sudden the robust woman seemed to go into decline. The weather was cool, but she perspired too profusely. Mary was out of sorts, never having seen her sister disposed in any way before and voiced this to Darby.

Wild thoughts assailed her. What if Aunt Bea were to die? Bea had been so kind, taking Darby under her wing, offering her room and board, and her heart's desire: schooling. If she recovers, Darby decided she'd be kinder to her. She was indebted to her aunt and felt she owed her so much. Then other practical thoughts sprang into her mind. There would be no more money for school and books. How could she go home without finishing her education? Where would she find a job? Mary will inherit the house, but she has no head for business. How selfish to think of all these things when the woman is so ill.

Darby sat at the dinner table, scribbled and sketched, but she was not studying.

Mary came in to the kitchen and prepared some lemonade. "Don't you have an examination this afternoon with Miss Violet?"

Darby shook her head. "Mary, I can't concentrate." She pointed to the frosty glass that Mary prepared to carry up to Bea. "May I have some, too?"

"Of course, but I thought you'd prefer tea." After Mary placed the glass in front of Darby, she said. "Make an effort."

Darby stood. "I can't. What if Aunt Bea—"

"Let's not think the worst. We'll wait until tomorrow."

Darby held out her paper to Mary. "I'm a failure."

"Don't fret. Violet will give you another chance. When she comes, I'll simply tell her you were unable to prepare. Now then, I'm going to dash off a note to Dr. Marsh and then I'll tend to Bea. Darby, you don't mind walking a few blocks to where he lives and has a practice, do you?"

"Not at all. I could use the air and happy to have something to do besides fret." Darby plopped down in the seat next to where Mary sat writing a note. Her aunt put the paper in an envelope. "Here's an introduction and a brief summary of what's wrong with Bea. If he's not overly busy seeing patients, bring him back to visit her. I've told him you were my niece."

Darby walked along the streets, weary and worried. She picked up a stick and ran it across the gates of the imposing homes she passed. When she got to the proper address she flung the stick into the garden before ringing the bell at a side entrance as Mary had instructed her.

She was greeted by a nurse with a starched cap and when Darby gained entrance was asked to be seated and wait in the sitting room. She looked at magazines, out the window, and all around the place, feeling strange and uncomfortable. Finally, after a half-hour wait, the doctor emerged in a white coat.

Darby's jaw went slack. It was as if she knew him. He was so familiar. What was it about him? Her thoughts were interrupted when he cleared his throat and said, "Good day. May I help you?"

He was as tall as the lintel with broad shoulders and hair graying at the temples. He was as handsome as a picture of a Greek statue she'd just seen in the *St. Louis Dispatch;* the same cut of strong jaw, dimples, and curly hair. She wondered what his credentials were as she handed him the envelope Mary had given her. He took hold of it, but before opening it, looked Darby over as if she were a cadaver recently stolen from a grave he could use to cut up and do experiments on. She shuddered.

"And you are? The house servant?"

Darby flushed. She shook her head.

He extended his hand and she shook it. "Have you a tongue, girl?

"Of course, it's just that your cold" and wanted to add the word: *greeting,* but said instead, "hand made me feel chilled."

"I washed them with a mixture of alcohol and aloe. Germs all around." He withdrew his hand and read the slip of paper Mary had sent. "Are you ill as well as your Aunt Bea?"

She exhaled an annoyed breath and said, "Not a bit, sir."

"I'm not that old, even if I did serve as an Army corpsman in the Civil War."

She looked at him confused.

"A medic. I was very young, but advanced in my studies and anxious to be a war hero, like most of the other idiots who enlisted in the Army."

She smirked and relaxed. He was disarmingly—for lack of a better word, she thought—beautiful.

His eyes sparkled and he smiled. "Ah, you're human, after all. Thought at first you were a sphinx."

She smiled at that.

He removed his coat. "Mind if I walk you back to Bea's? I'm done seeing patients for the day."

"That's fine. Mary wanted me to bring you back. What do you think is wrong with Aunt Bea? She has night sweats. Mary sponges her down. They seem to be up at all hours. I hope it's nothing serious."

"Please." He indicated a chair. "Sit. I'll be only a minute." He hung his professional coat on the back of the door he opened. "Need to grab my bag."

As soon as he disappeared behind the door, Darby tried to imagine what it was about the doctor that made him so familiar to her, and then it dawned on her, like lighting a lamp in the dark. Cayo. Not his looks, of course, but his build. The broad shoulders. The narrow waist. The back she could imagine rippled with muscles like Cayo's. Yes, even his stature and the assured confidence in his movements: a bit of a swagger. He was a man secure in his own hide. He had lived through difficulty and come out basically unscathed. Since when was Darby so knowledgeable, worldly and reflective? Of late she'd been looking deeper than mere face value presentations. She now considered a person's character, personality when she was introduced. People were complex beings. Neither all good nor all bad and it was this that fascinated her. What made him the way he was? What did his humanity encompass?

The doctor held the door for her when they left his outer office. She noticed that he took a key from his pocket chain and locked the door. She had never seen anyone lock their door before.

"Are you afraid of thieves?"

He pocked the keychain. "Let's say I don't want anyone getting into my experiments by mistake."

Shoulder to shoulder they walked back to her aunt's. He was a head taller, and so vivacious, Darby could barely keep step with his long strides or the many questions he cross-examined her with when all the while she searched for some pithy answer. She didn't want to come across as a country bumpkin.

When he stopped asking questions, she was embarrassed with the silence and to fill it, she said, "You have a beautiful home and waiting room."

"A detached house. My father was in the mercantile class, what's known today as a captain of industry. He made his fortune in manufacturing and wanted a home to reflect his wealth and economic status. Father purchased a very large lot and had an architect build the house to his specifications, including space for a waiting room and my office. He was a genius. Too bad he didn't live long enough to enjoy it. Almost when the last bit of mortar was applied he died and I inherited it. *"Casa pronto, morto sicuro.* It means, house ready, death certain."

That took Darby by surprise and she wanted to ask more, but felt it wasn't her place.

As they strolled along, he pointed to a stately house. "See that Victorian prize? His wife, my mother resides there. They were separated. He was—oh my, there I go again, telling too much family history."

"Please do finish—it's utterly fascinating."

"Utterly?"

"Wholly. I'm improving my vocabulary—please do go on—you're the first person to actually talk to me on a level of—"

He stopped and looked at her. "Yes?" he said.

"Continue, please," she stuttered.

"Father was a philanderer. Do you understand?"

"A whoremonger?"

He burst out laughing. "Well, I wouldn't put it quite like that, but yes, father did like his women—from all classes and societies. So he put mother up on a private street in a grand house near enough, yet not in spy-glass distance, gave her every comfort imaginable and begged her not to divorce him."

"Why did he only want to separate instead of being free of her permanently?"

"In his own peculiar way, he loved her and selfishly didn't want to see her with anyone else. She's an exquisite woman. A terrible snob. If you met her, she'd make you feel beneath her—you aren't, of course. She can't help it. Mother was raised in society, and—I shan't bore you with the other details."

They resumed walking but had slowed their pace, and Darby hoped it was because he found her engaging.

"Here we are. Arrived. Safe to your aunt's doorstep."

"I'm sorry," she said and stuck out her hand.

"Whatever for?" He shook her hand but didn't let go.

She regarded their grasped hands and gently tugged hers away. "Sorry for having arrived so quickly. It was a pleasure to meet you, Doctor Marsh."

He leaned in and said, "Call me Paul. You are?"

"In that case, Darby Mc Phee, lately of Parcel Bluffs, residing with Aunt Bea and studying to be a teacher," she said in a breathless manner.

"In that case, Darby McPhee, lately of Parcel Bluffs, residing with Aunt Bea, and studying to be a teacher," he repeated mocking her jovially, "the pleasure's all mine."

When the doctor had finished examining Aunt Bea, Mary had him sit in the parlor and served him a cordial as he'd declined his fee.

"You must tell us, Dr. Marsh, is it serious with Bea?" Mary asked.

He looked at Darby and back at Mary. "Aren't you ladies going to join me?"

Darby examined his glass with a hankering look on her face.

"No, we don't imbibe, do we now?" Mary said. She looked at Darby, whose eyes became large with pleading. "Well," Mary hesitated, and in that brief instance Darby understood the relaxed atmosphere without Aunt Bea. "Just a drop." Mary stood and poured a thimble full of sweet vermouth into two tiny upside down etched bell-shaped stemmed glasses, handed one to Darby, and clinked glasses with her and saluted the doctor with her raised glass.

The doctor explained in a self-conscious manner that Aunt Bea wasn't suffering anything unusual, "It's a mild case of symptoms of adjustment —what Italians call *'la terza età'* or the third age."

"The third age?" Darby asked.

"No easy way to say this. It's the onset of old age for a woman past her prime. Her body is in decline. For example, she's no longer able to bear children."

"I see," said Mary. "The change."

"Precisely. She'll have these *vampate*," he said, and stopped himself realizing that wasn't the right word and continued in English, "flushes of heat every now and again," his voice indicating an end to the discussion. "Darby," he said, "tell me more of your studies. Where do you plan to teach school?"

"Then Aunt Bea's problem isn't serious?" Darby sipped her cordial.

"Nothing to worry about," he said, "but about your plans?"

"I've been so concerned about my aunt I've let my studies go these past few days. I've never done that." She cast her eyes down. "I even failed an examination I should've passed easily."

"You can make it up, can't you?" he asked.

"I'm not used to failing anything I try for." Darby said, a hitch in her voice.

"But you just said—you hadn't studied, therefore, you really didn't try. Were you using your aunt's illness to avoid studying?"

Darby shot him a look. "You're right. I didn't try," she repeated. "I'll walk you to the door. Thank you for coming so quickly," she added.

"But, Darby, darling, Dr. Marsh hasn't finished his drink yet, and you didn't answer his question. What are your plans?" Mary said.

A little "Oh," escaped Darby's lips. "Do forgive me. Actually, I've left enquiries in several neighborhood schools for a teaching position.

I've written to some schools out west, but so far there aren't any possibilities except . . ."

"Yes?" Dr. Marsh asked.

"Teaching on Indian reservations, and I don't think that's my calling. I love English and writing and reading, but I'm not dedicated enough or capable of teaching English to non-speakers. And most of them are religious schools. I'm hardly a candidate for the cloister."

Dr. Marsh smiled. "I see. If you need a recommendation, would one from me help?"

"I doubt it. But thanks," Darby said. "What could possibly be the basis of your recommendation?"

"You could work for me as a secretary. Mine is leaving. The position is open at the end of the month."

Darby looked at Mary and both wore an expression of surprise. Darby stood and put her chin in her hand. She dropped her hand. "I appreciate the offer; however, I must finish school and I truly have no secretarial skills. Forgive me for saying so, but learning to take dictation seems like a most boring pursuit."

"And that, Miss Darby, is what I like about you most—you're forthright and honest. Now I must be going." Dr. Marsh stood up, gave a slight bow to Aunt Mary and turned to Darby. "Please accompany me to the door."

Darby inclined her head in accord, smoothed her skirt, and walked him to the front entrance. She opened the door, but hesitated. "Why did you use those Italian words before when you were explaining what's wrong with Aunt Bea?"

"Italian has its roots in Latin, the language of medicine and science. Besides, it comes easy to me. I was baptized Paulo Marciano before my father legally changed our name to Marsh. He didn't want me to suffer ridicule because of our heritage. In fact, he wanted me to be totally assimilated as an American, but we always spoke Italian when we were alone."

"Who do you speak Italian with now that he's passed?"

"My mother."

"The snob?"

Paul laughed. "My, but you're direct, aren't you? She'd probably like you. Curious to meet her?"

"Heavens, no! I barely know you, and I was quite bold answering you. I guarantee I'm going to receive a scolding from Mary for my improper behavior towards you." And all in one breath, she blurted out, "Why would you take me to meet your mother unless we've become engaged?" Darby swung the door forward and back.

"We can arrange that if you'd like." He leaned toward her as if he were a huge bear picking up honey scent.

"Hardly," she said, taking a step backward.

He straightened. "You're delightfully fresh and uncomplicated."

Darby opened the door wide. "I'm anything but that. Good day, Dr. Marsh."

He put on his hat. "You aren't a bit offended. Why the pose? In fact, you rather like the idea I said it. Come now. Drop the womanly guiles. They don't become you at all."

"Only if you do not persist in this conversation. And leave."

"I'll come by tomorrow to see how your aunt is doing. I'll call around midday. Consider my offer. Dinner. Saturday. Discuss it with Mary. Mother will fill your ears with the latest gossip around town. But give me your answer tomorrow, or I'll have to sit around by myself on a Saturday evening."

"I can't."

"Why not?"

"I don't think it's proper. I haven't—"

"But you will consider my invitation, won't you? Till tomorrow." He made a slight bow and was off. With that, Darby closed the door quickly and leaned against it, blowing out a huge breath. Then she dashed to the window on the far side of the parlor and caught sight of his long stride as he crossed the street.

As soon as she walked into the parlor, Mary said, "Charming, isn't he? But, I fancy, a bit of a rake. Sit down, child."

"What's the gossip he mentioned?"

"Aha! Forewarned you, did he? He's forthright too. He'd make some girl a great catch."

"He's invited me to dine with him on Saturday. But I think not—too sophisticated for me. I prefer rough and rugged. Like Cayo. Anyway, your sister would drop dead if I had even the slightest notion. Why she's practically handed me over on a platter to the pastor."

"Your Aunt Bea means well, but we're veering off in another direction. I want you to hear about the doctor.

"As I remember, he's recently broken with his future-intended. And in a most bizarre way. They'd been engaged to be married for about six months. A stunning couple. He escorted her to all the society functions. Balls and operas. And theater. She attended teas and church functions, and got on rather well with his mother who approved of her background and her—pardon this vulgarity—her wealth. But," she hesitated, "there was a scandal. I seem to remember she'd been rather flirtatious at a Maypole ball, last May, and our dear Paul socked the fellow who fell into the punch. Dreadful."

"That was the end of it?"

"Oh no. They must've reconciled, and she was to be a June bride, but at the last moment, it seems Paul had second thoughts and left her standing at the altar. Scandalous."

"Why would he do such a despicable thing? Why didn't he break it off with her civilly beforehand?"

Mary stood up and poured some more in her glass. She sipped. "I'm not sure, but from what I could piece together, his bride-to-be was the exact kind of social climber his mother is, and he realized he didn't want to marry his mother and have to put up with her double for life."

"I can't even begin to imagine the cost of a society wedding."

"It was splattered all over the newspaper. Ann McGovern, that was her name, was so disgraced she left St. Louis to visit relatives in Boston. I don't believe she's returned yet. "

"A whole year almost? That's like a mourning period."

"Precisely."

"Poor Ann McGovern."

"Poor Paul. His mother wanted to disown him. She has all the money. He only has the house his father left him. And his practice, of course. Why don't you accept his invitation to have dinner with him? He'll take you to one of the most posh restaurants in town. You're free. Cayo is far away and you think Erik is too close."

"Aren't you the daring one, Aunt Mary?"

"Not a bit. I only wish I had your pluck when I was your age. I might not be the old maid I am now."

"I've wounded you. Please take no offense."

"None taken, dear."

Dr. Marsh visited the next afternoon to see how Aunt Bea was feeling. On his way out, hat in hand, he looked at Darby and waited a full minute. "Well?"

Turning red-apple red, she managed to sound nonchalant. "What time will you call?"

He smiled. "I'll come round with a carriage at seven pm. Don't overdress. You're charming without all the accoutrements."

"Oh my." The second flush was worse and raced up from chest to neck to cheeks. Darby turned slightly so he wouldn't see. "Thank you." *Accoutrements?* She closed the door and dashed straight for the dictionary.

When Darby came home from her outing with Dr. Marsh, Mary greeted her, excited to find out about her dinner engagement. "Well? Isn't he charming?

"The Cinderella evening was more than I could dream, but—"

"There's a 'but' to this?" Mary asked, surprised.

"Aunt Mary! He kissed me in the carriage—"

"You're not so shocked, really, are you, dear?"

"That's not all. He tried to fondle my—I didn't like the fawning or pawing over me. I'm not a sophisticated city girl." She paced up and down as she removed her gloves, hat, reticule, and cape and tossed them on the sofa, whirling around. "He thought he could take advantage of me, the country bumpkin. Yes! He's charming, elegant. He's from high society. Everything I'm not."

"Maybe that's what interests him about you. Perhaps, that's the appeal."

"I'd never fit in his world. What's more, I don't even want to try. If I'm honest with myself—and you—it was an interesting experiment. I'm not worldly. I truly believed these physical longings only occur when you love someone."

"What a great deal you have to learn, my pet. I'm so glad you're here with us."

"You, dear aunt? Patronizing me?"

"Never. I was unprepared for the outside world much as you. I'm happy to know you'll be able to make informed decisions. I think you're very brave. Are you hurt?"

"Stunned."

"You didn't slap him?"

"Nothing so dramatic. It was my own fault for falling prey to his charms. I wrestled free of his grip, and said, 'You are no gentleman, sir.'"

A tiny 'oh' issued forth from Mary. "Whatever did he say to that?"

"The handsome scoundrel laughed and agreed with me. He said: 'You're right there.'"

Mary shook her head and smiled.

"I guess it is rather funny. My first excursion with a fine gentleman and I insulted him."

"Don't be surprised. He may not be deterred and may call on you again."

"I'll be prepared in that case. He's welcome in this house as Aunt Bea's doctor, and nothing more, I assure you of that."

Mary giggled. She kissed her niece on the forehead. "You're a survivor. I'm proud of you. Congratulations. Shall we have some hot chocolate?"

"Only if you let me lace it with some of that raspberry liqueur you keep hidden from your sister."

"Why you horrid little scamp. How did you know?"

"Not everything escapes me, Mary."

"In that case—" she took hold of Darby's arm and marched her into the kitchen. "Let's have some," she crooned.

A voice from the top of the stairs, called out, "What's going on there you two?"

"Just going to make some hot cocoa, sister, darling. Everything's fine."

"Peachy, dandy," Darby whispered to Mary.

"Goodnight then," Bea called sleep-deprived.

"Sweet dreams," Mary answered, taking hold of the cocoa tin, watching Darby scrounge about in back of the cabinet under the sink for the stashed bottle of liqueur.

On Monday, after classes, Darby met the mailman delivering the post outside the front door. Instead of dropping the mail in the letterbox, he handed her an envelope. It was from Fern. "Thank you," she said, and tore it open. A train ticket floated to the ground. It felt as if the letter scorched her hands and heart. She read it three times before stooping to pick up passage to Parcel Bluffs. Cayo had saved up money to purchase her fare to return to him. Her prayers were answered only they weren't. She couldn't leave now with Aunt Bea on the mend, and her classes about to be completed. She dashed into the house, told Mary, and sat to write Cayo and Fern. Would he understand? Would he ever forgive her? Choices. Each one of them that a person makes has consequences.

Chapter Sixteen

The Cattle Roundup

As weeks rolled into months, Cayo became anxious for change. He liked ranching, enjoyed being with animals maybe even more than the men he worked with, but he found he was not able to concentrate on his daily routine and jobs that were second nature became a drudge. One night when he couldn't sleep, he walked out of the bunkhouse and sipped some tequila from a canteen. Then he took another sip and before you know it, he was tipsy and tired and ready to try sleep once more.

That night he dreamt he ran like a coyote—he was the coyote running straight for the brush. Then he soared high, flying over clouds, watching the coyote run and as he flew by, he became an eagle watching the coyote—but at the same time, he was still the coyote. That's how it is in dreams and the mind doesn't know it's a delusion, until one awakens. When he opened his eyes, questions started forming. Where had he been running to? Where was he flying? To that faraway place where she was. Wondering why he hadn't gotten her pregnant. She sure as hell wouldn't have gone off to St. Louis in that condition. He'd let Darby get away, yet had no one to blame but himself, but now things were different. He'd tried to rectify his blunder of letting her depart by sending her passage home. She'd refused him. He was stunned with disbelief.

After the summer roundup, a beef roundup segued—the collecting of cattle in good enough shape for market. Once Darby left, Cayo had no other interest except working long hours to set aside all the pay he could muster. He wanted to convince her to come back sooner, and had bought her the train ticket. She'd said, no, but kept the ticket, saying when her lessons were done.

After the cattle roundup, he might go locate his parents' spread. The animals would be ready for shipping to market in October. That's when he thought to go.

It was early autumn when Captain Pederson started showing particular interest in being a wealthy stockman, wanting to learn what his profits would be. What in tarnation had the man been doing and thinking before this time, Cayo wondered, dismayed.

Captain Pederson had sent for Roddy and Cayo and all three rode out to a nearby pasture where some of the herd grazed. They stopped their horses by a wooden fence, looking over a large patch of grassland.

"My sole purpose in raising cattle, men, is to make money," the Captain said.

"How much you think they'll render, sir?" Roddy looked over the herd, seemingly doing a calculation in his head.

"I'd be happy if this beef herd of a thousand returned me a thousand dollars. Why a return such as that would be most agreeable to me in these most congenial Indian summer days." Pointing to Cayo, he continued. "It's no wonder this here stockman's at peace with the world, I tell you true, at peace with this wild world." The Captain made an expansive wave of his arm. "Next batch of these fat cattle, I'm sending on by rail to market, just like neighbor Mc Phee and those boys of his do, and probably to the same places—Kansas City and Chicago. We're hundreds of miles away from market and it's no small feat conveying cattle—why that's some kind of distance, you agree?"

Cayo took off his hat and wiped his forehead with his sleeve, put his hat back on. "Yes, sir."

Roddy nodded. "Our herd's close to a hundred miles away from the railroad and we've got to drive them over this big distance, subject to the changing weather."

"As long as we don't head into some unforeseen rare seasonal snow-storm—in which case both cowpoke and cow suffer. But once they reach the railroad station, they'll find suitable corrals and an enclosure space near the freight cars, I'll see to it," Cayo said.

"We've got to move quickly next couple of days," Captain Pederson said.

Cayo, wondering why he'd been invited to this discussion, decided he should add something more. "I heard tell of a stockman who had to wait a week of days in a snowstorm with sleet too. He waited in them open pens for the expected train cars, both man and beasts pained and afflicted."

"That won't happen to us, will it, sir?" Roddy said, pointedly waiting for a response from the Captain.

"That's right. You'll see to it, eh, Roddy?" Captain Pederson said, and not waiting for an answer, headed back to the ranch.

"Guess the discussion's over," Cayo said and rode on ahead towards the branding station.

"Hey, Cayo, today after branding," Roddy yelled, "don't bring them extra horses home—just turn 'em loose. Worse'n damn cattle for eating on the spot."

Later in the day, Cayo got back to the bunkhouse before the others and was first to see a sign tacked up by Roddy, who considered himself the boss. The message on the door stated:

Points to Remember
1. Keep castration and dehorning instruments clean.

2. **Disinfect for each animal.**
3. **These calves are worth money!**
4. **Dehorn, castrate, brand and handle properly and with respect.**
5. **Keep an eye out for *fiebre aftosa*, or hoof and mouth disease in any animal. Highly contagious. Must be reported immediately. Animals must be put down and buried in lime pits. Could lose the entire herd.**

The Boss, in accordance with Captain Pederson

Cayo looked it over, took it down and handed it to Roddy. "Read it to me."

Roddy said, "You're serious?"

"Apache don't teach reading and writing." Cayo said.

When he'd finished, Cayo, wore an embarrassed look on his face. "Can you help me learn to read and write?"

Chapter Seventeen

The New Year in St. Louis

It was a blustery New Year's Eve. There was a small celebration with a unique gathering of friends and distant relatives in the parlor of the house that Darby had come to love. The drafty rooms of her aunts' home were once again warm with new velvet curtains at the windows and fireplaces that glowed with flames replenished by a cord of fragrant wood on the back covered porch.

She wanted to look her best. Paul Marsh attended the gathering. She had been charmed by him, but now was wary of his advances, and quite over any initial attraction.

At the stroke of midnight, Darby made sure she was nowhere in kissing distance to Dr. Marsh or the pastor. She was, in fact, on the other side of the room, hugging her tutor, Miss Violet, and wishing her every possible happiness for the year to come.

Darby sensed that the pastor saw her quick move away from the men, and gave her a tiny salute. Was it for the adroit movement or because she had outwitted them, not wanting any physical contact? It probably would have only been a polite bussing of her cheek, but the remembrance of her carriage experience—the idea of it, nauseated her.

She had a bubbly feeling in her stomach with the mere remembrance of Cayo's kiss. She wondered then if he'd be invited to the annual jamboree to usher in the New Year that the Pederson's held in the town hall. And where exactly would Hanna position herself? Beneath the mistletoe? She breathed out an audible sigh.

"What is it, dear heart?' Mary said.

"Nothing. Happy New Year. I need some air. I'll just pop out the back door for a minute. Don't worry, I won't fall in a snowdrift."

She took down Mary's old work sweater from the hook by the back door, and threw it around her shoulders, opened the door to the back garden, and stepped outside. The chilled air made her hot breath cloudy as she meandered along all the slate stones to a small hothouse. She glided along the path carefully as it was slick with snow.

She reached the hothouse, entered and closed the latch, touching a nearby wrought-iron bench. Ice cold. She pulled the sweater beneath her thighs and sat down. The minute she did, she heard the rustling of the hasp and startled, looked up to see Pastor Erik.

"I hope I'm not intruding on your privacy, Miss Darby, but I've come to collect."

"Collect? What?"

"The New Year's kiss you gave so freely to everyone else but me."

"Pastor Erik!"

"Please. My name isn't pastor, so make the effort to call me Erik." He sat next to her and kissed her cheek. "Well?" he said.

"You can't be serious. You're a man of the cloth and—"

He turned her shoulders toward him and kissed her forehead; then his lips slipped down her pert nose and travelled to her lips where they pressed hers and lingered.

She was amused that she knew how to kiss and he didn't. She was also too shocked to push him away and far too intrigued to know what on earth he saw in her uncouth western ways when he was gentrified, citified and every other *fied* she could think of.

When he caught his breath, he breathed into the hair behind her ear, "Happy New Year."

"Why?" she said. "Why, when you're so—" she thought a second and then threw out the new vocabulary she'd learned—"why, when you're so urban, cosmopolitan and suave would you want to kiss a country hick like me?"

"You're fascinating, yet uncomplicated. You do know your aunt has intended us to become—"

"Hold it, sir." She put up her hands, palms toward him. "Stop right there." She put her hands in her lap and exhaled. "What my aunt pretends has nothing to do with my desires or goals. You realize that my objective in coming here has nothing whatsoever to do with your wishes to find a wife. You need a companion who is religious. Someone who is a believer in your faith," she hesitated a second, "and in you. How could you think that I—?" Darby stood up. "How could you entertain the idea of marrying a silly, uneducated country girl, one who doesn't even know the proper fork or etiquette to use when she'd like to push a certain preacher into the snow for daring to take advantage of her and kiss her? It's improper to say the least. Where's your sense of decorum?"

"Who said anything about getting married? Your aunt Bea was hoping we'd become friends."

"Oh." She was embarrassed, but hoped he was sufficiently warned off. And for good. With that theatrical bit of dialogue delivered in a resolute voice, she flew out the door, only to find that it was snowing hard and with the intention of sticking. Her step immediately faltered. She slipped on a flagstone, landing unceremoniously on her *derriere*, another newly acquired word!

She looked upward and back to see him standing over her smirking. He covered his mouth with his hand in an obvious gesture of embarrassed laughter.

"Don't just stand there gaping and gawking. Help me up!"

He walked around to face her, bent down and lifted her up. This time he kissed her with surprising passion. And she kissed him back, imagining Cayo.

Breathless, she pushed back from him. "Is this what they teach you in theological seminary?"

"I've wanted to do that since the minute I met you sitting prim and proper in your aunt's drawing room."

Darby dusted the snow off of her backside. When she'd finished she looked at him steadily. "Now that you've succeeded what do you think will come of it?" Not waiting for an answer, she trod off in the direction of the house.

Inside once again, her cheeks burned. Was it the raw cold? Or was it the fact that she'd betrayed the memory of Cayo's kiss? Or was it because she had enjoyed the kiss? Darby went to join the gathering and poured a glass of punch. How she wished it contained some of the hard cider and whiskey that Cayo had introduced her to. As soon as Pastor Erik came into the room, she put down her cup and said a quick good-night to all of the guests. Except him.

The next morning, in the breakfast nook, Darby was prepared for Aunt Bea's reprimand, but she was greeted by her aunt's smile as she handed over a calling card.

"It seems, my dear, you've made a conquest in Pastor Erik." Aunt Bea poured some coffee in a delicate porcelain cup and handed it to her niece, who turned the card over and read that the pastor would like to pay call in the afternoon.

"Whatever have you done to captivate him and make the pastor so forward?"

Darby wanted to say, I fell on my ass and he picked me up like a sack of beans, kissed me till I was breathless, but simply smiled and said, "I haven't the foggiest notion."

Back in her room, Darby threw herself on the bed and covered her eyes with a forearm. "This man," she said aloud "can never replace Cayo. How will I find a space in this world without the man I love?" She twisted her head from side to side. Next, Darby envisioned a scene with Cayo—a daydream sequence so real she felt as though she was living it. She imagined finding herself with Cayo as he pulled his poncho over his head. He laid the other blanket on the ground. He sat down. "Here," he said, patting the spot next to him. Habit made him reach for his holstered guns and belt and tuck them under the blanket near him. He covered her with the poncho. "Hungry?"

"Famished. Does that always happen afterward?"

He laughed. "Sometimes."

"I brought fry bread and a Spanish tortilla of potatoes and onions, but I'm loath to move from this nice warm spot. Can you get my satchel?"

"For a price." He leaned into her and kissed her.

"Air hunger comes before food, you know," she said, inhaling a lungful. "Your kiss—" she began, but cut herself off. He looked puzzled. "Makes me want to crawl out of my skin into yours." He nodded. The smile that played around the corners of his mouth was almost a smirk, confusing her. It made her feel foolish. She'd exposed herself raw and felt like hiding. But then he grinned at her and touched her cheek with tenderness and strode off.

He brought the satchel of food and placed it down, then he gave her a handful of pine nuts and offered his Army canteen. "Take a swig of this. It'll warm you."

"River water?"

"Why waste a canteen full of what we got right here," he said with a wave of his arm toward the river. "No, little darling, it's apple cider laced with whiskey."

On the verge of sleep, Darby covered herself with a crocheted afghan. When she began to feel warm, she continued her musing.

Behind closed eyes, she watched him build a fire. She took a swig and her throat burned and her eyes teared.

"Potent brew, you got there, cowpoke."

Cayo stoked the fire to a controlled blaze. He sat next to her and took a long pull on the canteen. He leaned on an elbow, his breath close to her cheek.

"I dreamed," he said.

Darby felt his breath warm, sweet with apple cider and piñon, his voice at once disembodied from earth yet tinged with desperation.

"What of?"

"You'll leave soon on the Iron Horse instead of for our cabin in the foothills. I'll travel alone and swiftly, followed by a posse and men armed with rifles as if to do battle."

"You think there'll be some sort of uprising?"

"I think I'm destined to go on a vision quest that'll reveal a piece of hell—if you leave me."

What if she hadn't left? What if she'd said, "I'm not going, Cayo. I told you so."

"In your Book, it's written that a man named Peter denied—"

"The Bible? You're quoting me the Bible?"

"In the dream, I saw a hawk feed on the helpless—I'll be feeble and weak without you."

"Even if I were to go, which I'm not, you're not weak—who would dare take advantage of you? There isn't a man who'd challenge you with whip, knife or pistol—"

"There are other arms far more dangerous because they're human."

"You're just trying to scare me—what're you talking about?"

She didn't need an answer because she understood he was talking about another woman.

That night Darby fell asleep with all her clothes on and in the middle of the night heard a scratching at her window. Who was it? What was it? She roused, walked to the window and threw it open to the cold and snowy night. It was merely the howling wind blowing a branch too close. Too close, she thought, remembering her daydream. She shivered from the frigid air and from the thought of something bad happening to Cayo while she was away from him—something that would cause a posse to chase him.

Darby made a decision to throw herself into her studies. What was done, was done and could never be undone. The curriculum at the new school included writing, with special importance placed on grammar and reading literature, solving arithmetic, algebraic and geometrical problems, and a smattering of foreign languages, music, and art. Determination, she concluded was key to success. She set herself the task of the hard work and study with a fervor few teachers had ever seen in their pupils.

By 1875 several private schools began springing up and one was under the auspices of the Reverend Oglethorpe Piper, Mr. Anders Volkman, and Mr. Harold Woodspin. They hired Mrs. Theodora Riggs who had acted as head governess of the school Darby attended. Rev. Piper also chose Mrs. Rigby's assistant, Mrs. Alberta Longshank, along with the music and art teacher, Mrs. Vita Castle to become members of the board. It was a great honor for these ladies to be considered by the reverend, since he deemed himself a modern thinker.

Darby was far advanced and had made such tremendous strides that Mrs. Riggs suggested she join the staff as an assistant. In lieu of a stipend she would continue to receive, tuition free, the rest of her schooling. Darby accepted. She was thrilled to relieve Aunt Bea of some of the monetary responsibility Darby's education had incurred. This opportunity to become a student-teacher would serve her in future.

"Truth and wisdom are like pebbles and stones on the beach," Mrs. Riggs was fond of saying. "One merely needs to sort them out." Darby understood that. Though some truths are difficult to discern. She visualized pebbles along the beachy stretch where she and Cayo had picnicked. Till the end of her life she'd carry with her images of loam and fern, babbling waters gathering in eddies, spilling, trilling over smooth gray-green and black stones. Leaves that had been green in summer and in fall were golden, red, and deep umber, were now covered with snow.

There was a pool by the gazebo at the back of the house and along the surface skimmed a few scant dead leaves—daubs of oils on a painter's dark pallet. While Aunt Mary painted at an easel inside a sun room that faced the garden, Darby remembered her time along the banks of the river, how the last time they'd been there they had sat on his poncho. She took hold of his shoulders, pulling him close so that her face rested on his chest. She murmured, "Not just me, but you and I—we are forever changed." His scent, she knew then as now, would permeate her senses for a lifetime.

Not the repetition of vacuous days, nor the replication of frivolous ones, could diminish the wild and unbridled skipping, singing stones Cayo had flung out in the Rio Grande. The flute notes they sang were conserved in her mind as if jotted down in India ink upon a music sheet.

Aunt Mary gave Darby a notebook, a sketchbook, and paints—water colors, pencils, crayons and oils. Aunt Mary insisted on loaning her easel to Darby. She had clucked and cooed about it so much that Darby was ashamed not to accept it, but she kept refusing it just the same and all the more Aunt Mary insisted she take it. Finally, Darby gave up.

Memory brought Darby strains of musical notes like spiraling whirlpools and moving water. River sounds played in her ears. They welled-up in Darby so much that they cancelled out every word of dialogue she'd pretended to hear from Aunt Bea, just now coming into the sun room. Such chatter!

It was breaking up her reverie as she'd struggled to focus on the image of Cayo's face by the Rio Grande. Darby recalled July and longed for the heat of it. Riding back on the Pederson's buggy, Cayo had called the yellow orb in the sky, summer ripe-corn moon—before the fruit moon. Before evening had fallen and that full moon glittered its outrageous pure light shimmering on the river, soaring above the mountains, she wanted him desperately. She knew she had the combustible heat to warm him the way he wanted to be warmed. He had called to her softly in so many of her dreams, Darby. Darby.

"Darby." Aunt Bea called from the back porch. Darby snapped out of her fantasy, aware that Aunt Mary had packed up her painting gear and she and Aunt Bea had gone indoors. "Don't stay outdoors too long, dear."

Darby reached for the ostrich-skin covered travel journal Aunt Bea had given her for Christmas the year before and now used as her diary. "Coming, Aunt Bea." Darby went inside and sat at the kitchen table. She wrote in her book: May the warmth of spring usher me through to summer's end, carrying me to autumn's rich store for winter. How can I cancel his image from my brain?

She began to pray for guidance and a way to assuage her thoughts of him, thoughts fringed with designs of Cayo. Fringed like his chamois shirt. Soft to touch, warm like his skin in the sun by the river. She hoped that she might be able to read some of her ideas to him someday, and tell him how much she'd missed him during this time of self-imposed separation.

She looked out the window. Butterflies abounded in the Dutchman's Pipe bush, and cardinals sprang from branch to branch in the potted bougainvillea that Erik had brought her. She couldn't understand why such a colorful species was attracted to the thorny bush, she deemed so appropriate for her own nature. She smiled at that analogy—like that flamboyant bird, Erik, flitting around her. He made her feel shy and reticent—like she was constantly making a gaff or saying the wrong thing at an inappropriate time. So lost in her thoughts she was surprised at a sprinkling of raindrops on the windowpane. Darkness hooded the sky. Darkness enveloped her to her core and with a horrible realization: Cayo had never told her he loved her. Not once. Never said the words. But he did, didn't he? He must. She had given herself to him. She had jumped up and ensnared him with her legs, hadn't that meant anything? Hadn't he touched her in unimaginable ways in places she'd never been touched.

Aunt Bea turned the wick up on the lamp. "Come away from your thoughts, dear. It's time to lay the cloth for supper. You've been sitting here all afternoon."

Darby said, "I've been in a reverie with a sullen sky, a rising moon bereft with clouds."

Chapter Eighteen

The Outlaws

Winter had not quite ended yet when Cayo got permission to ride out and look for his family's spread with Roddy and one other ranch hand named Sully. They rode all day as the snow kept falling. The deep snow was a hindrance as they trudged along. Roddy, Cayo, and Sully kept their ropes on the right side of their saddle horns. Long purple and mauve shadows began to fall, shrouding everything in sight.

"Enough for today," Cayo called. "I've had it and don't want to put my horse at risk in deep snow."

"Yeah, been a rough day riding and night's coming on quickly," Roddy agreed.

"Let's camp over there," he pointed, "in that gully by the rocks in the pinon stand," Sully said. "I'm faint from hunger, boys."

"Got some prairie oysters here," Roddy said, smacking his saddle-bag. "Bull, sheep, and pig. And cold packed bear grease will melt nicely over a fire so we can fry 'em up."

They dismounted, unsaddled the horses, fed and watered them. Roddy banked a fire out of the wind and cold. He stacked the frypan on an angle, cut off a hunk of cold grease and melted it. Before it began to bubble hot, he'd already cut off the thick membranes and flattened several pieces of cowboy caviar out on a levelled stone. He tossed the testicles into a mixture of flour, salt and pepper, and flung them in the frying pan to watch them sizzle. They ate and sopped up the grease with stale cuts of sourdough bread, and passed around a canteen of mescal.

Roddy lit a rolled cigarette, and Sully melted snow in the frypan, tossed it out, and wiped it with a kerchief that had seen better days.

Cayo whistled a low tune, forlorn yet lovely while the other two men began to speak of things they'd wished they'd done in younger days. "But you've still got time, Cayo," Roddy said. Then they all went quiet with the sound of horses' hooves coming into the warmed space of the gorge.

Three horsemen approached, wearing slick black parkas with extra shoulder capes, wide-brimmed black hats with the front covered in fresh-powdered snow. Their hats were tipped low to cover their eyes, faces shadowed. All three men wore thick facial hair, two had mustaches and one had a short beard. The two men with the mustaches had cheeks the color of burning coals in an open hearth, obviously weathered. They did not dismount.

Cayo was suddenly wary. His senses sharp, on edge.

The ugliest man with a scar on his lip said, "I'm Sherriff Deveraux and these two men are my sworn deputies. We've been searching for a desperado named Bob Dalton. Murdered a whore, took her money, and stole a horse. Mean sonofabitch. Wanted for other crimes and misde-meanors against women. No guts to stand up against a man. We're tired and hungry and wouldn't mind camping here next to that welcoming fire. What do you say, gents?"

Roddy started to shake his head, but Cayo said, "Sure. But we just cleaned our pot, and got only bear grease and bread if you'd care to fry it."

"Sounds good to put with some pemmican we got off a dead Injun."

Cayo's ears perked up. Roddy stiffened slightly.

"Yeah. Dead on account of the Sherriff here shot him dead," the man hanging back on a roan said.

Cayo comprehended in that instant that these men were not who they said they were but outlaws and outliers. He made no sudden move but gently slipped a knife from its sheath at the side of his leg, and asked, "What crime was he guilty of?"

"Weren't no goddamned crime. He was Injun, that's all," said the same man.

"Ain't that enough?" asked the Sherriff, and spat on the ground.

"Alone and with a fine horse, a rifle and this here pemmican. Now all ours," the third man said.

Cayo saw that statement warn Roddy, who moved slow and careful. "I'll get the frypan from my saddle bag. Sully, you get the bear grease and bread from your horse." All of the gear was with Roddy, so Cayo knew he and Sully were free to make their moves. His men knew as he did, they were in danger.

All three kept talking softly as they shifted positions like a well-oiled machine, each in a different direction. The sheriff made a sudden move. Cayo flung the knife and it caught the Sherriff's throat. Sully spun away from his horse, aimed his pistol, and shot the man who had his gun out, seated on the roan. At the same time, Roddy swung the frypan from low to high and hit the third man square in the face. He fell from his horse, landing in the fire and started screaming. Roddy ran at him; hit him across the jaw and over the head until he stopped yelling.

When the three of them had relaxed again, Roddy said, "What now, Cayo?"

"He's no more a sheriff than I'm a king. He went for his shooter, and if'n them critters hadn'ta made their play now, they would've slit our throats in the night. Felt it in my bones."

"Bones? I'm bone weary but we have to bury them now," Roddy said.

"Bury? Hell. We dump them over the canyon, and each of us now owns a fine new horse to sell next town we come to," Cayo said.

"And that Indian pony? The pinto makes four—" Sully started to say.

"Sell her and split the profit. I'll take the paint horse for now, and try to soothe her." Cayo sauntered slowly towards the wild-eyed horse calling out in Spanish. He took hold of the tether, gently petted the horse, and then scratched with a bit more pressure in his fingertips. He leaned in towards the head. "*Escúchame, dulce*," he began, practically in a whisper, stroking the horse behind one ear. Cayo led her around in a tight circle; then stopped. "*Estás bien, chica.*" When he saw that the horse had calmed, he led her away from the fire and tied her to a tree, but not too close to the other horses.

Cayo heard Roddy call out, "Check they're not stolen army issue, Sully."

"What about the saddles?" Sully asked. "How about a hat?" he said, taking hold of one. Sure could use a new—"

Cayo whirled on him and grabbed the hat out of Sully's hands and tossed it in the fire. "I owe you a new one."

"The other two hats go over the side with the men. No use taking chances. The horses are even a bit of a risk, but I looked them over and there are no brands. Probably stolen. We'll worry over that tomorrow, but we'll need to curry and clean them up at first light."

Sully smiled as he walked back to the circle of fire. "No special markings, and sure enough these bastards had the pemmican and this." He held up a bone and bead chest plate. "Comanche, ya think?"

"Navajo," Cayo said.

"We'll breakfast on the loaf of dried meat, but the Indian souvenir goes with the saddles," Roddy said.

Sully tossed the pemmican to Roddy.

Roddy caught it and looked it over. "Got berries in it, along with grease. Well prepared."

Sully turned to Roddy. "Who do we report this to?"

"A priest in confession. This stays here. It goes no farther. It never happened, got it?" Roddy leaned down and started dragging one of the corpses.

As they rid themselves of the dead men, Sully said he thought he'd take one of the fine black riding coats, but Cayo shook his head. "No guns either. Easy to recognize. Throw them down the canyon and then we'll settle the horses."

"Cayo was right. That sheriff was no lawman. No star on him," Roddy said.

Sully removed all the bullets, and pitched the guns and rifles over the embankment. He looked in the pockets of the man he shot. "Well, lookie here," he said, holding up a paper. "They's wanted men after all. We done society a favor."

Roddy read the folded poster. "He's right, but no reward money." He handed it to Cayo. "Can you make out some words now?"

"A few. Thanks to you."

When they'd finished disposing the bodies, Roddy wrapped himself in a serape and a horse blanket, turned away from the fire.

Before Cayo fell into a deep sleep, he gazed up. "Strange sky," he said.

Roddy turned to take notice. "Moonbroch," he said.

"What?" Cayo asked, sleep in his voice.

"You know, when there's a hazy halo of cloud around the moon— probably bad weather tomorrow. Aye, t'will be," Roddy said, and banked the fire.

Sully was asleep and snoring instantly.

Cayo didn't sleep well. He dreamed of branding—searing hot iron into animal hide. Skin. The smell of burnt flesh and squeals of cattle, cruelty and torture. His head was full of conflicting thoughts—hot burning flesh of cattle. His mind took flight, enlivened by the smell of burnt hair in close proximity. He was an eagle with a huge wing span that carried both the recently dead men and the lost living.

***

In a semi-awake state, he spotted the Indian pony and its unshod hooves. Cayo recalled having left the Jicarilla village on his unshod horse. He was clothed in his Indian leggings of dressed deerskin. He had ridden many days to the town of Cerrillos, near Santa Fe. Images of the town came back to him. He had stolen clothes from a wash load strung out to dry in back of a well-built log home, running hell for leather as a dog barked a warning to wake the dead. Luckily the dog was tied or he'd have given chase. Cayo changed by a quick-moving stream and rode into a town some twenty miles away. He needed a hat, boots, and a saddle. He rode to a livery stable, where, speaking slowly and hesitantly so as not to indicate his unfamiliarity with English after so many years.

Cayo met Ben Star, a smithy with the skin as dark as midnight on a moonless night, and asked him for a job. Ben tried out Cayo, who exhibited ease and care with Ben's horses, so he hired Cayo, looking down at his feet covered in moccasins. Ben picked up a hoof on Cayo's horse. "First off, let's get this animal shod, or someone could take it for an Indian pony. You're going to need a saddle, too. You can work to pay one off. That is—ever ride seated in saddle?"

"Years ago," Cayo said.

"And here," Ben said, try these boots on for size. Got others if they don't fit. Sheriff gives them to me cheap—they're off the dead men he hangs. Got a problem with wearing a dead man's—"

"No problem, sir," Cayo said, reaching out. "It ain't that thery're dead man's, it's just that I ain't worn boots for some," he hesitated, "time."

Cayo sat on a tree stump and tried on the boots. It wasn't that they didn't fit, it was that his feet so unaccustomed to the constriction of the leather, pained him. What seemed even more torturous was that the boots came up to his calf and dug in like a sonofabitch.

"Take a while to get used to. Better wear some socks. Got those, too, but in need of a wash."

Cayo said he was grateful. "I'll work to pay for these—"

"You'll work all right, but not for no dead man's boots."

Ben Star showed him a stall he could bunk in, and said, "You eaten?"

Cayo licked his lips, but a sense of wounded pride kept him from answering he was starved, but what hurt worse than his growling stomach, were his feet squished into the confines of leather.

"Any way to soften these here things?" he asked, pointing to the scuffed, worn boots.

"Rain helps. Getting them soaked in a river and letting them dry on you, maybe."

"Taking them off would for sure," Cayo said, yanking them off.

Ben Star bent his head, looked him up and down. "Out back by the forge, you'll find a pan and some eggs to scramble up. Help yourself, but clean the pot—you can scorch it dry."

Cayo had never seen a free black man, but he figured a man is a man and if he had to work, best be with a hard-working man. That was where he needed to be. When he'd finally saved enough to buy boots that fit and a saddle, he decided to stay on and Star was fine with the decision. Cayo worked hard and began taking extra jobs so he could save enough to buy a rifle and scabbard, gun and holster, bullets and new clothes.

He stayed for about a year, long enough for his feet to become accustomed to wearing the boots. Then he left New Mexico and rode up to the high plains of Colorado on to Denver. It was 1871 and he worked at a construction site of a hotel being built called the Brown Palace Hotel. After the opening of the hotel he rode for an outfit moving cattle to Texas, and then skirted back to New Mexico. Two years had passed in the blink of an eye. He was lonely and missed New Mexico.

On the trip back, he suffered wild nightmares. He attributed these to the fact that he kept the dream catcher his grandmother had made for him hidden away in his saddlebag. Coyote rode by pink and tawny adobe outbuildings and four huge spreads: the Hermosa, the Buttes, the San Marcos and the Mariah. These huge *fincas,* estates side by side, were owned and operated by the three Martinez brothers and their sister, Barbara, who ran the Mariah for the brothers, but didn't own it. These vast spreads were situated outside of Cerrillos. He found work on Barbara's ranch, and was relieved to be hired quickly as he was carrying only dust and fluff in his pockets, and was tired and sore from being on the trail.

Coyote kept having bad dreams. At breakfast one morning, the men in the bunkhouse talked about the wild nightmares Coyote had the night before. At breakfast, Barbara Martinez served *huevos rancheros,* tacos and tamales and strong, wicked coffee with honey to sweeten its bitterness. She listened to the men talk about Coyote.

"Coyote, your dreaming keeps a man from getting a good night's sleep," Jose, a ranch hand, said, then added, maybe you should bunk in the barn. The owls don't mind if you wrestle yourself."

As if to emphasize the point, a barn owl hooted, a raspy, ghostly, eerie sound, so different than other owls. Coyote couldn't see the nocturnal bird of prey, but knew the spectral white animal lay in wait to quarry rodents. Still, it sent a shiver down his shoulders, and pitched his memory back to the cave, and his sisters.

Coyote sat at the long rectangular table after the men left. He was exhausted by the ghostly visitation of his sisters. What was worse, the dream conjured Red Willow bleeding to death in the snow. Was she alive?

There was an elfin Indian maiden of marrying age who helped Luisa, the cook on the Mariah's spread, who reigned supreme in the kitchen. The Indian girl, Utahna, was a Ute, and Coyote wondered how she'd gotten here. She did the cleaning up and odd jobs around for Barbara. He tried to steer clear of her, because she put him in mind of Red Willow, but noticed that she was somehow always in his path, making herself not only visible but available. Then one day, he found out why she was in Cerrillos. Barbara's head man Jose had won her in a gambling debt. The shock of the tale turned Coyote's stomach. How could anyone gamble away the life of another into slavery? Jose probably didn't even notice how comely she was, just used her at will.

"Coyote, you're daydreaming is going to get this coffee poured right into your lap," Barbara said.

Everyone laughed, and Coyote tilted his cup, and Barbara filled it. The other men scattered, but he lingered just to get a few more moments in Barbara's pleasing company. She told him of a holy shrine that had consecrated dirt on the floor of a blessed ante-room attached to an old chapel built in the 1600s. She'd heard that the Indians and Mexicans went there to take some of this dirt for special blessings for crippled children. The hole never went deep, yet somehow it was always full of the red-brown dirt, the same dirt used to build *adobes*.

As miracles happened, the sanctuary grew in fame for the local gentry. Barbara herself walked with special boots. Her father had had them made in St. Louis to straighten her feet, but nothing worked. "Until," she said, lifting her skirt and showing a normal pair of feet in normal shoes, "I was cured by Our Blessed Lady. My mother placed the holy dirt on my feet. She prayed every day for months, and then finally one day, when I was stepping into the bathtub, my mother grabbed hold of one of my feet and screamed: 'It's perfect, *Santa Madre querida, gracias. Mil gracias.*' She fell to the floor and cried. When she stopped crying, she took my boots and made a pilgrimage to the shrine to pray for me and give thanks. My mother walked all the way to Chimayo. When she arrived at the sanctuary, she dropped down and continued from the entranceway along the winding road to the chapel on bloody knees. She'd brought my special boots to the chapel and left them there for all to see as proof of the Virgin's powers."

Coyote didn't think he was born Catholic, but he had believed all the wonderful things the Apache had told him about the Great Spirit and walking the Milky Way at the end of life's journey.

"If you go there," Barbara said, "you can get the holy dirt and rub a little on your temples. Perhaps your demons will leave you. You can confess all of your past sins, and the priest, Father Gonzaga, who lives there and cares for the chapel and the grounds, will give you absolution. The old mission is called El Santuario de Chimayo. I can take you there."

"I'll go," he said. "I'll do anything, but I don't think no priest or no Santa Maria can cure the kind of inward sickness I have."

"You must have faith," and with those words, Barbara did something uncharacteristic. She brushed the hair out of Coyote's eyes. She rubbed his temples as if to sooth the nightmares away. All he could think of was, *Here I go again, falling off the ledge of the world for a girl I've no business even looking at.*

He wanted to go there before he took off with the cattle run, he wanted to be forgiven. He wanted to see the holy shrine of Chimayo with Barbara. The next day before dawn, Barbara rode off with him. She left everything prepared with the cook, Luisa, saying she needed to see the priest and get some more holy dirt for her feet as they were starting to hurt her again. Since it was still dark out, she was taking Cayo with her as an escort. They rode climbing until they came to a narrow winding road. The cottonwoods were waving a welcome, and he felt an astonishing peace as soon as he entered the grounds. He sat for a while on a rough-hewn stone bench outside under a canopy of morning stars. A savory sweet something was in the air, what was it? Red, white and yellow honeysuckle crawled its way up and around the altar where he sat. The air was thick, but a sensation of peace and well-being had taken hold of him. Barbara had gone to find the priest. Coyote stayed outside so he could sleep till she got back, and laid down on a stone bench, his saddlebag for a pillow. He was deep in a dreamless sleep when she returned, but there was no priest with her.

She saw surprise in his face and answered it with, "Padre Gonzaga is in the church. Light a candle and go to the confession box. Relieve your guilt. Tell him your sins. He will forgive you."

"But can I forgive myself?" He stood up and stretched.

"I don't know what your sin is, but whatever it is it's a heavy burden you've carried for a long time. Seek redemption. Reconcile yourself to God."

"You're so darn pretty in this early light, you know that?"

"Go now. And pray. I will also pray and then we will get the holy dirt. I have brought my mother's ring case to put it in so you will keep it with you."

"Why are you so good to me?"

"It is my calling."

"Your what?"

"I'll explain later. *Vamonos.*"

After they returned to the hacienda, he still had brutal thoughts and scene flashes in day-dreams, but the nightmares had stopped, and it seemed for good. Every once in a while, he dipped his finger into the holy dirt and tapped his temple on both sides to keep the nightmares in check, and just to make sure, he tacked up his grandmother's dream catcher on his bunk. He made certain to pack both items in his saddle bag when he left for the cattle round-up.

When he and the crew got back from the round-up, even before he took care of his horse or stowed his gear, he went to see Barbara to thank her for everything she'd done to help him.

Barbara wasn't in the kitchen, in fact she was no longer there. Luisa said that Barbara had taken the veil and entered the convent. "Didn't you know she was preparing herself to become a bride of Christ?"

"No, Ma'm, I just know she's beautiful and a good person. She cares about people. Why would she close herself away like that?"

"Perhaps she loves God more than she could ever love a man." Luisa moved a heavy frying pan from the front burner to the back. She took a wooden spoon and started stirring—a punctuation to Coyote's talk with her—it was over.

He took it as a sign that since Barbara was no longer there, it was time for him to move on again. Sometimes, if he slept indoors for long periods, he felt his lungs constricting, and thoughts of his dead sisters, Red Willow being carried off, and Little Fawn seemed to drown him in his own fluids. Then he'd dash outside, feeling relief only breathing the fresh air outdoors.

He left the ranch and went back to Denver where he worked as a dish washer in the Brown Palace Hotel until someone planted the thought in his ear to go panning for gold. But he was a drifter and the idea of digging in a cave or sifting pans of sand and pebbles in streams just didn't appeal to him.

He had picked up Spanish and good lessons in roping and tying, steering cattle in drives. So after leaving the Indians and Mexicans, Coyote lived among the Whites, but was often taken for a half-breed. Life was rough, and he began to think how it would have been for his sisters if they had also lived with the Indians and had been released into White society again, only to be spurned and treated like scum. Little Fawn had been right to stay with the People.

He found work as a cowhand and tracker for a mean cattle boss named Rufus Ahearn. Four of his cowboys, including Coyote, were taking a small herd of cattle to a train depot a hundred miles away. One night, two of the men returned to the ranch, the other man was going to look for any scattered calves the next morning. They left Coyote out on the trail with Ahearn. They had built a small fire, eaten, and then Ahearn started swilling liquor. Coyote watched as Ahearn took swig after swig from his bottle of hooch. "Yous all look alike—ya hear what I'm saying, boy? Lazy bunch of thieving Injuns—" How many times had Coyote heard that from Ahearn's mouth?

Ahearn tripped backwards over a log and fell splat on his ass, somehow without spilling a drop or losing his grip on the bottle, but something flashed around his neck, and he righted it.

Coyote figured Ahearn to be quite drunk. He didn't flinch, but the fall must have injured his tailbone because he went down on top of a rock. As Ahearn continued to heap insults, he began a story that at first Coyote couldn't keep up with. He raised his hand, and Ahearn slowed his talking, wanting Coyote to understand every drunken word he was spewing.

"I said, you heathen Apache brave, I raped an Injun girl—a skinny slip of a thing—no good for nothing much less sticking it to her. She was apart off from her people, alone gathering berries. I made sure there weren't no other Injun woman with her—they's usually in twos or threes. But this here one was by her lonesome self, sad-looking thing—crying to make your heart sore. No brave to protect her—on the outskirts of the village. Easy pickings. I seen her and watched her like I was out hunting small game. I got me some Apache ways too—can move like a ghost, I can, sometimes just fading myself into the landscape—like one of them critters." He lifted a locket from inside his shirt, and then put it inside again. Coyote thought he recognized it. The thought of that locket touching Ahearn's vile skin turned Coyote's stomach, but he was more Apache than he knew. He waited.

"This one, she did water hauling, and found sticks for the cook fire. I stole up behind her and got a choke-hold on her—she passed out on me giving a poke to her. When she came to, fought me like a tiger she did before I run my knife in under her ribs to the hilt. The yowling and crying bitch went slack on me. Like nothing mattered any more, not even my giving it to her. I did her a favor and when I'd done with her, slit her throat to make sure she was dead, that's how I got this here locket. Didn't need a scalp. Took this instead." Ahearn held up the locket. "Funny thing, though, seems like her parents was white folks. Look here." He opened the locket, but Coyote knew before glancing at it whose parents they were, and they were not Red Willow's.

"Whites for parents or not, she was nothing but a dark savage. Why my dog had more manners," he slurred. He took a long pull on the whiskey, and nodded off.

Coyote had heard all he wanted to hear from this brute. Coyote would wait, and when Ahearn woke again, Coyote would kill him.

Coyote drew up tighter, and wrapped his arms around his legs, put his forehead on his knees and rocked himself to a keening rhythm and repeating over and over, Red Willow, Red Willow, my wife, my love, Red Willow, Red Willow, Red Willow. As a captive, he thought, she would have lived, even thrived, but knowing she'd been violated and savagely killed was a thing he could not, would not abide.

He looked up when Ahearn groaned. Coyote spat into the fire. He waited. He took the spurs off his boots and laid them aside. When Ahearn was snoring and his breathing had rendered a pitch and timbre that signaled the drunk was passed out in a stupor, Coyote moved with stealth away from the small bivouac, carrying Ahearn's saddle and boots toward the arbor where their horses grazed. Coyote saddled his own horse and gathered his gear: scabbard rifle, and canteen. He tied it up with his bedroll. Next, he dug a hole and threw in some of Ahearn's things, but kept the saddle, rifle, and pistol. Coyote sweated profusely when he'd finished.

He undid the hobble, removing the stake in the ground and was just about to smack Ahearn's horse's rump smartly and send the mare running off into the shadowy night, when he had second thoughts. He checked to see there were no markings. He re-saddled the horse and tied the bit rope and reins to his own horse. Coyote circled back to the camp. In the man's drunken stupor, Coyote hog-tied him and took whatever money Ahearn had and tucked it into a shirt pocket. Coyote figured it was his due. Ahearn started to regain consciousness, Coyote picked up Ahearn's Colt pistol, knocking him senseless with the gun butt. Then Coyote slipped the chain and locket from the drunk's head, and held it over the fire to burn off as much of the devil as he could. He wiped the locket on his pants, put it in the breast pocket of his shirt and buttoned it.

He doused the fire, but from the outer vestiges, he pinched some ashes in his fingers, faced the moon, and knelt. Whorls of smoke poured skyward. Just beyond the ring of fire, he sprinkled ash onto his head, drew a line across his forehead and one down each cheek. He scattered the rest round him. He prayed, then removed any sign he'd ever been there. He wanted to scalp the pig, but thought better of it, so he left that place behind him, the man cinched, ready to be skewered for any beast of prey, human or animal wanting a piece.

He rode for about a mile, jumped down from his horse and tethered him. Then he knelt and howled to the moon. He kept howling and the night animals howled back. But there was nothing for it—nothing could erase the image of that pig Ahearn with his precious Red Willow, and he had a new understanding and respect for her lover, Starfall, who had tried to save Red Willow from the Comanche warrior. She had loved his Red Willow as he had, maybe even more, for she had sacrificed her own life.

Coyote rode back to the camp, Ahearn was coming out of it, the look on his face comical, if it wasn't so pathetic.

"Vengeance is mine, sayeth the Lord," Coyote yelled. "Ain't that in your Bible?" He rode around and around the hog-tied man, at a dizzying pace, yelping and yelling like the Apache he was. He jumped down off his horse, knocked Ahearn off balance with the butt of his rifle, counting coup, and tossed the rifle aside, grabbing the man by his hair pulled his head backwards, and with a flash of his knife, took his first scalp. All the while, Ahearn screamed mercy, screamed for his life, blood pouring down his face.

Coyote yelled for him to shut up. In a hushed voice, he said, "You killed my wife, and I'm going to cut your heart out."

Over the hills, he rode, covering his tracks, using occasional switch-backs, climbing rocky outcroppings, sweeping large swaths with pine brush to hide his tracks. He left false trails: a broken tree branch, a trampled bush, a dropped piece of rag Ahearn used to clean his rifle. Coyote killed a rabbit with a simple snare and used its blood to throw off his and his horse's scent. He cut the rabbit in pieces, dredged the raw meat in pepper and dropped the bait at intervals to dissuade any dog from sniffing further. He collected horse droppings; backtracked and left the dung in a cove with hoof prints leading in the wrong direction. He tied Ahearn's horse, led his own horse forward for some distance, and then with practiced precision, walked his horse backwards over its own hoof marks in a sandy trace.

Coyote tied up Ahearn's horse once again with his own and traveled in streambeds for miles, crosscutting through bottomland. He traversed unmarked roadways, trod in the river shallows and crossed coulees from side to side, and rode ancient turnings, winding along forgotten paths. For three days with just the sound of the two horses' hooves pounding the earth and airstream rustling through the trees for company, he moved west, leaping over an arroyo until he came to a culvert and made his way around it. He switched horses so his weight would be evenly distributed and he wouldn't tire his own horse, Wind. When finally he crossed a deep gulch of standing water, he followed a small stream until he reached a bigger body of fresh moving water. Then he halted and surveyed the land. In high grass in a stand of cottonwoods, he pushed the horses forward no more. He watered and fed them each a handful of oats, and let them eat some grass. He ate a piece of hardtack and some pemmican and drank huge amounts of water. He tied and knotted the reins on a nearby low poplar branch, pulled the saddle down and rested next to where it fell in the shade of a sycamore.

At dawn he mounted again and rode long into the night. Coming up the leeward side of a hill, he climbed out of a ravine until he reached a plateau, paused, and dismounted.

Long silences roared except for the swish and swoosh of wind blowing leaves asunder at his feet. Coyote heard a suite of notes, a swoop overhead, and then an owl in the distance, hopping away on one foot. Clever, Coyote thought. A long-eared owl used a ruse to lead Coyote away from its nesting eggs. "I'm hungry enough to eat them," he said aloud to the owl. "Better come back, or I will."

When the owl returned, he swept away the forest duff, scooped up a handful of clay and flung it at the owl, who immediately soared back to the nest. Still holding the horse's reins, he sat down. He shuffled the duff around and measured its depth—two fingers—like his own deep emotional wounds. Cicatrices within himself as yet unhealed. He harkened back to warrior chants that had sundered around him after his first buffalo hunt when he'd saved Mbai". Surrounding him and within him, there had been a temporal, corporeal existence fathomed of live beings, but also of spirits from other times in other divides. That night so long ago had held magic. He almost felt redeemed by the life he'd saved and on the brink of reparation for the lives he'd taken.

***

When he gathered his strength, he built a fire. He sat a long time looking into the blaze. He tossed in Ahearn's scalp and watched it burn. He wafted the smoke toward him bowing his head, repeating incantations from another time, another life left behind.

He took off his boots, undid his belt buckle and took off his pants. He set them aside and tossed his shirt on top. Then from his saddlebag he took out the last pair of breeches that grandmother had made him, and the moccasins Red Willow had given him on their wedding day. He'd kept them all this time, worn, disheveled, and useless. He pulled on the breeches. Grandmother had sewn fringe on the bottoms with sinew, thinking he might grow even more, and he smiled with the thought of her trying to make them last a little longer.

His crisp, live, dramatic, internal turmoil sizzled outward to the flames and flashes of burning logs. The splintered wood poured smoke into the air, heavy with the scent of pinesap, small sage twigs, jimson brush and the bay he'd used for kindling. He stood, stripped and beheld his discarded leather breeches in his hands. Then he threw them onto the fire, knowing this part of his life was over, forever.

He began to chant in his breechclout. He ripped this from his body and threw it on the fire. He began a dance, circling and moving with his arms extended as if flying to his own music around the fire. Only sounds and utterances, but no distinguishable words—no diction, no speech, not any recognizable linguistic echo other than guttural noises produced by tongue against palate, upon the roof, in back of the front teeth, delivered of the throat, through the mouth. Tearing his moccasins from his feet he threw them on top of the pyre and danced on the balls of his feet, his calf muscles flexed and taut, his torso forward, erupting backward, keening. His chant sundered the night with volleys of sobs and plaintiff cries.

When his dance ceased, he took hold of his knife. He stood in a wide stance and faced the four points, all directions from where the wind is born. He held his arms straight overhead. "I am Connor no more. Dinizhi is no more. Mbá is no more. Coyote is no more. In my heart, I am now Cayo Bradley. Invisible until he will be no more." With sawing cuts he chopped at his long hair until he became just a no-name cowboy.

He slept, and in the morning, he bathed in a swift-running cold creek, dressed, and rode south to Mexico where he sold Ahearn's saddle, horse and rifle for gold pesos, a pair of ivory and silver-handled pistols, and a

Mexican tooled belt with holsters fitting two guns. He bought chaps that in Colorado or New Mexico would have cost him a month's salary. Then he bought himself two bottles of mescal. When he came to his senses a day later, he was asked to leave the cantina. He had broken the bed, a chair, the window and one of the empty bottles of mescal over the patron's head when the owner tried to restrain him from breaking anything else. Cayo paid the patron what he owed for the mess, asked for directions to the bathhouse, went for a bath, a shave and a decent haircut. He bought a new shirt, taking the locket out of the old one, and putting it over his head, tucking it inside his shirt. He gave his old shirt to the patron of the cantina.

Cayo made his way back through Nogales into Arizona where he stayed for a few months till he made his way back to Santa Fe by way of Cerrillos, wanting to know if he was or wasn't a wanted man with a price on his head. He loved the Rio Grande and the feel of the wind in his hair from the hilltops.

Back in Cerrillos he rode slowly through the sleepy town up to the Post Office. Cayo saw what he was looking for: a weathered and torn Wanted Poster.

$500 REWARD!
Disappearance and probable Murder!
In accordance with an order
of the: City Council of Cerrillos,
a reward of Five Hundred Dollars
is hereby issued for the detection
and conviction of the person or persons
who, on the 20th ultimo, are in connection
with the disappearance and possible murder

of Rufus Ahearn, cow herder,
aged approximately 40 years.

Samuel R. Cotton, Mayor

Cayo wondered how long it had been up as he ripped the poster down from where it was tacked up on a column outside the Post Office, folded it and put it inside his shirt. He rode around the town looking for other posters, but there were none. He turned his horse and headed out of the town of Cerrillos in the direction of Santa Fe.

On the opposite side of Santa Fe, he rode toward the sleepy town of Parcel Bluffs. About an hour later, he saw a horse and cabriolet go out of control from the driver's grip, and although he chased after them to try to catch up, they'd been running too far ahead. The horse got hooked up in sage brush and low junipers, crashing far from a stand of cottonwoods where every inch of land was covered with dust. The driver had managed to save the buggy from completely tipping over by shifting her weight and some of the gear and sacks carried alongside in the second front seat.

Cayo all but flew off his horse, and put his back to the buggy, lifting it till it righted and he could toss the sacks in.

Out of breath, the driver managed finally to say, "How can I ever thank you? I've not seen you around here. Where you from?"

"From parts unknown, Ma'm," he said, tipping his hat, searching his memory for every polite thing his mother'd taught him, and a few Indian manners as well, but he didn't look her directly in the eyes.

"At least tell me your name, stranger, so I can return the favor one day."

"Cayo—" He thought fast, but not fast enough to think of a Bible name. "Huh? Why it's Cayo, Ma'am, Cayo that's me."

"Much obliged, Mr. Cayo what?"

He hesitated. "Bradley."

"I'm Zora Pederson. Our place isn't far from here, if you'd like to come and refresh yourself."

Cayo thought a minute, stepping into a fresh name, trying on his new identity. Good as any name, he guessed.

"I'm heading to town for a bath and shave. Maybe get me some refried beans."

"After that? Plan on staying long?"

"Depends."

"On?"

"I'm trying out the town to see if'n she fits. Have to eat— I'll have to find work to pay for it."

"Eat with us. Come tomorrow. Dinner's early. Come by before dusk. Straight as an arrow, straight along this road. Ask anyone for Captain Pederson's ranch."

Arrow was the word that triggered his thoughts. Had he stayed with the Apache he'd be fighting other tribes, and Whites—but these had been his people before. Could he ever really settle in with them again, knowing what he knew, knowing how honorable and kind and religious the Indian people were?

The lady had been babbling all the time he'd been lost in thought— he missed everything she'd said.

"Hey, you listening to me?"

"Yes, Ma'm." He yanked on the reins to pull his horse's head up from grazing.

"I said you can't miss our spread, as the crow flies. See there, ahead," and she pointed in the direction. "My husband can always use another willing hand. Drives cattle. Know anything about herding?"

More than I care to, he thought, but answered, "Some." He pictured Ahearn's head snapping back before he'd taken his scalp.

"Get up, get on," Mrs. Pederson said to the horse with a snap of the reins. "See you tomorrow, Cayo Bradley."

She'd gotten some distance, then turned and smiled.

He tipped his hat. "My, oh my," he said under his breath. She waved. *Wonder how she'd have reacted to an Apache pulling her out of that ditch?*

He turned his horse and headed for town.

Chapter Nineteen

Ensconced in St. Louis

On a quiet Sunday after church, Darby changed her frock into something more suitable for the garden. That afternoon, Darby sat in a wicker chair with a chintz pillow behind her back and read in the paper that a year before she'd arrived in St. Louis in 1874, Montgomery Ward had already started selling to rural customers by mail.

"Look, Aunt Bea," Darby said pointing to the advertisement. "Do you think I could have some things shipped to Papa and the boys from Montgomery Ward? I'd sure like to see their faces when they get packages for Christmas from me." And how would she get one to Cayo? She wouldn't be able to send it to the Pederson ranch. What if that Hanna saw it, would she be so spiteful as to take and open it and not give it to Cayo? The only way she could write him was through Fern. That's exactly what she'd do.

Then something else caught her eye. Darby read aloud from the paper that Susan B. Anthony tried to vote!

"Nonsense," Aunt Bea said, with an authority belying her ignorance.

"Please put the paper down. I must talk to you seriously, dear. Your father wants you to consider staying here in St. Louis and making a life for yourself. You could teach school until you marry. I know just someone who's looking for a wife."

"Dear, dear Aunt Bea, I must talk to you seriously, too. I don't think your Pastor Erik even knows I exist on the same planet he's on, much less belong to the same congregation and church!

"There's something I think you should know. A letter came from your father this week along with this." Aunt Bea handed a pure white envelope to Darby.

"Why, it's from Hanna. When did it arrive? I'd know that chicken scratch handwriting anywhere." Darby turned the envelope over and looked at her aunt quizzically. "It's been opened."

"Forgive me, darling, but as I said, I had news from your father and I didn't want you to be shocked, so I opened your mail."

"You did what? But why? Why would you do that?"

"You see, dear, it's a wedding announcement."

"From Hanna? She's getting married?"

"It seems that your friend is already married. She must have given in to temptation and your, well, your fellow Cayo, well ... Hanna found herself in a family way. They're married now. At least he did the honorable—"

Darby stood and ran from the room, knocking over the small sewing table and a lamp.

After a while, there was a light knock on the door. "Go away, Aunt Bea," Darby said. "Have some compassion and let me be."

"It's Aunt Mary, darling. Please let me in."

Darby opened the door. Mary handed her a handkerchief and Hanna's envelope and Darby blanched white as the paper. "How could she have opened my mail? How did she dare?"

"Come, dear," Mary said, "sit on the bed." Aunt Mary also sat on the bed. She sighed and without preamble began her story. "Years ago, I was betrothed to a young man. Uncle Cyrus did some investigating and it seems that the man was a seeker of fortune. He was known in the nearby town of Dupo, Illinois. He'd broken the heart of a young heiress;

swindled her father, and left the poor girl heartbroken with a ruined reputation, and destitute. I was saved."

"Were you? Saved from what? Not spinsterhood. So what if he was the scoundrel they say he was. You loved him, didn't you? You thought he could make you happy, didn't you?"

"Stop. Now. Please. I don't know for sure. I'll never know, will I? But my family tried to protect me from being taken advantage of and save me heartache. I have to believe it was for the best."

"Not yours, surely. Perhaps the family's best."

"Don't be cruel. You're hurt and you—"

"I'll never go back home. Never. How could I see her with him? A baby? Who would have thought Hanna would have thrown herself at him like that. He loved me. I know he did."

"Love is not the only thing that matters in choosing a life's mate."

"It isn't? What is? Money? Position? What's a life without love? What is a union of souls without love? Answer me! I am in a state of surrender. There's nothing more for me to fight for, is there?"

"I didn't know you were battling anything?"

"I should have gone back sooner."

"Destiny. It wasn't yours. It was not mine." Mary took the handkerchief from Darby, who had wrung it into a rope. She flattened it out, got up, and dipped it into the basin of water on the dresser. She washed Darby's tear-stained face and said gently, "I survived. You will, too, my child."

When her Aunt Mary left the room, Darby thought, Ah, so this is the beginning. The quiet sound of loneliness. Unexpectedly, she was overcome with the sensation of wanting to make love. She pulled back the curtains and flung open the window. There hung in the sky was a bleached skull moon. How in God's name would she conquer this hunger? Her hands instinctively moved to her breasts. She closed her eyes and it was like feeling Cayo's hands on her. She ripped her hands away from her bodice and yelped, a wounded animal. She refused to give in to this craving. She slammed the window shut—it rattled like wind through hollow bones—what a squall must sound like on that faraway moon. She drew back the curtain and sat on the bed. What was her fate now? Where would her fortune lead her? Certainly not back into the arms of the man she loved. But a feeling of lightness stole into her heaving chest, and she understood that the one thing she could never, would never succumb to was the feeling of grief without hope. Somewhere on this planet, she'd find a chance and she'd gamble on it. She felt her mother hovering over her. Hadn't it been her expressed desire that Darby get an education to better herself in this world? This then was what she was meant to do. For now. She wouldn't, couldn't wallow in sorrow, and she sure as hell wasn't going to waste money on a Christmas gift for a married man!

Chapter Twenty

Wild Things

Cayo woke thinking of Darby. How long had she been gone now? He heard the toots of a saw-whet owl. He sat up and listened to the call come through the window. Sure enough the toot, toot, toot. He thought he'd spotted one while riding along a ridge a week ago in the Sangre de Cristo wilderness, but seemed too far afield. He wondered if they nested in the mountains.

Cayo worked all day hanging fence for a corral about a mile from the homestead. He kept at it all day, wanting to finish it, so he could do a more interesting job tomorrow. It was close to six in the evening when he called a halt to it.

He took off his shirt, washed his face and neck at the trough. He grasped the brown soap off the lip ledge of the trough and lathered up, rinsed, and dripping, doused his chest and arms, armpits. He lathered up and as the soap and water spumed and frothed, he thought of naught but Darby, forming her image in his mind. Pop! He burst a pretty bubble. He dried himself with his shirt, hung it over his shoulder, and walked to the bunkhouse where he changed into clean clothes. Cayo asked Harry, one of the gaff boys, handy with a hook and rope, if he was headed over to the chuck room. They sauntered out of the bunkhouse together talking about the day—Harry said he'd rounded up some strays, but Cayo didn't speak. What could he say about what had gone on at the corral? Weren't a thing to say about busting your hump putting up a post and rail fence.

Then he remembered there'd been a wild little mustang Cayo had his eye on when the herd had been brought in the day before yesterday and he asked Harry about her. About to leave, Harry said that the horse couldn't be broken.

Cayo smiled. "Bet I could've broke her, but I was out hanging fences."

"Bet you could've. Never seen anyone stay a horse, or break one like you. Almost like your legs are part of the horse's body," Harry said, and shook his head.

"Couldn't put it better myself. Exactly. Me—a part of the horse."

"Wild things know each other, I suppose," Harry said.

Strange, how a word like *wild* signaled in Cayo a vivid picture of Hanna. She loved taming wild stray dogs and seeing the mustangs. Two things, then, that they had in common: the love of wild things and horses. He pictured her with her hat tipped forward; eyes squinted against the sun, and her gloved hands holding on to the fence. She always seemed to be around, sitting on the fence watching when he was trying to stay on a bucking horse. She was often there, too, when horses were taken one by one into the small arena, some being led by a lead rope, ankles tied above the hooves, and slowly trotted around until finally made to lie down. Hanna could be such a little viper at times, but when it came to horses, her face glowed with some inner calm that appeared to Cayo to be a sign of contentment. The only times he saw the girl without the bristly coat of protection she often wore.

When Cayo had a horse down and gained the animal's trust, he'd stroke him, pet him and speak softly to him. Sometimes, the horse had already been saddled, and took the rider for a bucking ride. Once he'd gotten thrown and smacked his shoulder against the fence post. Hanna had gotten to him first, to see how badly he was hurt. Another thing they had in common, getting hurt by people and circumstances.

Harry ate a piece of fry bread, then picked the meat off a rabbit haunch and shoved it inside a biscuit. He wiped his hands on the seat of his pants.

Cayo looked at the food on the table, picking at this and that.

"What's the matter with my food? Ain't good enough?" Russ one of the hands asked.

"Nah. Smells great, but I'm not all that hungry." Cayo said.

"Oh, you're hungry all right—just not for food. You're the last one. Guess everybody'll be spending pay and the night in town, it being Independence Day and all," Grant the cook said.

"Not me. Lost nothing there I got to look for," Cayo said.

"Ain't you making a plate and setting a spell? Got apple pie. Miss Hanna made it with cinnamon."

"No time, Grant," Cayo said and winked. "I'm a man on the move this evening."

Cayo pocketed two biscuits, picked up a haunch of rabbit and walked out, eating his dinner on the way to the stable to saddle his horse. When he reached the barn, he stopped and thrust a dipper into a bucket of water, rinsed his mouth out and spat. He repeated the gesture a second time, but the slight taste of the Javel used to disinfect it soured his stomach on top of the wolfed-down meal.

He walked on, reached the stable and waited a few minutes for his eyes to adjust to the light. He approached his horse Wind's stall, and said, "Whoa, Nlch'í, *soy yo*— Mbá. *Hola, lindo. Yo te quiero como siempre, pero en estos días no tenía tiempo para verte, y mandé el muchacho para cuidarti. Veo que hizo un buen trabajo. Espero que te sientas mejor.*"

Stepping back from the horse somewhat and patting its neck, he inspected Wind's currycombed coat. Yes, he thought Harry had done a good job of grooming. Later, when the boy had told him how beautiful the horse looked, Cayo remembered flipping two bits, flashing with light in an upwards spin, and the boy catching it midair.

He saddled the horse and led him out before mounting up. He left the ranch at a slow trot. Riding away, he looked toward the Sangre de Cristos Mountains and wondered if they felt as stirred by him, as he did seeing them. Gazing at the mountains, he recognized he was not apart from them, nor they from him, but rather the two were as one, both united, belonging each to the moment, to each other in the mystery of Nature. The evening was pure and sweet as Darby's skin. With the full moon rising and the sun setting, and just a handful of twinkling stars, Cayo set out to mark his 25th birthday. In his heart he didn't feel like celebrating, not at all like having fun, no siree, as Captain Pederson would say. He just wanted to forget there was a moon, a sun and stars, and a girl named Darby who lived under them in a place he couldn't even spell.

He remembered nothing of his time in town, or the ride back to the ranch, nor the fact that he'd fallen into his bunk in a drunken stupor, until he woke with a start and smacked his forehead on the bunk above his. He was looking for a cup of water he'd put by his bedside, knowing he'd wake with a severe thirst.

"Well, lookie here what the cat drug in." Cayo shook his head, reached for the tin cup of water and downed it almost all in one gulp.

Hanna sat on his bunk bed in what Cayo thought was a pose he'd seen in a girlie magazine. Not a stitch on her. Cayo looked around, reached down, picked up a bundle on the side of the narrow bed and tossed Hanna her clothes. He looked at them, but something was wrong.

"Thought you had eyes for Ben? Are we involved in something I ain't quite privy too?" he said, still rubbing his head.

"Figured you'd be needing some physical comfort now that Darby's up and left you for good," she said.

"I got plenty physical making myself sick at my stomach with all that hooch I downed."

"I said comfort, not getting sick."

"And I said I got comforted when I threw up so bad, but that's not half what I'm going to do now." With that, he leaned over and puked into the spittoon.

"Guess you really ought to get some rest. But by the way you rode me, buckeroo, I thought you were cured," Hanna said, lifting her hair off her neck and letting it fall again.

"Wipe the smug off your face, Miss Hanna. You must've had a bad dream. If I was with anyone, it weren't you."

"I don't care if you called out another name, you rode me, cowboy."

"See that was a bad dream." He flicked his thumb toward the door. "Don't mean no disrespect, Miss Hanna, but get your sass and your ass out my bunkhouse." The smell of vomit and piss mixed with Hanna's perfume and sex was sickening. He wanted a bath, or at the very least to throw himself in the water troth out back of the stable.

"You can drop the *Miss*, now we've been intimate, and remember it's my Daddy's bunkhouse."

The light of day was making its presence through the narrow aspen-framed window, though Cayo still felt the reverberations of the moon and moonshine. He squinted to keep her face in focus. "Yes Ma'am. Sure is your Daddy's bunkhouse, but while I'm still riding shotgun over his herds, get off my bunk."

With more haughtiness than he'd ever seen her display, she reached for her robe, and stepped into her slippers.

That's what's wrong—they ain't day clothes.

At the door she turned, and let the robe fall to one side, exposing her breast, before pulling it closed. "I could have you horse-whipped for violating me."

"Miss Hanna, you've got that turned clear around, just like that head of yours. I was in no condition to know who you were or where I was, but I do remember hurting so bad wanting Darby's legs wrapped around me. Guess your Daddy's going to have to put some of that barbed wire he's so fond of smack around the bunkhouse. You're some kind of rustler—trying to steal a branded animal."

"Ah, so then you did take her—"

"I ain't never said that—all's I said was I hurt with wanting her. Now get."

She put her hand on the latch. "Don't treat me mean, Cayo, you'll be sorry if you do."

"I don't hold kindly to threats." He rubbed his bleary eyes.

"No threat. That's a promise."

As Hanna slammed the door on her way out, Cayo shook his head with shame. How he wished he could take back having said anything at all about Darby. And just what was that little molly-cat Hanna up to, he wondered.

He went for a ride. What had he remembered of last night? In the late evening of yesterday, the rain poured off his hat brim. A waterslide gushed down narrow canyon shoots of his oilskin parka and into the creases where little flooded gullies formed. His gloves were soaked through, the reins squished if he drew them in tight. He wished the rain could wash away his dread, but knew it wouldn't. He didn't care. Not for the wind, not for the rain, not for the mud, nor for the flash floods in the arroyos. He only cared about the letter he was writing in his head.

"D for Darby, my little darlin'," he said. "I'm learning to write." Somehow his brain got stuck on the letter D and so his brain's pencil moved along the empty page of his heart. "Dark out. I miss the bright days when you was here—miss you 'cause the dawn light no longer brings any hope of seeing you at the dry-goods store—does it even exist without you? Dazed every daybreak—wallowing in pity: a debtor, confined to prison with no doorway out. No way to dispel this dread for I despise my life—it ain't no life—all's I feel is death—I'm deaf to the howls of the wind." And with that Cayo let out a yowl, and a run of coyotes called back to him in their crazy kind of singing. He called out, "Whatcha all doing out in the rain, anyways?"

When the pack of desert wolves quieted and their echoes died, his brain picked up where it had left off: *Deceived by your parting, I'm a slain deer, an arrow through my lungs as I run, bleeding, wanting to deliver myself dead to your doorstop.*

I depended on you. I ain't been with no woman till now, but I swear I was dead drunk last night or that little bitch is lying. Did that she-devil Hanna come to me in the bunkhouse while the others were out carousing, having a high time in town? Why didn't I stay in town with them? Shit. She come to me, but I could've sworn it weren't real, just a dream, and I knowed for sure. I called you, Darby, oh no! Did I enter her with want and wanting and wanting you?

Cayo's mind letter-writing stopped. He leaned on the horn of his saddle. Horny, that's what he'd been, and should have done something about it with a woman in town. *Cristo.*

"*Caramba*," he whispered to Wind with the shadow of remembrance overtaking him, as if the horse, savvy and smart, understood with his neighing and whinnying, and shook an affirmative with his head to each and every phrase Cayo spoke. His heart's tender and weary story poured forth. He started to remember. He recounted to himself the vile actions the previous night, overwhelmed by shame. Sick and dirty, he had violated Hanna. He recalled blood smeared on her body, not his but hers.

She'd taken hold of his shirt to wipe it, but that didn't deter him from his gruesome purpose: a hungered animal that tore up her insides with an insatiable hunger for Darby. He had yelled Darby's name as if he stood on a mountain top calling the Great Spirit to forgive him. There was no forgiveness for every unforgiving and brutal thrust. He had poked her violently until he'd wailed and whooped, wild and untamed, the smell of blood. He saw the corners of her mouth wrenched into a satisfactory grin, gruesome as the emptied well of sadness in him. His mind called up Mbai', as he'd counted coup in the cave when he was a boy standing over his lifeless sisters. That image had stayed with him, riding like wings on the back of his guilt and self-hatred. He was able to forgive Mbai', but never able to absolve himself.

He stopped the horse and let him graze. He leaned forward over Wind's neck and cried against the heat of his flesh. Water funneled down the back of his head and neck into his shirt. When he ceased to sob, he raised his head and said aloud, "Darby, Darby, I'm damned without you."

He yanked the horse's head up, turned his reins toward the pasture. Cayo kicked and spurred Wind into a trot, putting the horse forward into a cantor, then a gallop at ferocious speed. With the wind whistling past him, he wanted to ride straight off the high ridge of the canyon and into life beyond this one, to death, to the spirit world, where he knew he'd be numbered among the lost, the aimless for eternity. He would never walk across the stars in the Great Beyond.

Hanna had accused him of rape and his first instinct was to run, and he did, but soon a posse of about five riders came after him. He lost them by covering up his tracks, riding in a creek beds, and using sagebrush to cover over hoof prints, even picking up Wind's shit to hide it. But in the end, he knew he'd circle back and come face to face with Pederson.

Hate was a hopeless disease, a waste of time and energy. It consumed. Ate away through the pores out of the skin, a blister that breaks, solving nothing but oozing. Hate, he decided was an offshoot of anger; an oppressive tumor growing from a root of discontent, a malady one cannot rid himself of—a consuming cancer.

How many times had he dreamed of Darby? Only recently he'd fancied the abandoned hacienda—how it haunted him. The wall, dense and cool. How they'd washed each other, her hair thick and ropy, streaks the color of white corn and wheat.

He wanted to hate Darby, despise her for leaving him. He wanted to despise himself for his weakness of the flesh—for the consuming act of ravishing Hanna, even though he thought it was Darby in his drunken stupor. How he wanted her, took her with passion, entered Darby, over and over.

Cayo leaned against a cottonwood and thought again. Could he do it still—settle somewhere with Darby, build a place, cut out a piece of land? Grow corn? What good was it to think like this? He couldn't do any of those things. By now Pederson and his gang of men had already judged him and found him guilty.

A posse of men would want to hang him for a crime he didn't believe he'd committed, and he knew a posse was following him. Drunk, even hung over, he had evaded them, though for a time he felt lost. Lost because he had drunk too much, and was fighting off a brutal headache and hunger for something to quell the stomach pains that wracked his body.

Lost because of the blinding freak snowstorm. Lost because he despaired and didn't care where he was going or if he would arrive. He wanted to die. This wasn't the first time he considered his life so worthless that it didn't matter if he continued living. He wanted to die when he killed his sisters. He wanted to die again now. Yet there was no way he could do the ultimate cowardly deed and end his life. He'd been taught by his Christian mother and by his Apache grandmother that suicide was the ultimate despicable deed. Judas Iscariot betrayed Jesus and hanged himself. That was understandable—Cayo wanted to do that, too. Shoot his brains to the other side of eternity the same way he did to his sisters. *Was being ravished by an Indian really worse than death?* How many times had he asked his dead mother, asked himself that very question, especially now that he understood that his white race and not the red-skinned people were the savages.

He came upon a deserted cabin in the high hills, found a rusty axe embedded in a sawed-off tree trunk. The wind canted, sluicing through his sleeve as he worked the axe free, picked it up, brought it up over his head and threw his weight into it. He slammed it down over and over again, chopping some wood, until one last time when it sank deep into the cut-off tree trunk and the shudder in his arms made him howl. He picked up the wood and carried it into a cabin and started a fire.

He couldn't take his own life. Instead, he did the only thing he could do. He slept off his drunk in a cabin in the woods, used for summer grazing. When he woke, he melted the last of the snow and drank to slake his thirst. Then he mounted his horse and rode back to the Pederson place.

When he returned, the place look deserted. He tied up his horse at the hitching post, went to the big house knocked on the door. Zora Pederson answered.

She whispered, "Thank God you're back. Harry and some of the boys are getting up a lynching party. What really happened, Cayo?"

"I need to talk with the Captain, Ma'm."

"He's in the parlor. Please let me help you," she murmured.

"Ain't no living human can do that, I'm afraid."

"I know the Captain's daughter's no saint, but—rape?" She paused. "Here, let me take your hat."

Cayo took off his hat and handed it to her.

"She's accusing you of rape, Cayo. You barely look at her. Why?"

"What I done was wrong. But she came to me and I was drunk, Ma'm. Imagined she was Darby, the girl I love. But ain't no excuse."

"She's got your bloody shirt, and to my shame, has been waving it like a trophy in front of the men. I—"

"Only thing I can say is, she weren't untouched, and she come to me. I never looked for her." He hung his head in shame.

"Not according to my husband's lying daughter." The scent of baking of apples reached him like a balm. This was real, then. He was here in the foyer. Confessing. Cayo looked up, understanding now why this woman wanted to help him. The little bitch weren't even hers. That's why they're so different. But as much as he hated Hanna in that moment, he felt sorry for her. She was a girl looking for someone to care for—the way she cared for those wild horses.

"You'd best go in," Zora Pederson said.

Cayo walked a few feet, knocked on the door and entered the room. "Captain Pederson, sir, I'm here to offer my apologies and ask for forgiveness and Hanna's hand."

"You animal. You have the audacity to enter my home because of my wife's goodness, and this is the thanks and respect and payment I get back for giving you employment?"

He picked up his cane and cracked it over his knee. "That's what I should do to you."

"Sir, I was dead drunk."

"You were drunk? Too bad you weren't dead. That's your excuse for violating a pure virginal creature like this?" He pointed to where Hanna sat whimpering into a hanky by the fireplace. She looked up at him, a face that made her look like the kitty cat that just swallowed her first canary, but no way was she going to take the blame for it.

"I brought my girl up to be raped by some savage?"

At this, Cayo flinched.

"Our name to be defiled by scum like you?" Captain Pederson turned toward his daughter. "What makes you think I'd let him marry you?"

"Oh, now, Father, please don't—"

"Quiet, Hanna or I'll send you to your room."

Hanna stood up, grabbed her handkerchief, and began to sob. "He really cares for me, Father, I told you he was drunk or he'd never have laid a hand on me." She was quiet for a minute.

"Now ain't that the truth about being drunk," he said and thought, you little skunk, you know I'm in love with Darby.

"He wants to marry me," she said, turning to face Cayo, "don't you?"

"Cayo. Is it true? Do you want that?" Zora asked.

"No, Ma'm, don't want no such thing. Never aimed to marry her at all, but I'll make an honest woman of her, if I have to, but see no sense in her wanting a man she knows for a fact's in love with her best friend."

"You brigand! How dare you!" Hanna beat Cayo's chest, but he grabbed her wrists, and pulled them off him. "You're hurting me! Father," she said, turning her head toward him.

Captain Pederson said, "Let her go before I—"

"Please," Zora Pederson said.

"Then tell the little she-devil to keep her claws offen me," Cayo smoothed down the front of his shirt.

Captain Pederson turned to his daughter and said in a cold, calculating voice, "Are you sure, Hanna, you want a man who might beat you and treat you like a squaw?"

"He wouldn't, Pa, I know he wouldn't." Hanna clasped her hands together in supplication.

"He already has." Captain Pederson picked up his broken cane and with an anguished cry, threw it into the hearth.

Cayo saw this as his only chance and looked down at Hana and said through his teeth, "If you didn't know it, you know it now, I'm Apache, and men don't take crap from women lightly."

Chapter Twenty-One

Holidays

The seasons were crowding in on themselves and time was passing. It was now late autumn and Darby had been in St. Louis for two full years. She was eighteen years old and her long blonde hair was now worn in an upturned, elegant style piled high on her head, a style that suited her face with a smattering of freckles she often dusted with powder to conceal. She knew she was a becoming girl by the looks she received from the neighborhood errand boys and passersby in the street as she walked to school.

Erik had invited her to walk in the woods near an old settlement to cut down a tree for the holidays. Mary packed them a big picnic basket. Off they went in a buggy that he drove—both of them covered with quilts and each with a foot warmer of boiling water in a cylindrical ceramic. Darby thought about how her feet would feel on the ride home, when they'd be freezing without heat exuding from the foot warmers, and was glad she'd listened to Mary and changed her leather boots for felt ones with thick woolen socks Mary had knitted for her. For once, Darby hadn't been pig-headed.

When they returned Mary had hot drinks waiting with a light supper. After they'd eaten, he brought in the medium-sized Christmas tree that fit perfectly in an angle of the parlor that seemed to invite its arrival. Without asking permission, Erik sat at the kitchen table and helped Darby and Mary make decorations to dress the tree. They made red paper bells that folded outward, white paper stars and angels, and lace decorated clothespin dolls. There was a box of striped candy canes left by Dr. Marsh which they hung from tree limbs partially garlanded with strung popcorn and dried cranberries. Antique German silver tinsel streamed over the branches, and here and there were red bows. Mary said she hoped that the centerpiece of twelve red burning beeswax candles wouldn't create a fire hazard. Aunt Bea made sure the lighted centerpiece was surrounded by a circlet of live holly and small pinecones with an outer ring of buttery-gold and rust-colored chrysanthemums. Darby set it on a large silver tray in the middle of the wooden mahogany dining-room table. There were trays of sugar, butter and ginger-bread cookies and fruit trays of apples and pears and nuts set out on the sideboard. Darby had prepared date-nut bread that Mary had taught her to make and another of walnuts and bananas, lest they waste the over-ripened bananas. It was getting late so Mary suggested some spiced eggnog, topped with imported nutmeg near the fireplace.

The eggnog propelled Darby back in time when she remembered collecting eggs one morning and putting them in an oval woven wicker basket when a shadow had made her start and almost drop the basket, eggs and all. Cayo had caught it just in time. The barn door stood open and there in a peg of light he plucked an egg out of her basket. He held it in his left hand and with his right pinky nail punctured one end and then the other. He held up the egg and sucked the insides out, tossed the shell on the earth and ground it with his heel.

"I've never seen anyone do that."

"That's because you don't know anyone who was raised by Indians or raided farms for food when he got hungry. That's a high energy staple for men being chased and on the run. He hadn't shaved and his cheeks were covered with a fine sheen of light hair growth and sweat. Cayo was so enticing to her, she almost forgot she needed to get the eggs in the house and prepare breakfast.

"What are you doing here? I can't dally now. You must know that."
"Not here to see you. Your Pa hired me as an extra hand today.
They'll be branding the calves."

The word branding seemed stuck in her head—the way he'd branded
her, and she came back from her reverie thinking about him. It echoed in
her ears so loudly she thought for sure Mary had heard. Darby glanced at
Mary as if Mary would know she'd been thinking about Cayo. Gradually
Darby came back to the present and had the feeling Mary was anxious to
observe the young pastor around her niece. Darby caught her aunt
unabashedly gaping at Erik when he made the slightest movement in
Darby's direction, as if Mary wanted to protect Darby.

**

After Easter, Darby read in the paper that Yellow Fever was again
raging in Central Texas, as was small pox in Chambers County. Beau-
mont in east Texas had posted guards at several points, with apparent
success, to keep infected travelers out of the city.

News spread quickly and two-thirds or more of the mail volume
reaching Jefferson County, Texas, consisted of the Houston and Galves-
ton newspapers, as well as such periodicals as *Godey's Ladies Book,*
DeBow's Review, and *Harper's Weekly*. However old each letter or
publication was, Darby knew it was read and reread many times before it
finally arrived from Texas to Parcel Bluffs, New Mexico. The news,
passed along to friends and neighbors, provided a momentary diversion
from the harshness and monotony of frontier living.

Along with the papers, disease somehow spread and reached the
west. A few cases were found in Darby's hometown. It had been a spell
since she or Aunt Bea had received mail from out west, and when letters

finally did arrive they carried with them horrible, unwelcomed news. Two letters landed in their St. Louis mailbox on the same day: one for Aunt Bea and one for Darby. Both carried the sad summary of Darby's father's illness. He was lingering, suffering, but Garrett didn't think he had much more time to live.

Darby faced Aunt Bea. "I must leave before he succumbs—Momma would've wanted me to be with him before he joins her in the next life. I need to be there for Pa. I was with Momma when it was her time. His age is against him and I'd never forgive myself if I didn't see him before he passed." She quickly erased the image of the front door of the ranch house draped in mourning colors.

Darby begged her aunt in a tearful manner to buy her a ticket to allow her time to grieve with her brothers, but Aunt Bea refused. "Pull yourself together," she said to Darby in the parlor, saying that her father would probably be dead and buried by the time she got there.

"What's the point now, dearest? He'll be gone to his just reward. The only thing you can do now is pray for the repose of his dear soul and hope to meet him in Paradise when your own time comes."

Stunned beyond words, Darby retreated to the loving arms of Mary, who comforted her as best she could.

Darby turned toward Bea. "You don't know that for sure. It's a gamble I'd be willing to take."

"You know how exhausting the trip here was. You can imagine how bad it will be returning there," Aunt Bea said, wringing her hands.

"Makes no never mind, dear aunt. I must go to him. I'd never forgive myself. I promise to pay you back the money for the ticket."

"It's not the money," Bea hedged.

"Then what?" Darby asked, her voice excited.

"Darby," Mary said in a stern voice. "My sister is practical. Besides, child, how could you ever pay her back?"

"I'll teach here instead of returning to Parcel Bluffs. I'll sign a paper. I'll stay for a year," she said, her voice in a crescendo, tapering to find a balance between the fine line of hysterics and normalcy.

"Come with me to the kitchen now. We'll have tea," said Mary. She pulled out a tin of freshly baked ginger snap cookies and set a plateful near Darby, who said, "Instead of tea, why not make sweet hot chocolate with fresh whipped cream on top?"

"If only that could assuage the bitter reality you mightn't arrive in time to see—"

Darby cried out, "Oh, Lord, never again to see my father on this earth."

***

That evening, Aunt Bea came into the kitchen where Darby sat with her books open on the table staring off into space.

"What's wrong? Are you feeling ill?" Aunt Bea asked.

"I can't concentrate on books and reading. Everything seems so trivial and unimportant. I should be with my father. I should be the one taking care of him, offering some succor at his last." She burst into tears.

"If it's God's will you'll arrive in time. If not," she said handing over a train ticket, then you will know it was his time, and you couldn't have done anything to save him."

Darby jumped up. "Oh, bless you, Aunt Bea." She embraced her aunt. "But I don't need it. I'd forgotten that I have a ticket—the one Cayo sent me that I was foolish enough not to use." She flushed at the mere mention of his name.

"Then, go, my dear, and show your father kindness and affection. Your brothers are wonderful men, but they are gruff."

"If it eases your conscience a bit, I've had a letter from Garrett, and he said Hanna was there to tend to him. Your—" she hesitated, "friend Cayo brought her around to the house to visit your father." Bea filled a vase with water for some cut flowers.

A bad-tasting, ugly bile raised itself in Darby's throat and she felt like throwing up. Not only wasn't she there for him, but Hanna was usurping her of her last filial duties. And with Cayo to ferry her back and forth. How cozy. Just as quickly as Darby had thought this, she rebuked herself for her jealousy.

"Do you want Mary to accompany you?" Aunt Bea asked.

Darby shook her head.

Chapter Twenty-Two

Return to Parcel Bluffs

Garrett met Darby at the train station, and picked her up in his arms like a featherweight and swung her around. "It's so good to see you. I never would have dreamed that I'd have missed you so much. Even your notes pinned to the curtains."

But Darby was not in the mood for frivolity. "How's Pa?" she said, her voice shaky.

"Old Doc Benson was out to see him this morning. He's on his last but he knows you're coming and promised to hold on. It will take you by surprise—he's not the strong Pa you left."

Darby entered the house and was immediately struck by the smell of sickness. Pa's bed had been moved into the great room and the windows were heavily curtained. She tiptoed over to him but he was sleeping. She touched his forehead, but he didn't stir, and she covered him lightly with the counterpane.

She turned to Garrett, who was standing with her luggage in hand. "Open the curtains and windows and get some fresh air in here."

"But the Doc said—"

"Never mind what he said. The new medical thinking is fresh air and sunshine. I read an article about it in the *St. Louis Gazette,* and Aunt Bea says her Dr. Marsh insists on outings and good country air. We have to leave the city for good air, do you believe that? Here" she made an expansive movement with her hand, "you've got it all around you."

"I'll put your gear in your old room," Garrett said.

"Coffeepot still in the same place?" she asked.

"Sure," he called from the hallway.

"Want a cup?" There was no answer, so she took that to mean yes. She washed her hands and took hold of the enamel dipper and filled the coffee pot. She set out two tin cups and hunted around for some sugar.

When they'd finished their second cup of coffee, Darby heard horses approaching and glanced out the window. "Oh, my, what's he doing here?"

Garrett leaned over her shoulder and peered out. "I've got some business with Cayo."

"I'll just go in my room to unpack. I really don't want to see him."

"Can't blame you."

"Let me know when he leaves."

Darby heard muffled voices. She leaned her back against the door and pictured Cayo. The thought of his nearness made her pulse seem to buzz in her ears and she cupped her hands over them. She took her hands down and shook her head, walked over to the water stand and poured water from the pitcher into the bowl. Darby undid the top four buttons of her bodice and splashed water on her cheeks and neck, dried her face with the rough linen towel. When it was quiet, she walked into the kitchen, primed the pump, and poured a glass of water and drank as if she'd never be able to slake her thirst.

How she had thirsted for him in the beginning when she'd first left Parcel Bluffs. How she had lied to Aunt Bea to cover up her real feelings for Cayo. Standing with only a door between them now, she had to see his face. Had to know why he did what he did. She wrenched open the front door. Garrett was already mounted on his horse and Cayo was about ready to mount his but turned at the noise of the door opening, and she saw that he caught his breath at the sight of her.

Garrett took one look at both of them, tipped his hat. "Be back soon," he said, and rode off.

Cayo loved her. Loved her still. Then why? "Oh dear God, why?" escaped her lips and her hands flew to her mouth to cover a cry.

He took his foot from the stirrup and rushed up the steps as she stepped back inside. Cayo entered and closed the door behind him and said, "Darby," in a plaintive voice that made her want to strike him. Instead, she ran to him and threw her arms around him, kissing him with rage and desire. He kissed her back, hunger in it.

She broke free after some time. "How could you? Damn you! How could you?" She pounded his chest over and over, until he grabbed her by the wrists.

"I must see you. Alone. I beg you. You got to know how it was."

He pushed his hat off his head, and it hung back by the string around his neck.

"I don't want to hear about you and her and your sordid affair."

His face was riddled with pain. He was hurt and she'd caused it, but at the same time, she relished his anguish, despite hating herself for it.

"It wasn't like that. I was drunk." He adjusted his hat string.

"And that, I suppose, excuses your giving her a poke for the fun of it."

"Darby. I thought I was with you. I kept calling your name."

"Oh how convenient to remember that little detail." She wiped tears off her cheek.

"It was Hanna who told me that, and she said I asked her over and over why she didn't have your vibrant color hair, your soft eyes."

"Take a look at my eyes now, Cayo. They're anything but soft, I guarantee it." She swiped the dish towel at a fly.

"How is it you remember all that yet say you were drunk?"

"Because Hanna spewed venom the next day and said, 'No matter what you think you were doing to or with Darby, it was me you were rutting and you're going to face the dire consequence.' Somehow she got herself pregnant."

"Somehow?"

"I swear. Not mine. I should have figured it out when Ben Star left in a hurry and I was forced to marry—one look at that child will convince you, Darby. She was sporting a pouch far too big for a one night poke, and in less than a month, she announces the fact she's carrying."

"Are you saying she's a fine little actress?" Darby asked.

"Please, let me tell you how it really was. I heard after from Zora that Hanna went crying to her father, her dress all torn, her hair a mess. I never done that. Not even drunk, have I ever forced a woman. She left the bunkhouse in a robe, bare beneath it. It was like a theater show and I was in the audience watching her playact, except I was also part of it. I went for a ride, spent the night in a cabin. I came back to face the Captain, who threatened to whip me with a cane or riding crop, and yelled, 'You'll pay for this savage act.' All a bad dream."

Darby glared at him, shaking her head, but said nothing. She saw how the hurt washed visible over his deep, brooding eyes, and his handsome face contorted. She was the cause of it and relished his anguish, stood ramrod straight to savor every minute of his bleeding out, but bile rose within her and she hated herself for gloating.

"Meet me at our—our spot on the river. Please say you'll come to me," he said, his voice tender and pleading.

"At the river, there is no longer our spot—just a place along the banks. Why don't you take Hanna there?" she said, her voice sounding disembodied, not hers, yet spiced with a cruelty she couldn't reckon as her own.

"Please," he said.

"I can't leave my father alone."

"Garrett should be back soon. Or one of the boys," Cayo said. "Come to me then."

Before Garrett returned, Darby changed into riding clothes, and then sat by her father's bedside. He had not stirred once, and as soon as Garrett came into the house, she told him so, and that she was going for a ride to sort out some thinking.

She saddled a horse. A horse she knew was way too much for her to handle, but no other horse was in the stable. Her fury made her think she could handle him. She rode out in a fast cantor that soon turned to a gallop with her heart racing along with the horse's hooves as they kicked up clods of earth springing forth toward the river.

She rode, trying to slow the pace, but the horse's rhythm in the gallop was too much and then she figured it was just as well, switching the crop from side to side, in a steady beating motion all the while thinking, *I'm injured. Inside. A part of me will never heal. I wish I could vomit up all the hurt pulsing in my innards, or run with this demon horse to the end of the world. What have I done? What have I gambled and lost?* Crying and calling out Cayo's name over and over, she finally brought the steed under control and trotted him to the river.

He was there. Pacing. A caged animal without a cage. He stopped. Hunched and then turned toward her and ran flat out. He reached up and pulled her off the horse. They fell onto the hard-packed earth with her twirled and tangled in his arms as if they'd never been apart. Never separated. And the love they gave each other was real and tormented and passionate until they both lay breathless and spent upon the river bank.

When Darby caught her breath, she sat up and said softly, "It's over between us. No matter what you do about Hanna. You and I are done."

Cayo took her tenderly by the shoulders as if she might break, and then crushed her in his arms until he stopped quaking and she no longer cried.

"I'll cherish you forever," he said.

She glanced up and face to face said, "Always and forever are words beyond eternity—neither one of us can make that kind of promise any more. Maybe once—a long time ago in another life. But now?"

"Then, please. Once. Call my name. Once. I'm Connor Bradley, and I'll worship you past the grave."

"Connor Bradley," she said, as if meeting a stranger for the first time and being utterly enthralled by him. They sat in silence for a while.

The oaths, the promises, the simple words she wanted to speak, to say to him, were hindered, hampered by the sensation that this was final. These feelings for him stayed inside of her, and just possibly it was a saving grace and better that way. *For God be my judge, I loved him, loved him, love him still and until I stop breathing on this earth, and if there's truly a world beyond death—I'll take his love with me to a so-called Heaven— love him there too. But I can't burden him now with these profound feelings. He needs to be set free to endure without even the thought of me.*

She broke into tears.

He said softly, "Hush now. It's just you and me. Let the world fall away."

***

Darby's father never regained consciousness, although somehow she felt he knew she was there, holding his hand, bathing him, caressing his sunken cheeks. The funerary procession followed the casket to a hill overlooking the McPhee ranch. There, with a sky full of mournful gray clouds, they consigned Darby's father to the depth of the grave dug out for him by his sons. Garrett was the first to toss in a handful of dirt, then each in his turn, Darby's other brothers. Lastly, she plucked a daisy from a bouquet and tossed it in her father's grave. Then she picked up a handful of dirt and threw that in, too.

Darby walked past the mourners, shaking hands, talking for a moment, saying thanks. She saw Cayo and his bride toward the back of the congregation. Passing them and the little boy in Hanna's arms, gripping her hand, Darby nodded by way of thanks for coming to see her father off to a time without end. She couldn't speak one word to them or she'd fall apart.

Later that day, Darby looked at her face in the mirror and saw her cheeks aglow and her eyes glistening still with wanting him . . . wanting him to kiss every part of her body. Oh, God, oh God. *What have I done?* That's the physical side—but was it love between Cayo and Hanna? She knew of love . . . that overwhelming power that engulfs you till you can't stand to be in your own skin. She knew it, knew it to the core of her. Only yesterday, he'd said goodbye to her with tears in his eyes, and how his words stung her now: "Darby, girl, how can you walk away from me? I'm lost without you."

She had gone though, riding back to Garrett and the boys, like so many times before. And now. Again, she rode straight through the gate, looking up at the ranch sign *Tess,* named for her momma, but this time Pa wouldn't be there waiting for her.

She wanted so much to ride over to that hellion's place and drag Hanna through the dust. But instead, she reasoned that Hanna loved Cayo in her own way. Back in her family kitchen, Darby scrubbed three pots, and had finished drying them when she heard a buggy approach. She looked out the window. *My, oh my, the Captain and Mrs. Pederson coming to call.* The visit, Darby thought, would be as stiff as she felt. Then again, Mrs. Pederson always had a soft spot for Darby—it was obvious to everyone, especially Hanna.

Garrett and Captain Pederson started talking about the herds and branding and the weather, when they finally decided to go outside on the porch for a smoke.

Mrs. Pederson got up, closed the door and walked over to where Darby was sitting on a small settee and sat next to her. She took both of Darby's hands in hers, and said, "I'm so sorry."

"My father was very ill. It was his time."

"I meant I'm sorry about you losing Cayo to Hanna."

Darby's head jerked up. "I'm not. Really." She blew out a gush of air. "If he'd been meant for me, he would've waited."

"Sometimes, Darby, life contrives against us, and—"

"Mrs. Pederson, please. I beg you—please don't do this. I'm hurting plenty all by myself."

"I never want to hurt you, dear. I'm quite fond—"

"I know that," Darby snapped. "Sorry."

"I've always admired your spunk. You're a hard-working girl, and—"

"Guess hard working girls shouldn't want to better themselves and get some education."

"You're wrong and you know it." She pulled her hands away from Darby's. "Maybe he just wasn't the right man for you. He could have attacked you the way he did—"

"That's a downright lie and you know it. He never—"

"Look at me. Darby, damn it, look at me. For his sake, I'm begging you as a mother, to let him think you believe he raped Hanna."

"That girl is your daughter." Darby played with the hem of her apron.

"The hell she is. She's a demon, and no blood of mine flows in her viper's cold heart."

"Mrs. Pederson, what're you saying?"

"You know she's the Captain's daughter, don't you?"

"I mean what're you really saying about Cayo?"

"Simply this—she framed him for something she concocted. I bet my life on it."

"Oh my God. You know it, too."

Darby and Garrett said their goodbyes to the Pedersons. Darby attributed the quasi-smoothness of the visit to the absence of Hanna. Darby and Garrett watched the Pedersons ride away. When their buggy reached the bend where she would sometimes meet Cayo, she said to Garrett. "I'd like to walk some. Be back soon."

"You go on. Do you some good."

"Need to get the kinks out. Been sitting too much in this old house."

"Don't worry. I'll be moseying my way to town. We all ate too much after the burial."

"Where are the boys? Gone to town to get drunk? Keep an eye out and don't let them get too bruised, if they pick a fight."

Not ten minutes after Garrett left on his horse, Darby went for a slow walk. A rider passed way to the left of her. He was moving in the opposite direction, wanting to get someplace fast. All of a sudden he twisted and coaxed the horse out of a spin that almost toppled him and came at her full speed.

He's out of his mind. Oh, God, no one handles a horse like that except . . .

She moved out of the way just as he pulled his horse to a stop and jumped off.

"Hello, Darby girl," he said out of breath.

She wanted to die, right there on the spot, but tried to keep tears in check, only to cry inside. Wishing wouldn't get her over this dilemma. This was real. Here stood the man she loved in front of her—seemingly as tall as a quaking aspen, but sometimes as prickly as cactus, more drinkable than buttermilk, more edible than fry bread. An apple core stuck in her throat, impeding words to come out. Not even, "How you been keeping?" Her lips were drawn together tight and thin, making her look severe and older than her eighteen years.

A screech owl flapped its wings and soared overhead.

She never meant for this to happen. She had taken the road that circled wide of the ranch to avoid seeing anyone. Darby knew facing him would be like falling into a well. Here was trouble—a porcupine with his hackles up and it was going to hurt.

But here he was.

She looked out over the land and saw yellow yucca flowers, and remembered a hat that her father gave her one Easter—a Sunday go-to-meeting-bonnet, he'd called it. She stood stone still, recalling things she didn't care to think about, like all those times she'd thought about Cayo and the day she got the news he was married.

She found her voice. "How many times I conjured up your voice when the wind went rustling though a plum tree in Aunt Bea's garden?"

"I'm here. This is real. We're talking."

Indecision, she knew now was her weakness.

"There's a rock wall, what's left of an ancient presidio, out yonder and beyond the pasture. Sit with me a spell?" he asked, as if he only wanted to pass the time of day. She thought about sitting on it—straddling her legs—one on this side, and one on that. Fence-sitting—that's what had made her decide too late to leave and go to her aunt's to study. She'd have had it all done if she'd begun earlier, but no, she had sat that fence, legs dangling till she knew she loved him more than anything and needed him to feed her heart and soul. Yet, she wanted schooling and knowledge to feed her curious mind.

"So it's come to this," he said, "you can't even talk to me?"

"We never did much of that anyway, Cayo."

Darby had a peculiar sense about her. She always longed to be where she wasn't. When she'd been home, before she'd gone to St. Louis and Aunt Bea's, Darby had wanted books to learn the mysteries of life held therein. And when she was surrounded by her books, her thoughts would be sparked by a word or description that would bring her mind galloping straight back home and the sparse good looks of the man who was asking her to speak, to say something to him now.

"You told me you wanted to come with me and start a home and family," he said.

"That's true, I did, way back when. But I also wanted to study and to learn things you couldn't teach me."

They walked on in silence, his horse trailing.

Her mind wrote a message she'd scribbled into a journal before coming back: *Shattered. I stand under this fading sun and must bear the digging, the scraping, the scaling of me, grappling to surmount my stalwart, never-yielding self.*

She stopped and looked at him. "Why? Why and how could you?"

He bent his head down close to her face. "I told you the truth, why don't you believe me?" He took the reins of his horse and tied them to a stunted juniper.

"Try to make me understand what happened?" She tilted her neck away from him and stepped sideward.

"I ached for you. I needed you. I wanted you. Forgive me for not going to get you—fear paralyzed me. If I'd a come, you might've scorned me. Hanna flung herself into my bunk when I was dead drunk. Like it or not, that's what really happened."

"Then why'd you have to go and marry her? Mrs. Pederson says you really did what they're saying and she told me to believe it for your good."

"Did you ever hear a mob cry out for a lynching?" He faced her and grabbed her upper arms with a fierce grip.

"Why didn't you come back? I sent you the ticket. You knew Hanna and what might happen? You could've saved me, Darby. You hear that?"

She cried, but never answered.

He took her face in his hands and kissed her with ravenous hunger. She couldn't think. She could only lean into his arms and let him kiss her face and her neck and then they were struggling at their buttons, falling behind the wall at sunset. He loved her like never before. She whispered, "Oh, God, Cayo, what are we to do?"

"If you don't leave with me now—then, nothing. You'll go back to your life in the East and be a teacher, and I'll be a father to that whore's son."

"Oh, no, oh, no, no," she wailed, until he held her tight, muffling her sobs in his chest, her arms flailing at him.

"Then come with me. I'll leave her."

Darby cried harder.

"Please calm yourself! You put me in mind of a young bride keening a warrior husband just killed. Don't do what she did—gash your leg with a knife and cut your hair like you was slashing rope. Don't leave me." He ran his hand down her hair.

"Cayo, we're doomed." She moaned.

"When can I hold you again?"

"In Hell. Let me go. Let me go." She pushed back from him.

"Mount my horse. You ain't walking back to your daddy's empty place."

"Are you crazy? I don't know you anymore. I heard things about you—not just this forcing yourself upon Hanna. They call you Injun lover. Said you married a squaw."

"I'm Apache—sure I had a woman. I was a kid. They dangle a pretty thing in front of a young warrior like a carrot in front of a horse." He lowered his voice, "But she's in the spirit world now." He took hold of Darby's arms.

"Leave me be." She wriggled free.

"I can't. I can't. Hate me if you will. But I can't leave you here."

"I don't know you. The man I love, why he—who are you really, Cayo?"

"An unlucky and lonely man, maybe. One thing for sure, a man in love with you. I'm devoted to you, cherish you."

They mounted his horse and he rode her home, she leaning into his back, never wanting to let go. They dismounted. He picked her up and carried her up the steps. She opened the door, and when they were inside, kicked it closed. He carried her right into her room and made love to her on her girlhood bed as if it were the end of the world.

He kissed her shoulder. "How will I live without you?"

She reached for something on the side of the bed. "You've got to leave before the boys get home. And take this."

Without a word, he took hold of the medicine bag, set it down beside her sewing basket.

"I want you—you're the breath in my body. I don't want to live a second without you near." He shrugged into his shirt.

"It'll be no life for me either, but you've learned survival from your people. You'll survive. I'll survive—with you in my heart, in my soul, in my gut for eternity. We will live, knowing we once were alive and in each other's arms."

"Come with me," he begged, his chiseled face so close to her in this light, impossibly close.

"You don't play by their rules—" she uttered.

"Enlighten me," he said, pulling on his boots.

"I can't picture our life together, knowing I stole someone's lawful husband—I'm an adulteress now—but I couldn't live the rest of my life as one. I'm not cut of that cloth."

"Adulteress? What's the law compared to us being together? Never separated again. I need you no end. Without yesterday and no tomorrow. Be with me." He kissed her softly.

She shook her head in slow motion from side to side. Her crying, a soft breeze sloughing through branches.

He clasped her to him. Their bodies pressed together in a tight hold that they could've endured forever. Then he broke from her, stood by her bureau, and reached for a pair of shears in a sewing basket. He bent and took hold of her hair, shining bright in the light of the candle—the scissors glinted, her eyes glowed. He cut off a lock of her hair and held it in front of her. "Forever," he whispered and dropped the shears on the bed. He took the deed out of the medicine pouch and walked out of her room. She followed, watching as he stepped out the door into the dawn light and onto the veranda.

She called to him in the sweetest voice, "Cayo."

He turned a slight bit, and she flung her arms around his back and shoulders. He spun into her and in a frantic embrace, they kissed. He broke from her. "The end of the world has just begun for me."

She slept poorly, and dressed without bathing, wanting the scent of him on her for as long as possible. Her brothers had all left for work after she'd fixed them breakfast. Cleaning up and washing the dishes, she sat by the window sipping a cup of coffee, calling up and memorizing each word, every look and action of the past night until dawn.

A little later that morning, Hanna stood in front of the McPhee door draped with a black mourning cloth. Darby opened it. She'd just made love to this woman's husband hours ago, but she wouldn't consider this a sin. It felt like coming home.

Hanna walked through the foyer carrying a cake covered with a fine embroidered linen cloth and set it down on top of a dry sink. "Thought you could use something sweet mother made for you and the boys."

Darby looked at the torte covered in icing and then back up at Hanna. "Pick up that cake before you wear it. I'm rankled and don't care for propriety's sake or good manners." Darby walked toward Hanna, cinched her by the upper arm with a death grip, fingertips digging into her, Hanna resisting as Darby's nails sunk into the muscle. She dragged Hanna screeching over to the window.

"Go ahead and yell your head off. There's nobody here but me and you."

Hanna calmed and fell silent and fell into a chair. "You shouldn't have left him, or you should have come back sooner. You knew I always fancied him."

"I don't know how you tricked him to lay with you and then convince your father he raped you, and tell the world you were pregnant with Cayo's baby. But that child of yours was hatched of an illicit relationship before Cayo. I saw your son at the funeral. Not Cayo's offspring." She spewed the words through gritted teeth as if they held poison. She bent over Hanna—too close, too intimidatingly close.

Hanna stretched backwards, trying to pull away. "Why, Darby, how can you—"

"That child of yours was spawned of someone other than a white man. I'm guessing it was that kind Mr. Star you bedeviled into sleeping with you—the baby's a handsome little tyke—great resemblance to the smithy."

"How dare you accuse—"

In a calm voice, Darby declared, "That boy has darkie blood in him. His features are anything but Cayo's. Drop the pretense. For all times since we were girls, you've had a hankering for my Cayo. Miss Hanna, you should've never confided in me. Like I should never have trusted you with my feelings for him."

"Such venomous words! You can't have him and you're jealous—" Hanna wrangled out of the chair and moved away from Darby.

"Jealous?" It was all Darby could do to keep from slapping Hanna so hard she'd topple to the floor. "His heart's mine until the day he dies, or I do."

"Liar."

"Mendacity? No, that's your game. You were a spoiled child, and you've grown into an indecent human specimen—fraudulent and conniving. Oh don't worry, I won't tell your darling, ailing father, blind soul he's ever been concerning you. You can pull his nightcap over his eyes, but you can't fool me."

"Don't fling your fancy words at me. What're you saying? Have you seen Cayo? What untruths have you filled my husband's head with about me, his lawful wife?"

"Cayo knows the boy's not his. Don't believe for a minute Cayo doesn't get how you tricked him. You may think—" she double-tapped her temple with a finger, "he's married to you, but you don't know him. No white man's law or marriage vow taken under duress will ever bind his heathen heart to you or your bastard son. Cayo's decrees and edicts are one and the same with nature. His own. He was raised Apache. His culture isn't mine, isn't yours. A gross miscalculation and something you obviously failed to understand."

"Lies. A pack of lies."

"You hoodwinked the wrong man. Your marriage act isn't worth the paper it was written on. Cayo is his own law—"

"It ain't true. You're lying. He'll stand by me—he has to," Hanna said, shaking her head, raising her hand to untie her bonnet bow and pull it off, her long, dark hair spilling out. She tossed the hat on the chair.

Darby felt her fury unleashed. "Here's the unveiled truth: not for you, not for your ranch, nor your daddy's herd of cattle. Maybe he would've stayed, if you'd have staked him to the ground. Now take your cake, mount your buggy and go home to your father."

Darby picked up the cake.

"Exactly what're you saying?" Hanna said with sweat curling the tendrils of her hair on her forehead and framing her face.

"Cayo's gone. He left after he kissed me goodbye at dawn. I don't suppose you can rustle up a posse fast enough or big enough to dry gulch him a second time. He'll cover his tracks."

Darby put the cake into Hanna's hands, wanting to push it in her face, but controlled herself. She reached for the bonnet and plopped it lopsided on Hanna's head. "I never want to see you again as long as there's breath in my body."

"Well, Miss High and Mighty, you don't have him either and you never will."

Darby smiled a half smile and shook her head. "What I carry with me for the rest of my life is Cayo's love—an enduring love—words you'll never understand. Get out of my sight, you cold-hearted bitch." She opened the door, wanting to boot Hanna in the rear.

Chapter Twenty-Three

Baseball

Darby returned to St. Louis and before long, she fell in love, but this time it was with the game of baseball. The game had been played in St. Louis for about ten years before a truly professional league was formed and scheduled to play its first season in 1871. Darby always liked the game and had begun watching amateur teams throughout the seasons of 1874-75. Although her Aunt Bea was not exactly thrilled that Darby attended many of the games, but since she enlisted Aunt Mary for a companion to go to the games as a chaperone, Aunt Bea relented. Darby learned the rules as well as anyone on the field. She was thoroughly captivated by the sport and played catch with young Matteo Silenzi, the wise-cracking little Italian neighbor in their adjacent backyards when no one was home. She'd seen how swiftly he ran around the makeshift bases he'd made in the field, which put her in mind of the Ceremonial Relay Race of the Jicarilla Apache's that Cayo had told her about.

But today Matteo wanted to practice his batting in the vacant field near Aunt Bea's house.

Darby threw a wild pitch and Matteo ducked.

"Here," he said, tossing his bat aside and walking towards her. "Let me show you again. "You have to step into it, like this," he said demonstrating, and tossing the ball underhand. He retrieved the ball and said, "Control the ball with your fingers. Think of the flight path it's going to take and where it's heading before you release it. See," he said and lobbed a perfect ball over his chalked "plate."

"How old are you anyway? And where did you learn this?"

"I watch practice games over at the big field and the boys down the street and I have started a team of our own. Want to come see us play?"

"Sure." Darby took the ball and tossed it up in the air and caught it. "Maybe you should pitch and I should hit."

"Darby, if you can't throw, and you can't catch, you sure can't hit."

"Try me." She walked toward home plate. "And I can throw—overhand and I can catch too."

"Only because I taught you to keep your eyes on the ball when it's coming at you."

"Then teach me to hit."

"All right. Do everything I say. First, stand left side to the plate, feet apart. Bring the bat back and over your right shoulder, left hand closest to you, right above it, but don't separate the hands. Next. Bring your right elbow back. Step into the swing as the ball comes so you can connect with it."

"Ready. Try me."

"Remember, don't close your eyes!"

***

One day while they were tossing the ball around and arguing like a couple of pros, Pastor Erik peeked around the corner of the house spying on them. Darby flushed red when she saw him and immediately thought of the embarrassment this was going to cause Aunt Bea. But he smiled amiably and said, "If you two will make up, I'd like to take you to see two teams from St. Louis that are participating in the final season of the National Association of Professional Baseball Players of St. Louis in the major leagues."

Darby couldn't believe her ears, and Matteo whooped for joy. He's human, after all, she thought.

And so Darby had her first date with Pastor Erik Anderson with Matteo as chaperone. Off they went to see the first professional league game when the St. Louis Red Stockings hosted the St. Louis Brown Stockings at their home field on Compton Avenue.

They ate peanuts and watched the game. Every once in a while, Matteo explained what was happening on the field, or Erik would ask Darby a question and she'd answer him. At the end of the game Matteo proclaimed: "What a great game."

"Nothing to do with you rooting for the Brown Stockings by any chance?" Erik asked.

"I suppose so, *padre,*" Matteo said.

"It's pastor," Darby said."

"That's all right," Erik said. "He means well." Their eyes held each other's glance for a few seconds too long before Matteo said, "But what a score—15 to 9, pastor."

The three of them began to stroll towards home. "What was all that yelling about from the bench back there?"

"Oh, just words to cheer them on." Matteo shrugged his shoulders.

"Why do I have the feeling it was some sort of oath or profanity?" Erik said, watching Matteo's face color.

"You must have imagined that *pad*—pastor. It's simply the tone of voice. The guys get excited," Matteo said, putting his fingertips together in an attitude of prayer and shaking his hands forward twice. "Got to forgive them if they get a little out of control. It's the thrill of the game, pastor."

"Why don't you just call me Erik? I'd like that better."

"Me, too," Matteo said with emphasis. "Especially as my mother's a Catholic religious fanatic. Wouldn't want her to think you're trying to convert me."

"Matteo, you're either going to make a great politician or drive some poor woman straight to the insane asylum," Darby said and ruffled his hair.

Erik looked at his pocket watch. "Oh heavens. I've got to pass by the parish rectory, so I'll be off in the other direction. Matteo, you'll see Miss Darby home, won't you?" Erik said.

"My pleasure, Erik," Matteo said and beamed.

"Darby," Erik said, bowed and turned to go.

When Erik was out of earshot, Darby looked at Matteo with a serious expression. "Sometimes he makes me feel like I should curtsy!"

"Me, too," Matteo said.

Darby smiled and they continued walking. Every once in a while Matteo would fling a stone in the air, and pretend to swing at it.

That evening after dinner Darby sat on the swing on the front porch. She watched the fireflies flit among the flowering shrubs along the alleyway to the house and by the hedge. She was thinking of Cayo, scolding herself for having left him twice, her only love. How could she have let him slip through her fingers and into Hanna's den of inequity?

His voice had been in her ear, just as though he were sitting next to her. Once again she had been in his embrace. He had her for his own again. Slower this time, without the chill of the water, merely the soft, sighing, soughing of the breeze through nearby junipers and alders and a smattering of quaking aspens. This time she writhed upon his body, a rider on a bronco, pitched and unbalanced until she hiccupped a cry of urgency and satisfaction, when he placed her on her feet. He stepped away several paces from her. There he stood. His face and body gleaming with sweat as if he'd just been smeared with bear grease and rubbed with buffalo grass. Lean angles and bones caught frozen, a sun-downing ice-covered time frame, naked sheen flashes of a promised moonlight.

He backtracked to his horse, untied the rolled blanket at the back of his saddle. He walked toward her, and tossed it around her, covering her shoulders with it, drawing her close to him.

"Did I hurt you, little one?"

She stood on tiptoes for his kiss. "A little at first."

"It'll get better. I promise."

Instinct told her it would.

She hadn't even realized she was crying until someone stood behind and covered up her eyes. She took his hands in hers. "Let me guess now, whoever could this be? The mailman, Mr. Bixby, comes by in the morning and the milkman too. My aunts are both at a music concert in the park, so this must be my busy-body neighbor, Matteo."

Instead, Pastor Erik came around to face her in the light of the full moon. "Why are you crying? Let me guess, and he started finger writing something on her forehead.

"What're you writing?" Darby asked and sniffled. He handed her his handkerchief. "Ever since I was a boy my mother would write JM on our foreheads. It stands for Jesus and Mary. If we were going someplace or taking a test, or whatever. Tonight you look sad, but I'm praying you'll smile and be happy again, soon."

"Is that what you wrote on my head?" Darby asked.

He took his finger and wrote some more and then rubbed it out as if canceling a word.

Finally she said, "What are you writing and erasing on my poor forehead?"

He said, "Jesus is watching over you—how do you spell: watching? I need a dictionary."

She laughed and he sat on the swing next to her. She flung her arms around herself to control the urge of wanting to hug him. "Sit down, please," she said, realizing he was already seated next to her. She smiled.

"If you were Matteo I'd offer you some milk and cookies."

"You spoil him. But that does sounds tempting."

"All right. Hold on and I'll get you a plate." She stood up and started walking toward the screen door.

He took hold of her wrist and drew her back to sit on the swing. "Why were you crying, Darby? Is it because your friend Hanna got married?"

She turned around to face him. "Who told you that?"

"I cannot tell a lie. It was your Aunt—"

"Aunt Busybody Bea."

He smiled. "How can I distract you from your unhappiness? Shall I croon beneath your balcony? You won't give me the time of day."

She dragged her feet and stopped the swing. "What are you talking about? Are you daft?"

"Daffy. Yes. I guess so."

"What are you saying?" She started swinging again.

"You know. Moonstruck."

"Erik?"

"Now how about those cookies?"

"Erik—"

"I know you think I'm reserved—a little formal."

"Forgive me. We've never ever had a real conversation. Two words, maybe."

"I'm a dud. That's what you think, right?"

"I never said that."

"But you thought it. A dud—like when a child's cap gun doesn't fire—you're not going back to him, are you?"

"Who?"

"That cowboy back home?"

"I haven't thought—about Cayo in a while," she said and crossed her fingers in back of her.

"Yes, him." Erik swung slowly back and forth.

"No. His dance card is filled. For life. And my name isn't on it."

"But you don't just stop caring for a person—maybe like in baseball, it's—what do they call it? A time out?"

"Excuse me but how did we go from cookies and milk to this?" She gave him back his handkerchief.

"It's because we had our first date and I'd like to ask if I can see you again. Not as a man of the cloth, but as a—"

"Yes?" She inclined her head.

"Well, as a suitor?"

"Come to think of it, maybe it's too hot for milk, how would you like something cold?"

When she returned with a plate of cookies, two glasses, and a pitcher of lemonade, Erik stood and opened the screen door for her. He watched her juggle the tray and finally settled it down on a small glass and wrought-iron table on the side of the swing.

"You never talk to me," Darby said.

"Of course I do. I even wrote you a penny postcard when I went to Springfield, Illinois."

"I know where Springfield is. You wrote to me? I never got it." She picked up one glass at a time, filled it, and placed it on the tray.

"I never mailed it."

"You're off the subject just like Aunt Bea does when she doesn't want Mary to know something." She handed him a glass.

"Mmmm, I'm trying to find the right words to tell you."

"Don't hunt for the right ones, please, just use any old ones, as long as they're true ones." She sipped some lemonade.

"All right then. Do you still care for him?" He sat on the swing and patted the space next to him.

She put her cold glass down and sat next to him. Slowly, she looked at him, as if it were the first time she'd ever really seen him. "Those aren't any old words. That's what's known as a sucker-punch. I learned that from Matteo. But here's the thing . . ." She hesitated, then said all in a rush, "Cayo's married. Or was. He left her. It's a Frontier Divorce. I couldn't spend the rest of my life looking over my shoulder for a law-man or sheriff to haul us off to jail."

"You gave him up without a fight. Why didn't you scratch her eyes out?"

"Excuse me? Where's the Christian: 'turn the other cheek' in that?"

"St. Michael the Archangel would've defended you."

"I was defeated before I had a chance to fight. With or without an assisting archangel. Too many things against me. I would've had to live life as an adulteress. Besides, weak as it sounds, I'm graduating soon. I owe that much to Aunt Bea, and myself."

"Oh, now you're crying again. I'm sorry. Me and my big mouth."

"Give me a few minutes by myself, will you, Erik?"

"No. I think you need a shoulder to cry on."

She turned and leaned her head on his shoulder and sobbed. *Cayo, damn your eyes—how you hurt my heart—is this survival, then?*

When she'd quieted, Erik touched her cheek gently and asked, "Shall I pour some more lemonade?"

"That's a fine idea, but our glasses are still full." He smiled and his gentle eyes sought hers tenderly.

He tipped her chin up and kissed her tears, and whispered, "Earth angel." Then with softness, he kissed her.

Chapter Twenty-Four

Cayo

Cayo rode practically non-stop and finally camped a two-day ride from Parcel Bluffs. He took down his saddlebag and sat by a stream. He stretched but ached all over and the worst ache of all was inside of him. Losing Darby. Forever. Would he ever be able to have a real family life? He stripped and swam for a long time, then dried off in the sun.

After he dressed, he opened his saddlebag and took out the deed to his parents' ranch. Where would he go now? What would he do with the rest of his life? Life, so precious. He could only think of his brother White Feather. Probably married now to Little Fawn. Maybe even with a baby. He pictured sweet Little Fawn carrying her child in a papoose, going about her chores, humming softly to the babe.

He decided to go where he had once been loved and accepted. He was free of Hanna. In his heart, he'd never married her, and felt no legal bond. Darby had called this kind of separation, a Frontier Divorce. No union, for sure. He'd never touched her again after the night she'd come to his bunk, and was glad he hadn't once her child was born two months early. Ben Star's son, now carrying Bradley as his surname. Cayo wondered how no one else ever said nothing about the child's resemblance to his true daddy.

Funny thing about names, how many he'd had? And all he'd wanted was for Darby to call him one time by his birth name: Connor Bradley. She knew he'd go back to his father's land, now he had the deed. Just as he knew that she'd never come to him there.

He fell asleep. Someone called as if speaking through a tunnel. "Darby. Darby, Darby." Cayo recognized his own voice, sounding far away: "By the light of stars, by the bright moon, by every heavenly creature who's seen the sun, we are one."

Afraid. Had something happened to her? Was she dead? No, she surely was merely listening as he had been doing to the cooing of doves above him, the quavering of his heart relieved his worry. Stillness settled. And he knew that miles away, Darby heard the shrill three-note trilling, as the dove's call rent the air, stirring the curtains of her window with the soft entry of spring.

She had to go. I had to let her go, but for the rest of my life, I have her in every heartbeat.

Coyote rode to the village of the People and found Little Fawn. She had indeed had a baby boy, but was in mourning for her husband. White Feather had been killed in a skirmish in a Comanche raid. Coyote spoke with her for quite some time before he left to pay his respects to Mbai'.

He sat at the campfire with Mbai'. They spoke of happier days, of Coyote's youth with his brother, White Feather, without ever mentioning his name. They were both sorrowful, but their hearts swelled with joy when Little Fawn brought the baby in to say goodnight to his Grandfather.

"Your son lives now in your grandson." Coyote smiled, a wry smile.

"But now my other son will take my grandson away. You are here because his father went to the Spirit World. You are here for Little Fawn." Mbai' turned to her, "You will mourn no more."

Little Fawn hushed the child and handed him to Coyote, who picked him up and smiled. He is strong, my brother's son." After a while, he handed the baby back to his mother.

Little Fawn cradled the baby in her arms and was about to leave, but Coyote asked Mbai' if she could stay. "There is something she needs to hear."

They were quiet for some time. Coyote smoked the pipe. "If Little Fawn is willing to come with me," he said, thinking perhaps this would redeem him for his monstrous act against his sisters, "then I will teach the boy our ways—to hunt and fish."

Mbai' nodded. "And you will name him?"

"I will."

They smoked the pipe and spoke of familiar things. It was peaceful listening to Mbai' talk of the old days, of battles, hunts, and the fierceness of the People.

Without a mention of their names, Coyote spoke of his fondness for his Grandmother and the awe with which he had esteemed Red Hawk. "I learned his teachings. Many times, I became invisible in the land of the Whites."

"You survived, but were not happy among the people of your birth?"

"They are not like the ones I remembered. Times have changed. The World is getting smaller. The earth seems to be shrinking, holding so many. And many more will come."

"Something you are not telling me?" Mbai' puffed on his pipe and passed it to Coyote.

Coyote held the pipe and looked at Little Fawn. "My two-spirit wife," Coyote said, without calling her Red Willow, "walks among the others in the world beyond. I met the man who killed her."

Mbai' waited. Little Fawn's eyes were wide with anticipation.

Coyote unbuttoned his shirt and held up the locket he had gifted Red Willow. "I killed him."

"That is not all, my son?"

"I left a woman who was not my choice. I may be hunted, though it is not certain."

Mbai' said, "What will happen now?"

"Knowing this, will Little Fawn want to follow me to the land of our forefathers and settle on a ranch west of here?"

She looked at her father-in-law and Coyote saw in her eyes a fierce loyalty. "She will go," Mbai' said. "But if you are a wanted man, would it not be better for my grandson to stay?"

"Look at her, my Father. She will not leave without the child. I will raise my brother's son as my own."

Mbai' reached for a knife and sheath and handed it to Coyote, who recognized it as his brother's. Coyote took his mother's locket and chain off his neck and handed them to Mbai', realizing this was the second time he'd be in possession of it.

The next morning, Coyote and Little Fawn parted on two horses. He rode Wind and Little Fawn with the papoose rode White Feather's horse. They also had a packhorse, a gift from the baby's grandfather.

Mbai' took hold of Coyote's rein. "I will see you once more before I no longer walk this earth, my son."

"I will bring your grandson when he's as tall as a sapling."

Chapter Twenty-Five

Thoughts Changing Like the Seasons

Darby mused about the conversation she had had the night before with Erik as she straightened her bed. She was once again lost in thought as she smoothed the chenille coverlet and then pulled it up and tucked it under her pillows. Her thoughts soon ran to daydreaming, as she wondered what it would be like to spend a night in Erik's arms. Could she? An unexpected flush came over her. She felt warm all over. She opened the window, hoping for a breeze, sat in the rocker and crossed her legs, but the feeling persisted. She tried to banish Cayo's face, his lips from her mind, but to no avail. She needed to concentrate on what Erik had said to her. The chilling truth: "You gave him up without a fight."

Later, having tea, Mary and Darby sat in the parlor room when Aunt Bea walked in with a downtrodden air and said, "I'll take my supper in my room, Mary."

Mary and Darby glanced in Bea's direction.

"You needn't bother about it—I'll tend to it myself," Aunt Bea said.

Darby looked at Mary, both knowing immediately something was wrong.

"Aunt Bea, did I offend you in some way?"

"Oh, no, child," she said, on the verge of tears, "I really want to be by myself for a little while," Aunt Bea said.

Mary gave Darby a nudge to stay put.

When Aunt Bea went upstairs with her tray, Darby asked Mary, "Did I do something, I oughtn't?"

Mary said, "Your Aunt Bea has been trying to see to your future, perhaps in ways that may not suit you. I wouldn't worry about it were I you; she's given me the silent treatment for years, and I've learned to cope."

"The silent treatment?"

"It's her way of making me pay for offenses. She tries hard, and even though in my heart I've forgiven her—" Mary stopped short with a look that Darby understood to mean she'd said too much already.

Darby said, "I'm up to the gills with wondering."

"What is it, little fish?"

"This pond is bigger than I bargained for, Mary." Darby poured a cup of tea.

"It's never too late, and by the mature look on your face I think—" but Mary cut herself short. "However, do make sure you put 'auntie' before my name in front of Bea. She'll hate that we've become such good chums—she's very old school proper."

Mary stopped short, for the second time and bit her bottom lip.

Darby put her hands on her hips "She was the one who interfered with your relationship with the fortune seeker, wasn't she?"

Mary didn't answer. She stirred a spoonful of sugar into her tisane.

"Mary, your silence speaks parables."

Mary tilted her head, but still said nothing, waiting to see just where this was going and how much Darby understood. Then she said, "His name was Captain Jordan Williams. Tall as the lintel. He had a cleft in his chin."

"I'm sure Aunt Bea loves us both, but she didn't think your Captain Williams was a good suitor for you. She squelched it, nipped it in the bud, as you say."

Mary sighed, and with a gesture of hands up, acquiesced that Darby was certainly on the right track.

"She's trying to do the opposite with me."

Mary said, "How do you mean?" She picked up her cup, blew on the hot tea, and sipped.

"Erik," Darby said, as if she'd smashed her teacup against the wall. "She means well—"

"She was in an arranged marriage to a man twenty years older, and doesn't understand the first thing about romantic love." Darby pulled her long hair in back of her ears.

"And you do?" Mary asked.

"I know what a spring breeze feels like on your arm—the way the hair stands up on the back of your neck when you picture the man you can't stop thinking about. I've seen wheat dance in a field and I've known that same sway closing my eyes and envisioning him. Is that love? To desire someone's look, his touch, his connection with you, but now it's only in dreams."

Darby took a deep breath. She thought of what she'd really like to say, tell her the feelings she had while fixing the bed that morning, but didn't want to shock the knickers off sweet Mary. "I can't say what love is for sure. I only know I felt every sense alive when I thought of or saw Cayo. I swear at times, I think I would have killed for him. Loving Cayo was like having a butterfly land on my palm and begging it to linger, knowing it would be gone in an instant." Her brain sparkled with images of her and Cayo together. "But that's over and done with." *I love Cayo, although I can't pretend what happened last night on the porch, didn't happen and I can't fool myself into thinking what happened this morning didn't take place. I want Erik to hold me, touch me, possess every inch of my body the way Cayo did, though I don't believe that'll ever happen with him. More than this, I want to be a mother and have children—I doubt that would've been possible with Cayo. I hope my prayer will be answered. Why did I scoff at the thought of being a mail-*

order bride for a pastor? How immature of me! Maybe what I'm seeking isn't independence but security.

"Maybe, Mary, love can be an acquired virtue. I think my mother loved my father."

Mary patted her hand. "You're very wise for one so young. Yes, Tess of the three of us, was the lucky one."

"Why did you let Bea?" Darby sipped her tea.

"What?"

"Ruin your life." She put the cup down and it chinked against the spoon in the saucer.

"I wasn't brave like you." Mary ran her hand down her bodice and smoothed the folds of her skirt.

"Me? Brave? I threw away my only chance with Cayo out of a self-ish motive to want to better myself. Only to discover there ain't nobody better'n him," slipping back to a familiar, younger voice, "and he sure as shootin' didn't need no educated wife."

"When you talk about Cayo, you slip back into improper speech patterns. Why?"

"I guess I want to stress what I'm saying. Seems unimportant, I suppose, when you make the comparison to what I've lost out of stupid pride and hubris."

Darby looked out the window distracted by the splendor of nature. The purple pentas were in bloom again; forsythia and lily of the valley, and pansies . . . and daffodils. There were rambling tea roses such a light shade of pink that they seemed white, clinging and crawling up the wall of the carriage shed. The dogwoods and a single lone peach tree were in bloom.

"You're so quiet all of a sudden. What are you thinking?" Mary smoothed back her hair.

"I'm blessed. Not the religious kind of sit-me-down-in-a-church pew-for- an-hour-to-lecture-me, but spiritually, I truly think I was saved coming here, and I've been given a second chance at life with a man I was too stubborn or blind to see."

"You look a bit tired, dear. Why don't you take a rest or read for a while."

"Good idea. I'll go upstairs, but not to read. I want to jot down something so I won't ever forget it."

From the window in her bedroom, her eyes were, of a sudden, trained on the carriage-house wall and she remembered another noontime, long ago as she glanced out the window when she'd heard the three-note hoot of a dove. She focused on the wall of the carriage house until those thoughts made the wall shimmer like summer heat waves rising from a sun-scorched paved stone pathway. Shimmering heat waves, but she felt cold. Where had that been?

A decaying hacienda in ruins. Instantly she felt the pressure of the wall on her back and the insistent pressure of Cayo's lips bearing down on hers, pressing into hers, and she was overcome with melancholy and desire. She hugged her arms around herself to keep from falling off the edge of eternity. Would he forever be her scourge? Despite her new regard for Erik, could she ever cast off Cayo and rid herself from wanting him?

She stepped away from the window and sat at the small mariner captain's desk, lit the hurricane lamp on the flat surface above the slanted top, opened it and took out her diary. She unfastened it, dipped her pen in the inkwell and wrote:

Cayo—
The wind has blown through me. You are gone.

Can you hear my plea of loneliness in the place where you now dwell? How much I want to tell you that my life is impoverished—diminished forever without your loving light.

***

It was Sunday and Darby was running late. She rushed down the stairs, holding a bonnet in one hand and a prayer book in the other. Late for church. How could she have overslept? And why had she wasted so much time day-dreaming, sitting on the window bench, looking out at the lilacs, and wisteria so lacy and lovely the racemes dripping with the weight of spring. She dressed in Cayo's favorite color, *azul,* a sure sign she wanted to feel confident and self-contained.

She had listened and watched the meadowlarks as they ran, stopped, ran, foraging on the ground. Approaching the nest, one bird, yellow-breasted with a thick black cowl around its neck, walked more stealthily, its body closer to ground. Darby had looked toward the birdbath iris-ringed, alternating purple and white. There was a family of birds, a friendly group at least, preening, head scratching, and bathing. Some stretched like old men, the only thing missing, she thought, was an accompanying yawn. But she knew they were females because it was early morning and that was their habit. She also noticed their behavior after they had copulated. All around her were signs of rebirth, fertility . . . mating . . . and her thoughts drifted to the grove and the soft loam beach near the Rio Grande, where she and Cayo picnicked eons ago.

She refused to let him rob her tranquil spirit and quickly thought of the man she was going to hear preach the Sunday sermon in the little stone and mortar chapel not ten minutes from the house. But for how long had she tarried within Cayo's arms, lost in the wonder of his eyes?

And what did it mean to yearn to linger there? Would she ever rid her psyche of him? Purge the physical need of him that she could only have now in uncalled for wanton dreams and summoned daydreams where she longed to wander? *Give over. Give over or perish.*

She called after her aunts, but Aunt Bea had said they'd be going ahead and to please hurry and follow as soon as she could. Aunt Bea still scolding as she stepped out the front door.

"Darby, must you always be tardy?"

Rushing toward church, of a sudden she slowed her steps. *How boring to have to bear the thought of another homily.* How would she be able to sit still and feign attention when her thoughts traveled so often back to Parcel Bluffs? She might as well delay and bear the wrath of her aunt after services.

From the church window, Darby heard a police whistle, and the sound sparked the strongest urge in her to drop her hymnal and run out the door. Just run to feel the air lift her skirt and petticoat, riffle through her unpinned hair. How would she ever tame these wild, unconstrained fantasies? Would she ever be able to slow these coiled emotions, pick up her feet and move in lady-like manner in the direction they should go? She dashed unbidden tears from her face, braced her shoulders. When the sermon had finished, she carried herself forward, greeting other parishioners. She must banish Cayo from her spirit, but now she understood it would be like truncating a limb.

***

On a sun-filled Saturday afternoon, June 24, 1876, there was a centennial celebration for the birth of the United States of America. Forest Park officially opened to the public. It was located in St. Louis County, almost two miles west of the St. Louis City limits. It took Aunt Bea,

Mary, Darby and her new beau Erik, now considered good husband material, a forty-minute carriage ride from downtown to reach the park.

Forest Park's dedication ceremony took place at the park's center, built near the De Baliviere entrance. The little group walked around and when they reached the bandstand, a decorated wooden music pagoda on an island in Pagoda Lake, they stopped and found chairs. Darby admired the wooden structure and said, "My but aren't the statues lovely."

"A bit ornate," Aunt Bea said, tucking her skirt beneath her.

"They represent the four seasons. See?" Darby said to her aunt and pointed.

Aunt Bea put her hand on top of Darby's and pushed it down. "Lower your hand, dear, this isn't a circus."

Erik held each of their chairs, and when they were all comfortably seated, despite the heat, Darby watched her aunt open her parasol, heedless of the view of the person in back of her. Darby nudged her and her aunt shifted in her chair and lowered, but did not close her parasol. The man in back of her changed seats. The band played and then a hush came over the crowd.

Darby felt a bit nauseated, and started to fan herself. Mary noticed her distress and said, "Let's walk to the refreshment stand for a soda pop."

"Really? Is that quite necessary now that we're all settled?" Aunt Bea said.

"Yes. I'm terribly thirsty," Mary said. "Darby needs to move. Her foot fell asleep."

Darby stood, amazed at how quickly Mary had lied to her sister to get her own way. She stepped in front of Erik, who gave her a puzzled look. Darby hunched her shoulders as if to say, she didn't quite get Mary's uncomfortable state but needed to accompany her. Inwardly grateful for Mary's fib, Darby shook her foot on purpose for effect.

***

When they returned, Darby was distracted by the heat, but was close enough to listen to the opening remarks made by Chauncy F. Schultz. *"I present to you, the people of St. Louis, your own, this large and beautiful Forest Park for enjoyment of yourselves, your children and your children's children forever...The rich and poor, the merchant and mechanic, the professional man and day laborer, each with his family and lunch basket, can come here and enjoy his own...all without stint or hindrance...and there will be no notice put up, Keep Off the Grass."*

Darby muttered, "Thank Heavens," and applauded loudly. She loved open spaces and parks. She knew them well—Carondelet Park in the south; Forest Park in the center and O'Fallon Park on the north.

The next day on the front porch, Darby sipped sweet lemonade and read in the *Globe-Democrat* that the opening day ceremony at Forest Park attracted fifty thousand people. She tried to do the math of what percentage that would be when the population of the city was three hundred-fifty thousand. The newspaper reported that the park was on a railroad line, opened a week ago. The train ride from downtown took twenty minutes—half the time as by carriage, and she could go unescorted. The city was booming. Access had been one of the parks commission's first problems, but a bill providing roads was approved by the legislature. Darby had witnessed a great deal of construction, by-passing much of the work on these projects. By the dedication date, roads, lakes, bridges and landscaping were completed. The city looked re-born and splendid. A growing metropolis, like the feeling she got sometimes discovering something heretofore unknown. She was almost happy. Almost.

Maybe the feeling was more like contentment, as long as she didn't allow herself to let memories of Cayo trespass. One thought of his high cheekbones, the small shy smile he gave her at the sight of a pressed buttercup and she'd come undone. Then she'd be abjectly cast down into the doldrums, and it was difficult to shift the cogs and gears of her mind to set herself at peace again.

She tried to convince herself that she could do it now, but doubts crept in. Although. Had she really learned to be in harmony with her new life surroundings? Hadn't Cayo been that way? Did she learn this lesson from him? We meet people along the way, helter-skelter, but do they come into our lives for a purpose? And is that purpose to teach us how to go on living while forgetting? Darby finally knew how this had to come about one vesper evening after church a mere two weeks ago. Standing side by side with her pastor—through the grace of God and this man of God—she'd understood at last that his gentle strength had the ability to cosset her, to cradle, to comfort and to guide her through the tempest of difficult memories and of longing.

***

Now she paced the room, then finally quieted and stood by her bedroom window, as she usually did when thinking. She placed her hand under her heart. What was she to do? Not much of a choice, now that she knew for sure she was expecting. *It's the devil in front of me or the devil behind. Keep Cayo's babe, lose Erik.* She decided to walk over to Dr. Marsh and confide in him. She certainly couldn't tell Mary, at least not yet.

On the walk to the doctor's office, Darby heard a coach's whistle from the playing field where Matteo was. He waved to her and she stopped, waved back, facing the boys throwing and catching, and practicing batting at a makeshift plate. She continued walking, address-ing the infant she was carrying, she whispered: *If you're a boy, I want you to play baseball. I can teach you how to position your body and keep your eye on the ball when you catch.*

She sat on the opposite side of Dr. Marsh's large Louis XV Style Ormolu-Mounted writing desk. Inwardly, pleased she'd learned to identify the furniture, but the grandeur of it unsettled her, and she had to take several deep breaths before she could say why she was consulting him.

He saw her nervous demeanor and waited.

When she finished telling him, he sat shaking his head. "If you tell your aunt, you'll be an outcast. *Persona non grata* at Bea's. Do you understand? She may put you out into the street. She'd resent it terribly after all she's given you. But," he hesitated, "you could on the other hand miscarry."

"You mean abort?" Darby gripped the arms of the chair.

"You don't seem to have much of a choice. Or," he hesitated, stood and walked to the end of the desk and looked down at her, "perhaps, be the devil incarnate and sleep with that good pastor to make him believe the child is his and at its birth, pretend it came early. Take that appalled look off your face. Women have been duping men like that since time immemorial."

"Not this woman. That's what Hanna did to Cayo. How could I de-ceive Erik? He's in love with me and has proposed. I haven't given him an answer yet but could never betray him like that."

"Do you love him?"

Darby didn't answer.

"Do you love him the way you loved your cowboy?"

"Love," she corrected. She shook her head.

"You're still in love with him?" He asked, his tone exacting.

"He's a ghost of my past in my ever present."

"Then you've really only one choice."

"I must tell Erik. The gamble is great and I chance losing him. Or, if he's the kind of man I think he is he'll have spine enough, compassion even—"

"You're sweet but delusional. I don't think any man can love that much to sacrifice his life raising another man's bastard."

She fumbled in her reticule for a handkerchief. "You are so cold-hearted."

"Realistic, my dear. Although," he hesitated, "there's another possibility. Go to a convent and when the baby's born quietly give it up for adoption. The nuns will say the mother was lost in childbirth. You can tell your aunts you've accepted a job teaching in Chicago. I'll help you."

He poured whiskey from a decanter into a tumbler and handed her the glass. "You're going to need this, whatever you decide."

"But the baby?"

"You're not going to drink every day. Just today. Please consider me a friend. I'll stick by you whatever your decision. I've never had the pleasure of meeting a woman like you before. If I had I would've married her." He lit a pipe. "Will you tell Erik also that you don't love him?"

The question, like the smoke from the pungent tobacco, hung in the air for a minute, and then she stood to leave, her drink untouched. "I care for Erik—he's kind and considerate, and I'd make him a good wife. Perhaps I could learn to love such a man."

"But never like—"

"Cayo."

He opened the door for her, took her hand and kissed it.

"No, never like him," she said.

"You're lucky. Not everyone encounters love for a lifetime. Shall I see you home?"

"Please do."

As Paul opened the door, Darby said, "By the way, Aunt Bea is having a small celebration for the completion of my studies next Saturday evening. Will you come?"

"A graduation party. I'd be delighted."

That evening, awaiting Erik's arrival, Darby walked through the kitchen to open the porch door. Recently, she'd answered an advertisement for a school-teaching job out west at a mission school in Towaoc, the southwest corner of Colorado and had received an appointment. She'd be teaching children of the Weeminuche band of the Ute tribe. She stood at the porch railing, tapping the letter in her pocket—her back-up plan if things didn't go as she hoped. Hearing approaching footfalls on the path, she took her hand out of her pocket and turned to face Erik's approach. She placed a protective hand on the spot under her heart close to her newly conceived being, begged God to protect and bless her for this explosive yearning to mother Cayo's wild lovechild. She knew this might cause her to lose Erik. She'd have to confess to him. Confess? No. Speak to him. Of what? Of the love she had for a man no longer in her life. Although, how precious a gift to have his baby.

Darby jumped. It was only the neighbor's dog. She shooed him away, sat down, and began to swing slowly, willing herself to place Erik's face before her instead of the man she loved, would love for her whole life. *God forgive me.* Would Erik still want her as his bride? Would he be able to love her and raise a child not his blood? Would he want a soiled dove? Could he love and esteem a woman bearing another man's issue?

Darby stood on the back porch behind a trellis of blooming forsythia. Waiting is what she seemed to have been doing her whole life until now. It was time for her to act and do it quickly. The night air was pungent with blooming jasmine and renewal. Was Erik late? She started pacing, and then willed herself to calm down. She stopped, unclenched her fists, sat on the leafy lilac chintz-covered cushion on the swing, and began to rock back and forth. Memories of Cayo caused nervous flutters. How could she cancel him from her life? Especially now that she was carrying his child? She must force herself to forget him. But how? Forget that she loved him and loves him still? Forget that she had surrendered not only her maidenhead to him but herself entirely? She let out a deep breath at the sound of footfalls on the path, but they were not close by. Someone else's back garden.

The scent of Aunt Mary's baking biscuits awakened her from semi-torpor as Mary tapped on the window. "Are you all right, dear?"

"I was day-dreaming," she said, knowing she'd have to face reality in mere minutes. "I'm fine."

She closed her eyes again, wanting to sink back to the place of her fantasy, but it was impossible.

Erik mounted the stairs.

In a matter of minutes, she'd have the answers to all of the questions that weighed heavily on her heart. In that instant, he stepped up to the covered porch, the air rich with the scent of gardenia bushes below. Darby knew, no matter what the outcome, she'd never abandon this child, even if it meant she had to sell flowers on the street corner some-where, or beg with a tin cup on some cathedral steps.

She closed her eyes, and straightened her shoulders. When she gazed up, Erik's gentle eyes met hers, as he started to take hold of her hands.

Erik on the porch. Before her. Reaching for her hands, pulling her up and into an embrace. She could not allow any further intimacy between them and turned her head away so he couldn't kiss her.

"Please, Erik." She all but fell back onto the swing and patted the spot on the cushion next to her. "Sit here with me. I must talk to you about something that's praying heavily on my soul and in my heart."

"You're so serious. Why? This is a solemn occasion, guaranteed, but it's also a joyous one." Before she could object, he knelt before her and opened a ring box covered in mauve velvet. A breeze ruffled the loose tendrils of her hair at the back of her neck. Too soon. Too swift. She hadn't had time to say anything. She closed the box held in his fingers.

He looked bereft. "What is it? What's happened, Darby?"

"I can't accept your ring until you've heard what I have to say." She got up and closed the kitchen window.

He stood. "I assumed we'd agreed. I brought you my mother's wedding ring."

"It's beautiful. It's—more than any girl could hope for from a valiant, respectable suitor, but I don't think you'll feel I'm worthy of it, Erik."

He started to protest, moved closer to enfold her in his arms.

Darby held up her hand to shield her face, and then gently nudged him away from her. "Please. Please, hear me out."

Once again she sat on the rocker and Erik took his place next to her. He took hold of her hands, and though she wanted to resist, she let him.

Darby took in a few deep breaths before plunging into a discourse with him.

"Something happened when I went back to Parcel Bluffs for my father who was only a short time away from breathing his last. And then my brothers and I buried him."

"I know all this. Is this the reason you're hesitating?" Erik shrugged his shoulders.

"Heavens no. It's far more complex, it's" she sighed, "it's complicated—but that isn't even the right word. You see, Erik, I saw my cowboy Cayo while I was home." She'd said *"my"—such a possessive word.* "Cayo's still in love with me even though he married my best friend, and I—I don't know how to say this except to say it—I fell into temptation and well, I'm with child, Erik. His child."

"But it's so soon. How do you know? And why? Why did you fall? How could you, when you knew I was going to propose to you? But, of course, you didn't know."

She scanned his face and slowly withdrew her hands from his. "Why does a sunflower turn its head toward the sun?" Should she tell him it wasn't the first time? Because now that she thought about the way she'd said it, it sounded as if it were the only time.

He shook his head. His face wore an expression that was at once aggrieved, distraught and totally repelled, but then he relaxed.

"Cayo and I had been lovers before I came here."

Shock registered on his peaceful countenance. "But you were so young. Did he force you? Was he a brute?"

"I can't lie to you. I went with Cayo willingly. He was my moon and every star in the sky. I never stopped loving him until he married Hanna, and even then, I couldn't chase him from my thoughts or heart."

"This isn't about me taking you to wife—it's—can you cast him from your mind forever?"

Why in God's name hadn't she thought of that? She'd only thought of telling Erik about the pregnancy. She swiped at a truant tear and said, "I can only try, if you'll have me—us."

Erik stood and began to pace. He stopped short and looked at her sternly and raked his hands through his hair. "Listen, Darby. This is too much to filter and grasp. Please excuse me to your Aunt Mary. I won't be staying for dinner. I need to ponder this." With that hasty leave-taking, he all but leapt off the veranda and bounded down the steps.

Darby cried. She didn't sob, tears merely coursed down her cheeks as she searched in her sleeve for a handkerchief. She cried, not because Erik left her so abruptly, but because she knew in every sinew of her body, she would never, could never stop loving Cayo. How could she even think of spending the rest of her life with the good Pastor—how could she, knowing she could never feel for him the way she did for Cayo. Would Erik resent her love child? How would he treat the baby? She wondered if Erik would still want to marry her after this disclosure. How could she accept his proposal of matrimony when every moment she'd fear he'd change and perhaps become cruel to the infant, despite his kind nature? Hate and antipathy are vile poison in a snake, but no one knows if the snake will strike. Recently she'd read of a man who had exposed his baby to inclement weather and the child took chill, fevered and died. That child was his own baby who made him insanely jealous of his wife's affection for it.

Darby was a lost and lonely soul. On her own now. But damn! She stood and gripped the trellis, and looking out over the lush garden knew she was determined to have and keep her baby at any cost, even if she could never have his father, the man she'd love her whole life long.

Mary moved the curtain aside and rapped on the window. "Dinner's ready."

Darby went into the kitchen, took a calico apron off the hook in back of the door and put it on, tying the strings in a fluffy bow at her back.

"What are you doing? What's wrong? You were just speaking with Erik a minute ago. Where's our guest?"

Darby stood staring at the stone kitchen sink. "Gone," she finally said.

"What do you mean, dear? Where's Erik gone to?"

"Not staying for dinner. I chased him away."

Mary turned Darby's shoulders and looked at her. "You did what? Why in heaven's name? What happened?"

"Mary."

"Child. Please. You're frightening me."

"Oh, how I thank God Aunt Bea went to her whist group. She'll be late and sleep in. Please, darling, let's sit a minute before we eat. If I can eat."

They walked to the table set for three in the dining room. Darby sat down and looked at Mary and shook her head.

"Are you ready to tell me?"

Darby sipped some water from a jelly glass. "Have to sometime. Might as well be now."

She took hold of her aunt's folded hands. "Do you remember how upset I was that Aunt Bea interfered with your proposal?"

Mary nodded, never taking her eyes off Darby.

"Well." She sighed. "Now I've done just that. I have pretty much messed up positively the most wonderful chance of matrimony in the state of Missouri. Mary, close your mouth. Here it is in a nutshell, but first you must promise you'll never divulge this secret under pain of mortal sin and hell's fire and damnation as a final destination in the afterlife."

Mary jumped up. "Darby!" she screeched.

"Sit, sweet Mary. I'll tell it to you plain and simple. I'm in love with Cayo Bradley and have been in love with him since I was a girl. I'll love him till I die and go before St. Peter in the conclusive judgement of my life on earth. Do I have your promise never to reveal this to your sister or anyone else?"

Mary nodded and reached out for Darby's hands. "I swear," she said.

Darby sat straighter in the chair. "I'm with child."

"Lord, have mercy on us!"

"You mean, 'me.'"

"Impossible! I can't believe our placid Pastor took advantage of you—"

"Oh, he surely didn't. Did I not just say who I love? It was that devil of a coyote. I let him love me and begged him to keep on loving me and never stop. I'm carrying Cayo's child."

"Oh, dear. Oh my. Tell me that you didn't tell Erik—"

"But I did. I had to—"

"What did he say? What will you do? How can I help?"

"He's thinking it over. But it's not a matter of waiting until he thinks about it to decide. Maybe I'm judging him too harshly, but if he really cared for me—well, he should've said so on the porch. I know my course of action."

"You don't think he'll accept you and the baby, do you?"

"He's a man of the cloth. Dedicated and—"

"And?"

"Fearful of what genteel society may learn and castigate him for it. I may be wrong. I was hoping he'd be courageous enough, in love with me enough. But no, I feel in my heart he's not the man of backbone I'd hoped for."

"Oh but he is. You're expecting too much."

"Perhaps. No, it's not that I'm expecting— what may be of more consequence is the fact that I don't really love him. At all. Oh I admire him to be sure. But love? That's a whole different thing, isn't it? To understand, that's what love is, isn't it? That fire in the soul beneath the solar plexus—wanting to care for someone as they age, wanting to serve him his meals, wash his back in a steaming tub—"

"Darby, what are you saying?"

"That I'd do anything in the world for Cayo, and I don't give a hoot what happens to our dear parish minister. Let him save souls, let him be a martyr, let him marry a proper, prissy girl from around the corner. I don't give a damn. It's no longer his decision. It's mine."

Darby stood and started to walk out of the dining room.

"Where are you going?"

"To pack, Mary. To leave with my baby and the sweet time of waiting for his birthing, to go where I'm needed. To teach out west."

"But what about Aunt Bea?" Mary stood up and pointed at the dinner plates. "What about dinner?"

"You eat, darling. I'm not a bit hungry. Be an angel and pack me a lunch to take with me on the train. As for Aunt Bea—well, she can continue to adore her confessor from afar."

"Please. Don't leave me, Darby. Please," she said with a supplicant's bent head and tears rolling down her puffed, spidery cheeks.

Darby threw her a kiss. "I'll write you, but now I'm going to bundle up my wardrobe and tomorrow morning, I'll be purchasing a one way train ticket west. It's where I belong."

Mary took hold of the knob on the banister and looked up. "But where west? Parcel Bluffs?"

"No Ma'm. Colorado," Darby said, hiked up her skirt and petticoat and headed upstairs.

The next morning, Darby knew she had to face Aunt Bea. She rapped on her bedroom door.

"Come in, Mary, I'm reading.

"It's me, Aunt Bea."

"Why Darby, you're dressed in traveling garb."

"In fact, yes, because I'll be traveling."

Aunt Bea pushed the newspaper aside and sat up straight. "Where are you going? Why wasn't I told you were preparing a trip?" she asked in a tone anxious and alarmed.

Darby sat beside her aunt. She folded her hands. "I don't want you to think I'm ungrateful. You've given me what no one can take away from me—an education. Now I'm going to make use of it. I've had a job offering in Colorado on the border of New Mexico."

"But I assumed you and Erik were—"

"Aunt Bea, Erik has too much church responsibility for a flighty young thing like me. And I've no intention of becoming a staid, sedate matriarch. There's still too much unbroken horse in me. I belong out west—"

A tap on the door interrupted Darby. She rose and opened it. Mary whispered that a boy came round with a note from the Pastor. She handed it to Darby, who unfolded it and read: "I'll have you, after all." She shook her head. Kindly tell the boy the answer is: "No, thank you."

Aunt Bea called out from the bed, "What's all the hush–up about, you two?" She started to rise from the bed and almost collapsed, saying, "I'm not an invalid. Just tired."

"Stay calm, Aunt Bea." Darby turned back to Mary. "Tell the boy to hire me an extension-top Barouche cab and have it come within the top of the hour. Tip him for me please, Mary, I'll settle with you down-stairs."

"I'll be back to explain all the details in a moment, Aunt Bea."

Darby stepped outside with Mary who was flushed. "Well? What did he say?"

"He said, he'd have me, Mary, but it's too late—he should've said so instantly last night. It's no good—I could never love him the way I hunger for Cayo. However, do remind him to have enough delicacy to keep this from Bea—she's far too fragile."

Mary nodded, her expression solemn. "Am I growing a spine like you?"

"Dearest Mary, this isn't a funeral dirge—it's a call to life. Be happy for me."

"You're so brave. If I'd only had some of your pluck when I was your age."

"Never too late. You've got it now. When I'm settled come visit, won't you?"

"Could I?"

"Most definitely."

"Oh, I almost forgot what with all the commotion. You've had a letter." Mary handed Darby the envelope. She looked at the unfamiliar script quizzically.

"I'll read this in my room and gather the last of my belongings. But first Aunt Bea." She knocked quietly on the door and stepped inside.

"Where will you live teaching out west?"

"A mission school for Indian children with lodgings."

"But why there and not here?" Aunt Bea straightened her coverlet.

"I can only say, I don't belong here. I never did." She kissed her aunt's forehead.

Back in her room, Darby sat at the desk, took a peacock feathered letter opener from the drawer and ripped the envelope.

My darlin' Darby,

I'm telling this here letter to a town scribe. Paid him two bits and swore I'd shoot him dead if he told a living soul. He's signing down my words. For you. To tell it fair, heard Hanna run off with Ben, the blacksmith to Cerrillos. Took the wooly-haired love child—sweet, mild, like Ben. Nothing like his she-witch mamma. Never'd believe she'd of left her Daddy's ranch and all his silver dollars, but ain't life like a horse—you never know'd if it's gonna kick your head in.

When you left, I went to my people's village. My brother White Feather killed in a raid. I took his Little Fawn as my own—not in the Biblical sense—she was more a sister, and her son. We settled on my ranch. Still had the paper my Pa give me when the Apache attacked. I been out hunting with the boy one day. When we got back, ashes only. Marauders, whites, left Little Fawn to die, but not before they brutalized her outside the barn and burned my homestead—not a lucky place. The boy's with me now. I'm running cattle and breaking wild horses with my Ute friend Ndóicho. Cornerstone Ranch, Colorado, near the four corners in the Colorado plateau. Owners name Mc Dougal. Big Irisher with red whiskers. He ain't mean, though. Even when drunk.

I ain't good with words, Darby. Never was. I'm free. Come to me. Cayo.

X

Darby held the letter to her heart and then folded and put it in her reticule on the bed. She picked up the medicine bag Cayo had given her—the last object she wanted to pack in her valise. She caressed it, opened the flap, removed Cayo's mother's wedding ring and held it glinting in the sun from the window.

She slipped the gold band on her finger, and whispered, "I will."

Acknowledgements

A thousand and one thanks and all my love to my "Road Warrior" Felipe, my husband—the guy who drives me all over this beautiful country of ours, and especially for taking me to New Mexico countless times, and expressly for our many visits to Santa Fe.

Thanks to Duke Pennell, editor of *Frontier Tales* for publishing part of this novel as a short story entitled: "Cayo Bradley."

Before writing the second draft of this novel, I spent time, perused and frequented the Santa Fe Library, the New Mexico Museum of History, the Indian Arts and Cultural Museum, the Wheelwright Museum, and many wonderful bookstores and shops in Santa Fe. I would like to thank all of the congenial people I met and who patiently answered my many questions.

Most especially, I would like to express deep and sincere thanks to Docent Sue Knuth, of the Wheelwright Museum, Santa Fe, New Mexico, for her gracious assistance and handout materials from the art exhibition held at the museum by the Jicarilla Apache Nation in June 2017. I just missed seeing it by a week!

I'd also like to extend many thanks to the people of Santa Fe: the librarians, the barkeeps, the wait staff in cafes and restaurants, and passersby I encountered walking through the heart of the city and stopped to ask all manner of questions. The books that I found useful are numerous, but I'd like to cite a few of the most important ones that were beneficial to me:

A Brief History of New Mexico

Apache Warrior vs US Cavalryman: 1846–86 (Combat)

An Illustrated History of New Mexico

Images of America Historic Ranches of Northeastern New Mexico

The Dictionary of Jicarilla Apache
The Jicarilla Apache of Dulce (Images of America)
The Jicarilla Apache Tribe: A History, 1846-1970

As always, I bestow blessings and gratitude, to my friend, mentor, and advisor John Dufresne for his comments on the manuscript.

I can never thank Jane Brownley enough for her invaluable reading and commenting on the manuscript, draft after draft, numerous times. I sincerely thank Beth Morris for her analysis, edits, and suggestions. I appreciate the time and critique that Melissa Westemeier dedicated to my early drafts. For the discussions of the history and geography of the West, New Mexico, and the Jicarilla Apache Nation, I'd like to thank Cris Edwards. For his expertise and knowledge of guns and rifles of the West, I'd like to acknowledge the author Jim Ballou.

Heartfelt thanks to two wonderful writers who gave generously of their valuable time to read and blurb this novel: Ruth Hull Chatlien and Michelle Cox.

About the Author

Nina Romano is the author of the Wayfarer Trilogy. Book 1, *The Secret Language of Women,* was a Finalist *Foreword INDIES Reviews* and Independent Publishers Gold Medal IPPY Winner. Book 2, *Lemon Blossoms,* was a Finalist *Foreword INDIES Reviews*. Book 3, *In America,* was a Finalist *Chanticleer Media*.

Romano has published a short story collection, *The Other Side of the Gates*, five poetry collections, two poetry chapbooks, and one collaborative work of nonfiction, *Writing in a Changing World.* She has been twice nominated for the Pushcart Prize.

Her new novel, an historical thriller, *Dark Eyes*, is forthcoming from Speaking Volumes, Book Two of the series Darby's Quest, *Star on a Summer Morning*, is currently a work-in-progress.

COMING SOON!

NINA ROMANO'S
DARK EYES

In Soviet Leningrad, it's the eleventh hour for Anya Ivanovich Andreyeva, a down on her luck, ex-ballerina and unwed mother of neurologically deficient daughter, Iskra.

Anya becomes embroiled in the murder of two women, and although she mistrusts men in general, falls into a relationship with Andrei, a police photographer. Can she trust him?

Anya is being stalked by Nikolai, a rogue policeman, and discovers that her lover is also being pursued by him.

In a reversal of brutal and violent circumstances, the predators Anya and Andrei, become the stalkers and huntsmen.

For more information
visit: www.SpeakingVolumes.us

COMING SOON!

NINA ROMANO'S
STAR ON A SUMMER MORNING
DARBY'S QUEST SERIES
BOOK 2

Star on a Summer Morning, the sequel to *The Girl Who Loved Cayo Bradley*.

On her way to meet Cayo, Darby is beset with inconceivable events impeding her travels to Four Corners, Colorado. Surprisingly detained in Silverton until springtime, she becomes distressed and disheartened due to losing contact with Cayo. Rumors are he's on the trail after his Indian wife's killers.

Will Darby search for Cayo with the Ute Indian tracker, Silverthorne? Will she remain faithful to Cayo or fall for Silverthorne's enchantment?

For more information
visit: www.SpeakingVolumes.us

On Sale Now!

AWARD-WINNING AUTHOR
MARDI OAKLEY MEDAWAR

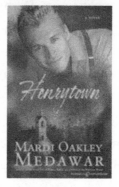

For more information:
visit: www.SpeakingVolumes.us

On Sale Now!

MICAH S. HACKLER'S
SHERIFF LANSING MYSTERIES
BOOKS 1 – 9

**For more information
visit:** www.SpeakingVolumes.us

On Sale Now!

ROBERT WESTBROOKS'S
HOWARD MOON DEER MYSTERIES
BOOKS 1 – 7

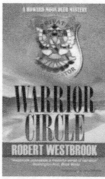

For more information
visit: www.SpeakingVolumes.us

Sign up for free and bargain books

Join the Speaking Volumes mailing list

Text

ILOVEBOOKS

to 22828 to get started.

Message and data rates may apply.

Made in the USA
Las Vegas, NV
15 December 2021